SEVENTY-TWO VIRGINS

'A hectic comedy thriller ... refreshingly unpompous and very funny.'   *Mail on Sunday*

'Johnson scores in his comic handling of those most sensitive issues ... he succeeds in being charming and sincere ... a witty page-turner.'   *Observer*

'Among the hilarious scenes of events and the wonderful dialogue which keeps the story moving at a cracking pace, Johnson uncovers some home truths ... I can give no higher praise to this book than to say that I lapped it up at a single uproarious sitting.'   *Irish Examiner*

'As an author, he is in a class of his own: ebullient, exhausting but irresistible.'   *Daily Mail*

'Fluent, funny material ... the writing is vintage, Wodehousian Boris ... it has been assembled with skill and terrific energy and will lift morale in the soul of many.'
Evening Standard

'At the centre of his first novel is a terrorist plot of frightening ingenuity ... the comedy is reminiscent of Tom Sharpe.'   *Sunday Times*

'This is a comic novel, but Johnson is never far away from making serious points, which he leads us towards with admirable stealth.'   *Daily Telegraph*

'A splendidly accomplished and gripping first novel ... Few authors could get away with it, but this one most certainly does. Highly recommended.'   *Sunday Telegraph*

By the same author

BORIS JOHNSON

Seventy-Two Virgins

HarperCollins*Publishers*

HarperCollins*Publishers*
77–85 Fulham Palace Road,
Hammersmith, London W6 8JB

www.harpercollins.co.uk

This paperback edition 2005
2

A catalogue record for this book
is available from the British Library

ISBN 0 00 719805 1

Set in Meridien by Palimpsest Book Production Limited,
Polmont, Sterlingshire

Printed and bound in Great Britain by
Clays Ltd, St Ives plc

Optimis parentibus

PART ONE

THE TROJAN AMBULANCE

CHAPTER ONE
0752 HRS

On what he had every reason to believe would be the last day of his undistinguished political career Roger Barlow awoke in a state of sexual excitement and with a gun to his head, the one fading as he became aware of the other.

The gun was equipped with an orange whale harpoon, and would have been lethal, had it been more than six inches long and made of something other than plastic.

'Say your prayers, buddy,' said the four-year-old. Roger's eyelid quivered.

If Sigmund Freud had been able to catch this kid's conversation, he would have been thrilled. Seldom had there been so exuberant and uninhibited an Oedipus complex.

One morning they were lying all three of them in bed, and Roger was trying to persuade the kid to go and watch *Scooby Doo*. The child turned to his mother.

He spoke prettily, in the kind of voice he might use for ordering another fish finger.

'I am going to kill Daddy, and then I am going to marry you.'

Today, Roger didn't want to be rude to the four-year-old, and he didn't want to exacerbate his complex, but he was damned if he was going to be treated in this way. He grunted, and rolled away, gripping his slumbering wife with both arms.

The four-year-old fired the plastic dart carefully into the back of Roger's neck.

Barlow's blow went wide. Ceding his place to his rival, he rose. He tended to wear T-shirts in bed, and this one was a relic of a brief but illustrious former Tory leadership under which he had been proud to serve.

'It's Time For Hague', proclaimed the T-shirt, while the back announced: 'The Common Sense Revolution'. As a piece of nightwear, his wife claimed that it had anti-aphrodisiacal properties of a barely credible order.

'MMM,' said his wife.

'Mmm,' said Roger. 'Back in a mo.'

As he went into the bathroom he heard the flap of the letterbox. *Cee-rist!* he thought, the papers . . .

He scooted downstairs and scooped them up off the mat. Quickly he went through the brutal tabloid that was most likely to have done him in, and then the ones that pretended to be more responsible.

Nope.

Nothing.

Nope. Nothing.

Phew.

Just the usual flammed-up load of old cobblers, masquerading as news.

There was allegedly a 'dirty bomb' threat to London, or so said 'sources' in the Home Office, with an eye, no doubt, to stirring up public alarm, and then introducing some fresh repression of liberty. There were acres of predictable drivel about the security arrangements for the celebrations today.

The police had launched some Al-Qaeda raid in Wolverhampton and Finsbury. But then there was one of those every month.

In other words, there was nothing important, and certainly nothing to feed his ludicrous paranoia. But some guilty instinct told him to purge the house of these bullying quires of paper.

So he stretched down the Common Sense Revolution to make it a kind of nightshirt (common sense, innit?) and zipped outside into the summer morning. He stuffed them into the fox-ravaged bin, and then checked that no one had seen him.

Drat. Someone had indeed seen him. It was that funny woman who was always muttering under her breath, and who had once seen him administering physical chastisement – in fact it was about the only occasion he had ever done so – to one of his other children.

He beamed at her, tugging the T-shirt over his hips.

With a shudder his neighbour hurried about her business, and Roger darted back up the steps to see the door shutting in his face.

'Oi. You. No!' he said.

He bent down to look through the flap.

'Please,' he said.

The child's sweet face came closer. He was now dressed in a red crusader's tabard, and brandished a plastic gladius or stabbing sword.

'You are not necessary,' he said to Roger through the letterbox. 'Mummy,' he called, looking back over his shoulder, 'do we know this man?'

Five minutes later, and with the help of his wife, Roger Barlow had regained access to his house, dressed, washed, and was thrashing around the kitchen looking for that . . . that thing.

'You know,' he said to his wife, 'the thing with the thing in it.'

His wife had been around long enough to know what to do in these circumstances. She got on with drinking her coffee. 'Ah yes,' she said, 'that thing.'

Barlow cast a worried glance at his watch. It was that green folder thing, the one all about poor Mrs Betts. They were threatening to close the respite centre she needed for her son, who had such severe learning difficulties that he had no realistic hope of education. And last night, in a fit of alcohol-induced elation, he had been staring at the autistic Betts kid's drawings, which were pretty good, and thought he had seen the answer. But he had had had HAD to have the file.

He was going to ring Mrs Betts that afternoon, and it was no use if he . . .

Maybe Cameron still had it. He looked again at his watch and wondered whether to dial his beautiful, omnicompetent American researcher. It was too early.

He searched again in his office, under the bed, under the sofa, under the doormat, in the stuff being put out for recycling. He had a sudden horror that he had accidentally thrown the folder away with the papers, and went back to the bins. And then he saw something under his son's chair, where the child was eating his second breakfast.

He had no time to ask how it had got there. He had no time to speculate on the industrial-strength adhesive with which it was now covered, and which is created by mixing Weetabix with milk.

He had no time because he had a speech to prepare, a respite centre to save, and he had to get to the Commons before the whole of Westminster was blockaded by the Americans.

The President was due to start speaking at 10 a.m., and Roger had to be in his seat in less than an hour. He pointed the bike south and started to churn his legs.

As for the President's breakfast, it differed from Roger's in almost every respect. It was a leisured and ruminative repast, taken at a round table in a vast bay window in the same vaulted apartments that have been given to every visiting head of state for the last fifty years.

Olaf of Norway had slept there. So had King Baudouin of

Belgium. So had the Pope, and come to that, President Marcos of the Philippines and sundry other thugs the Foreign Office had once thought fit to foist on Her Majesty, notably President Ceaucescu of Romania in 1978 and President Mugabe of Zimbabwe in 1994.

On the bedside table was a guide to the British Museum, a volume of Tennyson and a Dick Francis hardback that might have been new in 1973, when the room was used by President Mobutu Sese Seko of Zaire.

Now the President looked out over Windsor Great Park, at the ancient oaks, trussed and propped with iron, and the deer, and, in the distance, the looming turrets of Legoland; but what fascinated him most was the yellow packet of breakfast cereal, reposing in a specially constructed silver cruet.

'Say, honey, look at this,' he said to the First Lady, and read out the awesome royal warrants. 'By appointment to Her Majesty the Queen, Weetabix and Co., purveyors of breakfast cereals. And Prince Charles. And the Queen Mum. I thought she passed away.'

'Gee,' said the First Lady, who had also been trying to eat the Weetabix. 'Does that mean they make this stuff specially for the Queen?'

'I guess she has to sort of approve it.'

'How much does she have to eat?' asked the First Lady.

They both stared at their bowls. 'I dunno,' said the President. 'Kind of soaks up the milk, doesn't it?'

Like Barlow, the President considered the amazing physical properties of a Weetabix/milk solution, and its possible application in the construction industry. The First Lady fleetingly wondered what it would be like to have the Presidential seal on the back of a packet of Froot Loops.

There was a knock on the door.

'Sir,' said a US Secret Service man in a blue blazer, 'Colonel Bluett just called. He wanted to be sure you were aware of the security implications of the arrests last night.'

The President grimaced. He had naturally read the papers, but had been hoping not to bring the subject up in front of his wife.

'You bet,' he said. 'Good job by the Brits.'

'We should go now, sir, if you're ready, ma'am.'

'Too bad they didn't catch the main guy,' said the First Lady, who had also read the news.

That wasn't the only detail troubling Deputy Assistant Commissioner Stephen Purnell, who had been sitting at his desk since 6 a.m. in the New Scotland Yard Ops Room. News had come in of a vehicle theft in Wolverhampton, a crime that appeared to have taken place shortly before the not-quite-successful synchronized raids. It might mean something; it might mean nothing. But it was a very odd thing to steal, and his dilemma, now, was whether or not to share the information with the Americans. After ten days working on this visit with Colonel Bluett of the US Secret Service, he somehow couldn't face the conversation. 'Don't worry, sir,' said his assistant, who was called Grover. 'Even if it was our friends who took it, where the hell are they going to park it? I bet someone will find it within an hour.'

CHAPTER TWO
0824 HRS

It was going to be a beautiful day, thought William Eric Kinloch Onyeama, as he walked across Lambeth Bridge.

No. Wait.

He stopped, and his delighted eye scanned the landscape, dapply and wavy and branchy. He could do better than that.

He searched for his new favourite word. It was on the tip of his tongue. He had just confirmed its rough area of meaning with his teachers at the Euro language school in Peckham Rye.

He looked at the happy brown river, winking beneath the bituminous scum.

He looked at the gilt flèches and steeples of the Houses of Parliament, which inspired in him a deep and unfashionable reverence. That building was, in his view, heart-stoppingly lovely, but too spiky, surely, to qualify for the adjective he was now struggling to recall.

He took in the roses in Victoria Tower Gardens, and the red, white and blue flags that flew over the heart of Westminster on this day of glorious commemoration; the white ellipse of the London Eye; the leaves on the plane trees, turning up their light undersides in the breeze.

They were all beautiful, beautiful, but they were not exactly b— What was it again?

He looked down at his shoes, which he had polished the night before. They were fat Doc Martens, burnished and blushing like bumps or buns. They were bu— What was it? They were like the black rumps of the taxis, the bashful bums that beetled before him over the bridge. They were b—; they were bu— they were busty – no, they were buck, they were bucks—

That was it.

It was going to be a buxom day.

He grinned, and thought of all the things that might be classified as buxom.

Obviously there was Mrs (Nellie) Naaotwa Onyeama. She was as buxom as all get out. This he had amply confirmed a little while ago, just before he rose from her bed.

And the clouds above him were high and fleecy. How foolish they were to talk of rain, thought Eric; and how typically gloomy of the Apcoa people to make them take their pacamacs.

If you added it all together, thought Eric, if you looked at all the glitter and lustre and promise of the new summer's day, then you could argue – and he stood to be corrected – that this July morning stood fully in the semantic field of his new best word.

So he went on down Horseferry Road, past the obelisks with their odd pineapple finials, past the bearded stone Victorians who had conquered the continent from which he came, and he, the colonial, began to hunt in the former imperial metropolis.

He checked the Resparks. He checked the tax. If someone had stuck a ticket in the window, he noted the time of expiry and plotted his return.

All the while he was savouring this language which ruled the world, and over which he was acquiring mastery . . .

And there in Maunsel Street was his first prey of the morning, buxom in the curvature of its forequarters, a gleaming black four by four which had flouted the Respark and was therefore in defiance of Code 04 and a thoroughly ticketable vehicle.

He reached down for his Sanderson Huskie computer, the wizard device that has given the parkie the whip hand over the motorist. Eric started to record the time, place, and exact dereliction of a Pajero station wagon, licence plate L8 AG41N.

But now a woman was running back down the pavement towards him. She had a kid in tow, with a satchel and a blazer, and she wore an expression of tragic supplication.

'Oh please,' she wailed.

She was dressed with terrific chic. She had long blonde hair, dark eyebrows, a tight black T-shirt over a willowy figure and a belt made out of copper plates. It was hard to believe she could be the mother of a ten-year-old.

'I am very sorry,' he said and continued to tap.

'I'll be literally THREE minutes.'

'It is not for me to say. It is de rule.' Eric had caught a glimpse of himself in the smoked Pajero pane, and he knew what she was looking at: six foot two of anthracite hand-someness and power, as richly accoutred with high technology as an American infantryman. He had a smart peaked cap with the cap-badge of the council; he had metallic silver numbers on his epaulettes. He carried a TDS Huskie mini-computer. He had a two-way T8 288 Motorola radio. He had a Radix FP40 printer, ready to discharge his literary efforts, and he was about to print the ticket now.

'Oh please,' she said, 'I've got to drop him off at school, and he's got an exam.'

Eric smiled. 'What kind of exam?'

'It's a maths exam, isn't it, darling? Oh please, he's going to be late.'

'I don't care,' said the child.

'Oh darling.'

Eric approved of maths exams. A cadet branch of Eric's family had made a great deal of money by scamming arith-metically untalented Europeans, and he was generally in favour of encouraging our children to better themselves.

'Just one minute,' wheedled the woman.

The parkie considered. Many traffic wardens are traumatized by the verbals, as they are called. COON. NIGGER. MONKEY. APE.

Those were some of the names Eric had been called, shorn of their participial expletives.

IS THIS YOUR IDEA OF POWER? WHY DON'T YOU GET A BETTER JOB? These were some of the questions he was asked.

Faced with such disgusting behaviour, some traffic wardens respond with a merciless taciturnity. The louder the rant of the traffic offenders, the more acute are the wardens' feel-ings of pleasure that they, the stakeless, the outcasts, the niggers, are a valued part of the empire of law, and in a position to chastise the arrogance and selfishness of the indigenous people.

Eric was unusual in that he liked sometimes – every once in a while – to show mercy, as befitted his kingly lineage.

The scars on his cheeks denoted that he was a prince of the royal blood in the Hausa tribe, and it was only the evil of primogeniture that debarred him from substantial estates outside Lagos.

Sometimes he would exercise clemency, if he were offered a really rococo excuse, as a bored tutor will indulge a crapulous undergraduate if his reason for missing a class is truly bizarre and degenerate. Sometimes, as today, he could be moved by the appeal of a damn good-looking woman. But today he had a peculiar reason of his own for not wanting to prolong the conversation.

The night before Mrs Onyeama had been very good to him. She had made him his favourite meal, a chicken Kiev with a kind of special West African garlic called kulu, rather like the North American ramps, and he had slept well on it. But he knew from experience that Mrs Onyeama's chicken Kievs had an amazing effect on the digestive system. There was nothing normally detectable, but from time to time the kraken would wake, and then a globule of air would force itself up the oesophagus and press on the palate . . . until he was obliged to let it go.

It had happened to him at a wedding party recently. He had been telling a joke, and he came to the punchline, and everyone was crowded around him, like maternity unit staff, waiting for the birth of the joke, and he had suddenly felt – *whup* – this thing come out of him, involuntarily, rather like the thing in *Alien* coming out of John Hurt. His audience had reacted in much the same way as the characters in the movie.

So he beamed at her, without a word.

'Mmm-hmmm,' he murmured, and put down the Huskie.

'Really?' She couldn't believe it.

'Mmmmbmm.'

She gushed her thanks and was gone. And it was therefore with a faint sense of a hunter-gatherer who has missed one easy kill that he turned into Tufton Street, for the second time that morning.

He could hardly believe his eyes. It was still there.

It was the big one, el gordo. This was the white whale, and he was Ahab.

It had been there, to his certain knowledge, for half an hour, and probably far longer. The ambulance was on a single yellow. That was a Code 01 offence, and it was on the footway – that was Code 62. But what made it a legitimate target, in Eric's view, was that it was blocking the thoroughfare, in the sense that two cars could certainly not pass abreast.

It was not true – as the tabloids hinted – that he received a bounty for every car he successfully caused to be plucked from the streets. But it certainly was true that he received bonuses for 'productivity', and productivity was measured – well, how else could it be measured?

Eric and Naaotwa Onyeama were ambitious for their children, and on the televised urgings of Carol Vorderman they were currently investing in a series of expensive 'Kumon' maths text books. Since Eric Onyeama only made £340 per week, working from 8.30 a.m. to 6.30 p.m., this was not an opportunity he could responsibly pass up.

He reached for his Motorola and summoned the clampers. Then, since there could be no question of the vehicle staying where it was, he rang the tow-truck company.

Hee hee hee, chortled Eric, and he laughed at the multiple pleasures of the morning.

He knew all the tow-truck men, and Dragan Panic, the Serb, was the hungriest of the lot. Unless the mysterious crew of this ambulance returned within five minutes, the vehicle was a goner.

In the Tivoli café on the corner of Great Peter Street and Marsham Street three men and a kid of about nineteen were

13

coming to the end of breakfast. The restaurant was non-posh to the point of affectation. Up the nostrils of its diners rose the tang of vinegar, mothering in its bottle, mingling with the ammoniacal vapours that hummed from the cloth that was used to wipe the Formica.

But the four dark customers had done well. They had eaten a meal of Henrician proportions: eggs, beans, chips, chops, schnitzels, steaks. The proprietor was amazed, especially considering it was not yet nine in the morning.

They had swallowed draughts of milkless tea, turned into a kind of sugary quicksand, and then they had eaten the Danish pastry and the doughnuts, ancient thickly iced things that had been in the display so long he had feared he would have to reduce the price.

They had eaten, in fact, as if there were no tomorrow; but today their mortal frames required relief. Owing to their eccentric bivouac they had been unable to pass water all night.

'Quickly,' said the one called Jones, coming back from the toilets. 'The traffic wardens will be here.' There was certainly something lilting and eastern about his accent; but if you shut your eyes and ignored his brown skin, there were tonic effects – birdlike variations in pitch – that were positively Welsh.

'I must go too,' said one of his colleagues, who had a moustache.

'Well, hurry, God help us.'

Haroun scowled. It was obviously inequitable for their leader so to privilege his own requirements, but no doubt he was under pressure.

'Sir, please can I go?'

It was the kid. 'Quickly, Dean,' said the man called Jones.

There was only one toilet, identified by a pictogram on the door, of a Regency buck and a crinolined dame, to show it was for the use of both sexes, and by an unspoken agreement Dean went in first.

Full though his bladder was after a night of appalling discomfort on a stretcher in that airless vehicle, he found he was trembling too much.

'What is going on?' hissed the man called Jones.

'What are you doing in there?' Haroun banged on the door and Dean felt that any hope of micturition was gone. He respected Jones, but he was seriously frightened of Haroun, who had the pale blue eyes and tiny black pupils of a staring seagull.

Jones saw a traffic warden pass the window. Their researches had already established that the wardens around here were sticklers, and he had a sense of impending disaster.

He ran out and round the corner. He stood still. He shut his eyes. He clenched his fists.

'*Nooo*,' he called. 'Stop it, you!'

Already a clamp had appeared on the right-hand front wheel of the ambulance, a green clamp, moronic, infernal. He swore in Arabic.

Hmar. Jackass.

Yebnen kelp. Son of a bitch.

Hee hee hee, chortled Eric Onyeama.

Jones ran back into the Tivoli and rounded up his men. By now only Haroun had failed to make use of the facilities.

'Come,' said Jones.

'I must just go . . .' said Haroun, but such was the power of Jones, and so contemptuous was the expression in his eyes that Haroun followed him like a lamb and Jones ran back into the sunlight.

And now he couldn't believe it . . . He couldn't flipping well believe it. Surely he had been gone only seconds, and now the clamp had gone but the ambulance was being hoisted up into a kind of hammock by a hydraulic lift, and the parkie was standing there, still scribing zealously away into his Huskie computer.

'I am sorry, sir,' recited Eric, 'but once all four wheels are off the ground, you have lost control of the vehicle. It is now the responsibility of Westminster City Council.'

Jones waved the keys. 'But it is ours. Put it down.'

'All the craps are on,' said Eric.

'The craps?'

'Yessir, these are the craps. The metal craps.'

'You mean the crabs.'

'That is right, sir, they are the craps.'

Jones gave up. 'Did you say all four wheels?'

'Yes, that is correct, sir. Now that all four wheels are off the ground, it is the law that you no longer have any control over this vehicle.'

This was a big ambulance. Fully laden it weighed not far short of three and a half tonnes, with a 3.5 litre Rover V8 engine and bulky aluminium chassis, so that it was already astonishing that the tow-truck had been able to hoist it.

At that moment Jones had an inspiration. It was technically true that the wheels were off the ground. But the front pair were only a few inches up.

'What about now?' asked Jones. He and Haroun jumped on the bonnet of the Leyland Daf vehicle, painted with a blue star and caduceus, and it sunk its nose until the front offside wheel brushed the ground.

'See!' shouted Jones. 'Now it is ours again!'

CHAPTER THREE

0832 HRS

'Whose ambulance did you say it was?' asked Deputy Assistant Commissioner Purnell, who was, today, in charge of anti-terrorist and security operations throughout the Metropolis.

Grover entered the room with an air of satisfaction. 'What did I tell you? We've got it. An ambulance from the Bilston and Willenhall NHS Trust was seen at the Travelodge in Dunstable at one a.m.'

'Good. And it's still there, is it?'

'Er, no. It left.'

'Aha.'

'We're on the case.'

A second later, he was back again. 'I've got Bluett on the line.'

The two London policemen looked at each other. They knew – or strongly suspected – that the Americans were tuning in to their frequencies.

'Put him through,' said Deputy Assistant Commissioner Purnell.

He listened with half-closed eyes to the American's demands.

'You want a sniper on the roof of the Commons? What did you say his name was?' On a piece of headed notepaper Purnell printed 'PICKLE'. Then he crossed it out and wrote 'PICKEL'.

'I see, yes,' he said, 'I see, yes.'

He listened some more, and then said: 'Well, I can understand if the First Lady is a bit anxious but . . . Right you are, Colonel . . . Okeycokey, chum. Yep. See you later, I expect . . . No, no, everything else is, um, fine. We have no evidence of anything, you know, untoward.'

He disconnected with a groan.

'They want a sniper on the roof of the Commons, above New Palace Yard. I've said we'll oblige. Someone answering to this name will be presenting himself in a few minutes. Whatever happens, I am not having him sitting up there alone.'

He handed over the sheet of paper. 'And I want the choppers to start scanning Westminster for this flaming ambulance.'

High above Soho a Metropolitan Police Twin Squirrel Eurocopter AS 355N banked and turned down Shaftesbury Avenue.

* * *

17

It passed directly over the head of Roger Barlow, who looked up and felt vaguely resentful. Why did they hover in that threatening way over innocent streets? It was like some dreary lefty movie about Thatcher's Britain.

Then he continued to thread his way through the cars. That's what he loved about bicycles: the autonomy, the ability to put your wheel wherever you chose. As you looked over the handlebars you could see your front tyre as a snub-nosed cylinder, nosing at will down the open streets of London. He passed an *Evening Standard* hoarding, announcing full coverage of the state visit.

Uh-oh. The *Standard*. He had forgotten about the *Standard*. How would he stop his wife seeing that one?

The traffic was getting heavier. Now he understood. It was the exclusion zone. The American security people had insisted on a total ban on traffic in the area to be honoured by their presence, and the result was that a freeborn Englishman could not even move down the Queen's highway.

'Strewth,' he cursed, and used a disabled ramp to mount the pavement. He knew he shouldn't do it, but there you go. In any case, his political career might be over by tomorrow morning.

Then he was back on the road again, watching the shimmer starting to rise from the hot bonnets of the backed-up traffic, and *thugga thugga whok whok* the helicopter was ceasing to impinge on his consciousness.

CHAPTER FOUR
0833 HRS

In the Twin Squirrel Eurocopter the two sun-goggled officers peered into the hot canyons and smoking wadis of the city. 'So who's meant to be driving this ambulance?' said the pilot, as they passed over Trafalgar Square and made for the river. 'He's called Jones,' said Grover from New Scotland Yard.

'Jones? What's he look like?'

'Kind of Arab-type thing.'

Hundreds of miles away, at Fylingdales in Yorkshire, the word Arab triggered an automatic alert in the huge golfball-shaped American listening post, and within seconds the conversation was being monitored in Langley, Virginia.

The pilot continued: 'That's all we know: that he's a kind of Arab called Jones?'

'That, and he's on the CIA's most wanted list. His father was a gynaecologist in Karachi who was struck off for some reason. He knows a lot about explosives and is a serious wacko. That's what we know about Jones . . .'

Who at that moment was sliding with Haroun off the bonnet of the ambulance and on to Tufton Street, as the vehicle was jerked up into the air.

Dragan Panic was standing by his Renault 150 authorized removal unit, twiddling the vertical line of six hydraulic knobs, and grinning. It was always fun when they went doolally.

One chap had leapt aboard his Porsche Cayenne, mana-cled to the truck, and put it into reverse.

He took it up to about 7,000 revs, smoke pouring every-where, as the Bavarian beast struggled to escape the gin. There had been a bang and a fresh convexity appeared in the gleaming black bonnet, like a rat in a rubbish sack. That HAD been gratifying.

Jones decided to take a different tack with the traffic warden. He made the obvious point.

'But we are ambulance men.'

The parkie looked at him.

That was just it. He had watched the vehicle like a tethered goat. He had seen the men get out, leaving it parked in a disgracefully dangerous position.

He had seen them shamble into the Tivoli for breakfast. He didn't believe for one minute that they were ambulance men. They were the first ambulance men he had ever seen in scruffy old T-shirts and jeans, and he didn't see why they should be in possession of an ambulance belonging to the Bilston and Willenhall NHS Trust.

'Please, let us pay now.'

'No, you must come to the pound.'

'Why?'

'You must establish that the vehicle is yours.'

'But I have lost the papers.'

'Then you must come to the pound.'

The man called Jones went to the cabin of the ambulance and rootled in the glove box. He came back with a brick of cash, like the wodge the winner has at the end of a game of Monopoly, or what you get for a fiver in Zimbabwean dollars. Eric frowned and pretended to study his Huskie.

'Please do not force me to beg,' said Jones.

'I ain't forcing you to beg, sir.'

'My sister is pregnant.'

With every second that passed, Eric was surer that he had done the right thing. Now if they had said that they were taking the Duke of Edinburgh on a secret assignation with a nurse from St Thomas's hospital, that would have been one thing.

If they had said that they had a freshly excised human liver on board, and that it needed to be transferred in ten minutes to a terminally alcoholic football player, or if they had claimed to be part of Scotland Yard's counter-terrorist unit, they would have appealed to his imagination.

But to say that his sister was pregnant – that was sorry stuff. He looked at the four of them. He noticed that the youngest one was staring at him in a funny way, as if terrified.

Am I really so frightening? wondered Eric Onyeama, king of the kerb. He continued to tap into the Huskie.

'L64896P', 'Tufton Street', '02, 62' . . . The details were soon pinged into space, and stored in irrefutable perpetuity in the Apcoa computers. Somewhere in cyberspace the electronic data began to team up with other groups of electrons; in less than half a second they were having a vast symposium of sub-atomic particles, and among the preliminary conclusions would be that the vehicle was from Wolverhampton.

He looked up again, and saw the kindlier-looking one, Habib, who was cleaning his teeth with a carved juniper twig. But where was the other one?

Haroun had vanished.

He had stolen inside the machine and he was searching for something.

He knocked aside a cervical collar-set. He brushed a mouth-to-mouth ventilator to the floor. Ha, he thought to himself. This would unquestionably do the job, he decided. He extracted the prong of a pericardial puncture kit, and tested its needle point on his finger.

CHAPTER FIVE
0835 HRS

'Looks like a killer,' said Purnell. He gave a small shudder as he looked at the file on Haroun Abu Zahra, a slim docket. 'What do we know about him?'

'Not a lot,' said Grover, 'but the Yanks are pretty keen on talking to him as well. There is one thing, though.' He paused, as all subordinates will when they are keen to emphasize some tiny advance.

'Our lads were talking to the Travelodge, and they said there was something most peculiar about their room.'

'After they'd left?'

'Yeah. There's a picture by some posh artist on the wall, of a naked girl, you know, a print.'

'Uh-huh.'

'Tits out, very tasteful and all.'

'Go on.'

'And they had turned it to the wall. Twenty minutes later they checked out.'

'Wackos.'

The phone went in the outer room. They both knew it was Bluett.

Deputy Assistant Commissioner Purnell looked at the clock on the wall.

'They'll be on their way, won't they?'

'No way of stopping them now,' said Grover.

No fewer than fifteen BMW 750 police motorcycles were engaged in sheepdogging the traffic out of the way of the slowly oncoming cavalcade.

Now they were approaching Junction 4 for West Drayton and Heathrow, and seeing the signs the President looked over to his right.

He tried to spot the two Boeing 747-700s, painted in the eggshell blue livery of the President of the United States; but no sign. Perhaps they had been tactfully concealed in a hangar.

After the airport the wailing host of outriders and motorbike voortrekkers took the red route that runs from Heathrow to London. They shovelled the taxis aside and cowed the cursing commuters.

One woman tried to see into the tint-windowed limos and crashed her Nissan Micra into the back of an expensive but vulnerable Alfa 164. The ensuing delay added an average of fifteen minutes to the journeys of more than 1,000 motorists.

*   *   *

As the traffic thickened down the Charing Cross Road, it occurred to Roger that this security business would be no joke. What if he couldn't even get into his office?

Cameron. That was the answer.

Cameron would have all the passes necessary.

He reached into his breast pocket for his mobile, since he was all in favour of using his bike as his office.

Damn. Oh yes. He'd thrown it away the other day when it rang at the wrong moment. Straight out of the car window, as it happened, on the M25, landing safely in some buddleias in the central reservation.

He negotiated the Palio of Trafalgar Square and howled round into Whitehall. And here it was.

A fence. Ribbons of aluminium fences, and policemen in fluorescent yellow, sprouting like dandelions in the grey of the stone and the tarmac, and the *whok-whok-whok* of a helicopter in the distance.

'I'm sorry, sir, you'll have to dismount.'

'But I'm a Member of Parliament.'

The policeman looked at him with open disgust.

'I don't care if you're the Queen of Sheba, sir.'

And so it went on as Roger was shunted in a ludicrous arc westwards of the place to which his electors had sent him. Every time he attempted to penetrate the cordon of fencing he was sent off again in search of some mythical entry point.

'I'm sorry, sir, you can't take your bike through here.'

At one point, to his shame, he snapped at the men in blue.

'What's wrong with my bike?'

'It's a lethal weapon, sir.'

'You can say that again. It's almost killed me several times.'

'Now don't try to be funny, sir. I've seen these things packed with explosives. I've seen what they can do. Look, I know it's annoying, sir,' said the copper, seeing his expression, 'but please try to bear with us. We're all doing our best, but the whole caboodle has been agreed with the Americans.'

23

And so Roger Barlow tacked ever round and west, until he found himself in Pimlico and puffing up Tufton Street.

Where he saw Dragan Panic standing by the tiplift of his Renault 150, heaving some large white vehicle aboard.

'Come on, droogie moi, come on, my friend,' said Dragan to himself in Serbo-Croat.

In theory the Renault could lift 4,450 kilos, but the hydraulics were puffing a bit and the stabilizing rods were biting into the tarmac the way a heart attack victim clutches his chest.

Dragan wanted to take this bleeding ambulance, and then he wanted to scarper. Personally, he thought Eric the parkie was mad.

OK, so it was dangerously parked. But you didn't lift an ambulance. Nah, not an ambulance. Since fleeing Pristina in 1999 Dragan had slotted in nicely in the East End. His knuckles were richly scabbed and crusted with doubloons, and he dressed in trackie bums. At Christmas he sold Christmas trees on the street corner, thumping his mittened hands together. He did a bit of gamekeeping for some toffs out in Essex, place called Rayleigh, and he did like a high bird.

But lifting an ambulance – well, it was like shooting a white pheasant, wasn't it? He wasn't on for that. And above all he didn't like being in the company of Muslims. That wasn't just because he was a Serb killer from Pristina, and a former member of Arkan's Tigers.

It was also because he was as big a coward as ever set fire to a Muslim hayrick in the dark, and experience had taught him that you had to keep an eye on the sneaky bastards. Speaking of which . . .

A couple of them seemed to have vanished. Now there was just the young kid and the spooky-looking fellow, and the parkie taking his time.

CHAPTER SIX

0837 HRS

Eric Onyeama was struggling with the urge not to burp.

This man was rude, and Eric had to maintain his poise and dignity. It was impossible to do this while burping.

'Please . . . Oh you bastard,' said the man called Jones. 'Just do what I say or I'll . . .'

'I must warn you that it is the policy of our company to take legal action against anybody who uses the verbal or physical ab—'

As when scuba divers find a pocket of stale air in a sunken submarine, and the bubble rises to the surface in a distended globule, so the garlic vapours were released from Eric's stomach.

'Abuu—'

They passed in a gaseous bolus through his oesophagus, and slid out invisibly through the barrier of his teeth.

'Abuse,' he said, and a look of mystification, and then horror passed over the face of the man called Jones. He staggered back.

Ah yes, thought Roger Barlow, a classic scene of our modern vibrant multicultural society, a group of asylum seekers in dispute with a Nigerian traffic warden.

Poor bleeders, he thought. What were they? Albanians, Kosovars, Tajiks, Uzbeks, Martians? Now their day was wrecked. They would have to find the thick end of £200 just to spring their motor. How many windscreens would they have to wash to earn that back?

He composed a sorrowful speech in his head, to the effect that the law was cruel, but that its essence was impartiality. Hang about, he said to himself as he drew nearer. That's bonkers. They can't take an ambulance.

Barlow rescues ambulance, he said to himself reflexively. Have-a-go hero MP in mercy dash. 'I couldn't believe my eyes,' said Mr Barlow last night. The *Mail* asks: Has the world gone mad? He was thinking Newsroom Southeast, he was thinking Littlejohn. He was thinking Big Stuff. Well, this was a story, all right. That should get that awful Debbie woman off his back.

He saw the traffic warden say something to the olive-skinned man, and the olive-skinned man reeled; and no wonder he reeled, poor dutiful fellow. He could imagine that they were already late for a mission.

Across London, the mere act of getting up was taking a terrible toll. People were braining themselves in the shower, slicing their nostrils with Bic razors, brushing their teeth with their children's poisonous Quinoderm acne cream, sustaining cardiac infarcts at finding themselves misreported in the paper – and where was the ambulance?

It was outrageous! Roger braked and spoke in the mellow bedside tones of the MP's surgery.

CHAPTER SEVEN
0839 HRS

'Excuse me. I wonder if I can help.'

The traffic warden smiled bashfully. 'It's OK, sir, we do not need any help here. De law is de law.'

'I know it's none of my business, but are you seriously going to remove that ambulance?'

'Please, sir, do not get involved. I cannot make de rules. I can only enfoooo – *oo* excuse me, I can only enforce them.'

Barlow blinked as he was engulfed. 'But this is absurd,' he said, turning to the victims. 'I know this shouldn't make any difference,' he said superbly, 'but I am an MP.'

For the first time the olive-skinned man faced the MP. His

passport said his name was Jones, and that he had been born in Mold, Clwyd. Though it was true that he was currently a student at an institution implausibly called Llangollen University, these biographical details seemed unlikely.

Roger Barlow noticed something about his eyes. They had a kind of wobble. It was as though he was watching a very close-up game of ping-pong.

'Piss off,' he said. 'Piss off and die.'

'Eh?' Barlow gasped.

'Not necessarily in that order,' said Jones.

Barlow looked for guidance to the warden. There was something badly out of whack here. When all was said and done, were they not, he and the warden, part of the same team?

He made the law, the warden enforced it. They were like two china dogs, bracketing the sacred texts of statute.

'I'm sorry . . . ?' he said, pathetically.

Tee hee hee, sniggered Eric Onyeama, and shook his head at the busybody. He felt sure he had seen dis man before, maybe in church, or at a meeting of parents and teachers. But if Roger was looking for an ally now, he was out of luck.

'De man is right,' he said. 'You must go away.' And Roger did. For once he felt he could have made a difference. He could have improved things here. He cycled on. Was it getting hotter, or was that the sweat of embarrassment?

That man told me to piss off, he told himself. And die, too. He wondered whether anyone had seen his humiliation.

Had Barlow not been so mortified, he might have seen Haroun issue from the side of the van and pass something to Jones. The leader of the gang of four now looked at his watch and decided it was time to bring matters to a close.

'Please be so kind as to put the ambulance down now, and stop this damnfoolery.'

Hey dere, said Eric to himself. The Huskie was chirruping back to him.

I knew it, he thought. The ambulance had been reported stolen last night, from Dymock Street, Wolverhampton.

'Did you hear what I said?' Jones's voice had an evil snit to it.

'I'm sorry,' said Eric, thinking fast, 'but you must come with me to the pound.'

'I'm going to ask you one last time: give us back our vehicle.'

'You have broken de law.'

'No,' sneered Jones: 'you broke de fucking law. You lifted the thing off the ground while we were here.'

'I am sorry, but that is wrong.'

'You IDIOT! Tell him to put the ambulance down. Tell him to do it now.'

In defence of its parking attendants, men and women who must put up with some of the worst abuse known to this coarsened, selfish and irresponsible age, Westminster Council gives them cameras.

These are used not just to record the offence, but also to deter the protesting traffic offender just as he is about to bust a blood vessel or commit a common assault. Now Eric took out his Sony DSU-30 digital camera, and left the Huskie hanging by his neck. As he was doing this Haroun was creeping unseen up the side of the tow-truck.

In his hand he held a nasty-looking piece of medical equipment which was, did he but know it, a thorax draining kit. The man called Jones began to swear – never a good sign for those who had dealings with this horrid person.

'*Omak zanya fee erd.*' Your mother committed adultery with a donkey.

'I am sorry?' beamed Eric, who had decided to call the police.

'*Yen 'aal deen ommak!*' barked Jones. Damn your mother's rooster – a deadlier insult than you might think, if only to an Arab.

'What for do you need an ambulance anyway?' asked

Eric, and he took a couple of quick shots of Jones: billhook nose, grubby neck, short grey-flecked hair and peculiar eyes.

'It is for the disabled,' said Jones.

'Who are the disabled?'

Haroun tiptoed round the front of the Renault and prepared to lunge at Dragan Panic.

'I don't see a disabled person anywhere,' repeated Eric. 'Show me the disabled person.'

'Here is the disabled person,' said Jones.

'Where?'

'Here.'

The last noise Eric heard before he fainted with shock was the ripping of his own pericardium as it was punctured by the pericardial puncture unit. Then there was a scraping noise as the spike hit something hard that might have been bone.

'Help me,' shouted Jones to Dean, the nineteen-year-old, as he caught the falling warden.

Dean watched, mouth agape, as his boss buckled under the weight; and then leapt forward to help him arrange the traffic warden in the gutter.

CHAPTER EIGHT
0841 HRS

Dragan the Serb had been weaned on tales of heroic assassination and glorious betrayal. From the Battle of Kosovo Pole onwards, Serbs have learned to glory in a sense of victimhood. But today he decided to give the national myth a miss.

He pushed away Haroun and his spike, and thudded off, weaving and shoulders hunched, as though with every yard he expected a bullet in his back from the Kosovo Liberation Army.

He sprinted from the Muslim extremists, down Tufton Street, past the (former) Society for the Propagation of the Gospel in Foreign Parts, founded in 1701, and turned on to Great Peter Street. He weaved one way, he ducked the other.

Haroun watched him go.

'Leave him,' called Jones. 'We have no time.'

Dean already felt he had good reason to be admiring of Jones, but he was amazed at the self-possession with which his boss now began to unload the ambulance from the tow-truck.

'Whoa,' he called, as the telescopic arm of the crane jerked into life, and the vehicle was thrust out into the street.

The arm was powered by three separate hydraulic lifts, the first capable of carrying 2,500 kilos, the second 1,700 kilos and the third 1,300 kilos; and in theory they were well capable of lifting a three-and-a-half-tonne ambulance.

But Jones was in such a hurry that he neglected the basic laws of physics.

'Hey!' said Dean, as the white machine was swung out over the street, like some mad mediaeval siege engine.

Haroun gave a curse – something nasty about a dog, Dean guessed – and even Habib broke off from flossing with his juniper twig.

'Yow need to come back a bit,' shouted Dean over the roar of the Renault engine.

The front wheels of the tow-truck were now on the verge of leaving the ground; black smoke was coming from the exhaust; the whole thing was about to keel over, and Dean instinctively ran to drag the body of Eric the warden out of the way.

'It is fine, it is fine,' shouted Jones, and flipped the next toggle, so that their stolen machine crashed back towards them and bust a taillight on the bed of the tow-truck.

'Do it like this,' called Habib quietly in Arabic. Habib was also called Freddie, and came from a good Lebanese family.

He was a Takfiri, a man who masked the ferocity of his faith with a sympathetic worldliness; and he had spent enough time in gambling houses to understand the principles of the grabby machines you use to pick up a watch or a fluffy toy.

Together, and with what Dean thought was remarkable coolness, he and Jones worked out how to ease in the last extender arm and, in hydraulic pants, the van was lowered to the ground.

With the speed of Formula One pitstopmen they now undid the metal crabs and hessian straps, bunged them on the back of the tow-truck, and loaded poor Eric in the back of the ambulance.

Haroun paused only to read the sign on the side of the Renault.

'How ees my driving?' he said, and laughed, a horrible carking yelp.

It says something for the tranquillity that has descended on the Church of England that no one else observed these events outside Church House.

No one took any notice of them as they drove in full conformity with the laws of the road – apart from the tail-light – in the direction of the Palace of Westminster.

They began thereby to catch up with Roger Barlow, who was waiting with his bike at a red traffic light, as all good lawmakers must.

CHAPTER NINE
0843 HRS

Barlow's thoughts of political extinction had taken a philo-sophical turn. Did it matter? Of course not. The fate of the human race was hardly affected. The sun would still, at the appointed date four billion years hence, expand to the girth of a red giant and devour the planet. In the great scheme of things his extermination was about as important as the accidental squashing of a snail. The trouble was that until that happy day when he was reincarnated as a louse or a baked bean, he didn't know how he was going to explain the idiotic behaviour of his brief human avatar.

It wasn't the sex comedy side of things. It wasn't the waste of money, the cash that should have gone into Weetabix and plastic guns for shooting him in bed.

It was the gullibility – that was what worried him.

Should he wait for the papers to present this appalling Hieronymus Bosch version of his life? Or should he try to give his account first, and thereby win points for frankness?

Hang on a tick: there was a colleague. Swishing down the pavement, hair cut by Trumpers, suit cut by Savile Row – it was Adrian (Ziggy) Roberts. Bright. Forceful. Decisive. Very far from completely unbearable; in fact, by any standards really rather nice.

Roger conceived a desire to talk to him, not least because he could see under his arm the early edition of the *Evening Standard*.

'Ziggy, old man,' called Roger Barlow, kerb-crawling on his bike.

'Hombre!' replied Ziggy.

'You going to this Westminster Hall business?'

'God no,' said Ziggy, who had benefited from the most expensive education England can provide. 'Can't be arsed.'

Roger felt welling up in himself the urge to confide in a friend. A problem shared, he whispered to himself, is a problem halved.

'Can I ask you something, Zigs?'

'Of course.'

Roger looked at his colleague, his high, clear forehead, his myriad certainties. On second thoughts, no.

Ziggy counted as a friend, but it was, in the end, your

friends who did you in. And quite right, too. That was what friends were for.

'That posh suit,' said Barlow. 'Just tell me roughly how much.' But Ziggy's answer was lost in the noise of the Twin Squirrel Eurocopter. Blimey, thought Barlow: this was worse than the helicopter paranoia scene in *Goodfellas*.

'Wait a sec,' said the co-pilot of the chopper, as they bullocked over towards the Embankment. He craned backwards the way they had come, and the City of Westminster – touching in its majesty – was reflected in the black visor of his helmet.

'I just realized . . .'

'Say again?' yodelled the pilot into the mike on his chin.

'I think we just flew over it. It was on a tow-truck. I didn't really take it in . . .'

'On a tow-truck?'

'Yeah, you know, a council truck.'

'Bollocks,' said the pilot. 'No one lifts an ambulance.'

'Go on, it'll take thirty seconds. Just back there in that little street near Marsham Street.'

The pilot sighed and turned the joystick. 'Well,' he said a little later. 'There's your tow-truck, but I don't see any ambulance.'

The co-pilot stared. It may have been unusual for an ambulance to be hoisted, but it was positively unheard of for a vehicle of any kind to escape the clutches of a tow-truck operator.

'Where's the driver, anyway?' he asked himself.

Here, thought Dragan Panic. Down here! Look this way!

For a couple of seconds he jumped up and down, waving and staring at the police helicopter until his eyeballs began to ache from the glare.

No use. They couldn't see him.

Dragan had a pretty good idea what he had witnessed: the

shambolic beginning of something that might end with eternal loss and heartache for thousands of families. He had read about the idiotic punch-up outside Boston's Logan Airport on the morning of 9/11 itself, when the Islamic headcases left their maps and their Koran and their flight manuals in the stolen hire car. But mere incompetence was no guarantee of failure, as he knew from his own soldiering.

Dragan looked down towards Marsham Street. He saw a building site; he saw men in yellow hats and muddy boots. Tough men, who could help.

He was older and fatter than he had been as a purple-pyjamaed Serb MUP man, and he was soaked with sweat; and though he had absolutely no reason to love the United States, not after what they had done to Serbia, he stamped and grunted as fast as his Reeboks would carry him.

'Hey!' he shouted. 'Help, please!'

Dark faces looked up.

Dragan put his hands on his knees in exhaustion, and began to explain to the immigrant builders that there was a plot against America.

CHAPTER TEN

0844 HRS

'I'm starting to think we should warn the Yanks,' said Deputy Assistant Commissioner Purnell.

'You mean about the ambulance?' said Grover. 'What makes you think they don't know already?'

But when Purnell came to dial Bluett he once again found himself changing his mind. Why raise the temperature?

He cleared his throat when Bluett picked up, and was on the point of improvising some excuse when the American cut in.

'Mr Deputy Commissioner, we have a problem.'

'Oh yes,' said Purnell, 'I know. I mean, what problem?'

'We got reports of helicopter activity right over the cavalcade route, and the Black Hawk needs to go that way.'

'. . .' said Purnell.

'We need that Black Hawk in the aerial vicinity at all times, and neither of us wants a mid-air collision.'

Purnell found his eyes closing, and he listened some more.

'Unbelievable,' he told Grover, when the conversation was over. 'We've got just over an hour till the President starts speaking, and the Americans are fussing about the French Ambassador's girlfriend. They say they don't want her in the hall.

'And tell the boys in the chopper to clear out of the way, would you?'

The trouble with today, thought Purnell, was that if something did go wrong, no one could say they hadn't been warned.

BOMB SCARE HITS LONDON read Roger Barlow, continuing to steal shifty looks at Ziggy's *Standard*; and then page after page about the state visit.

Of course there was nothing about him. He felt like laughing at his own egocentricity.

There was something prurient about the way he wanted to read about his own destruction, just as there was something weird about the way he had been impelled down the course he had followed. Maybe he wasn't a genuine akratic. Maybe it would be more accurate to say he had a thanatos urge. By this time next week, he thought, there would be nothing left for him to do but go on daytime TV shows. Perhaps in ten years' time he might be sufficiently rehabilitated to be offered the part of Widow Twanky at the Salvation Army hall in Horsham.

'Catch you round, then,' said Barlow to Ziggy.

'Ciao-ciao,' called Ziggy, the man of efficiency and ambition. He flashed his pink 'P' form, and was admitted to the security bubble.

For the eighth time that morning, Barlow presented his bike for inspection by the authorities.

Roadblock was too modest a word for the Atlantic wall of concrete that the anti-terrorist mob had put in Parliament Square. Each lithon of black-painted aggregate was packed with steel and designed to withstand 83 newtons of force, or a suicide ram-raid with a Chieftain tank.

There was a gap through which cars were being admitted in drips, but all cycles were being stopped.

'Whoa there, sir,' said a sixteen-and-a-half-stone American man with a kind of transparent plastic Curly-Wurly coming out of his ear and disappearing into his collar. 'How are we today?'

'We're fine,' said Barlow shortly.

'I can't let you through without a pink pass with the letter P.' Barlow had grown up in the Cold War, and when at school he had read Thucydides. It had been obvious to him that America was the modern Athens – energetic, pluralistic, the guarantor of democracy and freedom; and therefore infinitely to be preferred to the Soviet Union, closed, nasty, militaristic, the modern Sparta. But now, on being intercepted by an enormous Kansan, just feet away from the statue of Winston Churchill, he felt his gorge rise. His eyes prickled with irritation. 'I am a Member of Parliament.

'Oh, damn it all,' he added; though as luck would have it his curse was lost in the noise of the Metropolitan Police Twin Squirrel swinging high and away towards Victoria.

Had he looked 200 feet behind him, he would have seen the ambulance come to a halt in the queue for the very same traffic lights-cum-checkpoint.

* * *

Sitting at the wheel, Jones swore. Any minute now the caval-cade would be upon them. He looked at the Americans, checking each vehicle with glacial deliberation, and checked his watch.

'*Aire fe Mabda'ak,*' he said, which means 'My cock in your principles'.

The cavalcade was now approximately twenty-seven minutes away from Parliament Square. Apart from the outriders, it consisted of thirty black vehicles, a mobile operating theatre complete with the appropriate blood supplies and a specially adapted Black Hawk helicopter in a continuous hover, intended to snatch the principals in the event of an ambush. The two 'permanent protectees', as they were known to the 950 American agents in London, were in a Cadillac De Ville so fortified it was a wonder it could move. The armour plating was five inches thick and designed to withstand direct fire from a bazooka or a mine placed beneath it. There was a tea-cosy of armour around the battery, the radiator and the engine block, to minimize the risk of the fuel catching fire. The glass was three inches of polycarbonate laminate and instead of allowing the driver simply to look through the windshield, an infra-red camera scanned the heat signa-ture of all the objects in the path of the car, and projected an image on the inside of the windscreen. But move the Cadillac did, though at something less than the US speed limit.

Permanent Protectee number one shuffled the papers of his speech and touched the hand of Permanent Protectee number two. It was an insane way to travel, but kind of fun. The cavalcade mounted the ramparted expressway at the end of the M4, and West London was spread out beneath them in the morning sun, like a beautiful woman surprised in bed without her make-up.

'Gee,' said the second Permanent Protectee, 'ain't that something?'

She smiled at her husband, but secretly she was worried.

She had been reading the papers; she knew about the abortive raids on the Islamist cells. That was why she had furtively telephoned Colonel Bluett and begged him to take extra precautions.

Bluett had been frankly amazed, but also pleased to be made her confidant.

'Yes, ma'am,' he said. 'Never mind what the Brits say: that place is gonna be full of my people. I mean some of our top men.'

As the cavalcade began to crawl the last nine miles of its journey, a hatch was opening on the roof of the east wing of the Palace of Westminster, in the cool shadow of Big Ben. Out scrambled the sizeable figure of Lieutenant Jason Pickel.

He stood for a moment on the duckboards, 120 feet above New Palace Yard, listening to the honking of horns down the Embankment, the protesters bleating to each other, like ewes in some distant fold. He held out his hand and squinted at it.

'Man oh man,' he said to himself. He stopped the tremor by gripping his sniper's rifle, and walked on down the duckboard until he found a point of vantage.

'Are you all right, Jason?' asked Sergeant Indira Nath, who had followed him up. Indira had been specifically deputed to stay with Pickel, on the orders of Deputy Assistant Commissioner Stephen Purnell.

Not that the British cops had any reason to think of Pickel as a risk. It was just that if they were going to have a Yank sharpshooter on the east wing roof – and Bluett was very keen – then there was damn well going to be a Brit to accompany him.

Indira was from the SO19 Firearms Unit. She had huge eyes, rosy lips, and tiny, delicate hands, in which she now toted an Arctic Warfare sniper rifle, built by Accuracy International of Portsmouth, capable in the hands of an average marksman of bunching bullets within a couple of inches at more than 600 yards. In the hands of Indira, the gun could shoot the horns off a snail.

'You OK?' she repeated.

'It's just that something gave me goosebumps here. I guess you could call it Dad flashbacks.'

Dad flashbacks? wondered Indira. It sounded like something worrying from Sheila Kitzinger's *Baby and Child Care*. She looked at her neighbour on the roof. He was big and blond, with a proud nose and heavy brow, and hands that made his rifle-barrel look like a pencil. He was dressed in olive drab fatigues, and had the name Pickel sewn in black capitals on his chest, as well as the American flag. She hoped he wasn't going to blab about some deathbed reconciliation with the father who never loved him.

'Yeah, honey, it's like a Nam flashback, 'cept it's about Baghdad.'

'Tell me about it, Jason,' said Indira as they settled down together. 'Were you scared?'

'Scared? Did you say scared? Jeez, I was—What the hell was that?'

The American went rigid as percussive waves filled the air. He instinctively eased off the safety catch and now *BONG* the second explosion assailed his eardrums.

The whole roof vibrated as Big Ben sounded the opening carillon of a quarter to nine.

CHAPTER ELEVEN

O845 HRS

The great clock struck, and Jones cursed (something about a dog, again). The longer they stayed in this traffic jam, the higher their chances of being spotted. Surely the tow-truck man would by now have raised the alarm?

'But why did he clamp us, sir?' asked Dean.

'I don't know.'

'Isn't that why we got an ambulance, so this couldn't happen?'

'Have faith, Dean. Has not Allah looked after us? Think of the prophet in his youth, how he became a warrior for God.'

An electronic voice interrupted them. It was female, and spoke in an American accent.

'Turn left now,' she said. Haroun cursed. It was the satnav, determined to take the vehicle back to Wolverhampton. Much to the irritation of Jones and his team, they could find no way of silencing her.

'Soon we will be in the belly of the beast,' said Jones.

'Make a U-turn,' said the satnav, 'and then turn right in 100 yards.'

The voice of the bossy little robot carried through the driver's window, and might have reached the ears of Roger Barlow, who was now only a matter of a few feet away; except that he was turned away and bent over.

He was trying to lock up his bike against the railings of St Margaret's, just until they sorted out this business with the pass.

'Not there, sir,' said an American.

'Where?'

'Not there, either, sir. I am afraid you will have to take it with you.'

'But I can't get into the Commons without a pass, can I?' The USSS man shrugged.

Barlow stood on the pavement with his bike, like some washed-up crab, as the tide of traffic lapped through the gap and continued around Parliament Square. As he approached his fifty-second year, Roger was conscious that his temper was decreasingly frenetic. He had long since ceased to rave at airport check-ins. If his train was delayed for two hours, it no longer occurred to him to sob and squeal into his mobile. But there was something about being told what to do by this gigantic gone-to-seed quarterback that got, frankly, on his tits.

The Yank was wearing those clodhopping American lace-ups with Cornish pasty welts, a Brooks Brothers button-down shirt, and a large blue blazer. He had the Kevin Costner-ish Germanic looks that you see in so many members of the American military.

'Well, can I borrow your mobile? I need to get this blasted pass from my assistant.'

'That's not allowed, sir.'

Barlow was fed up with the moronic anti-American protesters who were fringing the square and bawling their questions about oil and how many kids Nestlé had killed that day. But he was also fed up with being treated like a terrorist, when he was a bleeding Parliamentarian, and the people of Cirencester had sent him to this place, and it was frankly frigging outrageous that he should be denied access by this Yank. Not that he wanted to be anti-American, of course.

'They'll vouch for me,' he said, pointing to a trio of shirt-sleeved, flak-jacketed Heckler and Koch MP5-toting members of the Met.

No they wouldn't.

'Sorry, Mr Barlow, sir,' said one of them, 'I am afraid you've got to have a pink form today. It's all been agreed with the White House.'

'Well, can I use your phone, then?'

'They'll have my guts for garters, sir, but there you go.'

Cameron had just reached the office, and was tackling the mail. 'I'll come now,' she said, when he explained the problem.

Roger handed back the phone to the Metropolitan Policeman, and stared again at the American.

41

'Is it true that there are a thousand American Secret Service men here?'

'That's what I read, sir.'

Barlow couldn't help himself. He went back to Joe of the USSS.

'Excuse me. I think you really ought to let me through, because I was elected to serve in this building, and you have absolutely no jurisdiction here.'

'I know, sir,' said the human refrigerator, and he touched the Curly-Wurly tube in his ear and mumbled into the Smartie on his lapel. 'I'm not disagreeing with you, sir, not at all. I have no doubt that you are who you say you are, and I really apologize for this procedure. But my orders say clearly that I don't let anyone through today without a pink P form, and if anyone gets through today who shouldn't get through today, then my ass is grass. I'm not history, I'm not biology, I'm physics. Wait, Joe, who are those guys?'

Everything without a pass was being sent up Victoria Street, but now an ambulance had drawn up at the checkpoint. The linebacker was staring at it, but Roger wanted his attention.

'May I see your ID?' he said. He knew he was being a pompous twit, but honestly, this was London . . .

With great courtesy, considering what a nuisance the Brit MP was being, the American Secret Service man opened his wallet and produced a badge. It had a blue and red shield within a five-pointed gold star, and on the roundel was inscribed 'United States Secret Service'.

'There you go, sir. Is that OK?'

Roger couldn't help it. These credentials should mean nothing to him, not on the streets of London. But he felt a childish sense of reverence.

'Er, yes, that is . . . OK.'

'Just wait here, sir,' said the American, and he strolled towards the ambulance driven by the man whose passport said he was called Jones.

'How are you guys today?' he enquired, removing his shades, the ones with the little nick in the corner, and holding out his hand for their papers.

'At the next junction, turn left,' said the female Dalek of the ambulance satnav.

'What's that?' said Matt the USSS man.

'She is a machine,' said Jones. 'She is stupid. She is nothing.'

As Roger Barlow saw the Levantine-featured fellow hand over a pink P form, a thought penetrated his mental fog of guilt, depression and self-obsession.

'Oi,' he said to the American, but so feebly that he could scarcely be heard above the chanting. 'Hang on a mo,' he said, almost to himself.

'Joe,' called the vast American to one of his colleagues, 'would you mind checking in the back of the van here? You don't mind, sir,' he said to Jones, 'if we check in the back of your ambulance?'

'It's an ambulance, Matt,' said Joe.

'I know, but we gotta check.'

The queue behind set up a parping, and down the Embankment the noise of the protesters reached an aero engine howl.

All the Americans were now touching their trembling ears, and the men from the Met were listening on their walkie-talkies.

'Joe,' called Matt, as his colleague approached the rear of the ambulance, 'we gotta clear this stretch of road more quickly. We got the cavalcade in around twenty minutes. We've got POTUS coming through.'

'POTUS coming through,' said Joe, and slapped the flank of the ambulance as if it were a steer. 'You boys better git out of the way.'

'Hang on a tick,' said Roger Barlow, a little more assertively. 'You know it really isn't possible,' he murmured, as the ambulance went slowly round the back of the green and came to a halt at the traffic lights. 'I saw those guys a few moments ago.' Another thought half-formed in his depleted brain.

Jones stowed the forged pink P form on the dashboard and touched the accelerator.

CHAPTER TWELVE
0851 HRS

Six miles away the cavalcade circled the Hogarth round-about, and the first Permanent Protectee shifted in the bullet-proof undershirt he had been forced to wear. He looked out of the window and was startled to see a trio of English children, aged no more than eleven or twelve, leering in at him from the side of the road. They were 'thugged up' in their grey tracksuit hoods. They were spotty. They were giving him an enthusiastic two-fingered salute.

'I guess those guys would rather Saddam was still in power,' said the second Permanent Protectee indignantly, and took her husband's hand.

And now Bluett's top man, the sharpest sharpshooter in the US Army, was looking out from his eyrie across Parliament Square and trying to wish the bad feeling away.

Here and there across the crowd, the bleats were turning into an anti-American chorus; and it took Jason Pickel back to the rhythms of the cretinous song the Iraqis sang, the song of adulation of a man who had tortured and killed thousands, some said hundreds of thousands, of his own people.

'*Yefto, bildam! Eftikia Saddam!*'

After that statue had been pulled down, on the day of the 'liberation', they had briefly and obligingly changed the lyric.

'*Yefto, bildam! Eftikia – Bush!*' they sang, ingratiatingly. But it didn't have the same swing. It didn't last.

The trouble with Baghdad was that the fear never let up. You couldn't sleep at night because it was so hot, and they couldn't fix the air con in the Al-Mansouria Palace, one of Uday's little pied-à-terres, a hideous place constructed of marble, crystal and medium-density fibreboard. And even if they had been able to fix the air con, they wouldn't have gotten no electricity, because no one seemed able to get the generators to work; and even if the generators had worked, the juice wouldn't have made it across town, seeing as people kept ripping up the copper cables, and barbecuing off the plastic, and melting down the metal. And then the self-same looters, or their relatives, came and screamed outside your compound, and cursed America.

And when you had to go on patrol, in your Humvee, the crowds of protesters would part sullenly, and the sweat would run so badly down your legs that you would get nappy rash, even if you never got off the Humvee, and no one, to be honest, was very keen to get off the Humvee.

'We're going into the Garden of Eden, boys,' his commanding officer had told them as they flew over Turkey in the C-130s. 'It's the cradle of mankind, so I want you to treat the place with respect, and remember that these are an ancient people, and they want our help.'

Garden of Eden? thought Jason after he had been there for three weeks. Call it hell on earth.

The economy was shot to hell, the Baathist police wouldn't turn up for work; and almost the worst thing of all was the food. Wasn't this meant to be the Fertile Crescent? Surely this was a place so rich in alluvial salts that it had first occurred to mankind to scratch a bone in the earth and plant seeds.

And all they could get to eat was shoarma and chips, chicken and chips, shoarma and chips, chicken and chips. And you know what the Iraqis really loved, their number one smash hit recipe? They called it Khantooqi Fried. It was funny: back home, people complained about the imposition of American values on an ancient civilization.

Well, there was one delicacy that every Iraqi short-order chef could produce, and that was the brown-grey salty batter in which they caked the corpses of their poor, scraggy, underfed roosters. Long before General Tommy Franks, there was one American military figure who had conquered Iraq, and that was Colonel Sanders.

After a while McDonald's did arrive in the barracks. They installed Coke machines. The troops' skin began to suffer. All the guys were getting seriously homesick, and they were only allowed five minutes per week on the phone.

All of it might have been tolerable, however, had it not been for the streets. He hated the streets, walking among these skinny and malnourished people as though you were from an alien planet. You felt like Judge Dredd, with your big padded helmet, your flak jacket, your chest a kind of mobile drugstore: watch, radio, aspirin, scissors.

Always there was the heart-thud of anxiety when the cars cruised towards your station. Everyone was afraid of the guys with the mad eyes, who ran in from the crowds and *pop pop pop* they fired or *ka-boom* they blew their killer waistcoats. No damn good a flak jacket was going to do you, not against a man who really wanted to whack you.

Pickel had been standing on the mound outside the Al-Mansouria Palace, watering his geraniums. Actually, he wasn't watering them, he was Diet Coke-ing them, since some clerk's error in the Pentagon meant they were supplied with more Diet Coke than bottled water. The geraniums liked Diet Coke, even if it was bad for people, and Jason just loved the way they grew, the way they responded to him. He loved their geranium smell when he broke their stalks, to make them grow better. He stroked their pinks and reds and whites that mimicked his sunburnt Germanic skin. He marvelled at their long woody stalks, and thought how much bigger they were than the geraniums at home.

Thing was, he was worried about how things were at home. He hadn't talked to his wife for more than twenty minutes in the last month, and he missed her.

Anyhow, he was Diet Coke-ing the blooms, when the Humvee with Jerry Kuchma rolled up. They were already yelling for help as soon as they came in sight, and when they braked poor Jerry Kuchma's helmet rolled out into the yellow dust of the street. There was a big nametape stitched to the brim, as if he were at school, saying that it belonged to Kuchma, blood type A neg. But Jerry wasn't going to be needing a transfusion now. You only had to look at the exit wound in his back, when they rolled him over, to see that the blood wouldn't stay inside him.

Pickel was so horrified that he just stood there, and the only thing he managed to say was 'Hey'. He said 'hey' because at one point he was worried that the stretcher guys were going to damage his blooms.

But the worst bit was when the English journalist came.

Why the hell he had been picked to come to London he did not know. He'd told his superiors.

He'd explained how it left him with a rancorous feeling of resentment towards anyone with one of those smooth-talking freaking British accents. If Jason Pickel had been asked to do a word association test, and you had said the word 'British', he would have said 'rat' or 'fink' or 'shithead'.

So he was on geranium patrol, a week after Jerry Kuchma died, and it was meant to be extra-tight security because of some pow-wow or shindig inside. A lot sheikhs and mullahs and fat Iraqi businessmen were trying to sort out some blindingly obvious problem, that should have occurred to the Administration before it invaded the country, such as who was going to be Governor of the Reserve Bank of Iraq, and who was going to set monetary policy, and who was going

47

to be in charge of the Iraqi army, now that it had been routed, and who was going to be Foreign Minister, now that Tariq Aziz was being held out at the airport, or how they were going to get the air con back, that kind of thing.'

Then this guy walks down the street towards him, a white guy, wearing one of those special Giraldo Rivera war-zone waistcoats, with the pouches. Except that he had nothing in the pouches, and he was wearing stained chinos and trainers.

Thing Jason really noticed about him was his hair. His hair was like an Old Testament prophet, all silvery and swept back. But the detail that mattered, the thing Jason fixed his eye on with almost romantic excitement, was what was clamped to his ear.

'Yuh, yuh,' the man was saying, 'OK, I'll file 400 words about the scene of the American torture orgies. OK I understand. Listen, if you're tight for space, I'll just do 300.'

The reporter hung up, and then directed a look at Jason that was grave and charming. Jason knew he was going to be corrupted.

'I am so sorry to trouble you,' began the reporter.

'No trouble at all,' said Jason.

'My name is Barry White, and I am a reporter for the *Daily Mirror* of London, and I wonder if you would be so kind as to help me.'

'I'll surely do what I can,' said Jason.

'I'm trying to track down General Axelrod – hang on,' – he pretended to consult his notes – 'I'm sorry, Lieutenant Axelrod Zimmerman.'

'I am afraid I don't know Lieutenant Zimmerman,' said Pickel. 'You'll have to consult with the media department if you want to arrange an interview. You need to go back to the football stadium.'

'No, it's all right,' said the Moses-like reporter. 'I've just come from the media department and they said that Lieutenant Zimmerman would be expecting me here.'

'Sir, I am afraid I can't let anyone in here.'

'This is Uday's palace, isn't it, the one they call the love-nest?'

'It surely is, Mr White sir, but like I say, if you want to see that stuff, you've got to get clearance. Haven't you all done that torture story, anyhow?'

'Well, there's just a detail I'd like to check, and I was told that Lieutenant Zimmerman . . . Tell you what, I'll ring them up now, and you can talk to them . . .'

Jason Pickel felt his mouth go dry. He knew he was in the presence of a pusher. It was six days since he had talked to Wanda. Anyway, he needed to know about the soccer matches his kid was playing in, that kind of thing.

The Brit was dialling the number, and then he was offering the phone to him. Jason could see the screen lit up, the plump rectangles indicating a full battery, a clear signal. It was a Thuraya, a satphone. Jesus, he ached for a quick conversation.

'I'm really sorry,' he said, 'but my regulations state that I may not talk in public on a civilian telephone. One of our guys was killed doing that.'

'But that's absurd,' said Barry White, with the look of a headmaster uncovering a case of fourth form bullying. 'Why don't we just nip in there and you can use the phone in private?'

That was when the disaster happened, said Jason to Indira, as they sat on the duckboards, on the roof of the House of Commons, surrounded by pigeonshit.

What disaster? asked Indira. But Jason looked brooding, and in her imagination she supplied the answer.

It was the usual thing. Soldier rings home unexpectedly. Crack of dawn. Wife picks up. Sleepy male voice in background.

Before this conversation could go any further, there was another noise, said Jason, outside the gatehouse he was supposed to be guarding. It was like someone quickly popping bubble wrap next to your ear. It was the shooting, and cheering.

And then there was someone else yelling, almost screaming, in English, that unless someone else stopped now, and got out of the car, he was going to open fire.

By this time Barry White was running back outside, and Jason Pickel was following. When his ex-wife was later to sue the US Department of Defense for traumatic stress, it was on the grounds that he had failed to terminate the conversation, and she heard the whole thing.

But now there was a new noise in Parliament Square. The first BMW 750 motorbike had arrived at the traffic lights by St Margaret's, the forerunner of the precursors of the harbingers of the outriders of the cavalcade. A blue light flashed weakly in the sun. The cop waved a gauntleted arm.

Indira was glad of the interruption.

CHAPTER THIRTEEN

0854 HRS

And now that he could actually hear the police sirens, Dragan Panic began to wonder whether he had chosen the right place for succour.

The Serb tow-truck operative looked at the men standing around him on the building site. They observed his face, pasty, sweaty, the moles like fleshy Rice Krispies that were the legacy of the air pollution that had been part of childhood in communist Eastern Europe.

As soon as he had gasped 'Where is police?' he saw their burning eyes, hook noses and hairy black eyebrows that joined in the middle. He knew who they were.

They were Skiptars. They were Muslims, almost certainly from Pristina. And they knew who he was.

He was a Serb.

'Here is not police,' said the leading asylum-seeking brickie, whose family farm had been torched in a place called Suva Reka.

They pressed round him, breathing silently, as a bunch of bullocks will press round a terrified picnicker, and drove him backwards.

Handsomely rewarded under the terms of the Private Finance Initiative, the gang of Skiptars had efficiently driven in the piles of the new ministry. They had sunk huge corrugated sheets of steel into the grey loam of London, and now they were pouring lagoons of concrete between the sheets. Towards one of these pits of gravelly slurry they now herded their enemy.

'What do you want, Serb?'

Dragan saw it all. In fifty years' time this building would be torn down for reconstruction by the next lot of asylum-seekers, from China, or Pluto, or wherever, and they would break up these concrete blocks to find his whitened bones.

He dodged and ran. Then he tripped, and fell face first in the mud, and then he was up and running again, back down Horseferry Road towards the sirens and the chugging of another helicopter.

Of course he wouldn't admit it, not even to Grover, but Deputy Assistant Commissioner Purnell was deeply cheesed off by the arrival of the Black Hawk.

It was his airspace. He had sovereignty. But the Black Hawk had somehow bullied away his Twin Squirrel, in a humiliating vindication of their brand names.

'Are we going to tell them about it?' asked Grover. He was thinking of the ambulance.

'Let's just concentrate on finding the thing.'

Stuck in the gummy shade of London's plane trees, the ambulance was waiting at yet another traffic light, this one at the back of Parliament Square by a statue of Napier. It was getting hotter in the cabin; the rusty metallic smell of freshly spilt blood rose from the back, and Jones was conscious of a sense of mounting disorder.

Despite their enormous breakfast, Habib was now eating a tub of hummus, spooning it down with a tongue depressor he had found in the glove compartment.

'Why do you eat it now?' asked Haroun.

'Show me where it is written a man may not eat on the eve of battle.'

'But we are all about to die.'

'We'll be lucky,' said Jones bitterly.

He tried to concentrate on all the things he had to get right in the next five minutes.

On leaving Parliament Square, the plan was to turn left up Whitehall, and then, just before the Cenotaph, to turn right at the Red Lion pub. There Dr Adam would supply them with a parking permit.

It was very important, when they saw Dr Adam, that they acted their parts convincingly. The man called Adam knew something, but he did not know everything.

The only person who knew everything was Jones.

Then the lights changed and in defiance of the satnav they trickled forward to the last set, and came once again in full view of Roger Barlow – had he chanced to look that way.

Not that anyone in his right mind would look at an ambulance, when he could behold the face of Cameron Maclean.

He watched her come towards him across the road, and the crowd parted around her like a zip. She looked like a character in a hairspray ad, with glossy evangelical skin and lustrous eyes. She was twenty-four, full of energy and optimism, and she had the dubious honour of being Roger's research assistant.

Not for the first time, Barlow was seriously impressed by her efficiency. If his memory served him right – and he kept a vague eye on her romantic career – she had been off in Brussels last night, and here she was in less than five minutes.

He beamed. He knew that Cameron had long ago lost any reverence she may have had for him or his office, but what the hell.

'Your wife left a message on my mobile. It must have been while I was on the Tube.'

'My wife?' Barlow felt a prickling in the roots of his hair.

'Yeah. She sounded kind of pissed.'

'Pissed?' Roger's mind boggled. It was less than an hour since he had left home.

'I guess you guys would say pissed off.'

They sorted out the pink pass, and Barlow entered the security bubble.

'Did she say what about?' he asked, thinking as he did so what a foolish thing it was to ask.

'No, Roger.' He scrutinized her. Was that contempt? Was that pity? Who could tell?

Roger was indebted – England was indebted – to Cameron's former political science tutor. This was a languid Nozickian with whom she had been in love and who had baffled her, candidly, by his refusal to sleep with her. At the end of her last winter term she had come to see him in his study. The snow was falling outside.

'What shall I do, Franklin?' she had asked him, stretching her long legs on his zebra-skin rug. 'Where shall I go?'

'Go work in Yurp,' he said, meaning Europe. 'Go to London. Why don't you go work for one of those British Tories? They're in a whole lot of trouble right now.'

So she'd written to about ten MPs whose websites proclaimed them to be interested in North America. Barlow was the only one to answer, with a laconic scrawl, inviting her to appear for work in December. Eight months later, Cameron was finding that her political convictions were somehow wilting under prolonged exposure to Roger Herbert Barlow MP.

Her first job had been to sign all his Christmas cards. These were late.

'Uh, Roger,' she said, 'I don't know what style you want me to use. Do I say Mr and Mrs or do I say Justin and Nell? Or what do I say?'

'Tremendous, tremendous,' he said. 'Look, I'll catch you later.'

'But what do you want me to say? Best wishes Roger, or Love Roger, or Happy Christmas from Roger and Diana?'

'Yup yup yup yup,' he said. 'Gotta go.'

Since this was among her first meetings with Roger, she hardly dared say what she felt: that it was grossly rude to treat friends and constituents in this way.

So she knuckled under, and signed 500 cards 'Mr Roger Barlow Esquire MP' in that flagrantly American piggy-knitting handwriting, with the r like a Russian ya sign. It would have been more believable if she had written 'David Beckham'.

When, inevitably, there was a revolt in his constituency about this breach of etiquette, he was so low as to seek, somehow, to blame her.

'Oh Gaaad,' he said, groaning and running his hands through his hair, to the point where she felt like kicking him.

Just what kind of a Conservative was this guy, anyhow? It was *soooo* disappointing. She'd been with him at a meeting in a church hall in Cirencester, and someone had stood up and said, 'Mr Barlow, do you agree with me that there is far too much gratuitous and offensive sex on TV? And will you' – the man's hands were shaking as he read out his question – 'take steps to ensure that Ofcom protects children from the current tide of filth?' Barlow had given an intelligent answer, about the difficulties of censorship, and the watershed, and that kind of thing, and then thrown it all away with some flip aside.

'Of course, I tend to rely on my children to tell me what it's safe to watch, *ha ha ha* . . .'

Cameron felt her stomach contract with irritation. Didn't he understand that these guys cared about this question? He was their servant, paid with their tax dollars, to represent their views in Parliament.

A young lady had asked him about abortion, and his answer had been protozoan in its invertebracy. It was all about 'grey areas' and 'moral continuums'. The nearest he came to a statement of principle was to say, 'Frankly it's all a bit of a tricky one, really.' But the worst thing had been his answer on gay marriage. Now Cameron had graduated from Rochester University NY (motto: *Meliora*, or Better things) as a pretty straightforward moral authoritarian neoconservative. In the run-up to the war on Iraq, she had stuck a poster in her dorm, saying, 'Let's bomb France'.

At the height of Francophobia she had moved a motion in the student body. Many American colleges were to rebaptize French fries as 'freedom fries.' She wanted to go one better.

In honour of Tony Blair, she said Rochester should call them 'chips', like they did in Britain. The motion did not attract much support, but her Nozickian professor gave a wan smile.

Before she arrived in London, she had presumed that if Barlow were a Tory, he would be sound; he would be staunch; he would stand full-square and broad-beamed in favour of family values and all the rest of it.

By the time of the church hall meeting, barely a month ago, she had put up with a lot: his political evasiveness, his moral evasiveness, and indeed, dammit, his sheer physical evasiveness. Half the time he would give her some great project and then evaporate, muttering about the 'whips' or the '1922' or 'Standing Committee B'.

She coped with all that, and she endured his jelly-like answers about censorship and abortion; so she was thrilled when he seemed to take some sort of stand on gay marriage.

His answer was indistinct, no doubt deliberately so, but she heard him say something to the effect that gay marriage was 'a bit rum when you consider that marriage is normally thought of as taking place between a man and a woman'. Whoopee!

At once it was as though she had chanced upon a knuckle of principle in the opaque minestrone of his views. He was actually AGAINST something, she thought, almost hugging herself with excitement. He was against a cause espoused by people who might actually VOTE for him. And then, of course, came the disappointment.

She was charged with drafting an answer to a letter from a constituent, who sought the joys of matrimony with his same-sex 'partner'. She wrote a rather fierce letter, if not exactly consigning the man, an IT consultant, to the licking tongues of hellfire, then at least making it pretty clear what she, or Roger Barlow, whose name and superscription appeared on the letter, thought of the whole project. To her amazement he had crossed it out and written, 'Good on yer, matey, go right ahead. Frankly I don't see why the state should object to a union between three men and a dog. Yours sincerely.'

'But excuse me,' she said, and her lips grew tight and her eyes larger and more beautiful than ever, 'I thought you were against it. That's what you said in the church.'

'Oh did I?' said Roger. His own eyes were merry and dark. 'No, I think what I said, in the interests of total accuracy, was that it was a bit rum, and to say something is a bit rum is a long day's march from saying that you are against it. A long day's march.'

'Right,' said Cameron.

There were still ways she admired him. He worked prodigiously hard. He got things done. By dint of 5 a.m. vigils, and by writing innumerable letters, he undoubtedly lifted the odd pebble from the mountain of suffering that oppressed the losers of Cirencester. He cared a lot about some of his projects, and yet sometimes she couldn't help wondering about his IDEALS. His VALUES. His CORE BELIEFS.

Sometimes, it occurred to her, when she listened to Roger waffling about pornography or abortion, the mullahs had a point. No wonder the Christian churches seemed in permanent confusion and decline, and no wonder Islam was the fastest-growing religion in this country.

As they walked through the checkpoint and over the zebra crossing, the noise of the protesters became overpowering. They had whistles and rattles and bongos and steel drums. There was one man so covered in badges denouncing America that he looked like a pearly queen.

Seeing Barlow, he picked up his megaphone and bawled, 'There's that tosser, whatsisname! It's that jerk thingummy! It's old whodjamaflip, the complete prat. Sorry I can't remember your name, my old china, but I hope you accept that my sentiments are sincere. Come on everybody, let's have a chorus.' And he began to warble raggedly, jabbing a finger in the direction of Barlow and Cameron as they scuttled past. 'You're shit, and you know you are, you're shit and you know you are . . .'(repeat to fade).

Cameron scowled at the man, piqued in her basic sense of loyalty. She tried accelerating her gait, in the hope that Roger would walk faster.

Much earlier that morning she and Adam, her boyfriend, had been brushing their teeth in the Amigo hotel, Brussels. She had been nuzzling him, unable to speak for foam and love, when he spat out his own mouthful of Colgate and made a peculiar request.

She had agreed without thinking; of course she had. But now that she was with Roger, and now that she could hear the square full of the sounds of hate, it seemed a more difficult and dangerous proposition.

She felt uneasy that she had handed over Roger's car park pass; though Roger the cyclist had long since lost track of it, and probably didn't even know she had it in her handbag. Now she was dubious about the ethics of the other request that Adam had made.

'It's completely outrageous,' Adam had told her, as he outlined the callous discrimination against the journalists from Al-Khadija. 'They just want to make a film about parliamentary democracy. Aren't we supposed to be in favour of that kind of thing?'

She didn't have to do anything difficult, he said: she just had to pick them up, and obviously he couldn't do it himself because he didn't have a researcher's pass. And, by the way, could she get one for him, too?

So guiltily she tried to force Roger's pace, and turned her eyes away from the crowd, and didn't look twice at the white emergency services vehicle chuntering slowly round the corner to her left.

CHAPTER FOURTEEN
0857 HRS

'So one of our chopper boys thinks he saw an ambulance?' said Deputy Assistant Commissioner Purnell. 'Did he get the roof number?'

The Deputy Assistant Commissioner was thinking that there was a case for passing it on to the pilot of the Black Hawk.

'No,' said Grover. 'He can't remember it, and anyway he says it was half covered up by a tow-truck crane.'

'A tow-truck?'

'S'what he says.'

'Well, where's this tow-truck? Christ on a bike.'

* * *

58

Dragan Panic sighed. He was only second in the queue, but he seemed to have been here for some time.

At Horseferry Road police station Duty Officer Louise Botting was dealing with another victim of crime.

She was a woman of about fifty, with grey hair, and perfectly attired for cycling. She had a helmet with a red reflector, fluorescent yellow zig-zags on her torso, and an air of Anglo-Saxon indignation.

'I feel a bit silly reporting it, but I feel it's my duty. It's just so uncivilized.'

'I know, madam,' said Louise Botting, and passed her a form.

'Do you know why they do it?'

'No, I'm afraid I don't.'

'Is there ever any chance of catching them, do you think?'

'Well, there's always a chance, I s'pose.'

Behind her in the queue, Dragan groaned.

'What I would like to know,' said the woman loudly as she left, 'is what kind of person would steal my bike seat?'

No one in the room felt able to answer, least of all Dragan, who now bent towards the counter, his muscles still trembling with exertion.

'How can I help you, sir?' asked Louise Botting.

'They killed the traffic warden, didn't they,' said Dragan.

'Did they?' asked Sergeant Botting, and then listened with mounting amazement. At one point she interrupted him. 'Did you say you were removing an ambulance?'

'I told him not to. I was going to tell him not to.'

'And why are you covered in mud?'

Dragan thumped a weary fist on the attack-proof glass, like a drunk in a benefit office. 'I swear I am telling the truth.'

Louise Botting summoned the station commander, and together they took a full statement.

'Are you saying you lifted this ambulance? Right. And

where is this ambulance now? They drove off, you say, and you are sure they are Muslim terrorists. I see, Mr Panic. Now, what's your address? No. 10, Eaton Place, SW1. You're sure about that. I see.'

Then the station commander took a call, and when he explained its contents to Louise Botting, she looked at Dragan Panic with new and wondering eyes.

She filled in an Initial Crime Report, and timed the incident for 9 a.m.

CHAPTER FIFTEEN
0900 HRS

BONG Big Ben struck nine, and on the roof of the Commons, Pickel quivered again.

BONG The cavalcade effortfully turned right towards Chelsea, and the leaves of the Embankment waved beneath the passage of the Black Hawk.

BONG The Ambassador of the French Republic, M. Yves Charpentier, told his official driver to follow the Mall down to Parliament Square and make for St Stephen's Entrance. Then he sat back on the blue velour of the Renault and buried his nose in the hot black scented crown of his mistress, Benedicte al-Walibi.

BONG In a cave in the tribal areas of Pakistan, not far from the Afghan border, the BBC's coverage of the state visit was being closely monitored on TV.

BONG The British Prime Minister sat in his small office in Downing Street and gave heartfelt thanks, once again, to the protocol ruling which meant he did not have to attend the speech in Westminster Hall; the theory being that he had proposed the President's health last night at Windsor, and that was enough. John Major, it had been pointed out, was not there for Nelson Mandela. Nor for Bill Clinton, if his memory served him correctly.

BONG Colonel Bluett of the US Secret Service had decided that it was time to take a more active role in the security operation, and was now being driven in a blacked-out Ford from Grosvenor Square to Scotland Yard.

BONG In the White House in Washington, the Presidential red setter had a beautiful dream, in which he sunk his teeth into the neck of the Presidential cat.

BONG Roger Barlow's four-year-old heir was sitting cross-legged at school, and looking intently at some pictures of king-killing in old Dahomey.

BONG Jones felt the first drop of perspiration emerge from his temple and run down his cheek.

As Roger and Cameron gained the entrance to New Palace Yard, a taxi drew up. The policeman bent down to look through the window, and then let them through. After twenty-five years everyone knew Felix Thomson. Barlow knew him, too, and offered a mock-salute which was returned, though perhaps a little more mockingly than Barlow, in an ideal world, would have liked.

The policeman at the gate once more demanded production of the pink slip, though for some reason they waved Felix Thomson's taxi on without too much fuss. The vehicle rolled on a few yards down the cobbles to another barricade, a ramp with winking lights that came up and prevented access, just by the spot where Airey Neave had been blown up by the IRA.

'No, sorry, sir,' said the policeman. Barlow had made to follow the taxi, because he wanted to have a word with Felix Thomson, and now he was told this was not on. He'd have to go that way, through the turnstiles. Did he have his pass with him? He had his pass.

'Oh Cameron, by the way, I have a terrible feeling I have to make a speech in the debate this afternoon.'

'That's right, Roger. The whips have been on to us twice already. They are expecting it.'

'Oh lor', sighed the MP, stopping. 'Can you remember what it's all about?'

Why the hell, wondered Cameron, couldn't he ever concentrate on what she was saying? 'I sent you a speech. I mean I sent you a draft of the speech. It was in your mail on Friday.'

'Oh yes, and what's the Bill about?'

'It's the Water Utilities Bill (England and Wales). The whips thought you might be interested in speaking on fluoridation.'

'Mmmm,' said Roger, 'and what line am I taking?'

'Well, I sort of presumed you would be taking a libertarian line. A lot of people have been writing in, saying how much they dislike fluoridation. They say it's the nanny state.'

'Nasty stuff, is it, fluoride?'

'Well, it can be deadly poisonous, and they've done a lot of research on possible side-effects . . .'

'Don't tell me,' said Roger, 'I know what it does. It causes premature baldness in rhesus monkeys, hypertension in rats, and it changes the sex of cuttlefish.'

'If you say so, Roger.' She tried shifting forwards. Adam would be waiting.

'I mean, what if the whole libertarian argument is utter tosh? What if this stuff is really good for you, protects the nation's teeth, mmm? I think of my parents' generation.

They never had the stuff and they had terrible trouble. I remember my father taking a great bite of an apple, and crack. Very psychologically damaging, losing your teeth. It's all in Freud. You know, if you're an elephant, and you lose your teeth, you've had it.'

'I expect the same goes if you're a lion.'

'Good point,' said Roger. 'Here, just say aaah. Go on, open wide the pearly gates.' Cameron had the surreal experience of offering her teeth for inspection to the Member for Cirencester.

'See,' said Roger, 'inside every skull, thirty-two vital differences between the English and the Americans.' As he was looking his research assistant in the mouth, he became aware of two people craning their necks to watch him from 120 feet up. It was Jason Pickel and Indira, their scopes glinting in the sun.

'Can I stop now?' asked Cameron.

'Yeah, sure,' said Barlow, and they resumed their walk to the wrought-iron porch of the Members' Entrance.

'You're quite happy for me to check your teeth?'

'No, it's fine.'

'Ah,' said Roger, brightening again. 'Now that is what we call Barlow's Law of the Displaced Negative. In principle you are saying that you are happy for me to look at your teeth, but there is a stray negative, the no, which simply needs to be removed from the beginning of that sentence and inserted between subject and predicate, to give the real meaning. You secretly mean, "It's not fine." To give another example, men are often asked, "Do I look OK in this dress?" and they answer, "No, no, you look great." The displaced negative is a clue to their real thoughts. They should say, "Yes, darling, you look great." The female equivalent is "No, no, darling, you have got masses of hair."'

Cameron snorted, not altogether fondly. She was damned if she was going to ask Roger if she looked OK, mainly because she had no (real) doubts about the matter.

Finally she left Roger, berthing his bike in the cycle racks at the bottom of New Palace Yard. She felt she had done her best.

He knew about the fluoride speech. He was on top of the Betts case, and the plan to save the respite centre. He was, by his standards, under control.

Now she had to go quickly to find Adam.

CHAPTER SIXTEEN

0908 HRS

Even though it was a warm July morning, the man outside the Red Lion pub in Derby Gate was wearing an elbow-patched tweed jacket and faded cords. He had scuffed brown brogues from which emerged cheap towelling socks, one of which was blue, and one of which looked suspiciously like a trophy from the goody bag of Virgin Atlantic. When the authorities would come that evening to examine the contents of his wallet, they would confirm that he was Dr Adam Swallow, thirty-five, and that he had recently been travelling in Jordan, Syria, Lebanon and Iraq, to judge by the few decayed and crumpled low-denomination bills he had saved from his trips. He was a reader at the Pitt-Rivers Museum of Anthropology and Ethnography in Oxford, and a plastic badge suggested that he was director of Middle Eastern studies at the Royal Institute of International Affairs at Chatham House. The innermost fold of his wallet contained a forgotten condom of great antiquity and no contraceptive value whatever.

He was tall and lean and dark, and sitting forward on the beer-splashed bench, and between his thick wrists he held a tabloid paper. He was chuckling.

The centre page feature was a tremendous tub-thumping why oh why piece by Sir Trevor Hutchinson, a former editor of the *Daily Telegraph*. Entitled 'Our Shameful Surrender to Terror', it dilated on the various erosions of liberty entailed by the current obsession with security. Was it not outrageous, whinnied Sir Trev, that the Queen was being served with plastic cutlery, aboard the royal flight, all these years after 9/11? He gave a vigorous description of the Metropolitan Police Maginot Line around the Palace of Westminster. He railed against the frogmen in the Thames, the boom that had been constructed in the river, to protect the Commons Terrace from a riparian boarding party, the glass barrier in the Chamber, that shielded the electors from their representatives, or vice versa, for the first time in our island story. And then he related his almost insane irritation, when boarding a flight from Heathrow to Inverness to fulfil an important shooting engagement, at being asked to produce his passport. There being 300 words to supply after this opening lungful, Sir Trev went on to deplore the general phobia of risk in today's namby-pamby society, alighting on such diverse themes as the near cancellation, on insurance grounds, of the climactic firework display at the Henley Regatta, and the use of cup-holders and – *splutterissimo* – air-bags in the new American tanks which the army, in defiance of his advice, was on the verge of buying.

'Good stuff, good stuff,' chuckled Adam, who had written his own share of bilge in his time. He folded the paper carefully, and would have dropped it in the bin, had not the bins all been removed for security reasons from this part of Westminster. He checked his watch, stood up, and looked boldly out into the street, his bright brown eyes shining with tension. They should be here any minute, he thought.

Where was Cameron?

Now the drops were chasing each other down Jones's pitted temples, and he could hear the chatter of the Black Hawk, coming up the Embankment with the President underneath.

He wondered if there was a sign on the roof, a visible identification code, and then began to feel the ambulance shrieking their crime to the heavens.

As he waited for the last lights to turn, he rubbed his palms together, and made little black worms of dried blood.

'He says four of them killed the warden,' said the station commander into the phone.

'Killed a traffic warden? We all feel like that sometimes.'

'No, I think he's serious.'

'Can he identify the ambulance?'

'Sounds like he had to scarper pretty quick.'

'We'd better get on to the Deputy Assistant Commissioner's office.'

'Oh yeah,' said the station commander. 'I'll do that right away. I don't suppose you know the number, do you?'

'I'll get back to you in a minute. You've sent someone round to Tufton Street, have you?'

'Good thinking,' said the station commander.

'Does he have any idea where this ambulance has gone?'

CHAPTER SEVENTEEN
0909 HRS

'Continue for 200 yards,' said the satnav in the ambulance, still yearning in its silicon soul for Wolverhampton and home, 'and then try to make a U-turn.'

'Oh shut up, in the name of Allah,' said Haroun.

'Can't you work out how to make that thing stop?' said Jones.

'It is a *sharmoota*. It is a whore,' said Haroun.

'It's just a machine.'

'It is an American computer whore.'

Habib had been silent, playing with his prayer beads, a chunky collection of sickly lime-green onyx. He had smooth, rubbery, almost Disney-ish features, and crinkly hair which he concealed in all weathers beneath a woven black skullcap. Now he opened his sad brown eyes.

'The man from the truck will tell them about us.'

'What will he say? There are too many ambulances.'

'He may have seen our number.'

'Believe me,' said Haroun, still fantasizing about what he might have done with that thoracic spike, 'the heathen dog was too frightened. It's not him I'm worried about, it's him.' He jerked his head towards the back of the van.

Jones took a still bloodied hand off the wheel as they came round into Whitehall. He pointed to a packet of surgical wipes on the dashboard, next to a Unison coffee mug.

'Please pass me one,' he said to Haroun in Arabic, and then read out the English motto on the side of the box: '"Clean hands save lives". Indeed.'

'He could ruin it for everyone,' said Haroun in Arabic, passing the wipes like an airline stewardess.

'I know.'

'So what are we going to do?'

'Have faith,' said the man called Jones, sponging the blood off his hands, and dropping the tissues on to the floor. They were talking about Dean.

Haroun and Habib, in slightly different ways, were possessed of animal cruelty. Both men had trained with him in the deserts, at the camps in the Sudan and at Khalden in Afghanistan. Habib's tranquil exterior was deceptive, in that he liked to meditate on violence, and had devised some of the more baroque elements of the plan they were about to execute.

With his slanty eyes and triangular tongue, Haroun was like a priggish wolf. If that porky tow-van operator hadn't beaten it so quickly, Haroun would have done for him with all the dispatch of a halal butcher slicing the throat of a sacrificial kid.

In the view of Habib and Haroun, therefore, it was absurd to have Dean in this operation at all. It was just because he was British. It was just because he was the local talent. It was tokenism. It was political correctness gone mad.

As for his terroristic temperament, he seemed to have absorbed far too much of the risk-aversion of the modern British male.

It had only been a few minutes since the violence outside Church House, but any self-respecting terrorist would surely by now have steeled his nerves. Dean, if anything, seemed to be losing morale by the second. He was sitting in the back, by the exsanguinating form of Eric Onyeama, and he was beginning to keen in a frankly off-putting way.

'You guys,' he said, sticking his head through the door, 'are you sure we shouldn't just knock this on the head?' He said yow, rather than you, because he was from Wolverhampton.

'Why don't we just drive on here, and maybe we could like chill for a couple of days. Why don't we do like the machine says, and go back to Wolvo?'

Habib looked at Haroun. Haroun looked at Jones. Dean caught the glances. It would on the whole be better not to end up like the poor traffic warden, yerked beneath the breastbone, with the bright bronchial blood still bubbling about the nose and mouth.

'OK OK.' Dean sat back down on the plastic banquette. 'Forget I mentioned it.' Jones bore to the right on Whitehall, about 100 yards short of the Cenotaph, and indicated that he wished to cross the traffic.

'Please make a U-turn now,' said the satnav, as soon as she understood what he was trying to do.

Haroun said something truly awful to the computer about what he would do to her mother's rib cage.

Then he struck her on the fascia with a seat belt cutter. The machine started to squeak and gibber, sounding like Robert De Niro when he is hit repeatedly on the head at the end of *Cape Fear*.

Then she fell silent. The trouble was, thought Dean, she was right. Of all the great terrorist outrages of history, could any boast such screwed-up and hopeless beginnings? Dean tried to think himself into the mind of one who was about to fill the citadels of the West with death and despair, and to send a message to every dutiful Muslim of encouragement, gladness and strength. He sighed and blinked.

Jones turned and looked back at Dean as they waited to cross the traffic.

'Remember what it says in the Holy Koran, my young friend.

"'Slay the unbelievers wherever you can find them. Arrest them, besiege them, and lie in ambush for them everywhere.'"

'Yeah,' said Dean miserably. 'Right.'

'We will perform the jihad against the Kuffar, the unbelievers.'

'Yeah.'

'Remember that Allah is our ally, and they have no ally. We are the lions, Dean, we are the lions ready to set out. We will assault with speed, with the heart of a volcano, with the bombardment of thunders.'

The ambulance moved across Whitehall to the right, and Dean felt his mood lift.

'Think of the *hur*, the black-eyed virgins of Paradise, Dean. Would you like seventy-two black-eyed virgins, whose chastity has been violated neither by man nor djinn? Would you like that, Dean?'

The ambulance slowed as it approached a red and white boom that controlled access to their intended car park. Habib smiled, and so did Haroun.

Yeah, said Dean, he guessed he would like that, really.

It was no coincidence that Dean was born in March 1988, nine months after Margaret Thatcher's last election victory. His father was the manager of a previously union-ridden Black Country autoparts factory, and believed he had much to celebrate that night.

Already he relied on immigrant labour, many of them Muslim women, and it made his blood freeze to think of a return to the closed shop. Dean never knew his name or occupation, and for the time being all we need to know is that towards 3 a.m. on the morning of Friday 9 June a Midlands businessman called Sammy, of Viper Wipers, was cruising the Bilston Road in search, as he put it, of a 'bit of black'.

There is no need here to rehearse the details of that melancholy transaction: the slow prowling of the Ford Granada Ghia 2.1 down the sooty sodium streets, over bridges and culverts that had been here since the age of Telford and Macadam. We must take it that Dean's biological father cruised on, his eyes like an unblinking snake, past pairs of white girls in white socks, shivering on corners, until he found what he wanted. Neither party would remember exactly where or how Dean had been conceived. Was it beneath this spindly smokestack which 200 years ago had been a symbol of England's industrial dominance?

Was it beneath this hideously echoing arch, dripping with slime? And how did life begin? Was it a burst condom, that triumph of nature over artifice, or did Dean's father pay some trifling bonus for unprotected sex?

And yet when the feature writers came to look back at Dean's childhood and adolescence, they had to admit that England had done him proud. His mother had almost immediately given him up for adoption, and since he was only the faintest coffee colour, he was fostered with a white family who appeared on the face of things to express all that was most honourable about bourgeois Britain.

Dennis and Vera (or Vie) Faulkner were in their late forties when Dean came into their lives. They were considered by the system to be towards the upper limit of the age range, but there was some sympathy for Vie in the chilly hearts of the adoptocrats. She had been one of the would-be mothers who participated in Robert Winston and John Steptoe's first attempts to create a test-tube baby. It had worked for the others. It had worked for Louise Brown. It hadn't worked for Vie.

She loved little Dean. She boiled eggs for him every day (in fact, his first act of rebellion was to announce, 'No more eggs!') and Dennis, a fanatical monarchist whose family roots were in Northern Ireland, would puff around the garden, teaching him football and cricket. He went to a Montessori school, and learned to glue bits of spaghetti on paper, the discipline now known as Key Stage One. He went to Wolverhampton Grammar School, and though academically undistinguished he showed some talent for water polo.

You simply could not pretend that he was unhappy in that quiet house in Wednesbury. He went on holiday with Dennis and Vie, and learned to put up with the curious glances. When people at school made the mistake of asking 'where he was really from' he learned to blank them and to say that he was really from Wolverhampton. From time to time – about once every three years – he would receive small sums of money in badly hand-addressed envelopes, and Dennis would hand them over with a grimace.

All children probably fantasize, from time to time, that they are not really the offspring of their parents. Is there any half-sensitive kid who has not speculated that he was in fact discovered in a capsule in the Himalayas, concealed among the eggs of mutant pterodactyls from the planet Krypton? It was different for Dean. From the word go, Dean had unambiguous physical evidence that he was the subject – the victim – of a swap, and all his life he had to cope not with narcissistic fantasies of otherness, but with the secret thought that he wasn't meant to be here at all.

It wasn't as if he didn't love Dennis and Vie. Mostly he did love them. It was just that sometimes he couldn't help wondering if they loved him as much as they would love a natural child; and then he felt alienated. Matters came to a head shortly after his sixteenth birthday. He was growing tall, with an honest and engaging smile, and his skin, after some early unruliness, was clear and good. He went with Dennis to the golf club, and earned tips for caddying.

He helped Vie in the Sue Ryder shop. Dennis was an executive with Otis elevators, or had been until his retirement, and hoped that Dean might one day join the company. 'Get with Otis,' he would tell his adoptive son, 'get with Otis and go up in the world!'

It all went wrong for Dean when his adoptive parents became involved in a war. It was a war with the neighbours, and it was as full of malevolence as anything that took place in Bosnia. Next door was a man called Mr Price, who was, sociologically speaking, not so very unlike Dennis Faulkner. Instead of working for Otis elevators, Peter Price had been quite big in the Milk Marketing Board. The high moment of his career had come in the 1970s, when he had helped to formulate Lymeswold cheese, the Heatho-Walkerian plan to deal with the Milk Surplus. Alas, Lymeswold never caught on. It was likened fatally by Auberon Waugh, the journalist, to banana toothpaste, and as a piece of import substitution it was no match for the soft blue cheeses of France and Italy, let alone the great wagon wheels of industrially produced cambozola, the German cheese that trundled across the channel with the ruthless housewife appeal of a BMW. Like Dennis Faulkner, Peter Price was pensioned off early. But instead of just watching the television, or doing his roses, Price the Cheese was a man with a dream.

In his garage he had a row of vats and centrifuges and

skimmers and strainers. Day in, day out, he would clank and prod, sniffing and pressing and squeezing. From the age of ten or so, Dean would go and see Price the Cheese, and his extraordinary machines.

'Go on,' Price would say, 'try this one.' Price would cut the coagulum into strips, and Dean would put the latest radioactive isotope on his tongue.

'Or try this one, my dear sir,' the caseomaniac would say. 'I think you'll be amused by its presumption.'

'Mmmmbmm,' said Dean.

'Have you heard of Auberon Waugh?'

'No, sir.'

'You wouldn't say this tasted like banana toothpaste, would you?'

'No.'

One day, Price told himself, the garage would produce a cheese so startlingly magnificent that the humiliation of Lymeswold would be avenged. Tesco would buy it. Waitrose would certainly buy it. No one, not even a posh git like Auberon Waugh, would dare to brush his teeth with this one. This cheese would be pungent, and that was the problem. Most days, in fact 90 per cent of the time, his garage exuded nothing to trouble the nose. On a very few days, when he hadn't been perhaps quite liberal enough with the Milton disinfectant, there would be the faintest bouquet of udder, as of two lactating cows standing close to each other in a warm milking parlour. And once in a blue moon, when Price the Cheese hit on something sensationally ripe, he would open the garage door and emit.

On a still, hot summer's evening, he was capable of producing an odour that was probably bacteriologically identical to the substance generated between the fourth and fifth toes of a squaddie who has marched for twenty-four hours in the desert in rubber-soled boots. One these occasions Mr Faulkner complained, though if the truth be told the objection was not so much to the cheesy aromas. The real protester was Vie, who had once been having a bath in the upstairs bathroom, without drawing the curtains.

She had looked up, and had the sudden thrilling sensation that someone was watching her. From then on, Peter Price was in trouble. Perhaps Vie had conceived some feeling for the old cheese-fancier, some instinct that needed to be suppressed or sublimated into anger. Perhaps there was a subconscious sense in which Vie's real objection was not so much that he had looked, but that he had jerked his head away.

No matter. Price was a snoop. Together, with the lights out, Dennis and Vie stood and looked up at the neighbouring window. They felt the play of his binoculars over their possessions, their lives: the fitted green carpet in the living room, the coal effect fire, the *Daily Mail* reader offer carriage clock, the Royal Doulton Ware figurine of the Queen Mother. They felt his mocking beams assess their choice of television programme, and the sad secret reasons for adopting this coffee-coloured son. They seethed, with the first stirrings of feud. When someone trampled the ornamental poppy in the front garden, they had an inkling that it might be him; when Dennis could have sworn that the slug pellets had been moved from one end of the shed to the other, he had a sudden notion; when Royal Doulton Ware sent them a frankly obscene figurine, instead of the requested statuette of Lady Di, they both found it hard to fight the suspicion; and when the cat went missing they had no doubt.

'I tell you what, honeybunch,' said Dennis to Vie, 'I've got just the thing for him.'

His answer, of course, was cupressa leylandii, the nuclear weapon of suburban hate. When Dennis planted them, ten in a row, at the bottom of the garden, they were only eight feet tall. In two years they had almost doubled. Upwards, sideways and diagonally groped their spongy, aromatic fronds, dwarfing and in some places crushing the original wooden boundary fence. Twilight descended on the sunny little room where Price would take his breakfast. No longer could he range his little pots of curd on the sill, and watch them turn radioactive in the heat. A sanatorial gloom spread through the entire lower floor, turning all the cheese he made to a green thought in a green shade.

Soon the topmost sprigs were beginning to challenge the upper floor; soon, thought Price, he would need to keep the lights on all day, throughout the house. He began with letters; he invoked the council; he sent them the text of the High Hedges Bill, then making its progress through the Commons. But Dennis knew instinctively that his hedge was untouchable. An Englishman's home is his castle, and Parliament would surely find it impossible to give one man the right to compel the chopping-down of another man's trees. Price joined a leylandii victims' support group. He became party to a class action which intended to test, if necessary before the European Court of Human Rights in Strasbourg, the proposition that a man had not only the right to life, but the right to light.

It was no use. Sometimes, with much pleading, the council's hedge officer would persuade Dennis to make a few desultory abbreviations to the very top. But if ever Price pushed or moaned too much, Dennis would threaten to expose him as a 'peeping Tom' and cheese freak.

'I'll get the health and safety round to that garage,' he said. 'We all know what goes on there. It's disgoosting,' said Dean's adoptive father, and Dean felt a twinge of remorse.

And then one September, two and a half years after the deployment of the leylandii, Price exacted his appalling revenge. Dennis and Vie and Dean had been to Alicante, and things had not been easy. Dennis resented the way Dean kept his headphones on all day, and Dean was basically doing his nut. For seven solid days he had endured a beach holiday with his adoptive parents: Dennis with the Factor 15 glooped on top of his head, and every other extremity, Vie with her crispy hair and stunned blue eyes and pointless expensive jewellery; Dennis with his old man's tits, Vie with her evening lipstick running into the cracks around her mouth.

Dean would stare at the incredible girls, and feel a repeated sense of amazement that people were allowed to appear like this, before him, in public. He would lie on his back and squint at the surf, and observe the curious fact that when a beautiful girl emerged from the sea, you couldn't always tell how big she was. As she rose, with water running down her terrifying shape, he would assume she was a divinity, a Venus Anadyomene, a mega-titted six-footer. But then as she came closer, so close that sometimes she would drip all over him, he would see that she was really just a little Spanish girl, all in the same proportions, but with her dimensions magnified by the sun.

'Dean!' Vie had called to him at one stage, 'shouldn't you be going for a swim?' And he had leaned forward, flapping his hands in irritation. He had sulked, in fact, all holiday, and his sulk was the worse because he was ashamed of his sulking; and he was ashamed because he knew, with the good part of himself, that Dennis and Vie were only doing their best. He sulked, and felt guilty for sulking, in the taxi all the way from Birmingham Airport.

So when he saw what had happened to the hedge, he felt an almost superhuman surge of loyal rage. The desecration was bad enough on its own, the tremendous battlefield aura of aggression and violation that rose from the buzz-sawed stumps. It was insane, in itself, that Price should have felt able to cross the frontier, in broad daylight, and perpetrate this massacre. But the real offence was the insult that made Vie cry, and made Dennis sink to his knees in lamentation. 'My trees,' he cried, and his voice rose over Wednesbury like Rachel weeping for her children.

At the end of the lawn, next to a mound of hacked-off foliage, were the limbs and trunks of the victims, neatly hewn by this psychopath, into even lengths. Propped up, in felt tip, was an amateur advertisement: 'Logs for sale.'

'Haven't you heard?' said Price the Cheese. 'Law's been changed, hasn't it. The council sends you three warnings, and then they are entitled to chop down a vexatious tree.'

'I saw no warnings,' said Dennis Faulkner.

'Really?' Price cocked an eyebrow.

'What is this law?' wailed Vie.

'Check it out. It's called the High Hedges Act. Labour chap called Stephen Pound. First piece of Labour legislation I've agreed with, actually.'

For many human beings there is something psychologically disabling about an act of violence on this scale. Some will lash out, and let the instant flame of vengeance bloom in their hearts; others find themselves winded, depressed, and full of the loneliness of the victim. So Dennis and Vie made themselves a Baxter's mushroom-rich cuppasoup and retreated to their bedroom. As he lay in his own narrow cell, adorned with *Lord of the Rings* posters and a *Sunday Times* map of the Roman Empire, Dean listened to their defeated murmurs and fed his fury. He knew in his heart that Price had a point. They all knew it secretly, even Vie. But the coffee-coloured semi-detached adolescent saw in the disaster a chance for oneness with his parents.

He would fight their corner. He would make a great act of atonement for the fact of his difference. He lay and watched the car headlights pass with aqueous mystery across the ceiling. Perhaps he would execute some Godfather-type revenge, and cause Price to wake screaming, his sheets polluted with a gigantic truckle of one of his experimental fromages. Then he had a better idea. Expertly skipping the stair that creaked he went downstairs, equipped himself, and stole like the shadow of a panther into the garden of Price the Cheese.

In the months that followed his social workers and probation officers would often ask him where he had come by the idea; and though it was of course the classic culmination of neighbour disputes, from Birmingham to Bosnia, he always insisted that it was his own.

The first warning Price had was the *BANG* of the frosted glass on the front door, blown in by the heat from the banked bonfire of logs and kerosene-drenched brushwood. Immediately his house began to surrender itself to the flames. The junk mail writhed and was consumed on the mat. The mat offered no resistance. All along the corridor it was a tale of instant, ecstatic capitulation by the pictures and soft furnishings. All Price's possessions were ready to turn themselves in, without a fight, and might have betrayed their master to perdition, had he not heard the boom, nipped out from under his duvet in his Viyella pyjamas, opened the landing window, and leapt for the now non-existent branches.

So Price the Cheese fell with an oath, because he had no doubt who had done this to him, and bust his ankle.

As he stood with his parents watching several thousand gallons of water thud into the Hollyhocks, and as the glare of the last flames died on their aghast faces, Dean knew what to do. He took a snap decision. He would say nothing. It was certainly possible that Dennis would hail him as a hero, and love him forever more for visiting such destruction on his enemy. But as he looked at the soaking, carbonized living room, and as the night air of Wolverhampton was filled with the smell of toasted cheese, he decided not to take the risk.

As a strategy, it failed. The police came looking and found a jerry can covered with Dean's fingerprints, in the Faulkner shed. Dean was taken to the living room, and under the gaze of the Queen Mother, his adoptive parents, and two kindly members of the West Midlands Serious Crime Squad, he burst into tears. His mother said nothing, but it was the words of his father that he kept and nursed, coddling and crooning over them when he wanted to bruise his heart into hatred.

Poor Dennis had tried so hard, for Vie's sake, to love the kid with all his heart, but he had never utterly succeeded. 'Oh for God's sake!' he said now, swatting the side of his head as though a mosquito had landed on either ear.

'You stupid little . . . coon!'

As soon as the word was out he wanted to choke it back. Vie was furious. Dennis had never said anything like it before, and it was a complete rejection of everything she stood for, what with her work in the Sue Ryder shop and all.

'Dennis!' she snapped. 'Oh I'm sorry, my dear,' said the former lift executive, advancing on Dean.

One of the policemen scribbled 'coon' in his notebook. You never knew how these things would go. But Dean shrank before him, and the ambiguities in his status seemed to fade away.

There it was, *en clair*, decoded. He was a coon, and he was stupid, and he was stupid because he was a coon. And whenever he was subsequently affected by doubt or scruple about what he was doing, he would say 'stupid coon' to himself, and immediately the watertight bulkheads in his brain would come crashing down. Which was what Dean did now as he sat in the stifling heat in the back of the ambulance, assisting in a plot that had started to go wrong almost as soon as it began.

'Stupid little coon,' he said to himself, as though reciting a passage from the Holy Koran, and shut the gates of mercy on mankind.

'The train of death is on its way,' said Jones. 'Its riders are steadfast. Nothing will stop them or turn them back.'

'Yeah, all roight then,' said Dean.

Jones pulled up outside the Red Lion pub. The Muslim wrinkled his nose at the smell of beer. He could see the boom ahead, painted with red and white chevrons, and the car park beyond it, normally used by MPs, from which he proposed to set out on foot.

CHAPTER EIGHTEEN
0911 HRS

Adam Swallow rose and walked towards the driver's window.

'Are you the guys I am expecting?' Jones nodded. Adam looked into those eyes and felt a momentary lurch of uncertainty. He hoped to goodness that Benedicte had got this thing right.

He wondered how the hell he was going to pass this gang off as a TV crew. He looked at Habib, now playing again with his rosary; at Haroun with his expression of a camel about to spit; he saw the kid, blocking the gangway to the back.

Adam tried to peer into the darkness.

'So, which one of you is the victim?'

'He is behind,' said Jones, jerking his thumb. 'He is not very well. Please respect his condition.'

'I didn't realize he would still need an ambulance?'

'Certainly. We have many supporters in the healthcare services.'

'OK,' said Adam, and prepared to hand over the car park pass, thinking as he did so that he would ring Benedicte as soon as he could.

Just as Jones's hand was about to close on Roger's plastic card, emblazoned with the Portcullis of Parliament, Adam's hand twitched, and the pass jerked just out of reach. He couldn't help it. He had to ask.

'Do you mind telling me what kind of torture it was? Was it in Abu Ghraib?' he said, naming the notorious jail in Baghdad.

'The Americans did it,' said Jones.

'The American women did it,' said Haroun. 'They did it with the long sweeping brush handle and the dog.' He mimed, and Adam flinched.

Without a word, he handed over the plastic pass, and Jones reignited the engine, and drove towards the boom.

The Yanks would be here any minute.

'Worra you lot on about?' wailed Dean, and was hit by Haroun.

The cavalcade now found itself somewhat ahead of schedule as it pulled through Chelsea.

'Bloody Yanks,' said one Chelsea pensioner, as he sat champing and bemedalled in Ranelagh Gardens. 'All the gear and no idea.' Most of his life, post-war, had been dominated by a single controversy: who was the greater general, Monty or Eisenhower, and why did Monty dither at Caen? On this subject he literally bored for Britain.

POTUS in three minutes, crackled the news in the ears of Joe, Matt and all the other USSS men in Parliament Square.

More like Patton than Eisenhower, the cavalcade moved in its lightning thrust through London, and the upper air was full of American communications.

So huge, in fact, was the US Secret Service men's requirement for bandwidth that yesterday, at Windsor, they had disabled Her Majesty's TV aerial, and she had been unable to watch Channel Four racing. Conversation at dinner had been strained.

'I jes lurve to watch the horses,' the President said. 'Most afternoons I take a nap in the Oval Office, and I whack on that TV and watch a race. Don't you watch the races, ma'am?'

'Hmmf,' said the Queen.

This morning her TV was still on the blink, and so she felt

no particular obligation to watch the speech that was about to take place, without her, in Westminster Hall.

POTUS in two, came the whisper from the smarties on the lapels of the USSS men.

In the Ops Room at New Scotland Yard the London police were still analysing the implications of the news from Horseferry Road. Deputy Assistant Commissioner Stephen Purnell: 'How many ambulances are there right now in the Westminster area?'

'I don't know. A hundred. Tops.'

'If all this is true, we'll find the damn thing in five minutes. Roll the CCTV camera film. Oh, another thing. Your dead traffic warden is meant to have recorded all the details in his Huskie, isn't he?'

'Yessir.'

'Well, what are you waiting for? We'll be able to find out all about it from the Apcoa computers. There can't have been that many illegally parked ambulances in Tufton Street.'

'Right, sir. I just wondered, sir, given that the whole thing is about to start in a few minutes, whether we should, you know, tell the Americans . . .'

'I've got 14,000 officers in Central London. We ought to be able to find one rogue ambulance without involving 950 trigger-happy Americans.'

'Righty-ho, sir . . . But hang on, sir, I'll have to tell Colonel Bluett we're raising the alert threshold. What if he wants to know why?'

'Tell Bluett to call me,' said the ranking British officer.

Before they could dial him, Bluett was on the line.

POTUS in one minute said the headsets.

The ambulance lolloped down towards the police booth that guarded the Norman Shaw car park. Roger's open sesame was waved; the tank trap went down; the metal boom went up.

The fatal machine had penetrated the walls of the precincts of the Palace of Westminster, pregnant with arms. Jones parked it smartly and out of the way, in Bay 20 of the small tarmac yard.

As he walked towards it, using a spare visitor's pass from Cameron to clear the turnstile, Adam suddenly felt a fierce flush of righteousness. The logic of the ambulance now seemed obvious to him, and as he looked at the tinted side window, he speculated murderously about the condition of the poor man within.

He and Cameron had been together in his Holborn flat when, trawling the antiwar websites, he had come across the archive of horror from Abu Ghraib. It wasn't so much the cruelty that got her, the hooding and beating and killing. It was the female involvement, and the way the whole thing was conducted with the simpering, grinning crassness of pornoloop America.

'Now I understand it,' Cameron had said, when they looked together at one of the unprintable images, of a naked Iraqi corpse, and a rather pretty Virginia girl brainlessly mugging for the camera. 'Now I understand how you could become a suicide bomber.'

Of course, he couldn't tell Cameron about the stunt that Benedicte had outlined to him, and in which he was collaborating. He knew that she would be prevented by her obligation to Roger, and her instinctive deference towards the office of the President of the United States of America.

So they had worked out a story about a TV crew; and when the truth emerged, he would of course take the heat, and he knew she would forgive him.

As he walked towards the van, he wondered how exactly they would bring the injured man in, and what his injuries were. Would he need a wheelchair? Would they use a stretcher?

He wouldn't stay to find out, because his plan was to be there in the hall when they entered. He wanted to see the expression on the face of the President.

No one of importance had resigned, in the wake of the scandal. None of the crack-brained neocons had really been confronted with the full awfulness of their doctrines. Now was the time for a reckoning.

It would be worth it.

From the driver's window, Jones was gesturing at him to stay back.

'Everything all right?' said Adam.

'Please wait,' said Jones in a whisper. 'It is the time of prayer.'

Jones wound up his window again, and Adam nodded, and removed his presence some way.

He wished Cameron would hurry up.

CHAPTER NINETEEN

0914 HRS

Now the noise was rising from the square, to mark the imminent Presidential arrival, and the crowd was flagellating itself with posters, denouncing everything American from bombs to powdered baby milk, like distraught mullahs at an ayatollah's funeral.

And Cameron's anxiety was rising with every one of her accelerating steps, as she went down the cloister, her papers clutched to her bosom. Roger watched her go, and so did several others.

Just then a taxi pulled up outside the Members' Entrance. The occupant got out, tipped, and was rewarded with a blatant fistful of blank receipts. It was Felix Thomson, who had spent the last few minutes sitting in the back while rubber-gloved officers subjected the taxi to prostatic indignities, scoping and palping for bombs, and gazing with dental mirrors at the undercarriage.

'Ah, Felix,' said Roger, and they adopted attitudes as transparently insincere as Molotov hailing Ribbentrop.

'My dear fellow,' said Felix, shaking his grey locks.

'And how is Felix this fine morning?'

'Felix is little short of superb,' said Felix.

'I saw your proprietor the other night,' said Roger, who knew how to irritate a journalist.

'Ah,' said Felix, and made a face of holy hypocrisy, like a cardinal discussing the health of the Pope.

'I think I should let you know that he thinks the media are a seething mass of mushy-minded anti-American pinkos, especially on his own papers.'

'You amaze me.'

'Not that you'll be doing any of that anti-American stuff today, not in your sketch.'

'I'd sooner be dead,' said Felix.

'The usual knockabout?'

'Good, clean fun.'

'Tremendous.'

Felix had turned to go, fishing for his press gallery pass. Roger Barlow felt temptation welling up. 'Hey Felix.'

'Yes old man?'

'I wonder whether I could beg a favour off you.'

'Provided it doesn't mean reporting one of your speeches.'

'No, no, it's nothing, it's . . . Well, you know in newspapers . . .'

'Yes.'

'Well, in newspapers you chaps probably have a pretty good idea in the morning what you are going to put in the paper that day.'

'Well, I don't have the faintest idea.'

'Not you, I mean the chaps in general. The top chaps, what do you call them, the sub-editors and things, don't they draw up some kind of list of the main items of the day?'

'Yeah, yeah, the newslist, yeah.'

'Right. The newslist.'

'Is this going to take much longer, old boy, because I've got an urgent appointment with a cup of coffee and a jam doughnut.'

'Absolutely, we're just coming to the point here now. This newslist: this is something which is presumably accessible to anyone who is in the newspaper.'

'Yeah, but . . .'

'And you are in the newspaper.'

'Well, I am on the newspaper.'

'Exactly. You are on it. Is there any way, Felix, that you could have a squint at that newslist for today?'

'Well, I wouldn't normally.'

'I know, but if you had a spare second, do you think you could conceivably flip it up, dial it up, download it?'

'Do you mind my asking why?'

'To be perfectly honest, and this is very embarrassing, I want to know if they are doing an article about me.'

'An article about you?'

'Yes, and if they are I promise I won't make a fuss or do anything about it. I just kind of want to know, because it has been eating me up.'

'And what kind of article might this be? Are you making a speech?'

'Well, actually I am making a speech today.'

'About?'

'It's about water fluoridation, but I don't expect the article will be about that.'

'Right.'

'It may well be about something else.'

'Right you are, guv, I'll keep my eyes peeled for an article about Roger Barlow, not mentioning water fluoridation.'

Felix went into the press gallery whistling Papageno's Song, and Roger felt the accustomed sweat of shame and idiocy on his brow. Everywhere people were coming and going as they got ready for the ceremony: reporters, MPs, researchers, security men and camera crews.

POTUS coming through now.

The bawling in Parliament Square reached a crescendo. On the roofs of the Cabinet Office, Portcullis House, the Treasury, the Welsh Office, the Foreign Office and all the way down Whitehall, police marksmen lay in the July sunshine, their black weapons soaking up the heat.

Eyes gazed through scopes. Fingers curled on triggers.

Toes shifted in the guttering.

In plotting the route of the cavalcade, Colonel Bluett of the USSS had reasoned that the Embankment, being built up on only one side, offered fewer opportunities to the sniper. *Whoomf,* went the Chevrolet people carriers, stuffed with bulging security men, as they now approached Millbank, passing the knots of people behind the security barriers. It was not their speed that was impressive, so much as the air they displaced.

Whooomf went the Cadillacs, the hugest Cadillacs anyone had ever seen. With their high roofs, athletic flanks and shred-proof tyres they were preposterously suggestive of a domi-nating class, the functioning, air-conditioned American version of a discredited Soviet idea.

Whoomf went the first decoy presidential car. *Whoomf* went the second decoy presidential car. *Whoomf, whoomf, whoomf.*

Just so must the tribes of Britannia have stood by the same gleaming brown river in AD 43, not knowing whether to cheer or boo, as the muddy legions of Claudius marched into Londinium, fresh from settling the Atrebates or the Belgae. Just so had the Saxons crowded round when the Norman conqueror was crowned on Christmas Day 1066, setting up such an ambiguous roar that the knights thought it was a revolt, and cut them down.

Except that Britain wasn't a colony of America, was she? She could hardly be called a vassal state, could she? No, she was an ally, a close and trusted ally, though she stood in relation to America as the most loyal member of the Delian league had stood to Athens. Or so it seemed to some of the more cynical folk who lined the route.

'Fact is, America has got bases, military bases, in places like Uzbekistan,' said a scruffy history professor to his wife as they walked up behind the railings.

'I mean, twenty years ago those places had missiles pointed at us.'

'Unbelievable,' said his wife.

'Of course, most people in this country don't give a stuff about American dominance, do they? They just think all human civilization has been pyramidal in structure since, well, since the Pyramids. They just think America is the boss and that's all there is to it. No point moaning. And this demonstration is really pretty small beer compared to the anti-Vietnam demos in the sixties.'

'Didn't we use to go on pro-Vietnam demos?' asked his wife.

'We did, darling, but times have changed.' The professor and his wife sat on their shooting sticks and took out their placards. In quavering magic marker the mediaevalist had written: 'Hop it, Yanks!'

'I don't mean you, of course.' The professor smiled at a group from the Rutgers University debating team, who were out with plastic stars and stripes to support the President, and having a tough time of it.

'That's all right, sir,' said the well-bred students.

'Yay,' they shouted now as the cavalcade shot past them like a black river of steel, and their cries were drowned out by the British mob.

The noise of her President's arrival made the hairs prickle on Cameron's bare arms, and she clacked ever faster in her strappy shoes down the stone tunnel that led to Portcullis House, and the turquoise tiles of the Tube station.

She felt a pang. It was guilt. But – if you considered the enormity of what she was about to do – it was only the tiniest frisson of guilt. In her current mood she could feel herself squashing her guilt like an aphid on a rose.

When she had become a researcher at the House of Commons she had signed a formal promise, dedicated to the Serjeant-at-Arms, that she would never do precisely what she was about to do. Ah, so what, she thought: think of the men in your life, darling, and think of your loyalties. There was Barlow. *Yeuuech*.

What was it with these English guys? What did he think he was doing, grabbing her lower jaw and fiddling with her teeth?

And yet apart from Barlow's absent-minded attentions, her eight months in England had been an unremitting tale of tepidity, frustration, and – let's be brutal – flaccidity. She had been taken on 'dates' only to find that the man's idea of a romantic climax to the evening was to escort her to a bar and meet a couple of his 'mates' from 'school', where school meant Charterhouse or Bradfield or some other fee-paying haven of hunnish practices. She had fought down her incredulity when a series of good-looking and allegedly heterosexual men had taken her to the zoo, to a game of cricket, to an Inuit art-house movie, and to an ice-skating rink; and on one occasion it had been seriously suggested to her that she pay.

She had stood almost in tears amid pastry-cutters and casseroles as a supposedly red-blooded Englishman had baked, before her eyes, some kind of faggot upside down cake with pineapple and glacé cherries. At the crucial moment one man had slipped from the room and returned with a porn video, which he had laid before her with all the moronic enthusiasm of a cocker spaniel that has brought in something disgusting from a ditch.

And always, at the end of the evening, there were these delicate manoeuvrings that cast her as the naysayer, when she was not at all sure that she wanted to say nay. Was there no one in this goddamn country who wanted to take her firmly in his arms and give a girl the time of day? Sometimes she wondered if it was not fluoride in the water, but bromine. Sometimes as she lay awake, on her own, in her little flat in Claverton Street, Pimlico, she would wonder whether it was to do with their mothers, or public schools, or nannies, or hot water bottles. Sometimes, at her most vulnerable, she would open her mind to the (sob) possibility that it was something to do with her.

Which was absurd, because ever since she was a tiny little girl, she had been told how beautiful she was. Sometimes she began to worry that she was going to lose it altogether – not her virginity, obviously, but her initiate status. Perhaps her hymen would actually regrow. At one point she seriously considered the rights and wrongs of an affair with Roger. Once you got over the nicotine-stained teeth, and the goofy sense of humour, there was something vaguely compelling about him: the gaunt face, the brown eyes that seemed perpetually amused, the beer-drinker's thatch. She'd briefly taken to walking into his office and staring at him for no particular reason, but he hadn't seemed to notice; and she had soon given up.

Just when she was about to abandon the English male as a contradiction in terms, she met Dr Adam Swallow, former Hedley Bull reader in International Relations at Balliol, now director of Middle East studies at Chatham House.

90

In contrast to Roger, with his gelatinous ability to see both sides, Adam was a believer, a man of ideological certainty.

The first word she heard him utter was 'bollocks'.

That is, he said it once, and then he repeated it, and then he said it again.

He was sitting only two away from her in the Strangers' Gallery in the House of Commons, as steeply shelving as an ancient amphitheatre. In principle, she should have been offended.

By the second, and certainly by the third bollocks she should, in all propriety, have said: '*Sst*. Oi, do you mind?' Because there, the object of the apathetic attention of everyone who could be bothered to sit on these bum-polished green benches, was her poor Roger.

It was a big set-piece Iraq debate, on a weaselly Opposition motion, and the subject was Britain's continuing commitment. Loads of members on both sides had given vent to little peeps of concern. Cameron thought Roger was making, by his standards, a respectable speech, jabbing his scrunched-up notes and sometimes seeming quite emotional. From time to time, however, he let fall some parliamentary platitude, and this earned her scorn.

'And I just want to say, Mr Deputy Speaker,' he said somewhere near the beginning, 'that this has been a very good and important debate with many excellent contributions . . .' Cameron was actually groaning to herself, and wishing that MPs didn't always use this formula to describe a series of shallow and repetitive speeches by people who, as often as not, had been gestapoed into performance by the whips.

'Bollocks,' said the man to her right with the Aztec profile, and she shot him an approving glance.

'And it goes without saying, Mr Deputy Speaker, that we in this country have the best and most dedicated armed forces in the world, and I join other hon membs in paying tribute to the courage and professionalism with which every man or woman has been carrying out his or her duties.'

Just as Cameron was wondering why it was necessary to extol ALL members of the armed forces, down to the last pistol-whipping NCO or fornicating Wren, the dark-haired young man exploded again. Some people shifted and snorted at the blasphemy.

At the top of the stairs behind them a man appeared in the doorway. He was dressed in a black tailcoat with a huge gold seal at his belly; and since he was shaven-skulled and had the physique of Big Daddy, Cameron divined that he must be a parliamentary bouncer.

The Aztec's third interjection was provoked by what Cameron thought was one of Barlow's best passages.

'Many people on both sides of this House, and many people in this country, have the profoundest doubts about some of the reasons we were given for going to war. All those of us who took on trust the Prime Minister's claims about weapons of mass destruction have reason to feel let down. We were told that Saddam could launch a chemical or biological attack on Britain in the space of forty-five minutes. We were told that Saddam was buying uranium from Niger.

'These claims have not, to put it mildly, been vindicated, and I am sure that most people will have been as disgusted as I was by the Government's attempt to cover its embarrassment.

'And then we have had the appalling revelations from Abu Ghraib and other jails. There is no question but that we will pay a price for this disaster, and I am sure it is accepted on all sides of the House that nothing is more calculated to inflame Arab sentiment than the spectacle of female torturers.

'But that still does not mean that the case for the war has been entirely vitiated.

'I have recently been to Baghdad, with Unicef' – he paused,

looking as self-important as any other MP – 'and I saw some pretty awful things. This is a country in many ways still in shock. The electricity supply is fairly ropy. The sewage system is frankly screwed up.' Cameron winced, and there was an unintelligible intervention from one of the few Members who was listening. 'But everywhere I went, I kid you not, I met people who were genuinely cheered and bucked up – no, in some cases overjoyed,' he said, as though suddenly remembering a conversation, and there was a little catch in his throat, and people in the Chamber finally stopped gassing, and eyeballed him moodily, 'yes, in some cases overjoyed to have been liberated by American and British arms from one of the nastiest and most unscrupulous tyrannies of modern memory.

'To all those who opposed and oppose our allied action in Iraq, there is one overwhelming and unanswerable rejoinder: that whatever our intentions, the result was the freedom of a civilized people from a particularly miserable servitude, and of that I believe we can be very proud.'

There was quite a lot of hear-hearing on both sides of the House, and for the first time in a while, Cameron felt sensations of enthusiasm for her employer. So she was amazed, when the assenting groans had died away, to hear the Inca prince say Bollocks again, so loudly that he was heard by someone on the green benches.

This time Big Daddy in tails descended a few steps towards him, and if he had not risen of his own accord, it seemed quite likely that he would have been manhandled out.

That, however, was three months ago. To say that her feelings had changed would do scant justice to the endocrinal choir of happiness within. According to a reductionist account – probably from the pages of *Marie Claire* – it was all about phenylethylamine, which was in turn stimulating the production of norepinephrine and adrenalin, suppressing her appetite for food and filling her with a sense of excitement.

Her hypothalamus was producing serotonin, giving her a broad benignity, and out of the substantia nigra of her brain came the really good thing, the boy from the black stuff, the most powerful and addictive of all the drugs in her personal self-generated pharmacopoeia.

It was the dopamine that gave her the sense of invulnerability, the hormone that lets a boxer take his punches and helps a rugby player to get knocked down and get up again. It was the dopamine, the clinching intoxicant of sexual love, which now propelled her through the concourse of Portcullis House, approving glances pinging off her from all sides. Without that drug it is doubtful she would have gone, as she did now, to the Pass Office.

CHAPTER TWENTY

0916 HRS

Bluett was in a considerable taking. The various US listening posts had put together enough snatches of conversation to conclude that something was awry.

'I'm coming right over,' he told Deputy Assistant Commissioner Purnell, though in reality he was already on his way.

'Tremendous,' said Purnell. He waved at Grover, who was just coming in to tell him that the stolen ambulance had been located both on the CCTV and on the Apcoa computers. 'The Ops Room is all yours. Can I ask why?'

'I want you to explain why the alert status is now red plus.'

'Triff – I'll see you in a short while, Colonel.'

'No, I mean I want you to explain now.'

'I think we may have an incident involving an ambulance.'

'An ambulance, huh?' said Bluett, as if he didn't know.

* * *

94

Like big black birds of prey alighting one after the other on a telegraph wire, the cars of the cavalcade came to a halt in line. Exactly abreast of the red carpet that spilled from the steps of St Stephen's Entrance drew up the decoy Cadillac De Ville, and the crowd experienced a kind of orgasm of hatred.

'Incoming!' said the USSS men to each other, as the eggs volleyed over the road and the railings, and as soon as they splatted on the crimson cloth, the mess was cleared up by men in black tights with J-cloths. Then the second decoy Cadillac swooped in to land, and drew some more of the protesters' ammo. Then the first two Cadillacs shifted forward, and the real De Ville slid into its berth, right slap next to the candy-striped marquee they had erected in front of St Stephen's Entrance.

Inside were the battery of sensors and G-men that Jones had hoped to avoid by choosing his subterranean route. Permanent Protectees One and Two got out.

Almost unseen by the mob they slipped into the shelter of the marquee and went up the steps, hand in hand, for their first engagement, an audience with the Speaker of the House of Commons. Pressing up against the barricades, and the statue of Jan Christiaan Smuts, the crowd disgraced itself with its commentary.

When she entered the Pass Office Cameron found she was momentarily tongue-tied. Every yell and honk outside was turning into a beat of warning in her lovely head, that this was wrong, wrong, wrong.

Everyone knew the risks, and surely Adam could see that there was something weird about what he was asking her to do. Why was he rushing her? Why was she being given no real time to think?

Whatever you thought about the President, he was her leader, her head of state. If only in virtue of his office, he deserved her most devoted and assiduous protection.

She calmed herself down. Adam could not possibly have got this wrong. It was only a TV crew.

'Yes, m'dear,' said the man in the peaked cap, a cheerful father of three from Stogumber in Somerset, who would never forgive himself for what he was about to do. He knew Cameron's face and liked it.

'What can I do for you?'

'I've come to pick up four press passes in the name of Roger Barlow.'

The man looked confused. 'In the name of Roger Barlow? But he's a Member.'

'Yes, no, I mean they are one-day press passes and Roger Barlow has signed for them.'

'Okey dokey,' said the guard, and after rustling in a drawer he produced four laminated badges. 'Coo-er,' he said, 'I see Mr Barlow's got some interesting friends. The Al-Khadija network, eh? Cameraman, soundman, producer and reporter. Very good. There you are, m'dear,' and he handed them over, as a man might hand over four freshly microwaved Cornish pasties.

Cameron took them, and she was about to leave the Pass Office in search of Adam, when she felt faint.

She had been up since five a.m. – or four a.m., UK time – to catch the early flight back from Brussels. But that wasn't it. She felt suddenly queasy, looking at these four photographs, which Adam had given her, and which he said had come from Benedicte.

There was a bench just outside the office, and here she sat, with her head forward to promote blood supply.

CHAPTER TWENTY-ONE

0919 HRS

Inside the ambulance, Jones was giving instructions to Haroun and Habib.

'We've got about thirty minutes until the beginning of the speeches. That means we've got fifteen minutes to get into Westminster Hall, which isn't very long. As soon as the good doctor gives us the passes, we go.

'Everything OK now, Dean, my child?' he added, turning to look into the rank, blood-spattered shambles. 'Or am I going to have to shoot you now?'

Dean looked out of the dirty side window. He could see a lowered security boom and Metropolitan Policemen in shirt-sleeve order and carrying machine guns, and, some way off, Adam waiting.

Now Jones knew from his briefings that they would be required to negotiate a series of tunnels to attain Westminster Hall.

As soon as Adam had gone to take his place in the hall, they would emerge, and go through the basement of Norman Shaw South, the Scottish Baronial building behind them. They had worked out a route past the kitchens and the post room. Then they would come up the stairs and tack diagonally across the ground floor of Portcullis House, and then under the road and down the escalator to the colonnade of New Palace Yard. It was a bit complicated, but could be accomplished in a shade over five minutes.

'I'm coming, sir,' said Dean. There was a small clonk, and Dean froze. Slowly he rotated his eyes to the floor. Was it his imagination, or had one of those parking ticket gizmos slipped off the warden's chest? Surely he— No, thought Dean; no one could survive the loss of so much blood.

He squelched in search of the equipment.

Life had been tough for Dean since that dreadful night in Wednesbury. The magistrates had grasped pretty clearly what had happened, and in some ways they were even sympathetic. But he was still convicted, in a juvenile court, of arson. Price launched an action with more than twenty separate complaints, including destruction of intellectual property. He claimed that he had produced a new kind of hard cheese, dense, nutty and as fissile as Parmesan.

It was going to be unmistakable, he said, and he had already ordered the British racing green wax in which it was to be coated. He painted a picture of a revolution in taste, and not just in Britain. His green spheres would pop up in delicatessens across the planet.

'And what were you going to call this cheese?' asked the magistrate.

'It was going to be Old Wednesbury,' said Price, with tears in his eyes.

The magistrate had a holiday house in Normandy. He understood the backwardness of the British in the matter of cheese. He was enough of a patriot to resent the loss of Old Wednesbury.

'Four hundred hours' community service,' he said.

Shock and disappointment had now crowded in so fast on Dennis and Vie that Dennis had a kind of blip, a small cranial embolism that noticeably slowed him down, and Vie, poor Vie who had loved Dean, contracted ovarian cancer, cruel irony of fate. She faded to bones and was gone.

Dean left school. He felt, and sometimes claimed, that he had been vice-captain of the school's water polo team, even though that office was not recognized in the school's constitution. Otherwise his record was unblemished by achievement.

He fell in with a bad crowd while performing his community service. It was a soft job, scraping graffiti off gravestones, and his fellow-convicts, Wayne and Paulie, had no desire to move on to the next task, trying to move the gum which clung like huge pale lichen to Wolverhampton's desolate piazzas, testament to the frustrated oral desires of office workers prevented from smoking. Wayne and Paulie told Dean about the horrors of this Sisyphean task, how even if the gum came off the flag, it adhered so grimly to the scraper that it seemed nothing would shift it but a tactical nuclear weapon. So every night, when the cemetery was locked, Wayne, Dean and Paulie would shin over the gate, have some drugs, and then, like Penelope with her loom, they would busily undo the work of the day.

Here was the mossy tomb of Hannah, beloved wife of Tobias Horton, departed this world in the year of grace 1869. 'SCMU', wrote Dean. He meant to write scum, but was so stoned that dyslexia was added to his list of troubles.

Here were the higgledy-piggledy headstones of the Arbuthnot family, sticking out of the earth like carious teeth. 'Fuck off, wogs,' wrote Dean on the Arbuthnots. In view of his complexes, well known to his social workers, he thought this act unlikely to be blamed on him.

Shorn of Vie's mediation, his life at home had become almost satirically bad, he and Dennis timing their routines so as not even to meet in the kitchen. After a year of drifting, and rejecting every solution that Dennis could offer, Dean was, as the politicians like to put it, on the conveyor belt to crime. Twice on the urgings of Wayne and Paulie he had been involved in attempted joy riding. Once he had been caught. Once he had served as a look-out while Wayne and Paulie burgled a house in Willenhall, a bosky street with quiet villas set well back from the lamps, the residence, did he but know it, of his natural father, whose wiper business had been wiped out by Tory interest rates and who made a tidy living offering consultancy to fellow-victims on how to go bust in the most profitable possible way.

You could not really say that the state had failed young Dean, not for lack of resources.

If a heartless politician were to engage in gratuitous political point-scoring, he might note that Dean was cared for by a Substance Abuse Outreach Worker (£25,000 pa), a Crime Prevention Detached Youth Project Worker (£31,000), a Burglary Reduction Worker (£23,000), a Probation Officer (£26,000), a Vehicle Theft Reduction Worker (£28,000 plus cars) and a representative of DYSPEL, a state-funded body that sees to the needs of dyslexic young offenders (£36,000).

No single person really took an intelligent interest in him until one day some liberal genius in the Home Office came up with the FreshStart scheme. In a move evoking the excesses of 1970s Sweden, or the penal policies of Sir Wilfred Lucas-Dockery, the Home Secretary decided that there was only one way of getting Dean and his kind off their conveyor belt before they became fully assembled, galvanized and rustproofed criminals.

The idea was that they should all be given a £10,000 FreshStart fund, at the expense of the taxpayer. Wayne, Paulie and Dean could hardly believe their luck. They immediately rented a large house, where they lived in scenes of unremitting squalor. They relieved the sudden tedium of affluence with drink and drugs. They bought an orange Vauxhall Astra, which they ineffectively souped up and rammed through the window of RitePrice in Bilston. Wayne sustained such serious injuries that he spent much of the next few years shuttling, at indescribable public expense, between Stoke Mandeville and assorted respite centres.

Dean and Paulie were still more or less in one piece; and the bulk of their FreshStart funds was used to compensate RitePrice. It was furthermore decided by the parole officers and social workers that in so far as Dean and Paulie still had a debt to RitePrice, they should repay it by working there, free, as part of a Youth Training Scheme called Passport2Jobs. Under Passport2Jobs some of the least employable young people in Britain were allowed to sit picking their noses and reading *Fiesta* in the stock rooms of firms willing to accept the subsidies attached.

Dean was in some ways a gifted shelf-stacker. He devised a way of booby-trapping the Pampers nappies, so that a shopper couldn't pull out one of the plastic breeze blocks of Maxi-Pluses without the rest of them raining down on her, or, more gratifyingly still, on the head of the little brute in the buggy.

He was wholly absorbed, as though back at his Montessori school, in creating pyramids of oranges and nectarines. One week, to his shivering pleasure, a photocopied form was stuck on the board announcing that he was RitePrice's most useful employee of the month of June.

'Well done, Dean,' said curly-haired Vanessa at the checkout, and Dean shot a glance at her.

She was beaming at him, showing loads of pretty white teeth. There seemed no question about her sincerity. 'Thanks,' he said. It wasn't obvious, as he stomped over to the so-called Delicatessen section, but he was walking on air.

Over the next few days he started looking more closely at Vanessa who was – though he and Paulie argued about this to begin with – at least as pretty as some of the girls in the *Daily Star*. On any pretext he would wander past her checkout and make some remark, in the hope of eliciting a smile. He was usually successful. Every time he looked at her sweet oval face, and her tight white checkout coat, he felt the choky feeling in his lungs. Bashfully he would buy choco-lates at her till, with his own money, and *ching-ching* he would present them to her.

One day he asked her to the pub with Paulie, and as they said good night, she actually stuck out her cheek for a kiss. He took her out again, and when he got home, he looked at himself in the mirror. He hadn't told her his origins, and he wasn't sure what to say. The interesting thing about his half-caste looks, he decided, was that he didn't look Negroid.

He looked kind of Arab: dark skin, curly hair, a forceful but straight nose. Yes, for the purposes of conversation with Vanessa, he would be a sheikh.

One night in the pub he poured forth his life's story: the misery of his existence with Dennis and Vie, the burning of Price's cheesorium, the tragic ram-raid. He couldn't believe how much she wanted to know, and how saddened she seemed by the details of his shocking finances. For the first time in his life, it occurred to him that he might be an interesting person.

''Ere Vanessa,' said Dean, who was fairly sure he was on the right lines, 'has anyone ever told you how lovely you are?'

'Oh Dean,' said Vanessa, 'that's reely reely sweet.'

'Vanessa,' said Dean, knitting his fingers, 'I love you.'

'Oh Dean,' she said, and to his delirious stupefaction, she hugged him. But the following night, when he had summoned the bottle to ask her whether she would like, perhaps, to see a film, it turned out that she was busy. Something to do with her Nan, and a hip bath, and cuts in social services.

It was the same story the following night; or rather, it was a different story, but with the same result. This time there was something very slightly distant in her manner. That evening, when Paulie came back to their digs, Dean had a sudden suspicion. Next Monday evening came the moment of tragic revelation. It was not strictly true that it was a night he would never forget, since the memory became distorted over the years, depending on how much he wanted to torment himself.

Sometimes it was an X-rated scene, sometimes it was almost innocent. It involved Vanessa and Paulie, and a store room for cleaning things which they wrongly believed they had locked from the inside. Dean was so offended, so horrified, and of course so jealous that he could only think of one thing to do. He spent the rest of his brief career at RitePrice hiding in the store room to make sure it could never happen again. He was fired.

A few days later he was sitting at home, eating a pot noodle and watching *Countdown* when Paulie walked in. He was looking triumphant.

''Ere, look who I shagged.'

He was waving the *Guardian*, not a newspaper that normally came into this household. It was a long article by someone called Lucy Goodbody, in the G2 section, called 'Breadline Britain'.

It was all about being a checkout girl in a shop in Wolverhampton, and how tough it was. He looked at the picture by-line. That wasn't Lucy Goodbody.

That was Vanessa.

'What's this bollocks?' he asked, and read, with mounting despair, Lucy Goodbody's account of life in RitePrice Wolverhampton.

It seemed they were among the lowest paid workers in Britain, and according to Lucy Goodbody they all hated their jobs.

That's not true, thought Dean. He'd rather enjoyed bits of it. Then he came to the passage about him. She described someone called 'Dave, a young, painfully lost-looking Anglo-Caribbean with a beautiful smile'.

'To my shame and embarrassment,' recorded Lucy Goodbody in her diary-type report, 'young Dave is developing a crush on me. He uses any excuse to come to my checkout till, and buys me presents he really cannot afford.'

Dean could read no longer. His eyes were too full.

'I shagged her,' said Paulie. 'I shagged some reporter from the *Guardian*.'

That afternoon, Dean did something really stupid. It occurred to him that he knew where the *Guardian* was based. It was just down the road; at least it must be the local branch of the *Guardian*, because it had a big black and white sign over the shop front, saying *The Guardian/ The Observer*. The luckless newsagent's went the way of Price's cheese lab.

He had been in Her Majesty's Young Offenders' Institution at Feltham for two weeks when he became aware of Islam. 'What's all those shoes doing there?' he asked as he was walked down a dim corridor.

'It's the mosque, innit.'

Every Friday lunchtime he listened to the Khutab. He heard incredible things, and things that seemed to him to be obvious, that explained so much about the evils of his world. He couldn't believe, really, that a preacher was allowed by the authorities to speak so frankly to prisoners.

Apparently there was a satanic Zionist freemason plot to ban the hijab, or headscarf. That didn't seem too bad to Dean. He'd vaguely heard that they were doing something of the kind in France.

'Britain is a society of divorce and adultery, where women are not taught to respect their own bodies,' said the imam. Yeah. Dean felt sick as he thought of Vanessa writhing on the floor of the stock room.

'Thirty-five per cent of women in Britain have been abused,' said the imam, 'usually by someone known to them. In the Muslim religion, women are to be loved and respected, and not treated like a piece of meat.'

Yeah. Dean thought of Vanessa/Lucy Goodbody (the very name was now a provocation) and how she treated her own sexuality. He thought how she had obviously liked the piece-of-meat approach, and he shuddered with horror and desire and incomprehension.

He discovered that Islam meant surrender. It meant obedience. It meant a union with God and with the word of God, unmediated by human agency. It also meant specifically a rejection of a world which had rejected him. When he left Feltham six months later, there were all kinds of outreach workers ready to reach out for him, but Dean was now on a different conveyor belt.

It was at the Finsbury Park Islamic Welfare Centre, where he went to pray, that he fell in with the man called Jones. Jones was the disciple and lieutenant of a one-eyed, one-armed cleric who had survived and prospered despite, or perhaps because of, all the hatred heaped upon him by the tabloid papers. Faith was flowering here, in the most unpromising surroundings. Hard by a thundering railway bridge was a kind of concrete cattle yard, and here the faithful came in their hundreds, from all over the world, five times a day, to hear the militant Islamic teaching of the one-eyed mullah.

'The American Christian fundamentalists want to bring about Armageddon, which is preparatory to the second coming of Christ,' said the priest. His audience sat on the tarpaulins, listening with glassy appreciation.

'It is planned to have the first homosexual prime minister.

'They wish to clone human beings.

'They wish to legalize child prostitution.

'Marriage with animals will become legalized.

'The women will be allowed to beat the men with rods, like in the American jails.

'There will be microchipping of the entire population.

'GM crops will be introduced.' Yeah, thought Dean: you should see some of the things we used to sell at RitePrice.

'They want to destroy the Al-Aqsa mosque.'

Slowly Dean became not just spiritually awakened and doctrinally literate. He became politically engaged. They had videos at the Islamic Welfare Centre, documenting the struggle against the Israeli occupation; and they had videos narrating and celebrating the sacrifice of the suicide bombers.

He learned of Richard Reid, the heroic young man from South London, who tried to blow up his own shoe. He heard of other would-be heroes, who had so far gone undetected by the authorities: the sock bomber, the pants bomber, the vest

bomber, the biro bomber and – most rare and admirable –
the bra bomber.

Sometimes, after he had been brought to an ebullition of
anger, he started to wonder whether he might be made of
the same stuff. And so did Jones – Jones the Bomb.

'Remember,' said this prince of philosophers after their
first tutorial, 'he who does not fight is not a true believer.'
Every word Jones uttered seemed to slide into place like a
sweetly smacked nail. Now, as they sat in the Norman Shaw
North car park, Jones the Bomb repeated those words. Dean
found he needed no further prompting.

With dextrous shelf-stacker's hands he assembled the team's
gear, like a man in charge of a parachute jump or a dive.
They had a big DSR370P Sony Camcorder, with no battery,
to be carried by Habib. They had two big fluffy grey sound
booms, though anyone who knew anything about TV would
spot that this was unnecessary, and one of the sound booms
was no longer grey.

'Bloody hell,' said Dean, for such, since his conversion,
was the limit of his profanity, 'the bloody warden has bleeding
bled on everything.'

'Never mind, Dean,' said Jones.

CHAPTER TWENTY-TWO
0924 HRS

'All right,' said Deputy Assistant Commissioner Purnell to
Colonel Bluett, 'let's be practical. The President is due to start
speaking at ten a.m. In all candour, I think if we haven't
found this blasted ambulance by then, we should activate
Option Minicab.'

Bluett winced. Minicab was the emergency exit. It meant
bundling the two Permanent Protectees into the Black Hawk,

flying straight to Northolt, and putting them aboard Air Force One, the blue-painted 747.

'Shee-,' he said. It would go down as one of the most lamentable lapses in Presidential security since they shot Ronald Reagan. 'Let's run that tape again,' he said. Through the eye of a CCTV camera mounted on the Barry Tower of the House of Lords, they watched the ambulance make its jerky progress up Millbank. The shot was grey and fuzzy, but the licence plate L64896P was clear enough. Though they didn't know it, they also watched Barlow and Ziggy Roberts, moving in ten-yard leaps and making Chaplinesque gestures.

'That's our guys,' said Bluett, as they watched the ambulance being stopped by Joe and Matt the USSS men. 'What are they frigging playing at?'

'It's no one's fault,' said Deputy Assistant Commissioner Purnell.

'That,' said Bluett, 'may or may not turn out to be the verdict of history.'

'So now it goes up Whitehall, and then I am afraid we lose it.'

'We lose it?' said Bluett.

'Well, it seems one of the cameras has been vandalized.'

'Sheee-it,' said Bluett.

'There's a lot of ill-feeling against the congestion charge, you know.'

CHAPTER TWENTY-THREE
0926 HRS

The last Jason Pickel had seen of the ambulance was when it turned right, out of his field of vision, into Norman Shaw North. He had keen enough eyes to see that it had three Mediterranean or Middle Eastern types in the front seat, and though he knew he shouldn't be prejudiced, he was getting those Dad flashbacks again.

'Go on,' said Indira the friendly sniper, as he croaked to a halt, and once again checked his hand for tremor. 'What happened then?'

Jason got a grip and continued. 'You British have a great poet, Wystan Hugh Auden.'

'Mmm.' Indira couldn't remember much about Ordon.

'In his poem "Icarus" he makes a good point about any human disaster. Something terrible may be happening in one place, but just down the road people are getting on with their lives. In one corner of the canvas a tragedy is happening, a boy falling into the sea. But the ploughman gets on with his ploughing. The boat sails on.'

'Yeah,' said Indira, thinking he was a nice chap, the big depressed Yank, but hoping very much he wasn't about to recite poetry – or maybe he already was?

When he ran out into the street, and after the sunlight went off like a firework through his shades, what he mainly noticed, said Jason, was this incredibly peaceful scene. There were kids fishing in the Tigris, right by the American cantonment. In an instant, even while he could hear the screams of warning from the road, he took in their feet splayed in the mud, the way they cast their lines beyond the biblical rushes and the wavelets glittering. Then he saw the car coming down the road. The sweat was already coursing over his eyebrows and stinging his corneas, but he couldn't brush it away because he was carrying an M16 and a mobile, and anyway, there was no time.

'Stop or I fire!' yelled Sergeant Kennedy.

'Stop!' shouted GI Kovac.

'Stop!' shouted Jason. 'What part of stop don't you understand?'

The car rolling slowly towards them was a Chevrolet GMC, a big white shiny machine of a kind that could be seen all over Baghdad. Like every other example, the car had the letters TV extravagantly striped all over it in masking tape. It meant nothing. There were more 'TV' cars currently cruising Baghdad than there were TV stations on the planet. The Chevrolet GMC was the favoured vehicle of every Baathist kingpin turned looting gangster. Plenty of well-attested sightings had put Saddam himself behind the wheel of a GMC. The orders of Jason and the rest of the detail were clear. If the vehicle failed to stop within a reasonable delay, they were at liberty – no, they had a duty – to protect human life, Iraqi or American, from possible terrorist attack.

'Jesus Christ,' screamed Barry White the Limey journalist. 'What are you fucking well doing? He's not fucking stopping, is he?'

'Please keep calm, sir,' said Jason Pickel, and dropping the satphone still connected to his stunned and possibly faithless wife, he raised the carbine to his shoulder and shouted clearly, 'Driver, unless you halt I will open fire on the count of three. One.'

By some instinct the little fishermen of the Tigris flung themselves face-first into the reeds.

'Two.'

It does not take much to rob a British tabloid reporter – or indeed a broadsheet reporter – of his dignity, even if he has a hairstyle like Michelangelo's Moses. 'We're all going to fucking die,' shrieked Barry White as he hurled himself into the ditch, knocking over the last geranium as he went.

'Three.'

Because he had no choice, Jason Pickel opened fire, first at the windscreen and then at the bonnet.

'It's all right, Jason,' said Indira, touching his hand and noticing the vibration for the first time. It would be just her luck, she thought, if she and Jason actually had to DO something today.

Oh come on Cameron, darling girl, thought Adam Swallow. He looked at the ambulance and strained his ears for the sound of Islamic prayer. On no account must she see the mutilated man, or even see the men coming out of the ambulance.

He looked at his watch and yearned for the sight of her; partly because he was anxious, and partly because his feeling for her was turning day by day into the most heart-squeezing, throat-choking crush he had ever had on a woman.

In the office of the Speaker of the House of Commons there was a flap. The doorman at St Stephen's Entrance had just rung to say the President was on his way, and by their calculations he was almost ten minutes early.

The telephone rang again. 'It's the French Ambassador,' said Sir Edward Luce, the Deputy Serjeant-at-Arms, a spare, kindly man. 'He says it's about his partner, and he wants to speak to you personally.'

'His partner? What am I supposed to be doing with the French Ambassador's floozy?'

'He calls her his *petite amie*. You remember – Miss Benedicte al-Walibi. We had that trouble with the American Embassy.'

'*Nnnggh,*' the Speaker groaned. It was a low Scottish groan, an act of self-psyching-up, accepted within the Presbyterian sect to which he belonged as an expression of direct communication with the Almighty. Just such a noise had he produced in his youth, in the 1970s, when as an adroit convenor of the TGWU he had prepared to broker a deal between his lads and a once-great Coventry car firm. The deal might be inflation-busting; it might be unaffordable; it might accelerate the bringing of the hallowed marque to its knees. But with his broken prize-fighter's weariness he usually persuaded all sides that no better bargain could be struck. 'Tell him I'll call him right back,' said the Speaker. 'We've got the President coming in now.'

There was a silence in the Speaker's glorious apartments. The clock ticked a beat or two. Out of his nostrils came the soft, stertorous noise of a man digesting the traditional sheet-metal worker's breakfast of chitterlings and black pudding. But the Speaker's mind whirred with great precision as he worked on the problem of the French Ambassador's mistress.

Outside the Thames ran softly in the sun; inside the velvet brocaded wallpaper soared in plum and bottle green, like the luxurious trousers of some nineteenth-century clown, until it met the demented whorls and volutes of the Pugin entablature. Ranged at the back of the room was a glass-fronted case containing the gifts which successive Speakers had received from visiting dignitaries: a silver spittoon from the Speaker of the Chinese People's Assembly; a whip, its handle inlaid with topaz and jacinth, from the Majlis of Free Afghanistan; a drum from Uganda; a model ship from Moscow, and so on.

There was a rapping on the oak without. The Speaker stood. He clenched his buttocks. He stitched on his broadest smile. But it was not the President who entered. It was— Sir Perry Grainger, an MP for more than a quarter of a century, Chairman of the All-Party Foreign Affairs Committee, and a man of almost stratospheric pomposity.

'I am so sorry to raise this now, but the matter has only just come to my attention.' Sir Perry advanced to the middle of the carpet and beamed. It was an amphibian Roy Jenkinsesque beam of frightening intensity and insincerity.

'Someone has this morning informed me of the nature of the token which you will present on behalf of the House of Commons to the President. Is, ah, that it?'

Sir Perry's eye fell on the frankly unmissable object that stood on the Speaker's desk.

'Sir Perry,' said the Speaker, as patiently as he was able. 'You may not like it, but the President is going to be here any second.'

'My views are in a sense immaterial, but I think that there are many people, on both sides of the Atlantic, who might describe it as vulgar tat.'

'But I chose it myself,' said the Speaker, 'didn't I, Sir Edward?'

'You did, sir. You went to some considerable trouble.'

'I think it's just the job,' said the Speaker.

'It's certainly rather jolly,' said Sir Edward.

'The Americans are nuts about Churchill,' explained the Speaker. 'He's a hero to them. They canna get enough of him.'

Sir Perry looked at the enormous Toby jug of the wartime leader: mauve-cheeked, gooseberry-eyed and waving a V-sign. 'But the gesture is obscene.'

'Not in America,' said the Speaker. 'In America,' he demonstrated for Sir Perry's benefit – 'they use only one finger. I tell you what,' he continued, with the arm-round-the-shoulder voice he used for when the fix was coming, 'I believe that many colleagues on all sides of the House would think it right if you, Sir Perry, were to present him with this sign of transatlantic good wishes.'

'Well, I am not sure, Mr Speaker . . .' Vanity began to struggle with good taste in Sir Perry's mind, a short, one-sided conflict.

'The President is on his way now, sir,' said a man in tights, sticking his head round the door.

'And furthermore,' said the Speaker, as he reached into a humidor and produced a gorilla's fistful of nine-inch cigars, 'we will stuff it with Sir Winston's personal smokes.'

'But surely those aren't Winston's cigars?'

'They are now. Wah. I have spoken,' said the Speaker.

'But do you—?'

'I have spoken. That's what I'm paid to do,' and he raised his palm like a chief.

'Sir Edward, please ring the French Ambassador with my compliments, and tell him that he and his Palestinian doxy are fully expected in Westminster Hall. Their seats will be in the diplomatic section. This is the House of Commons, and no one tells us what to do, and certainly no foreign government.'

*　*　*

'Mr President, sir, it is an honour . . .'

And still Cameron sat on the bench in the corridor outside the Pass Office, not twenty yards from where Adam waited. She stared at the photos, of Jones with his livid mask, the slightly fatter one in the skullcap, the one with the killer eyes, and a young, good-looking boy. Was this really a TV crew?

Then she began to persuade herself that it must be, mainly because she had never known Adam to be wrong about anything.

Now that the President had gone inside, the shouting died down a little. The hard-core chanters continued to curse America, assisted by a steel band, but other protesters were taking things easy.

The July morning sun was gaining heat, and here and there it was almost what newspapers call a carnival atmosphere in Parliament Square. Some began to disrobe, to flop down on the chlorous stringy grass. The smell of fried onions rose from a pair of mobile hamburger stalls. Spliffs and cigarettes were produced, and soon the gathering had created a nice little nephos of polyaromatic hydrocarbons and benzo-pyrenes, as noxious in its way as a Kyoto-flouting gas-guzzling American traffic jam.

There were girls with bare belly buttons, and girls with rings through their belly buttons. There were girls with rings through their eyebrows, and young men with shaven skulls and beards so ridiculously sculpted that they ran like hairy caterpillars down their chins. There were pikeys with whippets and Sloanes with toe-rings. Here was a dreadlocked young black man flogging the *Socialist Worker*; here were Sir Harold and Lady Antonia, fingering cans of Special Brew; and every-where were people for whom this was only their second act of public protest, the first having been the countryside march. There was a curious confluence, in some old-fashioned

English minds: a simultaneous hatred of government interference in country pursuits, and a hatred of interference in Iraq.

Odd friendships were being forged and new romances beginning. Here was Raimondo Charles, a forty-two-year-old American website journalist with a dashing picture by-line, in which he appeared to be cupping his hands around a joint.

Raimondo liked to think of himself as a womanizing international dog of war. One moment he might be ferried around the backstreets of Beirut, blindfolded, in a Hezbollah taxi, with a gun to his neck. At another he might be in a darkened room in Rpublika Srpska, hearing the whingeing confessions of an ex-warlord. Raimondo had once persuaded a woman to go to bed with him by claiming to be an investigative reporter from *Rolling Stone* magazine. This was only true in the sense that he had contributed an interview (spiked) with an interesting fellow who claimed to have slept with Madonna's sister.

Now Raimondo had become part of the general anti-war movement – the people who thought the Pentagon was the greatest threat to global stability, and he was standing next to a very good-looking young woman, with an aristocratic manner. She had badges saying, 'Keep Britain Farming', 'Blair Doesn't Care', and 'Don't Attack Iraq'. Raimondo busily stoked her indignation.

'Yah,' she said, 'I think it's just outrageous the way America refuses to sign that Tokyo protocol on climate change.'

'Tchah.' Raimondo shook his head in disgusted assent, and offered her a cigarette.

'And then there's that other thing, that Hague thingummy about war criminals. What I'd like to know is why the hell we have to sign up for it and they don't.'

'You bet.'

'I've been reading this really good book, and you know

what I think?' Her eyes appeared particularly lustrous. Raimondo inched his muzzle closer.

'I think America is a rogue state!'

'You said it.'

'And all we do in this country is poodle, poodle, poodle, like' – she didn't want to say poodle again – 'like children who don't know any better. I mean, why the hell this government had to do what it did, and the Opposition, ugh. I tell you one thing,' she said, 'I bet you they wouldn't try to ban hunting in Iraq, whatever they say about Saddam.'

Not for the first time when making himself pleasant to a beautiful woman, Raimondo felt a fleeting challenge to his intellectual good faith. What she had said was balls. There have been only two governments in history that have preceded Britain's Labour Party in initiating a ban on hunting with dogs, and they are Adolf Hitler's Germany and Saddam Hussein's Iraq. Saddam banned the packs as somehow un-Baathist, though they have been a part of Mesopotamian life since Assurbanipal or Tiglath-Pileser set off in his chariot in search of a lion; and hunting survived only in the limited sense that Uday and Qusay Hussein would sometimes get up into a Hind Soviet-made helicopter gunship, fly over the marshes, and machine-gun anything larger than a rat.

He could have pointed this out, but for tactical reasons did not. 'So where have you guys come from this morning?' he asked, indicating the little coagulation of toff-ish protestors. Raimondo was a stealthy but dedicated snob.

'Oh, we're all down from Northamptonshire.'

'Oh yes, whereabouts?'

'From Knout, actually,' she said, meaning the famous stately home.

At once Raimondo seemed to see something familiar in that freckled little nose. Could this be – but of course it was! – Sharon, Marchioness of Kettering.

Raimondo's plans began to develop. He envisaged evenings

with Sharon at Annabel's; he seemed to see invitations to shoot. Perhaps, yes, why not, if he played it right, she might have him up to Northamptonshire for some eco-friendly blamming of the pheasant.

So he told her a little about Kosovo, and Afghanistan, and Somalia, and depleted uranium shells.

'Talking of which,' said the posh girl, finding a break in his recitation, 'guess what I've got in my knapsack.' She pulled it out. 'Freshly laid this morning. And I'm jolly well going to chuck it at someone!'

'Hold on,' said Raimondo, and just as he was about to say what he thought of this plan, there was a blaring of sirens in the corner of the square. There were police cars, and then ambulances, and they were screaming round from Victoria towards the Embankment.

'That's funny,' said Raimondo.

'I wonder what happened?' said the girl.

'There's a lot of violent men around,' said Raimondo.

'Crumbs,' said the posh girl. 'Shall we go and find out?'

'Come on,' said Raimondo, and began to lead her through the craning crowd. 'I didn't get your name.'

'I'm Sandra. I work for her ladyship. I'm the nanny,' said the girl.

The essence of being Raimondo is to get over this kind of disappointment quickly. 'Sandra,' he said, 'now whatever you do, don't throw that egg.' He waved not just at the British policemen, but at fridge-sized Matt, and Joe, and the other American security men. 'This place is swarming with security men from the most dangerous government on earth.'

Round the corner, outside Church House, assorted clerics were ministering to a sobbing woman, who had found a pool of blood on the pavement.

News of the horror fanned through the crowd, and was relayed to Purnell and Bluett in the Ops Room.

'Right,' said Bluett. 'That certainly stands up this guy's story.'

'Colonel,' said Purnell, 'I hate to admit defeat, but I think discretion may be the better part of valour here.'

'Meaning?'

'I mean let's knock this ceremony on the head.'

'You gotta be shitting me, Mr Deputy Assistant Commissioner.'

OK, thought Cameron, let's get on with this; and she prepared to get up from the bench. She just hoped to God that Roger didn't find out about it. After all, these passes were in his name, and if something went wrong, he would be in serious trouble.

CHAPTER TWENTY-FOUR

0935 HRS

Roger Barlow drifted on through the Members' cloakroom, where the coat racks are hung with red ribbons intended for MPs to hang their swords. He contemplated polishing his shoes, but some chap was already there. As he wandered on towards the stairs, he passed the double doors into Westminster Hall, and peeped in. Of all the chambers in the Palace of Westminster, this was by far his favourite. With its floor that seemed to have been laid with the sarsens of Stonehenge, with its perennial dungeon gloom and aimlessly colossal vaulted hammerbeam ceiling, Westminster Hall thrilled him as much as it sometimes left tourists cold.

It spoke of an age before the prinking pomposities of Puginism. The lifeblood of democracy might flow now through other chambers, but Westminster Hall waited, like some great underused ventricle, for those moments when it played its part at the heart of the nation. Kings and queens had lain in state here, and so had Winston Churchill. A king had been put on trial here, and condemned to death. When Parliament wished to honour some figure of global importance, he or she was allowed to speak in Westminster Hall, and the Lords and the Commons were assembled to perch on these same little gilt chairs, drawn up unevenly over the flags; and here, in less than half an hour, would speak the President of the United States. TV lights were already bisecting the gloom, and TV cables coiled over the floor like the roots of a banyan tree.

He shut the door and went on up through the Lobby to the Members' library. He quickly chose a computer terminal overlooked by no one else. He logged on to Google and searched for all entries under Roger Barlow.

Nope.

Nothing.

Nope. Nothing. Phew.

In a twinkling he checked his Hotmail account. Something from his wife at her office address. 'Call me.' Uh-oh.

He quit the email, and the machine was still attempting to execute this order when he became aware of footfalls behind him. He hit the little cross in the top right, and for some reason found himself in the list of the ten most recent Google searches conducted by the machine.

He clicked again in irritation, and a square popped up on his screen. He saw, too late, that it was headlined 'Put your nipple in my HOT mouth.' Soon he found that he was in a place called Boobtropolis, or Titty City, not, frankly, that he really cared.

'Ah, Roger.' His nape crawled. It was the pairing whip. 'Conducting some invaluable research, I see. I am so glad you are able to help us out this afternoon on the Water Bill. Stick to fluoridation, I would. That's the hot topic.'

'Right oh. Is there a line to take on fluoridation?'

'I don't care what line you take. As far as I am concerned, you can call for the nation's children to drink neat potassium cyanide, provided your speech lasts for more than ten minutes. We've got to avoid reaching clause twenty-four before the guillotine, so that it can go back to the Lords unamended.' Roger was about to indulge in some mordant (and probably uncalled-for) reflections on the health of parliamentary democracy, and what a shame it was that so many speeches were generated by the whips, purely to satisfy some timetabling requirement, when his pager went.

'Hmmm,' he said. Whips liked to see you fumbling with your pager. 'That's odd.'

The message said: PLEASE CALL JOHN WINZER PASS OFFICE X3621.

He excused himself and went to the phone in the corridor, where he first made contact with his wife.

'Hello, darling, everything all right?'

It seemed he was under suspicion. The four-year-old had watched him from the window, and seen him dispose furtively of the newspapers. The four-year-old had immediately dobbed him in.

His wife said: 'Is everything all right with you, darling?' She sounded more amused than anything else.

'Oh yes, it's fine. Just complete chaos, what with this state visit.'

'Oh yes. Are you going to listen to him?'

'I expect so. Look, gotta go, darling. Someone's trying to get me on my pager.'

'I am sorry to disturb you, Mr Barlow,' said the man from Stogumber. 'It's probably nothing, but your researcher has just been in, ever such a nice girl.'

'Oh yes, you mean Cameron.'

'That's right, sir, lovely girl. Well, I wouldn't trouble you with it, sir, but she said you had signed four passes for some foreign gentlemen.'

'Hang on. We are talking about the same person, aren't we? The girl I call Cameron is an exceptionally good-looking researcher of about twenty-three with good teeth and blonde hair.'

'I couldn't rightly zay about her teeth, zir, but the rest zounds right.' Winzer's accent was thickening with excitement.

'And who are these people I've asked to be given passes?'

'That's what worried me, zir. She said they wuz for four TV people from the Al-Khadija network. It's all above board and all that, but I thought I had better be safe than sorry. I mean they could be anybody, couldn't they, and what with everything happening here today, I just thought I'd give you a ring and anyway . . .'

'Well done, John,' said Barlow, whose dim, alcohol-drenched cerebral synapses were starting to see a pattern in the events of the day.

'Don't move from there, John,' he said, 'I am just on my way.'

'I am not moving anywhere,' said John Winzer. 'I am not allowed to.'

Cameron blinked as she came back out of the Pass Office and into the sunshine, and at first she couldn't spot Adam. Then he popped up from somewhere and kissed her on the cheek. She was pleased.

'I've got them,' she said, and handed them over.

'You're wonderful,' said Adam.

'Where are the men?' she asked. Her eye blanked the ambulance, searching instead the Rovers and Mercs.

'Oh they'll be along in a moment, but I'm worried that they won't have anywhere to sit down. Do you think you could possibly do me a huge favour and take these' – he produced four letrasetted signs saying 'reserved' – 'and put them on the chairs in Westminster Hall. They should be pretty close to the North Door.'

Cameron immediately saw how difficult this would be. All the good seats would be taken, and she didn't know what she would say if she were challenged, or whose authority she would cite.

She turned to go, but some instinct made her look back at him. 'But where are the people?'

'Oh, they are around. They'll be along in a minute.'

Cameron departed, out via the Embankment and Portcullis House. Adam was in some way fobbing her off. It was not a feeling she liked, and she had an idea. She stopped on the steps of Portcullis House.

She waited a beat, then doubled back, devising some question she might ask her beloved. As she looked round the corner into the car park, this is what she saw.

Adam Swallow walked quickly over to the ambulance and tapped on the window. After a bit a wiry fellow emerged, took the passes and disappeared back into the cabin, shutting the door.

At which point Adam turned on his heel and left, as if to go to Westminster Hall via the ground floor of Norman Shaw South.

Cameron made an involuntary noise and then beat it round the corner like a rabbit. An ambulance?

All her sense of panic and suspicion came flooding back, and with an effort she controlled it. She had to believe in Adam.

For God's sake, didn't she want someone unpredictable, who finally took charge? Wasn't that the whole point? In those long, wretched months of going to plays with dorks, the plays she called *les liaisons misérables* – she had done some pop psychology on herself.

Obviously she needed an alpha male. She needed an authority figure to supplant her father. But she had concluded – with the prosaic exactitude of a feature in *Honey* or *Bella* – that she needed someone who was both the same as and opposite to her father. She needed an alpha/gamma male, and Professor Adam Swallow surely fitted the bill.

He had a bust of Dante. He read a philosopher called Adorno. He collected 1920s Suprematist teacups. He went travelling to unexpected places, and in an elegant hand he recorded his thoughts – together with little doodles – on the pages of leather-bound notebooks.

He was furious about the treatment of the Palestinians, and resented America for her crass attempt to reconfigure, with bombs and dollars, the Muslim mentality, and to impose 'democracy' on societies that neither wanted nor understood the concept. Her father would have been scandalized by these attitudes. But maybe, for Cameron, that was part of the attraction.

Henry 'Hank' or 'Buster' Maclean was an alpha male so alpha that he would have been awarded a congratulatory first by the examiners in Advanced Virility. He commanded the Seymour Johnson US Air Force Base in North Carolina, and he believed firmly in the American imperium. He loathed the Democrats and he loathed the media, in particular their grotesque misreporting of the Tet offensive, which led to America's unnecessary withdrawal from Vietnam, and which he identified with current accounts of Iraq.

Not that he was a bigot, or anything like that. As a major employer, he saw the evil waste and stupidity of racism. He didn't care much about drugs either way. He was just innocently right wing in that he believed in the power of the will, the greatness of America, and the ability of a man to rise on the stepping-stones of his dead self to higher things. When Cameron was a little girl he would take her roaring out in his T-bird, a car on which he doted until one day he forgot to fill her with oil. Every year, on her birthday, he promised he would take her up in one of the Lockheed jets he was commanding in ever greater numbers, and every year she would look at him with shining eyes, secretly wish she could marry him, and yearn for the moment when she could be his co-pilot.

If Buster Maclean were to be portrayed by modern Hollywood, it would be considered theatrically indispensable to expose him, in the final reel, as a cross-dresser, a bra-fetishist, an alcoholic or an abuser of animals. He was none of these things. He simply had the right stuff exploding hormonally from every orifice. In fact his machismo was so intense that he was sometimes considered a danger to himself and the exorbitantly expensive technology he was paid to fly, and every time Cameron's mom heard him make his promise to her daughter, she would cross her fingers and hope, when the day came, for clear weather.

Nobody blamed Buster when his right-hand jet engine inhaled a turkey buzzard and forced him to eject at 5,000 feet. Nobody thought any the less of him when he was involved in a near miss with a Japanese Air Lines 747 approaching Baltimore Airport, forcing the commercial pilot to take such violent evasive action that upon landing a Matsushita executive was discovered in an overhead locker. But when he contrived to eject both his co-pilot and himself, without a cloud in the sky, leaving $60 million worth of taxpayer-funded fighter-bomber to fly on alone for almost 600 miles until it crashed into a convenience store in Nevada, it was decided there was only one thing to be done with Buster Maclean.

He was promoted to a position of real responsibility. By the time Cameron was twenty-one, and legally allowed to sit in an F15E Strike Eagle, capable of flying at twice the speed of sound while posting a bomb through the letterbox of Saddam Hussein, there was nothing and no one who could stop her father from taking her aloft. She remembered the day in delicious, lingering detail. She had just an apple and water for breakfast. There was no point in eating birthday cake if you were going to put your stomach through six Gs.

She remembered the fire engines and the ambulances nosing surreptitiously on to the tarmac (Buster's reputation as a prangmeister was still green). She remembered the pride in her father's voice as he said, 'Hang on, babe', and took off vertically, shooting up into the bright blue American sky like a firework. There was the awful pressure on her groin and legs from the G-suit, and then there was the joy, the ethereal unrepeatable joy, of being allowed by her father to co-pilot the plane. She simply held the joystick hard to the right, and the plane corkscrewed over and down magically at supersonic speed in an aileron roll towards the indigo sea. It was like a dream of death, or the animal exhilaration of some huge marine bird as it falls like a stone on some fish below; and so they might indeed have ganneted into the deep, had Buster not said to his daughter, 'OK, babe, I'll take back the plane, now,' and they flew back in contented silence as the afternoon sun gave its dying benediction on rural America, the little red barns, the cylindrical grain silos, the churches and the schoolhouses. Whatever man Cameron settled on, that was the intensity of experience he would have to replicate. Which was why she was so stunned by Adam.

Now she was making faster time than her new boyfriend as they both marched towards Westminster Hall, mainly because she knew the route, and he was momentarily lost in the ground-floor corridors of Norman Shaw South.

'You don't mind if I use the phone,' said Colonel Bluett to Deputy Assistant Commissioner Purnell.

Purnell indicated, again, that the entire Ops Room was at the Colonel's disposal.

'I'm jes gonna tell Ricasoli about this here ambulance,' said the Colonel.

'Ricasoli?' said Purnell.

'Captain Ricasoli, up there in the Black Hawk.'

Purnell looked at Grover, and Grover looked wordlessly back.

CHAPTER TWENTY-FIVE

0938 HRS

In the police booth that governs the entrance to Norman Shaw North car park, they were having an argument about multicultural Britain.

'It's all part of the diversity regulations, innit. You've got to treat all religions the same.'

'I don't know, mate,' said the other policeman. 'I've never heard of that one.'

''Course you do. You've got to have a Koran in every ambulance these days, in case you have to administer the last rites to a Muslim.'

'And you're sure it said it was the Koran?'

''Course I'm sure. It was right there on the dashboard, with a load of used tissues. Al Qur'an. That means the Koran in Arabian.'

The two coppers considered the implications.

'It's a different world, mate.'

'You can say that again.'

The second policeman's attention was briefly diverted to the *Sun* newspaper, which carried a big picture of Jordan's breasts. After a moment's thought he said: 'So every ambulance has to carry the Bible, too?'

'I 'spect so.'

'What if it's a Hindu accident victim? Do they have to carry the Bhagavad-Gita?'

'I shouldn't wonder.'

'What about the Book of Mormon?'

The two coppers brooded again. 'Tell you what,' said the first policeman, 'I reckon we just go and have a squint at that ambulance.'

'Right you are.'

They shut the door of the booth behind them and wandered

slowly over; with the result that they just missed the all points alert phone call, inviting them to keep an eye out for a stolen Wolverhampton ambulance, licence plate L64896P.

Inside that fatal machine Jones allowed himself to reflect, for one second, that so far they had been incredibly lucky. It could only be the will of Allah, blessings be upon his name, that they had not yet been detected.

Much of their plotting was amateurish. He thought with a shudder of the scene in the motel last night. But there was one detail which was both brilliant and revolutionary, and which would be copied by other terrorist cells. It was due entirely to him, the man whose passport said he was called Jones.

He was not called Jones, of course, but that was the name in which he enrolled at Llangollen, and which his fellow-students smirkingly accepted.

High above that North Welsh town, not far from the ruins of Dinas Bran and looking out over the foaming ale-coloured River Dee, are the delightful premises of a former mental home. Under the Learning and Skills Council it had been turned into a teacher training centre, where Welsh was dinned into the skulls of graduates, with a view to passing on this weird creole to the listless children of Denbighshire. The institution was then promoted into an Adult Education Centre, funded by the Higher Education Funding Council for England and Wales. Finally, in the great Stalinist push to expand the numbers in tertiary education, the place was rebaptized 'Llangollen University'.

Here Jones had arrived two years ago, and spurned the useless courses that occupied most of the students. He did not do Media Studies or Gender Awareness in Film. He did that proper old-fashioned twenty-first-century British university course. He majored in hairdressing, and was known to his sniggering fellow-students as Jones the Hair.

But his main interest seemed to be in the thick, sweet, colourless, odourless liquid which is applied to hair in pomades and unguents. It is called glycerin, $C_3H_5(OH)_3$, and when treated with nitric acid (HNO_3) and sulphuric acid (H_2SO_4) it produces something very remarkable.

One night there was a noise from Jones's room. Some drunken Media Studies louts had been out at the Wild Pheasant, and they burst into the toejam and cigarette infested quarters of Jones the Hair. He was lying stunned and blackened on the floor, and was known ever after as Jones the Bomb.

A few weeks later, he secretly propounded an advance in bomb-making techniques, which looks simple, like so many good ideas, but it had never been done before. It is true that a mobile phone has already been used as a bomb: in January 1996 Israel's internal security agency Shabak used an exploding phone to assassinate Palestinian bomb mastermind Yahya Ayash, known as the 'Engineer'. He blew his mind out on a call, as the Beatles sang. But until Jones hit upon the wheeze, no one had used a series of Nokias in suicide jackets.

Each jacket contained about six kilos of explosive and a small detonator. Sewn into a little pouch next to the detonator was the mobile. When the phone rang, a current was passed along a small wire, which in turn caused a bridge wire to heat-function, as physicists say: to get hot. This in turn ignited a match element, which set off the primary explosive of the detonator. This set off the secondary explosive of the detonator. This in turn detonated the nitroglycerine, which means that this substance was resolved, with incredible speed and violence, into nitrogen, water, carbon dioxide and oxygen. At this point, traditionally, the suicide bomber's head would fly off as though drop-kicked by Jonny Wilkinson, and in a confined space the ball bearings in the jacket would cause carnage and havoc. That was the idea.

Jones had all their numbers preset on his speed-dial. He couldn't dial all four at once: that would not be necessary; but he could ring them up one after the other, and get them on the blower, so to speak.

But there was one obvious point that had been oppressing Dean ever since their rehearsal.

'It's not fair, sir,' he said to Jones in what he hoped sounded a casual voice. 'You can dial us but we can't dial you.'

'It is fair, Dean. It is what we agreed.'

'Yeah, but how does your bomber jacket go off? You can't dial yourself, can you?'

'That is secret, Dean.'

'Well, I think we should be all in this together.' Nervous terror now propelled Dean's tongue. 'What's the difference? It's the four musketeers, innit.'

After this heretical speech, Dean opened the back door, without permission, and started to move the kit outside. In case this was a mutiny, Haroun and Habib went through the hatch to intercept him, and every time they stepped on poor Eric Onyeama, there was a nasty marshy sound.

Now Dean had begun to shift the jackets out through the back, and Haroun and Habib were obliged physically to restrain him. This was mad, thought Jones, and began seriously contemplating aborting the operation.

CHAPTER TWENTY-SIX
0940 HRS

Most MPs, even the most self-important, develop a kind of shuffling scamper from their offices to the Division Lobbies, from the Chamber to the TV studios of Millbank. If any of their constituents happened to spot them, they would get the impression of an exceedingly pressed and dedicated crew.

So no one looked twice at Roger Barlow as he loped across the ground floor of Portcullis House.

It could be nothing, Roger told himself.

By far the most likely thing was that Cameron had warned him of some arrangement – probably involving a Unicef delegation of Arab teenage journalists – and he had simply bleeped it out.

But the first thing to do was to find Cameron, and the most likely place was his office. So he went up the stairs in Norman Shaw South so as to cross by the passerelle that arched over the car park, and that took him almost directly to his office in Norman Shaw North.

And strike me pink, he thought, as he looked down from the passerelle to the left: there was that flipping ambulance again. It had to be the same one.

A darkish kid got out, holding some TV equipment, and gesticulating. Then he saw two Arabs hustle the dark young man into the back and close the door behind them.

'Christ on a bike,' muttered Barlow.

'Everything all right, Roger?' said Ziggy Roberts, scooting efficiently by, toting a bunch of girly swot papers about pensions, or the mobility component of incapacity benefit.

'You never know,' he called over his shoulder, in one of those phrases that made Roger want to punch the lights out of whoever said it, 'it may never happen.'

'But those chaps . . .' said Barlow. The ambulance was shut, and gave no hint of its cargo.

'I say, Ziggy, I couldn't borrow your mobile.'

'Yeah, of course. Oh sorry, I must have left it in the office.'

'Bloody hell, Ziggy, look at that.'

Both men turned to look as the back door slowly opened again, as unobtrusive and sinister as the nocturnal opening of that hatch, thousands of years ago, in the underside of the Greek offering.

A dark head poked out like a tortoise, and then slowly withdrew. The door shut behind it. 'Looks like an ambulance to me,' said Ziggy Roberts.

'Let's bloody hope so,' said Barlow, and double-timed across in search of Cameron. He was puffing a little when he opened the door, and found she wasn't there.

'What's the matter with yow?' demanded Dean, in the back of the ambulance. He struggled briefly in the grip of the two zealots, as they waited for their leader to apply discipline.

Haroun and Habib had worked before with young Dean, and Jones knew their views well.

Haroun and Habib belonged to the umma, the diaspora of aggrieved Islamic youth, whose hatred of the West was all the stronger because they lived in the West, and they were constantly exposed to its temptations and frustrations. Yes, their cause was officially Palestine, and yes, like so many men of their age, they watched the suicide bomber videos that are broadcast on satellite TV. They whipped themselves up with sentimental music, and sat in their bedsits, smoking, swearing, nostrils flaring as they saw the slow-motion balletic footage of the little kids (how expertly coached by their parents) provoking Israeli tanks to respond with shells to their stones.

They wept, as they saw the suicide bombers' home movies, the pukey little speeches of thanks to their parents and above all to Allah, the pornographic lingering of the camera on their dynamite waistcoats. They wept, they coughed, they swore, they spat; and then, quite often, they would go and get some of the other kind of pornography, and behold the self-defilement of the Western woman; provided, of course, that this was accompanied by a proper dose of Muslim self-flagellation.

The previous night, for instance, they had all originally checked into a Travelodge near Luton. But Haroun had been so outraged, on coming out of the bathroom, to find Habib watching *Angels of Lust*, the comically bowdlerized British soft porn movie set in the NHS, that he had insisted on moving out.

'It is the House of Sharmoota,' he said. It is the House of Harlot.

Habib had been so ashamed, and so admiring of Haroun's purity, that he had agreed; and Jones had sighed and driven on down the empty sodium-lit M1 until, out of sheer exhaustion, they had parked up in Tufton Street and sprawled in the back.

Because if Palestine was the cause for sickos like Haroun and Habib, it was only at best the proximate cause. There is one really psychologically satisfying explanation for the suicidal behaviour of young men, and it is something to do with sex, or at least with self-esteem. Somewhere in the background of their general screwed-up-ness was the cultural tectonic grinding between East and West, and the shaming, daring, tempting challenge presented to the Muslim man by the emancipated Western female. Which was why the Abu Ghraib scenes had been so catastrophic, and why the chuckling American servicewomen had been such efficient recruiting-sergeants for terror.

The pictures had so badly affected Haroun, in particular, that he had come to think that he had been himself in Abu Ghraib; naked, mocked, derided by these smoking, drinking Jezebels of the Appalachians. He had given instructions in a sealed letter to his imam in Tipton, that in the event of his death his body parts – should there be any remaining – were not to be touched by any female forensic officer or mortuary technician.

Habib, who wore the mask of a worldly Lebanese, was not as visibly disturbed, though his motives were very similar. These impulses had sent them both to train with the Sheikh, may Allah bring blessings on his head, in the camps in Sudan and at Khalden. But the kid from Wolverhampton was different, and in his wiser moments Jones knew it.

As soon as he found Dean in the Islamic Welfare Centre, Jones knew that he had a significant catch on his hands, and he also knew that it would be difficult to persuade others in the network of this fact. They saw a mixed-up, mixed race youth with only the vaguest knowledge of the Koran. Jones saw the makings of a small political coup. Not only did Dean have a phosphorescent hatred of bourgeois values, and an unconquerable will to undermine the dairy business, supermarkets, and other extensions of what he called the agro-industrial complex. He was also palpably – if anything, excessively – British.

He proved that British society was so corrupt that it engendered the very vipers that now sunk their fangs into its neck. If anyone could persuade the British intelligentsia to a bout of its favourite where-did-we-all-go-wrong-ery, it was surely Dean. Yet there had been times, even before the stressful events of today, when his optimism had been shaken. Last year the small remainder of Dean's FreshStart endowment had been spent flying him to Lahore, whence it was hoped he would trek to the border with Afghanistan and imbue himself with all that was most inhuman in the terrorist repertory.

Nothing was heard from the trainee operative for weeks. Jones dared to hope. Then he started to receive reverse-charge calls from a plainly dope-brained Dean, who seemed to be in a Peshawar doss-house. He complained vehemently about the Pakistani police who, he said, had impounded his passport. He added that ants were not only coming out of the shower drain but out of his armpits. There was nothing for it. Haroun and Habib were disturbed from their Prussian drill at Khalden. They left the red-rocked tranquillity of their desert camp, slunk down from the mountains, and at times with main force conveyed the tyro to Afghanistan.

It is hard to say which – Dean or the wolf twins – had the lesser affection for their partnership. A bad time was had by all. Haroun and Habib thought first to toughen him up. They yomped all day through vast and trackless systems of unpopulated valleys. Occasionally Dean's vestigial aesthetic sense allowed him to be penetrated by the beauty of the landscape, the rock turning with the sun from gold to ochre to reddish to purple and then to the blue-black of the night, with the white lamps of the stars shining on their sleeping bags in the very pattern they had shone on Alexander and his army. Mainly, however, he found himself thinking of the anti-smoking videos shown at Wolverhampton Grammar School as he gasped and gagged, through lack of fitness or oxygen, in the wake of the weaving wolves.

Soon the blood started to dry between his toes. Protective calluses formed. The soi-disant vice-captain of the school water polo team finally began to show some of the athleticism one might expect. He even started to look quite authentic, in his dish-dash and turban, and somewhat against their better judgement Haroun and Habib decided it was time to mount an operation. Dean would now prove his worth by striking a blow against the Western society he claimed to reject. The blow was to be all the more significant for being simultaneously vicious and pointless.

It was at a Chaikhana in the Panjshir valley that they came across their target. They were sitting at breakfast, Dean morosely drinking what he took to be fermented asses' milk, the wolves wolfing their nan, when they heard a voice on the stair. It was a high, camp, Oxonian voice, of a kind Dean had heard most often on TV in the mouths of characters who were meant to be absurd.

'I've got to go, darling, because I've just got to have breakfast and then go off and look at the Buddhas. Love you too. Big kiss. *Mwah mwah.*'

First down the stairs came a pair of sandals so evidently

travel-worn that one imagined they must be softer than the inner thigh of the sultan's favourite houri. Next were the infinitely fashionable baggy Afghan trousers and the Afghan waistcoat and then the long skinny brown arms decorated at the wrist with those epicene string bracelets affected by Prince William; and then six-foot, curly-haired Jamie Davenport emerged and embraced the whitewashed breakfast room with his radiant smile.

Not since the days of Eric Newby had a professional travel writer been through these parts, and come up with so much that was hilarious, fascinating, warm, witty and wise. At the age of twenty-three Davenport had dazzled London with his tale of escape from a shotgun marriage in the Khyber Pass, entitled 'A quick poke in the Hindu Bush'. Three years later 'Alph – the search for Kubla's Sacred River' had won just about every gong going. Now he was back on the ancient literary trail, in search of the usual farrago of wily Pathans and almond-eyed beauties with lotus-stud noses and peachlike bottoms and truculent, jezzail-wielding tribesmen who move, in the space of five pages, from desiring to cut your throat to desiring you to marry their sisters.

Wherever he went, his aerial was tuned for anything usable: snatches of sufi mumbo-jumbo, religious syncretism, gobbets of recondite fact, and if all else failed there were the charming mis-spellings of the menus. When he came down to breakfast, he was ready for anecdote, colour, quotes, personalities. What he found was Haroun, Habib and Dean, all in a pretty foul mood.

Dean was about to croak a greeting when Haroun kicked him under the table.

'But how,' asked Dean, when the team had assembled outside, 'and, you know, why?'

He stared into the fathomless brown eyes of the Islamofascists.

'He is a foreign pig,' said Haroun.

'He is part of the infidel desecration of this country,' said Habib.

'He is a Zionist pig,' said Haroun. The last was especially unfair, since Jamie Davenport's sympathies were very much in the opposite direction. Indeed, he had been known to attend parties with a little Arab tea towel at his throat.

'All right, all right,' said Dean. 'But how am I meant to do it?' In their hearts, the two Arabs were hoping he might be talked into the suicide option. Go off into the hot white noonday with the other irritating Englishman, take him to some deserted wadi, pull the ripcord and boom.

However, they doubted his competence, and whatever they said about sherbet and sloe-eyed virgins, they doubted his appetite for the job. So half an hour later Jamie Davenport found himself being driven in a Daewoo pick-up by two effusive Arabs, who swore they knew the whereabouts of a lost Buddha, and a seeming deaf-mute whose ethnic origins were not at all obvious.

'Look, is it much further?' he asked, after Dean had driven them erratically into the desert for several miles.

'Just five minutes, five minutes,' said Haroun.

'And did you say that this Buddha had Hellenistic influences?'

'Assuredly it is most Hellenistic.'

'Really? Does it have curly hair?'

Haroun appeared scandalized by the question. 'It is as curly as mine. Of course it is curly.'

Jamie Davenport settled back in his seat for a second. A syncretic Buddha. Good. Might be worth a couple of paragraphs, especially if he could contrive some kind of colourful incident or exchange with his guides.

'And you are sure it is syncretic?' he said absently.

'It is profoundly syncretic,' said Habib.

Dean was rehearsing his lines as he drove. In fact he had decided on only one line, the better to conceal his English voice. At a signal from Haroun and Habib he would stop. While the Englishman got out, he would take the automatic from the glove compartment. They would all four walk a little way. Then, when it was obvious that there was no Buddha, he would pull the automatic out, force the man of letters to his knees, hands behind back, head forward in the traditional position of execution, and he would say, with all due fanaticism, 'Die, foreign dog!'

Or should that be 'pig'? He was trying the words to himself, hunched over the steering wheel and moving his lips, when he saw an obstruction in the road. In fact, there were several obstructions, a row of boulders, each bigger than a melon.

After that things happened very fast.

Haroun and Habib screamed at him to reverse. Just as Dean was selecting the gear, a hairy face protruded itself through the driver's window, with dentition that was poor even by English standards, and an AK 47 was jammed beneath his jaw. Fifteen minutes later the team – Haroun, Habib, Dean – were standing by the side of the road. All three appeared to have been rolled in the dust like gingerbread men rolled in flour. They were minus their wallets, their mobiles, their car, and in Habib's case a tooth and a small amount of blood. They were also minus their shoes and their intended assassinee.

At one point during the exchanges, when Habib and Haroun had failed to persuade the badmashes to let them be, Dean had yelled at the robbers: ''Ere, mush, what's the matter with yow? Don't you know we wuz going to kill him anyway?'

After that Jamie Davenport the explorer was driven away by his new proprietors, his eyes wide with terror and his wits so scattered that he believed he had made an important discovery. Never mind the lost descendants of Alexander's hoplites. Here was a tribesman in the Panjshir valley who spoke with a strong Black Country accent. It was his most syncretic adventure for years.

Which wasn't exactly the opinion of Haroun and Habib. Never the jolliest pair, their eyes had bored into Dean, lacquered black and glittery with hatred.

So now, in the gloom of the back of the ambulance, Jones the Bomb did his usual trick. He took Dean's side. Over the recumbent form of the leaking Eric Onyeama, he put his hand on Dean's shoulder. He looked at him sympathetically. He gave him a kind of Vulcan nerve pinch.

'Come on, Dean, my son,' he said. 'We all need you. By tonight you will be world famous, and your name will be on every TV station and every newspaper on earth. We are all depending on you, and we cannot do it without you.

'O Lions of Islam,' he continued, addressing them all in a sacerdotal voice, 'may our appointed time be today and every day in the prayer niches of the exalted one, so that we may align our feet before Allah.'

We all have in our lives someone who controls our emotional thermostat. There is always someone whose function is to supply the pipette drops of praise, the intermittent goo' boy choc drops of external affirmation that get us through the day. The story of our lives is essentially the rotation of that person's identity: mother, father, teacher, girlfriend, boyfriend, spouse and so on. Dean's emotional thermostat was controlled by Jones, and had been ever since his arrival at the Islamic Welfare Centre.

'Yeah, man,' he said now, nodding. 'Come on then. Let's do it to it.'

He began again with the gear.

Roger Barlow was just about to shut the door of his office, and report the ambulance, when the phone started ringing. He hesitated. He ought to go straight down to the Pass Office, and get the police, but what if it was Felix Thomson? It was.

He sounded happy. 'Just thought I'd let you know that I've looked at the newslist.'

'Oh yes.' Barlow tried to inject a note of exquisite detachment into his voice, as though discussing the future of NATO.

'And there is a story about you listed at number 23.'

'Number 23?'

'Yes, it means, roughly speaking that there are twenty-two more important stories today, in the view of the news editor, many of them to do with the current festivities.'

Roger laughed, in what he hoped was a dry, amused chuckle. 'And, er, what does it say?'

'It just says, 23: Roger Barlow MP shocker.'

'Shocker?' said Barlow. It sounded like a frivolous media expression, that might be attached to a story of no real importance. 'Does that mean . . . . ?'

'Yeah,' said Felix Thomson. 'Or it could mean, you know, a shocker.'

In a transport of shame, Barlow thanked his journalistic contact, and ended the connection. He was about to dial security when the phone rang again.

It was Debbie from the *Daily Mirror*.

The ambulance would have to wait a tick.

'This is doing my head in,' said Deputy Assistant Commissioner Purnell. 'We've got footage of the flaming thing going up Whitehall, and we've got two cameras at the top end of Whitehall and they haven't seen it. This'll teach us to rely on those blasted CCTV things. It's just disappeared.'

'That sucker must have turned off somewhere,' said Bluett. He twizzled the map around to face him, spreading his hairy palm across it and pointing. 'It could have gone here, King Charles Street.'

'I suppose so,' said Purnell gloomily. 'That runs between the Foreign Office and the Treasury.'

'Or here. This little street called Downing Street?'

Purnell ground his teeth. 'You can't get in there,' he said.

'Commissioner Purnell,' said Bluett, 'we're running out of

time here. We've got twenty minutes before the speech begins, and I really don't want to interrupt the President during his speech.'

'I know,' said Purnell. 'But I'm the one who wants to pull the plug on it all now.'

'Hey man!' said Bluett, suddenly jovial and pulling out a cigar. 'We'll find it!' He clapped Purnell on the shoulder.

In the car park of Norman Shaw North the two policemen drifted closer to the mysterious vehicle.

Cameron heard the ambulances and the police cars but thought nothing of them. To anyone who lived in London a yowling police car was as banal as a bus. Perhaps her eyes were sensitized to beauty, but the capital did seem lovely today: the pattern of the sun on the river, like molten chicken wire, the whole thing a Monet of fluttering flags and snatches of cloud. There were Boadicea and her daughters, arms flung back in brazen-breasted defiance, shortly before they were crucified and flayed by the imperial power. Adam would know the history. He would have some mordant point to make. That was what she liked about him.

Ever since she had been in high school Cameron had a deep and sexist reverence for men who really knew stuff. It amazed her sometimes how little appearances mattered. He could be bald, he could be spindly or sweaty or tubby, but if that man's disquisition had enough interest, fluency and authority, it would speak directly to her groin. And Adam had the additional merit of good looks.

Such had been her wine-flown feelings yesterday in the Ogenblick restaurant, Brussels. There had been four of them: she, Adam and some kind of rumpled tobacco-wreathed Englishman who gave instruction in mediaeval something at a seminary in Rome, and his wife, who looked like the kind of woman who owns fifteen cats. The waiters finally removed the big glass bowl of chocolate mousse (licked out, in a hard-core performance, by the don's wife), and as they pompously swirled their calvados and tapped off fat turds of cigar ash, Adam Swallow and the dirty don started to rap about Britain and America.

The more they talked, the more keenly she desired to sit in Adam's lap. Their theme was not just that the special relationship was rubbish, an ignis fatuus, an unreciprocated teenage crush for America on the part of the British foreign policy establishment: that was taken for granted. The thought they developed by means of antiphonal examples was that at several key junctures in the twentieth century the Americans had actively sought to demolish the Empire and do down the British.

Adam: 'Look at what they did in the 1920s . . .'

The don: 'Stinging us for debt repayments . . .'

Adam: 'Making us reduce the Imperial fleet . . .'

The don: 'Swiping the Virgin Islands . . .'

Adam: ' . . . Think of Joe Kennedy during the war.'

The don: 'What a louse . . .'

Adam: 'Telling Roosevelt the Germans would win . . .'

The don: 'Irish bootlegger . . .'

Adam: 'And what about poor old Halifax in New York in 1940?'

The don: 'Pelted with eggs . . .'

Adam: 'To say nothing of Suez . . .'

The don: 'Leaving us twisting in the wind . . .'

Adam: 'Gangbanging the pound . . .'

The don: 'They still think they went to war to save Europe . . .'

Adam: ' . . . Total balls . . .'

The don: 'When the truth is that Hitler declared war on America!'

Adam: 'They'd have stayed out if they could . . .'

Cameron knew there was an answer to this, a simple

140

answer, but the nuisance of it was that she couldn't remember and she didn't really care. Invisibly as she stared at the interesting veins in Professor Swallow's hands, and that place in his neck where the pulse was beating, just above the clavicle, her endocrine system was re-ordering her loyalties and her geo-political assumptions.

'And now we just do whatever they tell us,' said the dirty don, and Cameron noticed that although the academic's cheeks were ruby coloured, the tip of his nose had become oddly white and protuberant. It was astonishing how much he could remember, but perhaps that was the alcohol, too. Perhaps each fact was pickled and preserved in the runnels of his cerebrum.

'I could go on,' said the don, 'and I will.'

'Go on then,' said Cameron.

'I give you Skybolt. Remember how they decided to get rid of Britain's independent nuclear deterrent, back in 1963, wasn't it? And who was responsible for that infamy? It was Kennedy, of course, the adored JFK, the son of the disgusting wartime Ambassador.'

Again Cameron had a vague feeling that there must be more to this story. Was it entirely America's fault that Britain hadn't been able to hack it as a nuclear power? But she had neither the inclination nor the knowledge to protest. She had never heard of Skybolt, this luckless British firecracker, jilted on the launching pad by JFK.

'Your witness,' said the don loudly to Adam.

Adam leant back. 'I tell you what amuses me. It's the way everybody sees everything through this roseate prism called the special relationship and people completely misremember events. Everybody now thinks of Reagan and Thatcher as this inseparable duo, she in her pearls, he in his aviator's jacket, each incarnating the eternal Anglo-Saxon struggle against tyranny, each pledged in blood to come to the aid of the other. Britain and America contra mundum, to the ends of the earth: that's how you remember it, isn't it? But look at what actually happened in 1982, when a deranged Argentinian junta violently seized a piece of sovereign British territory.

'Did Britain and America storm the beaches together? Like hell. If you look at the record the Americans – that includes Reagan – repeatedly refused to describe themselves as allies. British ships were being blown up in San Carlos Bay, British troops were being fried alive in the *Sheffield* and the *Sir Galahad* and the *Atlantic Conveyer* and what the hell were the Americans doing? They sent General Al Haig down to Peru to cook up some nauseating plan for shared sovereignty.'

'The Peruvian Peace Plan!' shouted the don. 'I spit on the memory of the Peruvian Peace Plan.'

'And people have forgotten Jeanne Kirkpatrick,' said Adam, and his voice, though not drunk, was also full of excitement.

'Jeane Kirkpatrick, my Gawd,' said the don. Cameron felt impelled to ask who this person was.

'Jeane Kirkpatrick was the US Ambassador to the UN during the Falklands Crisis. Irish,' said the don.

'Now, now,' said his wife.

'And there was one point at which Britain drew up a UN motion calling for an unconditional Argentinian withdrawal, and she actually vetoed it,' said Adam.

'Well,' said the don who had learned from the unparalleled viciousness of the academic world that you must never trifle with fact. 'She didn't actually veto it. She just said afterwards that if she had been asked again she would have abstained.'

'Frankly, I think that's just as bad,' said Adam.

'You're right,' said the don, anxious not to seem unpatriotic. 'Death to Jeane Kirkpatrick, always assuming her husband hasn't by now done the sensible thing and put ground glass in her tea.'

And the don and his wife laughed in the Brussels restaurant, weeping and guffawing like some masterpiece of Flemish tavern merriment, painted by Jan Steen. Adam laughed too, but more briefly, and that was just the point.

He took life seriously. To a man like Roger Barlow, the whole world just seemed to be a complicated joke, an accidental jumbling of ingredients on the cosmic stove, which had produced our selfish genes. For Barlow, everything was always up for grabs, capable of dispute; and religion, laws, principle, custom – these were nothing but sticks we plucked from the wayside to support our faltering steps.

That wasn't good enough for Adam, and Cameron thought it wasn't good enough for her. Clutching the reserved tickets, she now re-entered Portcullis House from the Embankment. She passed through the cylindrical glass security doors. She used her electronic pass to enter the main concourse, graciously received the smiles of the security men and descended the escalator towards the colonnade that leads to the Commons. Cameron walked fast, but MPs were now overtaking her in their haste to claim their seats.

She saw Ziggy Roberts zipping along ahead of her. He appeared to be wearing morning dress.

In one of the cafés in the Portcullis House concourse a large group of researchers and gofers – the taxpayer-funded clerisy of Parliament – was watching a live TV feed.

'Omigod,' shouted one excitable young man, as Sir Perry Grainger handed over the Staffordshire pottery tribute of both Houses of Parliament to the most powerful man in the world. 'What's he supposed to do with that?'

Raimondo squeezed his way through to the west of the square, the girl following.

'What's the story?' he asked a policeman.

'No idea,' said the copper, with a tight-lipped Knacker of the Yard expression.

Sandra had more luck. Another policeman said, 'Looks like they found a lot of blood in Tufton Street.'

'What did he say?' everyone asked.

'That girl just said the cops found a body in Tufton Street.'

'The police killed someone?'

'Somebody said the cops killed someone in Tufton Street.'

'A police horse killed somebody in the road.'

A death! Someone had paid with his life! Someone had come to London SW1 this fine July morning of argent and azure, and offered all he had for the cause. As so often, it took a death to give point to their campaign. The vaporous resentments – of America, the Pentagon, McDonald's, globalization, zero tax on air fuel, the Windows spell-check – suddenly achieved a crystalline form. Eyes that had been dulled with dope or hangover now gleamed fever-bright. On the brows of middle aged, Middle England protesters, people whose homes were called 'Whitt's End' or 'Jessamine', veins began to throb as they called for the martyr to be avenged. Killers. Pigs. *Oink oink oink*, leered the crusties at the police, and the police showed their customary restraint.

'We've got a bit of crowd trouble in Parliament Square, sir.' Grover indicated one of the monitors.

'Ricasoli,' said Colonel Bluett of the USSS, dialling up the Black Hawk, still in permahover, 'what's the story?'

'Can't say, sir,' yelled Ricasoli. 'Looks like they're kind of mad at something.'

To and fro the mob now began to wave, like a tentacled anemone under an incoming tide of rage. They knew not who their martyr was. They would have been interested to discover that the police had nothing to do with his injuries, but in no way deterred. Death had transformed an event into history, and at once they were glad they were there.

'Bastards!' yelled Sandra the nanny at no one in particular.

'Yeah,' said Raimondo, 'assholes.'

Thanks to the fluid dynamics of the crowd, they had ended up at the bottom left-hand corner of the square, the nearest point to St Stephen's Entrance. Ambassadors and other dignitaries were being dropped by car and scuttling into the porch, scalded by the blast of hate. A big blue limo of curious design drew up. Had Sandra but known it was a Renault, she might have stayed her hand. Had she spotted the blue, white and red tricolore on the bonnet, she might have thought twice.

A man got out, and there was something about his ineffable air, his swept-back hair, the weary glance he directed at the crowd; something which left her with no choice. She pulled the egg from her sack, and before Raimondo could do anything about it, she flung it.

As she had said, it had been laid that morning by the pride of the Knout flock, a seven foot hen called Kimberly. The egg weighed 1.9 kilos and was eleven inches in diameter and fourteen inches long.

Kimberly was an ostrich.

CHAPTER TWENTY-SEVEN
0942 HRS

'Oh, by the way,' said Bluett, 'there's one other thing I meant to ask you.'

Purnell was on the point of asking him not to smoke, but, maddeningly, he noticed that the cigar was unlit.

'Oh yes,' he replied. In only a matter of hours this wretched day would be over.

'I jes wanna check that you fellows blocked that Arab woman, al-Walibi, from getting into the hall today.'

'You mean Benedicte al-Walibi? I thought we'd told you:

we really didn't feel able to do anything there. She was vouched for personally by the French Ambassador.'

'Sheee . . .' said Bluett. 'Of course the Frog vouched for her. She's his fucking girlfriend. We don't like the look of some of the people she's been talking to lately.'

'Well, it's out of my hands. You'll really have to take it up with the Speaker.'

Barlow had been on the phone to the *Daily Mirror* for so long the receiver was blood warm and his fingers were beginning to ache. He kept remembering his duty to ring the House of Commons security people, or possibly just the police. He kept intending to put down the receiver, with a jovial farewell. But that was the trouble with these people. They had a way of draining your autonomy. It was as though they'd found a way to flip open the top of your head and pour in a bottle of ink to sink and settle in the fjords of your brain. The reporter was a woman with an Asian name, and from the minute she introduced herself, Barlow feared her.

He feared her as British soldiers on the Northwest Frontier once feared the Afghan daughters, and their knives, and their traditional knowledge of how to cut a live human being. 'I'm reely sorry,' she said, after his initial evasions, 'but I reely do feel you are going to be better off talking to me 'cos I've been asked to do this piece and your name's gonna be in it anyway.'

Barlow had asked her with a croak what the story was. 'Well, of course it's very embarrassing for me to talk to you like this,' she said, and then recited what purported to be a recent series of events in Barlow's life.

It was not the truth. It was an abstract impressionist representation: crude, impasto blotches that might or might not stand for an object in the 'real world'. But she knew she had enough to go on, and Barlow knew it, too.

At length he said: 'It's all rubbish, and besides, it was ages ago.'

The reporter went for the crack. 'It's either all bollocks or it happened ages ago. It can't be both.'

As when a stag is chased down the river, and his eyes roll, and the foam spackles his flanks, and the bracken and the alder hang in his antlers, and he drags himself to the bank and turns to face the music of the hounds in the knowledge that he can run no further, so Roger Barlow MP, almost fifty-one and pretty washed up, decided to speak his mind.

He thought of this woman, and all her ambition and aggression, and the pointless misery she was trying to cause him.

'Oh honestly,' he said, 'why can't you go and do something useful, like jump off a cliff?' As the seconds ticked away, he improvised a series of alternative careers for his tormentor.

'Where are they, anyway?' said the first policeman to the second policeman, as they wandered through Norman Shaw North car park in the direction of the ambulance. 'Are they all hiding in the back?'

'Tell you what,' said the second policeman, 'I reckon we should have a bet on this.'

'OK matey. Two pints of London Pride says yer gotta have a Koran in every ambulance.'

'Done.'

'Hang about,' said the first policeman. 'Is that the phone ringing in our booth?' They stopped and listened hard, turning back to look at the little black hut by the metal boom. The phone stopped and started again.

'I reckon it is and all.' Hands behind back, they drifted in the opposite direction.

The first policeman looked up at the sparkling morning. The clouds were still high and fleecy, but getting a little greyer and heavier about the bottom.

* * *

Jason Pickel's rooftop narrative had by now become so torpid and charged with horror that Indira, a sensible girl from Balham, was starting to feel quite tense.

'You know what a holocaust is?' said Pickel. Indira listened to the ambulance sirens in the square, and the unintelligible roar of the protesters.

Yeah, she said, it was a kind of terrible massacre, like what Hitler did to the Jews. She studied his hands. They were leaving damp marks on the barrel, but at least the safety catch was on.

'No, that's not a holocaust,' he said. 'In the ancient world a holocaust was when you sacrificed an animal and the flames took every part of it. It was wholly burned – holocaust – and every portion of the beast was offered to the god.' When the M16 bullets hit the fuel tank of the Datsun Sunny, said Jason, that was a holocaust.

There were six young Iraqi men in the car. Then there was this ball of flame. It was so big and so close that he smelt burning hair and realized it was his own eyebrows. The hairs shrivelled up on the back of his hands, like the nature films of ferns growing, except in reverse. When he came to describe the fate of the Iraqis, how they were first caramelized, then carbonized, and how their molten fat ran in rivulets down the sides of their incinerated car seats, Indira took a decision. She was going to report Jason. Someone should be told about this guy before he did any harm.

The fires had scarcely died down, said Jason, when the demonstrations began. They came from all sides, men slapping their hearts and their heads. They surrounded the torched car and screamed defiance when the Americans tried to approach it. They stuck their faces as close as they could to the Robocop-like Kovac and others, noses to chinstraps, and the curses spewed from their stained brown teeth and tongues that vibrated in the pink cavern of their mouths like a furious bird of prey.

It was a wedding party, they said. How could the GIs have failed to see that?

It was a victorious five-a-side soccer team.

Or they had just all passed their legal exams. They were brothers, uncles, fathers, sons, and they had been killed in cold blood by the crass and cowardly conquerors. It wasn't long before Captain Koch de Gooreynd came from his quarters and took charge. Shots were fired in the air. The mob drifted away. Jason was left with the car, and its contents, like something terrible left in the oven. Now he noticed Barry White, the British journalist, who at some stage had emerged from his ditch and was filling his notebook.

Jason was putting the geraniums back in a row and pathetically trying to patch up an earthenware pot.

'Ah, excuse me,' said the reporter, 'could I have my phone back, please?' The connection had been broken but a masochistic urge made him press the redial button.

The reporter was standing there with his arm held out as Jason listened first to the roaring of the electrons, and then to the effortful click as it dialled the phone number in Iowa. Someone picked it up.

'Honey,' said Jason. Whoever it was decided not to talk. After a short silence Jason disconnected and gave the satphone back. He stood in the orange dust, blinking back sweat with his singed lids, and jealousy began its throttling work on his gorge.

He wasn't listening as the Brit journalist – about six feet away – had a conversation with the foreign desk of his newspaper. Slowly, however, it permeated his consciousness that a story was being composed. What newspapermen call a piece, an article, was being dictated, about him and in his very presence.

'Yeah, OK, give me fifteen minutes,' said White. 'Tell you what, put me straight over to copy. Hello there, yes, Barry White for *Mirror* News. Let's call it "Massacre". Are you ready? Begins.'

Six Iraqis set off for a wedding yesterday morning.

They cleaned their shabby car. They put on their best suits.

They spent the day singing and dancing, as they celebrated a ritual as old as humanity, and tried to forget the misery which British and American forces have brought to their country.

And they were still singing when they came up to an American checkpoint at 5 p.m. local time.

They were told to stop.

They were ordered to get out of their car.

They were told to put up their hands and lie on the sand.

They were told to do these things in a language they did not understand.

They were screamed at by men who have no right, under international law, to be in their country.

For whatever reason, they did not obey. They continued to drive, waving and cheering.

When I saw the first 9mm parabellum round pass through the windscreen, and I saw the cloud of blood in the cabin, I shrieked at the Americans to stop.

I was ignored.

Burst after burst the huge American fired at the car, and I swear he smiled when the fuel tank went up.

There are no words to describe the fate of those six men.

We cannot begin to imagine the agony of their mothers, deprived even of a body to cradle.

There is now no way to tell them apart, save perhaps for the teeth which grin in their blackened skulls.

If you could come with me, and gaze at the dreadful cargo of this vehicle, and smell the unmistakable odour of burnt human being, you would never again tolerate the lie, that this was a war for the people of Iraq.

Is this the Pentagon's idea of liberation? What happened here today was evil.

It was a massacre. If there were any justice, it would join the list of other acts of brutality by American troops against Third World people.

It won't, of course. There will be no court-martial. There will be no inquiry.

The trigger-happy cowards who killed these six young men will say they were threatened.

They will say there were weapons in the car.

There were no weapons in the car, and none will be found.

And that, of course, is the central deception on which this war was fought.

Ends.

OK? Got that? Just whack that across to *Mirror* News and tell them I'll be filing more later.'

Before Jason could do anything to stop him, the reporter raised his camera and squeezed off several shots in his direction.

Then Barry White nodded amiably at Jason Pickel and strolled off down the road in the direction he had come. Jason looked up and down the street. A man on a donkey was approaching. The fisher boys had returned to their pitches on the Tigris.

Apart from the wreck of the car, and a helicopter buffeting the air overhead, it was as though normality had returned. He saw Kovac draw near, and the mere thought of talking to Kovac was enough.

He turned his carbine round, and would have added to the US fatality rate. But Kovac was quick, and knocked his arm down, and the bullet whanged aside. Not harmlessly, however. For the first time in his narrative, Pickel began to blub. The donkey stopped it, he said.

The donkey took the carbine round in his grizzled little donkey chest. They'd brought Jason over from Iowa. They'd screwed up his marriage. They'd equipped him with the most technically advanced weaponry in the world, and he'd ended up killing six young men who may or may not have been wedding guests, and he'd whacked a donkey.

Indira was no longer listening. She sidled away along the duckboards. Her orders were very clear. If you were in the slightest doubt about the mental state of anyone, it was your duty to get help.

Adam Swallow at last found his way through the corridors in Norman Shaw South, and could see his way out to New Palace Yard. It occurred to him that the route would present a considerable challenge to the Arab torture victim and his companions. Should he go back? He decided against. No doubt Benedicte had thought it through.

CHAPTER TWENTY-EIGHT

0944 HRS

Cameron was feeling irritated. The gloomy hall was starting to fill now, and it was with some difficulty that she had made her way to the steps at the far end. Why the hell had Adam given her these silly forged tickets? Where was she supposed to put them? Every seat in the place had 'reserved' on it. At length she found a seat, twenty feet away from the dais on the right, snaffled a reserved card, and sat down.

'*Excusez-moi, madame,*' said a voice immediately. 'I believe I am here. But I think we have met before. Yves Charpentier,' he said.

Cameron stood up. She saw a figure of Gallic nattiness, with the little red thread of the Légion d'Honneur, and a sense of disorder about his coiffure. 'I am the French Ambassador,' he explained. 'I believe we met in the company of the good Dr Swallow.'

It took Cameron a second or two to remember, but a man does not rise to the top of the French diplomatic service without possessing the nimblest grasp of situation. In a trice M. Charpentier had rearranged the placement in Westminster Hall, finding a place not only for Cameron but for a beautiful dark-skinned woman, who appeared to be his girlfriend, and two friendly Arabs in djelabahs.

'And here,' he said, sweeping up the place cards like a professional palmist, 'is the space for the good Swallow and his friends.' Cameron found herself sitting behind this comforting fellow, who kept up a lively chatter over his shoulder. But how could he forget meeting her, he asked? She had been there for his *petit vin d'honneur*, had she not? As she spoke, Cameron observed that his coat appeared to have been freshly sponged, and that there was some yellow gunk adhering to his hair.

'Ah yes,' said His Excellency, 'I was attacked. That is to say, I was ambushed by the cretins outside. Fortunately they did not hit me directly. That honour belonged unambiguously to my Dutch colleague, Mr Cornelijus.'

'What did they hit you with?'

'I cannot say. That is a question currently under investigation by the police. But I have my suspicions. It was a large white object containing a great quantity of albuminous matter. If I were forced to express an opinion, I should say it was an egg. It is so sad, of course,' said the Ambassador, smiling at her. 'They do not understand how many of us there are inside the hall, who sympathize with the objectives of those outside.'

M. Charpentier's girlfriend smiled. The two Arabs smiled.

'How true,' said Cameron. She shifted in her chair, and looked up at the stained glass of the north end. She deliberately set her mind upon a historical meditation, something about the antiquity of this hall, how it predated the discovery of her own country by 300 years. It was no use.

Soon she was once again daydreaming, in a happy mental fug, about the events of yesterday. She had been so frightened yesterday, with that row outside NATO, and the horrible pockmarked Flemish policeman going for his gun. She'd been impressed by the way Adam dealt with the guy, and at lunch, frankly, she had been dazzled.

Several times she almost cried out with anger at the coarseness and cynicism of their anti-American views. Every time she thought she would have to walk out or pop, they all laughingly paid out some slack and made her feel good again; and then slowly, ironically, gently, they'd begin the business of winding her up.

At one point she thought she was actually going to cry, when she heard her boyfriend — she had even had nesting thoughts about him — say that 'Osama bin Laden was more morally serious' than the American President.

They made jokes about American food, the cheese processed to the point of macrobiotic extermination, the bleached bread that bore no relation to wheat. Cameron looked around the smoky restaurant, where harassed Croats were dishing out steaming pots full of goo, the summit of Belgian civilization. There was waterzooi, a frightening salmonella-rich soup of fish and raw egg. There was steak tartare, so eloquent of toxoplasmosis that in her country it would have been banned by the Food and Drug Administration.

Yeah, she said, she had to hand it to the euros. They still had the edge when it came to lunch. Then they started laying into the American farm system that produced these culinary disasters, the depopulated prairies, harvested at night by huge computerized combines, the robot-controlled pig farms with their slurry lagoons. Did she not know that America was now the world's number one villain in dumping cotton on sub-Saharan Africa? Americans were obese. Americans were ignorant. They needed two airline seats per buttock. Most of them had never been to Yurp. Most of them didn't have passports.

Some of them, like Sylvester Stallone and Bruce Willis, were too terrified to get on a plane. Those that did travel abroad did not always leave their destination as they found it. Sometimes they blew up commuter trains on Balkan bridges, and sowed the fields with depleted uranium shells. Sometimes they bombed aspirin factories in the belief that they were making aflatoxin.

'Did I ever tell you about the whisky bottling plant?' said the don.

No, go on, they said.

'It was the funniest thing you ever heard.' They craned forward, their faces lurid and eerie in the half-light of the restaurant, and they awaited the nativity of the funniest thing you had ever heard.

'Some CIA guy was scanning the internet for suspicious sites and he came across this promotional video from Jura. He saw all these horrible bottles being filled with a mysterious yellow fluid. And you know what they did? They actually sent a team to Britain, in the belief that they were looking at weapons of mass destruction.'

The don put back his head and howled, and his wife howled back, like a pair of intellectual coyotes.

'Weapons of mass destruction is right,' she said.

Adam laughed, too. 'More dangerous than anything Saddam had,' he pointed out.

'Yeah,' said Cameron and her patriotic feelings evaporated as she joined their happy scorn. There was something adolescent about their laughter, as if they were conscious, for the first time, of mocking the pretensions of the grown-ups. And that was why their giggling was so intense, she decided.

Because it was only a few years ago that America would have inspired their undivided affection and respect. That was what made their ideological rebellion so naughty and so compulsive.

So she was in excellent fettle after lunch, when they went for a walk, and she found herself linking arms, first with the don and then with Adam. They walked down Boulevard Adolf Max, and Cameron felt the sun on her cheeks. Then they doubled back down the Rue Neuve and walked in the shade.

The pavement was cracked and bemerded, and she was watching her feet when she became aware of what she took, at first, to be a life-size poster of a naked woman on the wall. She turned her head and saw a window, and behind that window was indeed a semi-naked black girl.

She was reading a book, and as they walked past she looked up for a fraction of a second. 'Hey look,' whispered Cameron, 'is she doing what I think she's doing?'

'She's reading *Le Rouge et le Noir*,' said Adam.

That night they sat in the bar of the Amigo hotel drinking whisky, and she had not been surprised when he followed her up to her room.

And that was what Cameron was really thinking about, gawping up at the mutilated form of Eleanor of Aquitaine, the TV lights turning her hair into points of gleaming gold, until her eyes focused again on the person in front.

It was one of the Arab men, and he had disposed the skirts of his djelabah so that they were pushed out all the way through the hind legs of his chair. He appeared to have dropped something. He was leaning forward and scrabbling underneath himself. Cameron wondered whether she could help, and as she watched through a crack in the djelabah, she saw his hand at work. His chair was placed directly over a bronze plaque recording the spot where Sir Thomas More, the patron saint of politicians, was executed. She saw him finger the edge of the plaque and she saw – or thought she saw – him slip a key under the metal rim and lift it up.

She felt a panic, as one feels when coming across something secret and frightening in the place one doesn't expect it. She emitted the kind of noise you might hear from some tumbledown outside privy in Italy, where a well-brought-up girl has secluded herself on a hot day, and looked down to see a snake coiled in the bowl below.

The Arab straightened up. The crack in his skirts disappeared, and he was probing her with his brown eyes when they were interrupted. Hermanus Van Cornelijus was here, his thinning grey hair still wet from the sponge, and a band-aid on his Brueghelian nose.

CHAPTER TWENTY-NINE
0946 HRS

As soon as she had shot-putted the egg, Sandra melted away as efficiently as a Balkan bomb-thrower. Raimondo had been left watching at the railings as the sphere arced through the air.

'Yay,' he shouted, as it detonated on the dome of the Dutchman. 'Way to go,' he shouted, as if hailing some improbably brilliant piece of aerial billiards.

So it was not surprising that Matt, standing only an axe-handle away, should decide he was the culprit. As the cry died on his lips, the 220lb former linebacker lunged at Raimondo, not even bothering to draw his weapon, and flattening the crash barrier like an encephalopathic bullock. 'Sir!' shouted the White House man with instinctive extra-territoriality, 'you are under arrest.'

Raimondo had always scorned demonstrators. Nothing he

liked more in his younger days than seeing the fuzz break up some lefty protest. He remembered a pro-abortion march he'd seen in London, and his feeling of disgust at these scuzzy rentamob characters screaming for the right to kill the unborn. He remembered the way their voices rose to a studied shriek as soon as the police laid hands on them.

Now he yodelled at Matt in identical tones. 'Don't you touch me, you faggot!' he said.

'Yeah,' said the people next to him. 'Get off him!'

'Tosser!'

'Bastard!' they cried. When Matt, who did not like being called a faggot, began to use reasonable force to restrain the perp, the noise grew louder still. And when they saw the blood begin to stream down Raimondo's face, the crowd began to buck and sway. In no time there were two police helicopters overhead, and cops in Star Wars riot gear were climbing over towards them from the other side of the square. Even Jason Pickel was distracted from his daydream, and pointed his scope vaguely at the noise.

Debbie Gujaratne of the *Daily Mirror* had by now endured two minutes and 39 seconds of heady abuse from Roger Barlow, and the truth was that Roger was almost succeeding. Poor chap, thought Debbie as he ranted on. She could picture it all. The basically happy family life: the trips to the Science Museum, the kids on his shoulders, their sticky fingers in his ears; the long and formless Sunday afternoons of toys and fights and painting on the kitchen table; the cacophonous tea, the whimpering bath-time, the sweet breath of children asleep.

She imagined, because she had known them in her own childhood, all the longueurs of bourgeois domesticity, so boring and yet so desired. She pitied him, although she had no family herself (she was of course sleeping with her married news editor). And yet even as she pitied him, she knew she would have no mercy. It would be more than her job was worth.

Barlow had strayed outside the weird and hypocritical matrix that the tabloid imposed on the conduct of public and semi-public figures. He was a goner. 'I'm sorry, Mr Barlow, I don't want to be rude because I've reely enjoyed our chat, but I've got to go now.'

'You've got to go?' yipped Roger. 'You've got to go now, have you? Well, I haven't finished with you yet.' And he prepared to say what he thought.

'Oh for the Lord's sake,' said Deputy Assistant Commissioner Purnell, more to himself than to Bluett or anyone else. 'This isn't the Bermuda Triangle. This is Westminster and we've got 14,000 men on the job. It must have turned right on to Grosvenor Terrace and gone down the Embankment, but what I don't get is how we could have missed it.'

'Wait up,' said Bluett. He was bent over the map, and Purnell noticed that he was sweating, so that his scalp started to gleam under his thinning buzzcut hair like some denuded alpine forest. 'What's that in there? That kind of inlet thing?'

Purnell looked over. 'Oh that's Derby Gate. It's a place where loads of MPs have their offices. But I can assure you, Colonel, that it is crawling with my men, and they would all have been put in the picture by now.'

'Well, let's try them again,' said Bluett.

Purnell had eaten cornflakes for breakfast, and it is one of the world's great unreported truths that cornflakes give you indigestion. On even the most stress-free mornings, they are apt to send a vicious little acid flooding over your uvula, and today they were backing up something rotten on Deputy Assistant Commissioner Purnell. He prayed – since he was a religious man – that he would not be rude to the American.

'Colonel – can I call you Stuart?'

'You certainly can, sir.'

'Stuart, you know my view that we should in all prudence

tell the President and move him to a safe place until we've sorted this out. Where is he now, by the way, Grover?' he said, turning to his aide.

'He'll be with the Speaker of the House of Commons,' said Bluett, who had committed the President's schedule to memory. 'I respectfully say that we should spend the next eight minutes trying to find this goddam ambulance of yours.'

'Right,' said Purnell. Ever since he had been at primary school he had learned to fend off stress by stroking the underside of a table, where no one could see, and now he was stroking away like crazy. 'Get me Derby Gate,' he said.

Where Jones & Co. were trying on their equipment.

The skill of making a suicide bomber jacket is mainly in the sewing, and Jones knew plenty of women in the Finsbury area who were up to the job. One of the tasks facing the police, when they came later to sort out what had happened, was to analyse the ingredients. The results were banal.

The blue portabrace camera jackets, the Sony and the sound booms came from Euromedia in Hammersmith, a shop much used by the BBC. The wooden struts, used to separate the explosive charges, were of uncertain provenance, but seemed to have belonged to a fruit box, possibly one that had been used to contain Florida oranges.

The manager of RitePrice in Wolverhampton attempted to claim the batteries, though later, when his premises were stoned, he said that he had been trying to raise the profile of his store. As he complained to his insurers, 'All publicity is good publicity.'

It was fairly clear that the ball bearings, in two sizes, came from B&Q.

The nitroglycerin was easily and quickly traced back to a makeshift lab, which was discovered along with a fair number of toenail clippings under the Finsbury Park bed of Jones the Bomb. DNA tests on the toenails established that they came from more than one person, and rather like relics of the Beaker Folk, had been laid down in that site over a long period.

The Nokias had all come from a carphone warehouse in Wolverhampton, and had been paid for in cash, on a pay-as-you-talk basis, the day before. It was Dean's job now to turn them on, make sure they were charged up to last at least six hours, and to insert them into the right pocket in the appropriate jacket.

'Here you are, then,' he said to Haroun and Habib, opening the back of the ambulance and passing out the jackets.

'Nah,' said Habib almost immediately, passing it back to the quartermaster. 'This one is too tight for me. Give it me this one,' he said, turning to Haroun and speaking in Arabic.

Habib found that Haroun's waistcoat was also a bit of a squeeze.

'You then,' he said pointing at Dean, and offering a jocular Arab insult, such as an ill-mannered sheikh might bestow upon a slave. 'Give it me this one, then.'

'No, mush,' said Dean, whose cockiness was coming back. 'We've all got to have the right one.' He looked back into the cab for help from Jones the Bomb, but Jones appeared to be doing something elaborate with his own jacket. His shirt was off and he was sticking things to his chest with masking tape.

Dean stepped back, crushing the fingers of Eric Onyeama. For a second he had the impression that the corpse flinched, but he had no time to worry about that.

Habib looked at him shrewdly, and then gabbled something at Haroun. 'Why you no give it me him?' he asked, putting a foot on the rear running board of the ambulance. The two Arabs lunged and winkled Dean from the darkness.

'What's the matter you?' said Haroun, holding him from behind in a full Nelson.

'This is all wrong,' said Dean. 'I'm meant to be in charge of this bit.'

Just as the two policemen reached their black booth, the phone stopped ringing again.

'They'll call back,' said the first policeman.

They turned as one and looked back under the arch of the passerelle, towards the ambulance and the Embankment.

Like teenage sisters about to go to the disco, the enigmatic operatives were apparently squabbling over their attire.

Habib took Dean's jacket, tried it on, and gave it disgustedly to Haroun. Haroun took Dean's coat and gave it to Habib. Or was it that Habib mistakenly tried on Haroun's jacket twice, before settling for the one he first thought of, while Dean and Habib simply swapped over and back again? Jones was getting cross.

'*Inti mafish mukh*,' he spat. You have no brains. He jerked his head in the direction of the police, who were now walking back in their direction.

By the time they had shut and locked the ambulance, and begun the prescribed route through Westminster Hall, Dean's efforts at pelmanism had failed. They had done a three-card trick with the jackets.

As Roger Barlow ran back across the passerelle, he looked down again at the ambulance. It appeared to be deserted. Then he thought he saw a lupine figure, slinking through towards the Commons kitchens. Within a few seconds he had reached the Pass Office, still invigilated by the man from Stogumber. 'Those passes,' said Roger Barlow, 'can you deactivate them?'

Conscious that the two policemen were only a matter of fifty yards behind, Jones led them fast along the ordained route. First they crossed the threshold into Norman Shaw North, scampering over a yellow sign painted on the tarmac saying 'No pedestrians beyond this point'.

He then jinked confidently left and led them down past

the post office sorting room, then past the kitchens, and then to the first secure door, where a pass was needed. Fixed to the wall, on the right, was the little plastic swipe card socket familiar to anyone who has tried to get into a modern hotel room. The conspirators bunched in the corridor, a little spinney of sound booms and microphones and camcorders.

There was a hush, as Jones inserted the pass.

The door gave a click, and shifted open a fraction. A green light came on. Jones smiled. Dean froze. The lead terrorist pushed open the gleaming brushed steel door and Dean knew in his writhing intestines that whatever happened, he would not go through it. He understood that if he went through that door, and round that corner, he would die. Even if he failed to die by his own hand, Haroun and Habib would do for him, sure as eggs were eggs.

These two now followed Jones through the door; and as Dean was standing there mute, the door shut behind them. At the click of it, Jones turned round and came back to look through the porthole.

'Sorry,' said Dean, 'got held up.' He held up the sound boom and mimed the act of snagging it on something.

'Quickly,' hissed the mission leader, his voice muffled by the door. 'Stop being an old woman and use your card.' Dean looked at the oscillating brown irises of the man called Jones.

Trembling, he put the plastic pass into the pocket. He tried it one way. He tried it the other way. As Jones began to curse him, he genuinely tried to get it right, jiggling the card so as to produce a better contact between the magnetic strip and the electronic reader.

At the very moment when it should have done the trick, his card ceased to function at all. Now Dean was on one side of the barrier and his collaborators were on the other. Haroun and Habib joined Jones at the porthole, banging their noses like sharks at an aquarium. They started all three of them to say terrible things.

Bizzaz immak ala amood. Your mother's tits are on a pole.

Ma fish kahraba, said Habib, slapping the side of his head. There is no electricity.

Dean didn't speak their language, but he took them to be proposing, roughly speaking, to gouge out his eyes and piss on his brains. 'Oh I do wish yow would be quiet,' he said, 'it's not my fault.' Haroun started thumping the door, while Habib looked for a handle.

Had they spent perhaps another twenty seconds, they might have found the metal button, recessed in the tiles, that opens the door from the Commons side.

'There you go,' said a breathy voice. A figure appeared behind the three Arabs. It was a blazered and bouffant-haired junior foreign minister.

As he pressed the button he took a distinct pleasure in helping out these struggling journalists from a minority group. 'After you,' he said, holding open the door on the assumption that the trio wanted to go out.

'Thank you so much,' said Jones, indicating with a sweep that it was rather Dean who should come this way.

And Dean was unlocking his haunches to move, when a voice behind him said, 'I am sorry, sir, would you mind just staying there while I check your pass.' It was the first policeman, the other a few paces behind. He had observed Dean's difficulties with the swipe card.

'It's all right, officer,' oozed the young minister, passing through and holding the door open. 'I'm letting him through.'

'That's right, sir, but I can't let anyone through who doesn't have a valid pass.'

'I've got a valid pass. That's the whole point.' He nodded brightly at Dean. Dean stayed still.

The minister directed a quick but irrefutable wink at the terrorist conscript. Dean was rooted to the spot.

'Frankly, sir, I hope you won't mind my saying this, but I think it would be more appropriate from every point of view if we played this by the book. I am sure the young man won't mind coming to the office with me to revalidate his pass.'

. The minister turned to the policeman. His smile burst out like the sun over a meadow of alpine flowers. 'Look, I know you are only doing your job, and if I may say so doing it very well. But we have here a distinguished foreign news crew, and I think we should treat everyone the same, without the slightest suggestion of discrimination.'

Invisibly, behind the door, Haroun began to detach the still virgin thorax draining kit from its place of concealment in his sock.

At the mention of the word 'discrimination', the policeman stiffened. Jesus, but he hated that word.

'I have been working here for twelve years, sir,' he said, 'and I can assure you that I treat everyone the same . . .'

'I know that, officer,' said the politician, and his voice was like ginger beer, as it might trickle from an earthenware cruse on a hot summer's day, to quench a thirsty shepherd boy. 'I would not presume to tell you what to do.'

Haroun began steadily to draw the spike out of his trouser leg. Habib said something in Arabic.

'As you know, sir, my duty is to prevent access to the Palace of Westminster to any person or persons I see fit. I am not saying you are a security risk, by the way,' he said to Dean, 'but . . .'

'Now look here,' said the minister, and a frown had clouded his pallid brow, 'I really think . . .'

And so he might have continued, with one of those don't-you-know-who-I-am speeches he had given at perhaps a dozen check-in counters, when he had turned up late for a flight, with no better excuse than his own laziness and conceit. Matters might have seriously deteriorated. The puncture kit was now fully extracted from the sock, and was scintillating in the gloom.

Jones saw it, rested his fingers on Haroun's shoulder, and transmitted a message of calm and control. 'My dear sir,' he said to the politician, 'I am most terribly grateful for your help. But it is clear we have reached an impasse, and the last thing I want to do is cause any difficulties for our friend here.' He smiled at the policeman. Haroun smiled, and so did Habib.

They all beamed, like a bunch of Lebanese waiters who have been told to provide a birthday cake, gratis, for an orphan.

'So let us go back,' he said, coming out through the door, 'and see if we can find the document you have rightly requested,' he said, as the party straggled upwards and backwards to the car park in Norman Shaw North. Jones the Bomb set a brisk pace, conversing ceremoniously with the copper.

The politician fell in with Habib. 'Good Lord,' he said, looking at the terrorist's T-shirt, 'isn't that extraordinary!' Habib tried to hunch together the flaps of the suicide bomber jacket. There, smudged over the chest slogan, was a bloodstain. It was hand-shaped, presumably came from the blood of Eric the parkie, and had been made in the course of their bags-I-not struggle over the bomber jackets. 'Llangollen 3rd VIII University,' he read out. 'Isn't that a coincidence? Do you know that I am the MP for Llangollen?'

Habib gave a soft smile. Behind them walked Dean, who was trying to avoid the gaze of Haroun, while whistling 'Colonel Bogey'.

As soon as they emerged from the tunnel, they could hear the football-terrace roar from the square. It was now the middle of the passion of Raimondo Charles. As the Yankee fists pounded the glossy head of that innocent but irritating man, the wails of his supporters carried round the corner from Whitehall. It was quite frightening.

The minister decided to spend no more political capital on this incompetent TV crew, and with a final leer at Dean, he tootled off. He was going to watch the President's speech on television. Having been almost excessive in his gratitude to the emanations of the British state, Jones the Bomb turned to his underlings.

'Dean, you know how much I value you. You know how crucial you are to this operation, and how much the Sheikh, may Allah be with him, esteems the contribution you make. But I must confess that there are times when I wonder whether you do justice to your natural abilities.' Haroun spat at Dean's feet.

'Luckily,' continued Jones, 'I have already made plans for this contingency.' He took out the car key. 'This is why we are using an ambulance.'

Dean looked at him with the hunger of an eight-year-old being offered a ride on Disney's space mountain. 'Hey man,' he said, 'I know what. It's time for a bit of the old *nee-naw, nee-naw*, innit?' Then, once again, a film of fear came over his eyes.

Westminster Hall was now crowded to capacity, and here and there a terse dispute was taking place over the few unbagged seats, and the ethics of 'reserving' the chairs with scrawled bits of paper. Corpulent young MPs of all parties looked stonily into the distance, shifted their bottoms, and refused to meet the eyes of the peeresses who hobbled around in the hope of chivalry. Cameron was getting on famously with the French Ambassador and his girlfriend. She saw Adam walk up past her on her right, picking his way through the crowds against the wall. She waved, but he did not seem to see her. It was growing hotter and hotter under the klieg lights, and people were beginning to bend the programme, with its twin emblems, the Portcullis of the Commons and the Presidential Seal, and to fan their wide-pored faces. There was a sennet or a tucket or a fanfare and suddenly here they were.

First a group of trumpeters came on, in red and yellow tunics, white stockings, and odd little jockey caps. They lifted their long, valveless instruments, each with a heraldic flag suspended beneath it, and standing half a dozen on either side of the top dais, they parped a deafening salute.

Then came an assortment of dignified office-holders, mainly in tights, and all men. Then came a man walking backwards carrying a cushion with something on it, then the man carrying the Mace of the House of Commons, and then the Speaker of the House of Commons, and then there he was . . . all this for one man in a plain blue suit.

Cameron was surprised – since she had never seen her country's leader before, not in the flesh – by how tall he was. She felt herself flushing with simple patriotic pleasure and savoured the contrast between English flummery and the republican simplicity of America. He came down the steps from Central Lobby, shooting his cuffs and waiting until he and the First Lady could be escorted, with maximum pomp, to their chairs by the dais. Then the last echo of brass died away.

They stopped whispering and sniffing and bickering. In the silence that followed – and it seemed like silence, because the listeners automatically bleached out the quotidian noise of the emergency vehicle – the Speaker stood forward to speak.

CHAPTER THIRTY

0958 HRS

Roger Barlow and the man from Stogumber heard the siren and ran out of the Pass Office. Barlow established with a glance that it was the suspect ambulance. Blooming Bilston and Willenhall Primary Care Trust.

In the police booth they saw the machine hurtling towards them, flashing and wailing so loudly that it drowned out the noise of the telephone. Without a second's hesitation, the first policeman brought the palm of his hand down flat and hard on the big red button which lifted the boom.

Roger ran after it. He waved. He shouted inaudibly at the men in the booth. No good. It is one thing to clamp an ambulance when it is illegally parked. You don't stop it in mid-*nee-naw*.

Out of the parking lot lurched the terrorists, up past the Red Lion pub, whence a couple of piss-heads surveyed them apathetically, then round the corner on to Whitehall and they were gone from Barlow's view. He turned and double-timed down the tunnel towards Westminster Hall.

Dimly in the Scotland Yard Ops Room they could hear the noise of an ambulance; but it was the one that had been sent to assist the pool of blood in Tufton Street. All the evidence seems to agree that at this point, barely a minute before the President was due to open his mouth, the authorities had still failed to make any connection between the missing ambulance and the vehicle which had attracted such attention in Norman Shaw North.

Deputy Assistant Commissioner Purnell pressed 16 on his phone and spoke to Grover. 'Did we get through to Derby Gate?'

It took Grover a moment or two to find out the state of play. 'We tried to raise them, but there was no answer, and now it seems to be engaged.'

Purnell raised his eyes to Bluett, and the American stared unfathomably back.

In the booth at Derby Gate the policemen were trying to raise the Met Ops Room, since it was by now the considered view of them both that the ambulance was worthy of attention.

'It's bleeding engaged,' said the first policeman to the second policeman.

Bleeding Koran, thought the second policeman. They'd need more than the bleeding Koran if this thing turned out bad.

'Well, Bluett, old man,' said Purnell, trying to assert his authority in the mental arm-wrestle. 'It looks like we're going to let the programme proceed.'

'Yup,' said Bluett, sticking his cigar in his mouth and looking tough. 'Anything else would be a surrender to terrorism.'

PART TWO
THE SPECIAL RELATIONSHIP

CHAPTER THIRTY-ONE

1000 HRS

'My lords, ladies and gentlemen . . .'

The President looked over the lectern at upwards of 800 heads, goggling at him on either side of the central aisle. He was going to enjoy this, he thought. Whatever you said about the Brits, whatever their snobberies and limitations, they understood the relationship between the present and the past. They never pretended that their system of government was some ash-and-aluminum example of perfected modernity. They knew their democracy was an inherited conglomerate of traditions, bodged together, spatchcocked, barnacled and bubblegummed by fate and whimsy.

That's why, goddammit, he kept in the my lords bit. They might have been expelled or in some other way neutered by Blair (he was hazy on the details). But look at these guys, standing on the dais with him: get a load of their tights, their shapely calves, trimmed by tennis and hoofing it at posh nightclubs. Check out their crazy wigs, glowing like woolly haloes in the clerestory light. Dig those funky buckles and black satin rosettes like heraldic tarantulas crawling down the back of their tailcoats. Look at this fat guy next to him, this Scottish fellow who obviously ate nothing but fry-ups, with the rosy face and the whisky nose. Now this fellow, from what the President understood, had been the product of a Glasgow steel mill, and his hands were heavy and scarred with swarf. He spoke with so thick an accent that when the President had taken delivery of some freaky mug of Winston Churchill, he had barely understood a word. But he was the Speaker! He was in charge of this place, and in terms of troy ounces of bling-bling, he was more sumptuously attired than P Diddy himself.

He went on: 'It is a great honor to be speaking here today, and a rare honor, and I am proud to be speaking to you on a day when we commemorate a relationship that has had many triumphs and many perils. I know it is fashionable to say that the Special relationship does not exist. I have heard they say it in your Foreign Office, and in Foggy Bottom, in the State Department. But I know it exists, and you know that special friendship exists, and we know how much together we have achieved in the last hundred years, not least in the two great world conflicts whose successful conclusion we memorialize today.'

The President looked out at the vast windfarm of flapping programmes as his listeners struggled to keep cool. It wouldn't go down as a brilliant speech; he did not do brilliant speeches. But it had the small, additional merit that he believed every word of it, more or less. 'We stood firm in the Cold War, and we joined in bringing freedom and democracy to countries that were denied them for forty years. Together now, we work to liberate a region of the world' – this was the bit, to be frank, that he was worried about. Neocon though he was, he could imagine that this passage might grate with some of those Labor fellows, the Democratic Liberals, or whatever the hell they were called, and possibly even, for Chrissakes, some of the Conservatives. There were liberal squishes everywhere, these days, and he had been warned by the Ambassador that some of the MPs might try to make names for themselves by walking out – '. . . a region of the world where too many people are still forbidden from exercising their basic right to free assembly and free speech . . .'

Because he still had a reflex eye for these things the President noticed a good-looking blonde dressed smartly who was sitting three rows back on the left, and tilting her chin and the planes of her cheeks as if his words were some cooling shower to be caught and savoured on her skin. In front of her he dimly noted the swept-maned foreign guy, who had the air of some kind of composer or art critic, and next to him three Arabs, a girl and two men.

He looked at them now with the first stirrings of curiosity. One of them stirred abruptly in his seat. Was that a little protest brewing? But the President had no time, and his eyes flickered back to the big 28-point block capitals of his text.

'And I want to remind you of the origins of this great but mysteriously deprecated relationship, because its birth, like so many other births, was also the moment of greatest vulnerability. It was Oscar Wilde who said that we are two nations divided by a common language,' (the French Ambassador yawned so widely that Cameron began to feel reassured) 'and it would be fair to say, Mr Speaker, that there are some of your great traditions which doubtless through our own inadvertence we have failed to inherit. It is sometimes said that we lack the British sense of irony.'

A thousand toes curled: oh God, was he about to say how much he enjoyed the works of Monty Python? 'We do not as a rule drink our beer warm.'

The President simpered at the Speaker and the Speaker simpered back. In the game of tasteless presents the Scotsman had been out-generalled by the Texan: the appalling gargoyle mug of Sir Winston had been requited by a pair of cowboy boots in scarlet leather with the word 'Speaker' tooled on the shins.

'We do not populate our society with personages calling themselves knights or lords, which I think sometimes is a shame though I am afraid there are still people who complain that political office in our republic may be passed in dubious circumstances from father to son . . .' This sally earned the President his first desultory round of applause and reluctant laughter. The President gave his aw shucks expression and squinted his buzzard eyes on the script. He was coming to the meat of it.

'But perhaps the most obvious difference to an Englishman in New York or to an American arriving in London is that we do not drive on the same side of the road. It was that curious distinction, adopted on I know not what principle by our founding fathers which was almost fatal to this relationship at its moment of inception. It was in 1931 on Fifth Avenue that a great Englishman stepped into the traffic and was surprised to find it moving in an unexpected direction. We today must thank providence that the taxi driver braked before his fender connected with the form of—'

By this stage the audience of MPs had settled back. For a short moment some of them had hoped for an attack on the tyre approval of European motor cars, but they knew where he was going now. In any Anglo-American context his name was the name invoked with liturgical predictability.

'—Sir Winston Churchill. If that taxi had not braked, ladies and gentlemen, we in the United States would have lost the most fervent advocate and admirer to be found in all the ranks of European statesmen. If that taxi driver had not braked that vital friendship between the British Prime Minister and President Roosevelt would never have been forged. If that New York cabby had not been paying attention then your country would have lost its greatest wartime leader and the history of the world would have been bleak indeed.'

Bleak indeed! thought Sir Perry Grainger, who fancied himself as a bit of a rhetorician and never turned down an invitation to debate at the Oxford Union: that was a bit of a diminuendo, that wasn't exactly a climax for his ascending tricolon. But it was consonant with the general crapness of the speech, he thought.

Sir Perry was out of sorts. It had been embarrassing enough to present the leader of the free world with a Toby jug, worse to find the Americans had nothing for him, only a pair of boots for the Speaker. 'Mm,' he said as the President wittered on about Churchill's American mother and his odd habit of nudity in the White House. Like so many men faced with a choice between thoughts of nudity and listening to a speech, his mind wandered.

Nee-naw, naw-nee went the ambulance, straight through the traffic lights at the end of Whitehall. Quite a large proportion of the police manpower had now been diverted to suppressing the threat from Raimondo Charles, and those who did watch its progress made instinctive waving-on gestures.

As they turned into New Palace Yard, through the big wrought-iron gates, Jones hit the siren button on the far right of his console, and the machine changed its note.

Whoo-whup, whoo-wup, whoo-wup, said the ambulance, and the blue madness throbbed and strobed at its temples.

With the despairing entreaty of an emergency vehicle it approached the last security boom between the President and Jones the Bomb.

Cameron heard it, and knew in her heart that something was badly wrong. Adam heard it, and felt deeply puzzled. Surely this wasn't the plan? Or was it? What had Benedicte intended?

CHAPTER THIRTY-TWO
1007 HRS

Doo-whup, doo-whup, said the ambulance. In their black-painted booth, the police looked at it with bafflement. Under any normal circumstances, a vehicle was to be stopped before the tank-trap. It would be asked to ease gently over a device fitted with lights, cameras and mirrors, so that its underside could be properly surveyed. Its bonnet would be lifted, and only after a search lasting perhaps five or seven minutes would it be allowed down the cobbles and towards the colonnade and Westminster Hall. But these were not normal circumstances. The President had just begun speaking, according to their timetables. It might be, as the seconds crawled by, that to stick to routine was madness. The hand of authority hovered for a fraction over the phone, and over the red buzzer that lifted the boom; and for a fraction that hand hesitated between its options.

Such was the thickness of the ancient walls and so tiny the windows, that the audience in Westminster Hall had hardly heard the earlier sirens, let alone the tropic surf of the crowd.

This one was different. It sounded as though it was approaching the south of the hall by New Palace Yard and it was getting closer.

Up on the roof above the Press Gallery, deserted by Indira and with no one to keep him company but his gun, Jason Pickel now looked at the ambulance with all the acuity his training had imparted.

He had caught sight of the vehicle earlier, as it left the car park, because he could see perpendicularly between the blocks right down Cannon Row. But then it was lost in the buildings of Derby Gate, its siren muffled for the next seconds as it moved from Whitehall to Parliament Square. At first it did not occur to him to wonder why the British emergency services had stationed an ambulance in Norman Shaw North, nor did he attach any real interest to the emergency. Perhaps some conscientious old biddy had sustained a heart attack. Perhaps, God help him, some policeman had used too much force to restrain a rioter and bloodied his or her obstreperous nose. From his vantage Jason could make out the odd detachment of media representatives with their cameras and sound booms.

'Vermin,' he thought. 'Cockroaches.' And he looked at them as genocidally as a Hutu beholds a Tutsi. If it hadn't been for that *Daily Mirror* guy, thought Jason.

It is always a tricky moment in life and literature when a returning warrior opens his own white picket gate and walks up to the terrifying ambiguities of his own frost-paned front door. The Greeks called it nostos, the moment of return, and nostalgia is technically the longing for what should be a joyful occasion, but often isn't, of course.

Odysseus came back to find his house overrun by strange men trying to go to bed with his wife. Agamemnon returned to find the little woman in apparently good spirits. He gave her a loving kiss and said he was glad to be back after ten years. She congratulated him on capturing Troy, ran him a bath and stabbed him to death.

'Jason, honey,' his wife Wanda had exclaimed, with every sign of enthusiasm. But he was made nervous by the brightness of her eye and put off by her red lipstick.

In the days that followed he had entertained doubts about his wife, more than entertained them. He had invited them round, given them bed and board in his heart, he had listened with gloomy resignation as the doubts rabbited on into the night, refusing to take the hint no matter how much he coughed and stretched and signalled that their welcome was outstayed. And then she had clinched matters. She had referred to what had happened in Baghdad as a 'massacre', and lamely tried to excuse herself.

Pickel had hit the table, and she had cried. Two days later Wanda announced that she would be going scuba diving every evening after supper at the local pool. Sometimes she wouldn't come back until 10.30 p.m., and although she always seemed showered and shampooed, she sometimes smelled of chlorine and sometimes did not.

Jason would stand by the big picture window of the living room and wait until he could see her headlights come down the street; then he would quickly go to bed and pretend like a child to be asleep.

After a while he asked to be transferred, and nine months later, thanks to his skill as a sharpshooter, here he was.

About twenty feet below him, in one of the tall, badly ventilated chambers of the Parliamentary press gallery, a journalist opened a drawer. It had to be here somewhere. It just had to be somewhere. His fingers skittered like hamsters in litter until he found it.

'There,' he thought, pocketing an expenses form. It was the quickest way to make money and would give him something to do during this wretched speech.

As he rode down in the lift to the ground floor and Westminster Hall, he looked into the polished brass of the doors and admired for perhaps the 20 billionth time, his fantastic meringue of hair. Barry White pushed out his lips as if to blow himself a kiss.

Roger Barlow might not have admitted as much but he was naturally fitter than most men of his age. Late nights, cigarettes, alcohol: none of them had removed a certain undergraduate stamina. But now as he scooted back towards the colonnade, up the stairs, down the stairs, round the corner, along the corridor, he was starting to feel that burning sensation you get in your lungs at the end of a cross-country run.

The soles of his shoes were leather and he found it hard to gain traction on the polished tiles. His coat flapped, his shirt tails came out, his spongy elastic cufflink exploded, his cuffs waved in the air, and his tie slip-streamed behind him. In the fond imagination of one Commons secretary who crossed his path he had the air of a man who had just burst through a hedge after running through a garden having climbed down a drainpipe on being surprised in the wrong marital bed.

'You gotta help,' he gasped to that kindly face. 'Yes Roger,' she said. She felt the contrast between his hectic grip and her own, which she knew to be a lovely cool and calming thing, redolent of cold cream, and she transmitted through her palm her willingness, at least in that instant, to help him in any way he chose.

'We've got to get the ambulance,' he said.

'That's all right, Roger,' she said pointing up to the gates of New Palace Yard. 'I think it's on its way.'

Roger made a plosive noise, snatched away his hand and ran out of the colonnade on to the cobbles and up towards the gate where the ambulance was now dawdling before the barrier. Whop-doo-whop, it said, and now Barlow still had twenty yards to run before he reached the police box, where there must be men of good sense. He could just about see through the darkened panes of the booth where the coppers appeared to be having an argument. One of them was on the telephone and Barlow wondered who the hell he could be talking to, who could leave him in any doubt – surely to goodness old Stogumber, the Pass Office man, had let everyone know that this ambulance was travelling under false colours?

He was almost at the booth, waving his arms, when to his amazement he saw the boom go up. The ambulance yowled through the gap, bonnet bouncing, lights flashing. For a split second he stared into the eyes of Jones the Bomb. He stared for long enough to see that Jones would have no hesitation about running him down and then he jumped out of the way.

Fifty yards away, on the other side of the crowd control barriers, the two large Americans looked up from the agreeable business of beating up Raimondo Charles. Information was crackling into their ears via the Curly-Wurly tubes and they both turned to stare at the ambulance as it went through the gates into New Palace Yard. They dropped Raimondo back on the turf, bloodied and visibly reduced as a risk to presidential security. 'Bastards,' said the journalist. Though he was not in truth badly hurt, this marked his transition from a right-wing to left-wing polemicist.

'Yer bastards,' agreed a member of the crowd and others added their curses. The security men stood like bovine robocops as more news was pumped into their ears. Then as one, they reached into their blazers and drew out their big Glocks with the weird plastic oblong barrels.

The crowd screamed, and a figure emerged from their ranks.

Many artists have memorialized that pathetic moment when the battle is done, and the crows circle, and the warriors lie with broken helms and spears snapped asunder on the greasy grass, and the womenfolk come out to mourn. So Sandra the nanny, she who had chucked the ostrich egg, stood in pietà-like lamentation over the bashed-up Raimondo.

'Oh Raimondo,' she said.

'Sandra,' he replied, introducing for the hell of it an extra quaver into his voice.

'You meathead,' she shrieked at Matt, 'I threw the egg, not him.'

'I'm sorry, ma'am,' said Joe, turning. 'We have to go right now.'

With a yelp Sandra leapt up and fastened her limbs on his back, digging her fingers into his ears.

And as the siren wail could be heard moving round the yard, the American President had reached a moment of glutinous sentimentality. For ages his team had been looking for a testimonial to the special relationship by a British Prime Minister other than Winston Churchill. They had checked out Macmillan, but he was mainly famous for that crack, allegedly made to Eden, that the British were Greeks to the American Romans. Macmillan's point was that the Brits were learned, subtle and subservient, while the Americans were crude, energetic and dominating. This displeased the President's speechwriters as being patronizing to just about everyone. Also, it sounded kind of kinky, like something a prostitute might stick on a card in a phone booth. 'Greek Service Available', 'Roman Offered,' 'I'll be Greek to your Roman'.

Then they had found a few useful phrases from Margaret Thatcher, but were told that you could not mention Thatcher approvingly at a London dinner party any more, let alone in an important Presidential speech.

They briefly investigated the works of Edward Heath. A White House staffer read a book called *Sailing* in the hope that it might contain a reference to the beauty of trans-atlantic links, or an account of the shock of joy in the breast of that old matelot as he spied the coast of Newfoundland. He was disappointed. Heath did not seem to like America much.

The White House researcher did not bother to consult the oeuvre of Major or Wilson or Callaghan on the ground that any citation would lack the necessary uplift, and everyone had frankly forgotten about Sir Alec Douglas Home. So it was with a joyful cry that late one night in the West Wing a bright intern called Dee came upon the following emetic passage recited by A.J. Balfour to a Pilgrims' dinner on his return from a visit to America in 1917: 'We both spring from the same root. Are we not bound together forever? Will not our descendants say that we are brought together and united for one common purpose, in one common understanding – the two great branches of the English speaking race?'

Of course it was over the top and yet in a funny way it caught the imagination of hundreds of people in the hall. MPs thought mawkishly of the conflict they barely remem-bered but which their parents and grandparents certainly did, and perhaps took part in. Cameron felt a flush on her neck. How odd, she thought: for all his bumbling inarticulacy, this President had somehow captured her anterior feelings about Britain and America, before they had been stewed with the cynicism of Adam and his friends.

She liked the idea of two branches. For some reason she momentarily visualized this happy pair of boughs against the bright blue sky. She and Adam were the ultimate twigs of each vast ramification, caressing in the upper air before bringing forth their buds. Her eyes searched for him now, and found him standing up against the wall on the right on her side of the chamber.

He looked back at her so humorously, his teeth contrasting with his fabulous tan, like a row of Orbit sugar free chewing gum tablets, that she felt oddly ashamed. She felt embarrassed at having succumbed yet again to the pan Anglo-Saxon myth and bashful about loving him so much.

He mouthed something. Instinctively she knew the word must be 'bollocks'.

She sent back reciprocal waves of approval and between them the French Ambassador gave a saurian wink: 'C'est bien de bollocks, ça!' he whispered.

With a ping of sadness, Cameron whisked away her vision of the Anglo-American branches, as one might hide one's embarrassing painting at the school exhibition. Of course Adam was right, and she knew one of the points he would make.

Britain slavishly followed America in the war on terror. She helped her take out the Taliban. British taxpayers coughed up more than 5 billion pounds to gratify the neocons of Washington and remove Saddam Hussein. Whither thou goest I will go, said Britain to America as Ruth said to Naomi. When the war on terror yielded its first spoils and British subjects were arrested in Afghanistan on suspicion of being members of Al-Qaeda, Britain dutifully assented to their incarceration without trial, without due process, without any regard to the ancient principle of habeas corpus in a mysterious camp in Cuba.

From time to time the men were pictured in the British press, kneeling blindfolded behind barbed wire or being ferried on stretchers in their orange prison suits when they engaged in a hunger strike. British citizens were being held without charge or access to lawyers in the a-legal extraterritorial fourth dimension of an American army camp on a communist island on suspicion of being on the slightly more anti-Western side of a war between two sets of bearded Islamists somewhere in Central Asia. It requires concentration, however, to remain scandalized over a matter of principle.

Soon the British public had forgotten about the infamies of Camp X-ray, eclipsed as they were by the scandals of Abu Ghraib. The Prime Minister made the deathless remark that he would not seek the return of these Britons to Britain because there would not be much chance of securing a conviction. He got away with it, so completely was Britain prepared to subordinate her interests.

And how had the Americans behaved, Adam would say, when Britain was fighting her own war on terror? Irish Republicans blew up pubs and fish and chip shops, and cars and rubbish bins. They tried to blow up the stock exchange in Canary Wharf in plots that could have been as calamitous as the bombing of the Twin Towers. They murdered and maimed hundreds of civilians, and yet Americans moronically passed round the hat for them in Boston and in New York. American Presidents invited IRA leaders to the White House and shook hands with them on the lawn in defiance of the wishes of Downing Street.

They didn't care whether they gave legitimacy to these cruel and bitter men; they cared about the Irish vote. And when Britain wanted to extradite Irish terrorist suspects to the UK to face the due processes of the law, Washington did not want to know.

'That,' said Adam, 'is the American idea of a war on terror.'

Now she could hear – as could everyone else in the hall – the perplexing noise of a siren moving round the yard outside. It could be a police car, thought Cameron; it could at a pinch be a fire engine.

But deep in her guilty heart she knew it must be an ambulance. She looked again for Adam, but now he had his back to her.

In the Metropolitan Police Ops Room, both Purnell and Bluett were standing and shouting.

'Jesus H. Christ,' said Purnell.

'What in the name of holy fuck?' asked Bluett.

No fewer than five separate CCTV cameras were recording the fast advance of an ambulance, licence plate L64896P, and bearing the livery of the Bilston and Willenhall Primary Care Trust, round New Palace Yard towards the old glazed wrought-iron porch which is the Members' Entrance to the House of Commons.

'Abort, abort, abort, abort, abort,' said Deputy Assistant Commissioner Purnell.

'We don't abort yet, my friend,' said Bluett. 'We got snipers on the roof. We shoot on goddam sight.'

CHAPTER THIRTY-THREE
1010 HRS

Jason Pickel was still alone on the roof, waiting for Indira to come back, and yet he was surrounded by people. There were camp Plantagenets with tilted necks and two fingers raised in benediction, or they would be raised if the fingers had survived a century and a half of sulphur and pigeon dung.

There were carved princesses whose pie crust drapery had been eaten away by wind and rain. And there were beasts. There were heraldic animals on the roof of a kind not conducive to anyone's peace of mind. Jason stared at the gargoyle before him, crouched over the gutter. The elements had played leprosy with his features. Pollution and precipitation had made streaks on the limestone beneath his clammy paws as though they dripped black blood. His tail was nearly gone, his ear had been chewed off by time, his eye and nose had been devoured and his fanged jaws were open in a perpetual scream.

That's me, thought Jason Pickel. That's what they did to me. Because it might have been all right, he had long since decided, if that English reporter had shown the slightest sense of responsibility.

He had put Pickel's name in the story. Of course the US Army was good about it. He had been given counselling and support. It had been made clear to him that there was no question of inquiry or any other disciplinary procedure. But out there on the peacenik internet the name Pickel became a synonym for callous murder. When Iraqi rebels shot down helicopters full of American soldiers heading off R&R, or when GIs were bumped off on street corners, the' website polemicists always reminded their readers of the Pickel business.

It was just one example, they said, of the brutal fire-and-forget approach of the occupying power. In a long and ball-saching article in some left-wing magazine Barry White had returned to the subject. Was it not outrageous, he suggested, that the families of Pickel's victims were living without sanitation or electricity, deprived of their breadwinner, while Pickel lived it up in Iowa? A group called Wiltshire Women against War sent him a round robin letter addressed to Sergeant Pickel US Army. Some BBC producer had even rung his ex darling Wanda, and suggested he was a war criminal, and would Wanda like to come on a day-time TV show, and he wasn't too sure that Wanda had disagreed.

'Paw,' said Jason Junior one day when they were ambling along a mall in search of ice cream, 'how many guys did you kill out there in Eye-raq? Was it twenty?'

'No, son.'

'Because Carl's mum said you killed twenty.'

'No, Junior, there were six poor souls that died.'

'So was it you against six, then? I wish I could have seen it.'

'No you don't, kiddo.'

'I would of got my gun and aimed at them and *pow*, *pow*, *pow*, *pow*,' said Junior, massacring the waddling crowd of shoppers. 'Paw,' concluded the six-year-old, swelling with inspiration, 'if I'd been there I would of shot them all for you.'

At the memory of this conversation Jason was filled with such a flood of sentimental self-pity that his sniper's vision became blurred.

When the ambulance cleared the security barrier and braked noisily in front of the Members' Entrance, he was lost in meditation on the injustice of the world, and the willingness of citizens in a democracy to persecute those that protect them. He had so many denunciatory letters from anti-American ginger groups, from Balham to Helsinki, that he at one stage thought of changing his name. Now he wondered again: what kind of name did he want?

Down below him Jones the Bomb pulled the handbrake and got out of the driver's cabin. Sixty feet above him the sharpshooter rested his barrel on the gargoyle's ears and brooded again on the options.

For Pickel read gherkin, thought Pickel. Or perhaps O'Nion?

He looked absently at the ambulance men as they disembarked and then he looked again. Thought has no language. Our synapses work too fast for any verbal articulation and the same goes a fortiori for a US Army sharpshooter. The process of ratiocination is conducted in what computer programmers would call a machine language, in which concepts are spliced and bumped together at the speed of light, and it is only in retrospect that we can identify the path of our logic.

In the non-articulated machine language of thought, the following ideas tripped like bouncing electrons across his mental screen.

Dark men.

White van.

Ambulance.

Getting out.

Something funny.

Bulky waistcoats.

Terrorists.

Shoot them.

Dark men.

TV crew.

Could be nothing.

Could be something.

No time.

Dark men.

White van.

Car in Baghdad.

Could be innocent.

Could have been innocent.

No time.

Shoot first.

Wait a second.

Jason Pickel's pulse rate climbed. His palms began to sweat. He applied one big pale unblinking eye to the telescopic scope and located Habib in his sights.

The cross-hairs met exactly over the terrorist's breastbone, and a bar of sacred music started playing in his brain. He did not articulate the words, and he'd never worked out why that particular Anglican hymn was always associated in his mind with this terminal moment. The tune was 'When I survey the wondrous cross'.

Now the four men were moving over the cobbles towards the curlicued porch of the Members' Entrance. And all the while Jason Pickel was reminding himself that there could be a wholly innocent explanation, and all the while keeping Habib in his sights.

'What's all this, then?' asked one of the two policemen at the Members' Entrance. They were both in shirtsleeves, and carrying short nose submachine guns.

'Someone has been hurt!' yelled Jones the Bomb. 'He is injured.' At this stage, in all logic, the plot should have been thwarted. It was just conceivable that an ambulance – through the fault of no one in particular – could get past two police barriers. But it was incredible in retrospect that Jones, Dean, Haroun and Habib, should have somehow bluffed their way past two more armed and highly capable officers. And when the Metropolitan Police came to analyse what had gone wrong, they did indeed find it difficult to blame anyone.

When six months later an inquiry under Lord Justice Rushbrooke produced its findings, the conclusion, insofar as there was a conclusion, was that it was just one of those things. If the two armed policemen had been depicted by a cartoonist, they would have had big question marks in thought bubbles ballooning over their heads.

'Huh,' said their faces. 'Why is an Asian TV crew getting out of an ambulance?'

They could see there was something louche about the business. Jason could smell it from sixty feet up, and Roger Barlow, who was still charging across the yard, knew it for ding-dang sure.

No, when they came to work out how a quartet of barely competent suicide bombers had finally penetrated

Westminster Hall, they could not find it in their hearts to criticize the police, nor could they convincingly point the finger at the US Army sharpshooter, the Lieutenant formerly known as Pickel. Most newspapers leapt to the conclusion that he was suffering from a kind of nervous paralysis produced by his 'Dad' flashbacks.

Look at the analogies, they trilled. 'S obvious, innit!

Just like the fateful white GMC car of Baghdad, the ambulance challenged the poor Pickel to respect the sanctity of its insignia. The one was covered in duct tape spelling TV; the other had huge letters saying ambulance. No wonder, they postulated, that he had yibbed out.

Once again, they said, he saw dark young men of suspicious mien approaching in a mysterious vehicle.

Once more, he had only a few seconds in which to act. Either he could dispense lethal violence, or a calamity would befall those he was sworn to protect. At that critical moment, said the laptop psychoanalysts, Pickel's brain flopped over and died like a jellyfish with sunstroke.

He couldn't hack it, they suggested. They saw in their imaginations, and wrote without fear of contradiction, how the gun slipped from his wet fingers, how he vibrated like a medium, how his eyes rolled back like Baron Samedi and the perspiration sprung from his brow like the drops from a shaken colander.

His nostrils were filled with the flashback aroma of charred Iraqi, they said, and his throat, they suggested, was constricted by shame.

Not for the first time, they wrote rubbish. What happened was this.

With the help of the gargoyle's shoulder, Pickel was on the point of saving the day. He could have put Jones down with one high velocity round, and then the others as well, because he was not only the quickest and best, but he was also full of desire to vindicate his actions in Baghdad.

This time he would get it right, he would be Pickel the hero, not Pickel the walnut, and voices in his head were urging him on. And not just metaphorically.

'Come in Pickel!' yelled the furry receiver in his ear. It was Captain Ricasoli of the Presidential Protection Squad, suspended in the specially adapted Black Hawk. And even as Ricasoli was telling him the horrible truth about the ambulance, Pickel was bawling out his orders over New Palace Yard.

Roger Barlow jumped, the terrorists turned as one, the policeman boggled.

'Hold it!' yelled the sharpshooter. 'Hold it right there or I . . .'

Every sniper has the same phobia.

He takes his position as a big game hunter settles in his hide. He watches the tethered antelope and the trees, and the ripples on the river, and he stares so closely at the 180 degrees in front of him that he could draw it from memory. And in a hypnosis of intimate surveillance he forgets one possibility – that the tiger has been sensible enough to sneak up behind him and is about to bite his quivering rump.

So at the noise of the delicate subcontinental footfall Pickel turned around. Indira had not gone far away; she had merely climbed the ladder on to the pitched roof and stolen along the catwalk to a place out of earshot. There she had consulted her superiors and received unambiguous instructions from the Met.

Pickel was exhibiting signs of instability and she should do her best to disarm him, said her controller. It was only ten seconds later, so they later established, when the news came through about the rogue ambulance. They tried to reach the clever young Gujarati girl but she had turned off her radio, the better to steal up on her American colleague.

And now as he spun round she was almost upon him, looking at him with the motherly concern of a nurse in a loony bin.

'No, Jason,' she said and jumped him. She was brave, and other things being equal, right. Watching from the yard, Jones

& Co were puzzled to see the American officer disappear into a tangle of limbs, as Indira practised her jujitsu. It was long enough for Habib and Haroun to slink out of shot, one behind the protection of the Members' Entrance porch, the other in the lee of a policeman.

Even so Pickel might have pulled it off, once he had sat on Indira's head. He still had a clear shot at Jones, Dean and a good chance of hitting Haroun. He might still have earned a Congressional Medal of Honor. He might still have been graciously appointed by Her Majesty the Queen to the most excellent order of the British Empire, had he not spotted something out of the corner of his eye that made him think he was going mad.

It was that big puff of hair, that foaming crest he would know anywhere. It was that Limey journalist, it was that pisser of poison from the *Daily Mirror*. It was Barry White, who had used his disgusting good manners to seduce him with his satphone, and had fatally distracted him from his duties as a guard, and who had written his reputation into the dust, and his marriage into oblivion.

Barry White was ambling with his pass to the public entrance, thinking that the *Mirror* wouldn't conceivably want more than a couple of pars about the speech, and plotting his assignation for lunch, wondering why the people in the yard were all staring at the roof, and quite unaware that one of his most conspicuous victims had drawn a bead on his head and was fantasizing about how it would look when he pulled the trigger.

When he was a child in Iowa, Pickel used to look forward to visiting old Grandmaw Pickel, a woman as profoundly religious as she was deaf, who had a fetish for growing gigantic vegetables. Every year she would compete at the Town Fair with extra-large marrows, super-size squashes, and prodigious zucchini. Late one August evening she had taken him to the pumpkin patch and shown him her latest entrant, a colossal orange globe glowing in the gloom. He had never seen anything like it. It had winner written all over it, and as the day of the fair approached all Grandmaw's friends were invited to witness the almost visible expansion of its flesh, and to feel their morale sink.

Alas, Grandmaw had cheated. She had no special talent for manure; it was no priestly incantation that plumped the great gourd. When no one was looking she had tied a piece of cotton thread to the tap on the side of the house and she had run it to the pumpkin, and she had tied the thread to a needle, and stuck that in the top of the vegetable.

Then drip, drip, drip, she had opened the tap just a little and fed her pet continuously for weeks, with the pumpkin equivalent of anabolic steroids. Young Jason would never forget the moment of tragic revelation. On the day of the fair the whole family was assembled in the vegetable garden to see the raising of the pumpkin. Three male Pickels between them were scarcely able to hoist it on to a wheelbarrow, but Grandmaw wanted a photograph of herself holding it aloft, much as Hemingway would insist on commemorating the capture of an enormous marlin.

She reached down with both hands and gripped the freshly cut stalk as thick as a baby's arm, and she straddled her legs into a squat-thrust and heaved. And because it was she whose beefy genes had made Jason so big and strong, she prevailed. With the triumphant grunt of a female Ukrainian shot-putter, she lifted it up, first to chest height, then to her head. She smiled for the camera, and the scene was seared in Jason's memory, his grandmother backlit by the sun, and the fluorescent orange vegetable and everyone laughing and clapping.

Because all at once there occurred an event as sudden and horrifying as the conflagration of a hydrogen-filled airship. The pumpkin exploded. Fattened beyond endurance, unable to cope with the demands of gravity, the skin of the pumpkin popped like a balloon and splattered Grandmaw and Jason and everyone else with clods of waterlogged mulch and pulp and gunk.

Yeah, one moment a sphere, the next moment his grandmother holding nothing but a stalk, and that, thought Jason as he hummed his hymn and located Barry White in his sights, was what was about to happen to this guy's head. Except that Indira, dazed and winded beneath him, chose that moment to fight back.

Nothing could be worse, she decided, than the smegmatic oblivion of her current position. Rotating her head she bit what she took to be Jason Pickel's inner thigh, but was in fact his left testicle.

'Yowk,' said Jason Pickel, and his finger withdrew from the trigger guard.

Barry White walked on, quite oblivious, round the corner of the Members' Entrance and through the swing doors of the South Porch into Westminster Hall.

CHAPTER THIRTY-FOUR
1011 HRS

'Jeee-zus,' said Jason, and tried to fight back. This time his finger clinched the trigger. The gun bucked.

The bang scattered the group in the yard. The bullet whined off the cobble and into a tree.

Jason shoved his left forefinger into Indira's mouth as though to pacify a baby, and squeezed off two more rounds.

Even the sharpest sharpshooter finds it hard to cope with an Indian hellcat scratching and biting at his groin. *Pyo-yow-yoing* the first went over the heads of the policemen and they rolled into defensive positions, behind the porch and out of the line of sight of the deranged Yank on the roof.

Thwok, the next round took off the gargoyle's right ear

and a fourth ascended in a steep parabola, to land unnoticed ten miles away in a garden in Highbury. Jason did not fire a fifth shot. Barry White had eluded him. Indira was once more quiescent. The British police officers were pointing their trembling carbines at the roof.

Jones, Habib, Haroun and Dean had slipped into the Members' Entrance of the House of Commons, like deer suddenly lost in the woods. Roger Barlow ran after them.

On the roof Jason and Indira disentangled themselves, and stared at each other in a miserable post-coital way. 'Where are you going?' said Indira, as Pickel slung his rifle over his shoulder. But the American was off singing his song of crucifixion. 'When I survey the wondrous cross,' he hummed as he ran down the roof beam, sure footed as a marmoset, 'on which the Prince of Glory died, my richest gain I count but loss,' he puffed down the stairs and sprinted along the parapet in the direction of Westminster Hall, 'and pour contempt on all my pride.'

Pickel's gun was not especially loud, and the four seal-bark shots meant nothing to most people in the hall, least of all the President, who chuntered gently on. To Cameron, whose ears were pricked for the unusual, it sounded potentially bad. And for some of the audience at the far end there was certainly a distraction in the noise of Jones's entreaties, and the coppers falling over, and Jason Pickel's shouted orders. Some of them vaguely paid attention to the banging of the swing doors in the Members' Entrance, and the sound of running feet dimly in the corridor to their left.

But in the Ops Room, there was a kind of frenzy, and they boiled and thrashed and snatched at scraps of information, like a tankful of fish at feeding time.

'We've got shooting,' said Deputy Assistant Commissioner Purnell. 'We've got shooting in the yard. Four shots,' he said, holding the receiver to his ear.

'Four shots?' said Bluett. 'Didn't the tow-truck guy say there were four of them? *Whoo-hoo*. I bet damn Pickel has pegged those babies.'

'What do you mean, pegged them?'

'Shot their motherfucking asses.'

'Let's hope so, my old mate.'

Jones confidently led the way through the Members' cloak-room, a route he had long ago identified as the least heavily secured. No eyes beheld him, even at this stage, as he pushed open the oak swing doors, save the sightless bronze orbs of one Randall Cremer, parliamentarian of the nineteenth century.

No alarms sounded, no sensors were triggered. For a moment he thought he would be able to complete the twenty yards of the cloakroom entirely unseen . . .

Whoosh, whoosh went the shoe brush, wielded with manic zeal by Woodrow Watson, Labour MP for Pontefract and Castleford. He was standing in the corner of that dim silent place to which no one is admitted who has not been elected by the sovereign people of Britain. It is like a scene from a 1950s film about public school life. There is rank upon rank of coat hooks, with red tape nooses into which MPs are supposed to put their swords, and long-forgotten macs and duffle coats suspended as if in some spooky human abattoir.

At the far end is a mirror, a TV screen, a letter writing set, some scurvy hairbrushes and an ancient set of electric scales, which tired, fat, dejected MPs mount and remount, jettisoning still more from their pockets, in the hope of achieving a favourable reading. At the near end by the swing doors from New Palace Yard, are the shoeshine things.

Here, since the break-up of his marriage, Woodrow Watson was spending more and more time. He fully understood the psychological meaning of his actions. By shining his shoes he was doing what he could to bring back lustre and perfection to his life. His heart was a mess, scuffed, battered, shredded. But the shoes could be made whole and clean. The more he hurt the harder he polished. Around Westminster his colleagues bickered and plotted. Speeches were made. Reputations rose and fell. But Woodrow Watson stood in the twilight and buffed. He was a buffer, he told himself. At fifty-six he was on the threshold of bufferdom, and this was his buffer zone.

First he ground the polish in, smearing it over the welts and into the cavity in the instep. Then he left one shoe to dry while whoosh, whoosh, he began his obsessive frottage. His standards were by now very high. He no longer accepted the sheen of a polished apple. Even when his wrist ached and the lactic acid was building in his bicep, and he had produced the kind of vitreous surface that would get top marks at Sandhurst, Woodrow Watson was not satisfied. He liked it when all the crinkly surfaces of the leather sparkled with tinsel points of halogen brightness. That was the good bit; that made him feel calm. As he rotated the shoe like an Amsterdam jeweller, he felt momentarily proud of his work and with that brief surge of self-worth, he was able to obliterate his wife's desertion.

The trouble was that he needed his fix ever more frequently. He was getting through tins of taxpayers' polish. His nails looked as though he'd been mining coal, and though that was once a proper function of a Labour MP, his colleagues knew what he was up to, and he was starting to feel ashamed.

So when the funny Asian- or Arab-looking TV crew burst through the door, Woodrow Watson tensed. Hardly daring to breathe, one hand clenching the shoe, the other poised in mid-buff, his eyes locked involuntarily on Dean.

Oh God, thought Watson. It's probably a documentary about the peculiar habits of MPs. Blasted media. Don't they know they're not allowed in here?

The three others walked on quickly to the far door, but the young half-caste was still staring at him.

'Yer gotta stop it,' said the kid.

Watson thought he must be hallucinating. Who was this epiphany sent to piss around with his brain?

'It's madness,' said the hallucination, and Woodrow Watson could take it no more.

He knew it was eccentric to stand all day polishing his shoes, but he was damned if he was going to accept any kind of counsel from this intruder, who had in any event, no right to be here at all. He unstuck his terrified tongue from the roof of his mouth.

'You . . . You . . .'

But then one of the two Arab cameramen stalked back down the cloakroom. To the horror of Woodrow Watson, the young man stuck his face unconscionably close.

'Please, man,' said Dean, 'yow gotta get help.' It was too much. The shoe dropped from one hand, the brush from the other.

He had to get help.

He knew he had to get help. But he didn't need this squit to tell him.

Roger Barlow should easily have overhauled the four terrorists; and under any normal circumstances would have done so. But his legs were tired after so much running, and his feet were dragging.

The result was that he snared himself in one of the long black cables that coiled through the Members' Entrance and fed the TV lights and the cameras. He tripped, and fell flat on his face.

As he put out his arms to break his fall, both hands somehow became caught up in other rubbery snakes of electric flex. He righted himself, and the writhing lianas wrapped themselves about his arms and shoulders.

Oh for the Lord's sake, he said to himself.

Had Roger been in the mood for literary echoes, he might have caught his resemblance to the Vatican sculpture of Laocoon, who warned in vain of the Trojan horse, and who was devoured by sea-snakes.

Instead, he thought that even by his own energetic standards, he was making a bit of a berk of himself. He wondered what his wife and children would make of his performance, and remembered that it was the second time he had been shot at that day.

As the Oedipal four-year-old had once told him with a withering look, when refusing to unlock the French windows to let him in: 'I am sorry. You are not an Aztec.'

The President had reached a delicate point in his speech. He had invoked the spirit of Anglo-American cooperation. He had taken his audience with him and stormed the Normandy beaches hand in hand. Churchill had been cited so often that the French Ambassador was calling for *le sac de vomissement*.

Now, however, he was required to justify Anglo-American cooperation in Iraq. He sucked, and gave a birdy squint around the hall. So when the camera crew slipped in through the door down on the far right, the President was one of the few who noticed. He also observed the flustered fellow who followed them, a few seconds later, and stared around.

Not that the President saw anything sinister in these arrivals. He was just thinking what a grim old place this was and wouldn't it be nice if they covered those dungeon walls with paintings, but he got on with his homily. 'It's easy to have friends in the good times. Everybody wants to know a man when he's up. It's when you've taken a big knock and you're down and you're frightened. That's when you find out who really cares. That's how you know who your real friends are. And that's how we in America feel about Britain.' The President had felt so passionately about this bit that he had tried to draft it himself. He'd shoved in lots of biblical stuff about the road to Jericho and falling among thieves, and those who passed by on the other side.

The State Department had warned that his savage rebuke against the Priest and the Levite might be taken as some kind of reference to France and Germany, and the President had said too damn right it was a reference to France and Germany, but the striped pants would have none of it, not at a time of building bridges. So the President just got on with eulogizing Britain, the Good Samaritan, aware that his audience was becoming restless, and of the peculiar camera crew sidling fast up the right-hand wall.

Roger Barlow might have gone after them, and fully intended to raise the alarm. But he was intercepted. 'Roger,' cried someone, grabbing his arm and hauling him into the empty seat beside him.

'Oh, hello, Chester,' said Roger warily. He hadn't seen Chester for more than twenty years, or at least not in the flesh. He had seen him plenty of times on TV. He had watched *Chester Minute*, de Peverill's introduction to top speed cookery, and *Chester Little Bit More*. He had caught the tail end of *Chester's Gourmet Christmas*, whilst vaguely searching for something smutty on the high number satellite channels. In a hotly contested field there was no one on earth whom Roger found more deliriously irritating, though he sometimes felt rather ashamed of his feelings. In his heart, he knew that the TV chef might be bumptious, but was basically amiable. It had begun at university, when Roger had expended Herculean effort on persuading a very beautiful girl to go out with him. Barely had he succeeded when Chester started to pester her with lewd invitations.

'How do you know you prefer steak & chips,' read Chester's Valentine card, 'When you have never tried foie gras?' Roger thought this cheeky. To his slight annoyance his girlfriend thought it amusing. And so after university it was with some prickliness that he had watched Chester's TV chef persona – laddish but just pissionate, pissionate about food – rise and swell, like one of his very own soufflés.

What the hell was Chester doing here, anyhow?

'Oi,' he gasped, as the Arab film crew continued up the left-hand wall.

'What's up mate?' Chester whispered. Among the chef's affectations, even though his family came from Godalming, was a faux Australian accent.

'You see that lot there.'

'Which lot, Roger, mon ami?'

'The chaps with the cameras and what not.'

'The film crew?'

'Yes, I think something pretty ghastly might be about to happen.' Roger lurched to his feet and several people nearby went 'ssst'.

Chester gripped his arm again. 'Sit down, Rog, or you'll embarrass us all.'

'But I think they could be Arab terrorists.'

'If you want to make a complete wazzock of yourself in front of a thousand people while the President of the United States is speaking, you go right ahead.'

'But it's my fault they're in here.'

'Good for you, cocker, and frankly I'm glad to see that someone from your party is supporting a bit of ethnic TV.'

It came back to him that Chester de Peverill was thought to be stonkingly cool. His whole schtick was to recreate mankind as a hunter-gatherer with himself, Chester, leading the rediscovery of ancient flavours. He would be filmed scrumping for crab apples or gorging on offal rejected by even the most outré of game butchers. No weed or windfall was deemed too ridiculous for his hammered copper saucepans.

Across the Home Counties girls boiled up nettles for their men, so persuasive was his advocacy, and when suppertime ended in gagging on the hairy stalks, they didn't blame Chester; they always blamed themselves for getting the recipe wrong. They loved his 'I eat anything' approach, with its flagrant sexual message.

At one point Chester's PR people had let it be known that he had kept his wife's placenta in a fridge and then fried it up with some little Spanish onions – a revelation that was false, but which did nothing to damage his popularity. 'You poseur,' Roger thought, not without admiration, 'you shameless poseur with your clustering curls.' But he stayed in his seat.

'As you know,' the President went on, 'it has become a cliché to say that the terrorist is like a mosquito. He's difficult to spot, he causes an awful lot of bad feeling, a paranoia wherever he goes, and his bite is lethal. That's why it's no use just standing in the dark and slapping ourselves. That's why we decided to drain that swamp. We did it together in Afghanistan, we did it in Iraq. And I believe, in the words of Winston Churchill, that our liberation of those countries will go down as one of the most unsordid acts in history.'

The French Ambassador stuck out his tongue, placed his right index finger upon it and made a retching noise.

'Whatever people now say, we know that Iraqi regime had developed weapons of mass destruction, and had Saddam remained in power, we can be certain that he would either have used them or shipped them to other rogue states around the world.'

'Yeah,' said a satirical English voice, loud enough to be heard by ten rows forward and back. 'Like America.'

It was Barry White, who had slipped efficiently into a seat near the back. It would normally have been unthinkable even for a tosser like Barry to heckle the President, never mind that he was leader of the free world, whatever that meant these days.

He was a guest of the country and it was just rude to talk

during his speech. But there was something funny in the air, a pre-menstrual irrationality, the panting swollen-veined tension that precedes a downpour in July.

The President didn't catch the remark but he saw its effect ripple out as a gust might catch a particular patch of corn as it passes over a prairie, turning up the dark undersides of the ears. 'And we all know that there are people mad and sick enough to use those weapons.'

'Yeah, like you,' said Barry White, and the crowd swayed around him again, some indicating that he should put a sock in it.

'Upon innocent people.'

'You said it, pal,' said the heckler.

'And to all those who blamed my country for overreacting to the threat, I say to them that the terrorist is no respecter of frontiers or nationalities. There were 67 Britons who died in the World Trade Center. There were 23 Japanese, 16 Jamaicans, 17 Colombians, 15 Filipinos, and . . .'

'And a partridge in a pear tree,' said Barry White, to the disgust of those around him.

'. . . a total of 32 other nations lost lives. It was an attack upon the world, and I believe that it has been the world's fight that we in America have been fighting.' The President had feared that this was the most controversial part of his speech. It had echoes of that line – those who are not with us are against us – which had particularly cheesed off the cheese eaters. He feared with one lobe of his brain that the British Labor guys would all stand up now, and whip off their jackets and reveal 'Not In My Name' T-shirts, or perhaps that this would be the moment for the walk-out. But no, he appeared to have got away with it. He had a feeling that someone was heckling him, but the guy was too British or too cowardly to do it properly. What he noticed again as he flickered his gaze around the mediaeval hall, was the odd progress of that film crew.

You know how you spot a gecko on a wall and one moment it is in spot A and the next moment, when you glance again, it has somehow moved undetected to spot B. So the four characters were moving up towards him, hugging the grey cliff of stone, waggling their cameras at him. Had he looked harder, the President might have noticed that they had changed the order of march, so that the mixed-race-looking guy was being chivvied along by one of the darker-skinned fellows.

The President was more interested in finishing the text on his lectern. 'And never forget that among those who died on 9/11 were 58 entirely innocent Muslims. It cannot be repeated too often that this war on terrorism is not a war on Islam. We do not have any quarrel with any people in the Muslim world, and I want to say on a personal level as a Christian, how much I admire and respect their great religion.' There was some uncertain clapping at this point. People could see that there was much to respect in Islamic culture. It was not obvious why this should be particularly moving to a Christian unless the President was somehow asserting his approval of mutually antagonistic and fundamentalist creeds of all kinds.

'It is not Islam which drives young men and women brutally to take their lives and the lives of others.'

'No,' said Barry White in his irritating voice, much like Muttley, the dog that accompanies Dick Dastardly in the Wacky Races. 'It's the Israeli Defence Force.'

For some reason this sally was loud enough to reach a much larger section of the audience, and the President's own ears caught the word Israel.

He scowled. He didn't like it at all. He began to wonder whether indeed he would get to the end without some audience reaction so unacceptable that the US networks would be obliged to report it.

CHAPTER THIRTY-FIVE

1021 HRS

'It is not Islam that turns these sad and impressionable young men and women to terror. It is those who knowingly pervert the teachings of that great value system, and who corrupt these young people, and who lead them into the path of evil.' He looked up again and holy mackerel, the four Arab geckos had scooted a long way up the wall, they were there just off to his right, there where the skirt of grey stone steps began to rise from the floor to the dais from which he was speaking.

The President momentarily caught the eye of the leader. He was glancing up from his camera viewfinder and there was something in his manner that was, yes, reptilian.

'Our struggle and our fight is with those who would turn a religion of peace into a utensil of torture and killing . . .'

The word 'torture' produced a predictable heckle.

'. . . And I tell you all now, and I tell all those who may now be following this speech across the world, that as long as I am Commander in Chief, the United States will pay any price, we will bear any burden, we will travel any distance to track down those who would kill or harm our citizens or other innocents of the earths. My Lords, Ladies, Members of the House of Commons, Honourable and Esteemed Friends and Members of the British Cabinet . . .'

'Hey!' exclaimed Roger, quite loudly this time, as he saw Jones the Bomb begin his final scuttle towards the sweep of steps. 'Sscht,' said everyone. Chester de Peverill squeezed his arm in the most patronizing way, put his finger to his lips and winked. Roger gave up. He sat down and kept silent out of fear of embarrassment, the fear that prevents the Englishman from ever being as truly entrepreneurial as the

American, the fear that causes him to be exceptionally prone to prostate cancer.

From his vantage point leaning against the far wall, Adam Swallow looked with amazement at the group. But where was the cripple? Where was the man from Abu Ghraib? He wheeled around to find Benedicte, and she refused to meet his eyes.

In the Ops Room, Deputy Assistant Commissioner Purnell was filled with sudden and evanescent satisfaction. 'Quiet!' he yelled at Bluett and the rest of the room. 'I'm getting something about fatalities in New Palace Yard. What's that? A dark-skinned man has been shot, in the ambulance . . . What's that? A traffic warden? Oh Jesus, we know about him. What about the others? . . . The others, for Christ's sake. No, not the man on the roof. The man on the roof is on our side, you idiots. What happened to the four TV crew? What do you mean you thought they were just TV crew? You mean they aren't dead? Then where the hell are they? Oh sweet Mary mother of God, don't tell me you just let them in the frigging hall.'

'Where,' said Bluett, 'in the name of God is Pickel?'

The President glanced down at a group of the most senior British politicians from the Government and the Opposition who were sitting in the first three ranks. To his very slight surprise he saw that between him and the higher echelons of British politics, crawling towards him up the steps, was that Arab film crew. It seemed that the game of gecko grandmother's footsteps was about to come to an end.

The President had no time to pause, no time to think, but he thrust out his chin and filled his lungs.

'I thank you from the bottom of my heart and on behalf of all the people of my country for your steadfastness, your courage and the clarity with which you have seen the risk we all face and the readiness with which you have responded and I believe that future generations will look back on this alliance of ours and ponder the marvel that once again we too, Britain and America, stood firm against evil. Because I am certain that no matter how bitter the struggle may be, no matter how irksome the security precautions we must take, the time will surely come when we will overcome the – what the hell?'

Whatever abstract noun was fated, in the view of the President, to be overcome by the Atlantic Alliance, that audience would never know.

PART THREE

I COME TO BURY CAESAR

CHAPTER THIRTY-SIX

1024 HRS

Across the hall, behind pillars, behind doors, at strategic points in the audience, in helicopters overhead and wherever the speech was being monitored on television, American security men gasped or swore or howled and pulled out their weapons, just as the news was breaking in their Curly Wurlies.

They were too late. 'That will do, Mr President,' said Jones the Bomb, clicking the handcuff over the President's limp wrist. Then he held their hands up together, as the umpire raises the hand of a boxer to show that their fates are now conjoined.

That was it, thought Jones. He had done it. Whatever happened now, he would join the ranks of the immortals for this action. In Mecca, in Medina, in all the holy places of Islam, babes unborn would lisp the name of Jones. He was also aware that he was very likely to be shot dead in the next ten seconds, unless he could explain to the shooters that this was a bad idea.

'If you don't mind,' he said, taking the microphone, 'it will be simplest if I do the talking from now on. I should like to begin by pointing out to anyone who is thinking of shooting me that the bomb I am wearing is connected by electronic sensors to my heart and will detonate as soon as it senses that there is no pulse.

'If that happens, America will lose a president, Britain will lose much of its government and the rest of you will be in a very bad way. So here, as they say in the movies, are my demands.'

Cameron had already worked out what Benedicte and the two other Arabs, the ones sitting in front of her, would do next. The insight had been granted to another part of her brain, just as she watched Jones clicking on the handcuff. She was more interested in the behaviour of the French Ambassador. With what seemed now to be utter predictability, the man in the djelabah reached down under his seat in the movement she had seen him rehearse. He flipped off the brass plaque. It clacked backwards on to her toes, chipping the varnish.

'Hey,' said Cameron, and then regretted the incongruous pettiness of her complaint.

Here, the plaque reminded her, was the spot where Thomas More, patron saint of politicians, had been condemned to death. There was a point there somewhere, thought Cameron as she looked at the wrenched-off memorial, screws awry. The man's hairy wrist shot down into the darkness to produce a plastic bag marked 'RitePrice' out of which he removed two Schmidt MP rapid fire submachine guns, and gave one to his neighbour, and then produced another bag.

'*Mais Bénédicte,*' said the French Ambassador, turning to his girlfriend. The girl looked at the older man. She was beautiful, thought Cameron, with full red lips and skin that was startlingly pale for a Palestinian Arab.

'*Et alors?*'

'*Mais non,*' he shouted, and flung out an arm to restrain the two men as they rose. Benedicte al-Walibi kept her eyes fixed on the Ambassador but with one hand she tapped her Arab colleague on the arm, borrowed a Schmidt and shoved the muzzle hard into the soft fold under her lover's ribs.

'*Tais-toi, chéri,*' she said.

Out of the corner of her eye Cameron became suddenly aware that the Dutch Ambassador was on the verge of heroism. His father had fought the Nazis. His uncle had been present as one of the negotiators when South Moluccan terrorists had hijacked a Dutch train and started to massacre the passengers. He knew that violence sometimes had to be matched with violence for the salvation of society; and anyway he was full of the battle adrenalin and suppressed fury of one who has been freshly bombed by an ostrich egg.

He made a nostril noise like a kettle coming to the boil, and was on the point of hurling himself upon Benedicte when she whipped round and poked him in the chest with her gun. 'You shut up too, bald man,' she said. He slumped back.

When Cameron looked at him, with his morning dress streaked with the embryo of a flightless bird, with his expression of a stunned mullet, she felt instantly overcome. It was the shocking inversion of feminine aggression, it was the sight of the President, her President, handcuffed and humiliated. It was the gross impropriety of the submachine guns in this place to which even Parliamentarians were not allowed to bring their swords.

Along the bottom of her lashes brimmed tears as big as planets. She blinked. They splashed to the floor, on the plaque and on her feet. She looked up through the blur and saw someone walking through the rows towards her, unchecked by the gunmen.

He was someone she wanted to see, the man who would explain everything or at least provide her with a theory. 'Oh Adam,' she said, 'thank God.'

In the Scotland Yard Ops Room there was a moment of hush. Like all men in such positions, Deputy Assistant Commissioner Purnell and Colonel Bluett of the USSS were contemplating not just the imminence of carnage in Westminster Hall and the assassination of a president. They foresaw clearly the immolation of their own careers.

'Jesus Christ, what are we waiting for? I've got twenty-one guns in that hall.'

Without consulting Purnell, the American flipped open the switch that connected him to the earpieces of the men in the hall.

'Boys, this is Bluett. Who has got a line on these guys?'

From their vantage points around the hall, the lynx-eyed USSS men started to whisper their options into the Smarties on their lapels.

'Negative, sir: I've got a man with an Uzi at my gut.'

'Negative, sir: I'm way back here.'

'I got him, sir. I got that sucker whenever you want.' It was Lieutenant Alan Cabache.

High up and recessed into the east wall of Westminster Hall, just under the corbels of the hammerbeams, is a series of huge murky alcoves; hard to make out at any time, and almost invisible now in the overhead glow of the TV lights. In one of these alcoves Lieutenant Cabache had been waiting for an hour, hidden by the ancient friable skirts of Philippa of Hainault. He was covered with soot, and his legs ached from being braced against Philippa's rump. But it was all about to pay off.

Now he secretly slid his Glock barrel under Philippa's left breast and drew a bead on Jones, just fifty feet away, down and to his right.

'I got him, sir,' he repeated.

'Then whack him!' said Bluett.

'NO,' said Purnell. 'For God's sake, man, you heard what he said!'

'What's that, Stephen? Are you countermanding me here?'

'Too damn right, I am. You heard what he said. As soon as he dies, his fucking bomb goes off.'

'You believe that?'

Across the hall, the USSS men listened in despair. Who the hell was in charge here?

'I do believe it until we somehow find evidence to the contrary.'

'You do believe it.' A note of doubt had crept into Bluett's voice.

'Shall I shoot, sir?' asked Cabache, as quietly as he could.

'NO,' said Purnell.

'Uh, wait up, Cabache. Well, what do you frigging propose, Mr Commissioner?'

'Sir, I've got Downing Street on the line.' The Prime Minister, the head of MI5, the Cabinet Secretary, the Defence Secretary, the head of Counter-Intelligence and a new minister for Homeland Security were being hustled into Cabinet Office Briefing Room A, or Cobra. Normally, their number would have included the Home Secretary, but the Home Secretary was in Westminster Hall.

Now Purnell spoke to the British Prime Minister, on a 'secure' mobile, as he was jogged by his own agents towards the electronic nerve centre of Downing Street.

Like Purnell and Bluett, the Prime Minister had instantly seen that these events could be fatal to his career. So there was one point he stressed in his brief conversation with Purnell, namely that he, the Prime Minister, was taking political responsibility, of course, but no 'operational' responsibility. It would be quite wrong, the Prime Minister said, for him to second-guess the split-second decisions of the experts. That was why he, the Prime Minister, was going to leave such decisions to Purnell.

'With full cooperation, of course, with the Americans,' said the Prime Minister.

'Cooperation, sir?' said Purnell.

'And consultation.' Then the line went dead as the British leader was patched through to Washington.

'The first thing we do,' said Purnell, 'is find out about this business with the sensors. Is it possible to make a suicide bomb jacket like that?'

'I dunno, sir,' said Grover.

'Well don't hang around,' said Bluett. He didn't know whether he was entitled to give orders to Grover, but he was damn well going to give orders to someone.

The President and Jones the Bomb stood at the head of the congregation like a shackled pair of slaves about to be auctioned. As he waited for his yokemate to outline his demands the President looked and was not reassured. He saw a nose so hooked that Jones could easily touch it – and sometimes did, to the horror of anyone sitting opposite him in the Tube – with the tip of his tongue. He saw the bags under his eyes, shiny and dark as plum sauce; and now the eyes with their odd vibration were upon him.

'Out of the way,' hissed Jones.

The President was taken aback. 'Say what?'

'Move,' said Jones, shoving on the handcuff.

'Listen buddy, we're kind of hooked up here. If you want to let me go you'll be doing the right thing.'

'Shut up and move and say nothing more or else you'll be shot.' The President understood. So far they had been sharing the lectern, like a couple of pop stars crooning into the same microphone, and now Jones wanted to take charge. The President shuffled to the left and Jones began. He had been here a couple of times to case the joint and had picked up some of the essential history.

'Ladies and gentlemen, listen very carefully to me and do exactly as I say and no harm will come to you. I know that this is a traditional introduction to a speech by a lead terrorist, but in this case it happens to be true.

'Hundreds of years ago, more than 350 years ago, a king was put on trial on this very spot. His name was Charles and he was a bad king. He took the money that belonged to the poor people. He was oppressive and he acted in a way that was arrogant and outside the law. He believed that he had some kind of divine right to do what he wanted and so they brought him here and they put him on trial and then they chopp-ed off his head. In the country where I come from it is of course the practice that if people commit great crimes their heads are chopp-ed off. You like to say that this is barbaric and so I point out that all your great British democracy, all your Parliament comes from that moment when the King's head is chopp-ed and was that not the right thing to do?'

'No,' said Sir Perry Grainger, speaking for Henley-on-Thames in the royalist rump of Oxfordshire. 'It was completely wrong, and anyway, it's not chopp-ed, it's chopped.'

'Shut your face,' said Jones the Bomb, and located that bright red object eleven rows behind Cameron and the French Ambassador as he faced the hall and on the left.

'Well, you did ask,' said Sir Perry, but Jones had unstuck a Browning taped to the small of his back.

'Don't say another word or I will shoot.'

'All right, all right, keep your hair on.'

The noise of the automatic was so loud, reverberating off the flat flags and walls, that some thought the end had come and that Jones had let off his bomb.

The bullet was travelling in roughly the direction of Sir Perry, but connected first with the Dutch Ambassador's left ear. This was protected by a sturdy German-built hearing-aid, which clattered to the floor while the bullet flattened itself harmlessly 150 yards away against the far wall. The Dutchman groaned and started to bleed. Cameron put her arm around him. It really wasn't his day. A few seats away a distinguished lady peeress began to cry. A small puddle of pee formed beneath her chair. Black terror settled on the crowd.

'That bad king was put on trial by the people of England,' Jones resumed, 'and his head chop – his head was cut off.

Today' – he jerked the handcuff and the President's arm jerked in response – 'we have another bad ruler and another trial. This is a man who rules the world by force. He abuses human rights; he invades countries without any international authorization, just because he can, because he has the power. With his discriminatory trade policies he is keeping one billion people, the poorest people on earth, living on less than one dollar per day. With his depleted uranium shells he has been killing babies in Afghanistan.' At this the President rolled his eyes.

'Shut up,' said Jones, catching the movement from one of his panoptic irises.

'I didn't say anything,' said the President.

'Be quiet, you idiot!' said Jones and stuck his face so close, gun next to his cheek, that the President observed not just the eyes, but the awful pathology of a zit that had arisen when Jones was sixteen and exploded when he was seventeen, leaving a star-shaped depression in his forehead. The President was quiet. In the silence he could hear the sobbing that was spreading down the rows and the confused whispering of the security men into their lapels and the desperate chatter of the helicopter rotors overhead.

'Today is not just the trial of this bad man,' said Jones. 'It is the trial of America. Before the eyes of all the people of Britain and before the eyes of all the people of the world, I bring you this bad man to this place of history so that he and his country may answer for their crimes. But I do not presume to be the judge myself, I do not seize and abuse the law like this man does,' and he shook the cuffs again, so the President jerked like a crash dummy, 'nor will I even impose the death penalty like this man does' – *jerk jerk* – 'to poor mentally defective Negroes in Texas. Instead, everyone in this hall will have the chance to speak, yes, to speak in favour of him or against him, just like in a court of law, and then the world will judge him. Yes, the whole world will judge America and in a minute I will explain how it will be done, but first I must ask you all to surrender your mobile phones and I must ask all police and other agents to give up their weapons. Please throw them in the aisle; that's right, hurry up or else I'll shoot again and this time I may not miss.'

'Sir, it looks like he could easily be telling the truth on the heart sensor thing. Athletes buy them.'

'Thanks, Grover,' said Deputy Assistant Commissioner Purnell.

'Athletes?' said Bluett.

'Yessir. There's a thing called an exercise heart rate sensor. You could easily wire it up so that if the heart fails to beat for five or ten seconds, then it would complete a circuit and set off the detonator.'

'You see,' said Purnell.

They stared at the TV images of Jones the Bomb, which were now being watched in almost every country on earth. He looked mad enough to do anything.

'Shall I fire, sir?' asked Cabache, still locked in intimacy with Philippa of Hainault.

'Hold your horses, Cabache,' said Bluett.

CHAPTER THIRTY-SEVEN

1027 HRS

Dean stood at the top of the steps, looking out over the audience, as Benedicte and the four other Arabs moved up and down the aisle, harvesting the mobiles in big black sacks and disarming any obvious security men.

The cameras were allowed to function – indeed, they were essential for Jones's plan – and a close-up of the terrified kid was now flashed across the nation's TV screens and round the world. His large expressive eyes were so wide that the whites entirely surrounded the irises; his lips were grey, and he was holding a Schmidt, given to him by Benedicte, as if it were an adder.

In the house in Wolverhampton, Paulie was sitting on a scummy orange beanbag and eating Alpen with water, waiting to go in for the late shift at RitePrice.

'Nah,' he said. 'Nah.' He put his face right next to the screen, so that his features were bathed in the strobing panicky colours of his former colleague's skin.

'I just do not believe it,' he said. And the reaction was much the same in other parts of Wolverhampton.

'Oh for God's sake,' said Price the Cheese, and a ladle of whey dropped from his hand and clattered to the floor of the swish new cheesorium he had constructed with the insurance.

Next door, in the same old house in Wednesbury, Dennis Faulkner was so stunned that he thought he was having another little blip. He rose from his antimacassared Parker-Knoll and tried to loosen the tartan tie at his throat.

'*Huk hwork hwark*,' he said, and crashed back down again, knocking over various pottery objects ranged on the sideboard behind the chair.

There was even one person in the audience who thought she recognized Dean. She had been shivering, and praying, and crying with fear, and then she had opened her eyes and seen him. It couldn't be him; and yet it had to be.

In the Ops Room Bluett flipped the switch again, so as to communicate directly with his agents in the hall.

'This is Bluett,' he said.

'And this is Purnell,' said Purnell.

'Right. This is both of us,' said Bluett.

'They've taken my guns, sir,' said one USSS man.

'Mine too.'

'Mine too, sir.'

'I've still got a clear shot, sir,' said Cabache.

'Do not, repeat not, attempt to take these guys out. Please cooperate, and encourage the civilians to cooperate.'

'Yessir.'

'Sir?' said one agent.

'Yes.'

'What happens now? Do you guys have a plan?'

'We're working on that right now.'

There is an iron railing at the top end of Westminster Hall, equipped with a gate which is used to control access by the public as they come in through St Stephen's Entrance. Behind that fence was ranged an exotic collection from the great bestiary of British ceremonial. There was the Lord Chamberlain, an office now held by an epicene young coke-head whose family name may be found in the pages of Shakespeare.

He was wearing buckled shoes, tights, a stock and the kind of frilly frock coat favoured by Sir Mick Jagger in his *Sympathy for the Devil* phase. There was a man whose technical name was Silver Stick, but whose wife called him Algy, a super-annuated army officer whose creaking calves now sheathed in black silk had once propelled him over the tryline victoriously at Twickenham half a century ago. There was Rouge Dragon Poursuivant and Garter King of Arms and a man called the Earl Marshal whose job it was at the State Opening of Parliament every year to carry something called the Cap of Maintenance.

There was the Speaker and his clerks, all braided, wigged and frogged, and there to one side, standing nearest the gate and fingering with wet grip the old ebony staff, surmounted by a lion, which had been the mark of his office since it was created by deed patent in 1350, was the Gentleman Usher of the Black Rod, there, because he is Serjeant-at-Arms of the Lords, and it falls to Black Rod to officiate at all such encounters between Their Lordships and distinguished visitors.

Poor Black Rod. He had fought at Korea. With the utmost dash, gallantry and dispatch and with signal disregard for his own safety, he had led his SAS detachment by rope ladder up the cliffs of Aden. When he had successfully applied for his current position after seeing an advertisement in *The Times*, it was in the belief that he had all the calm and cunning to deal with any threat that might befall the Upper House; and now he had been out-manoeuvred.

Not since he had been a teenage lance corporal and guarded the wrong pylon in the freezing drizzle of Salisbury Plain had he experienced such a military reverse.

As Dean looked at Black Rod, he saw that his expression was shared by almost all the representatives of Britain's spavined *junker* aristocracy. They fingered the ancient maces and swords and pikes and halberds and rods by which it was their sworn duty in principle to defend this place, and a mood rose off them like a vapour. It was not alarm or fear. It was shame.

'I say,' whispered Silver Stick to the Earl Marshal, easing his sword perhaps half an inch out of his scabbard. 'You know what I think?'

'Don't be an idiot,' said the Earl Marshal.

'But I really feel we ought to do something.'

'Just don't even think about it.'

'It's all very well saying that, but . . .' Silver Stick was going to point out that a large proportion of his male relatives had died in engagement so heroic as to be ludicrous, charging machine gun nests with nothing but a whistle and a swagger stick, abseiling down smokestacks into the Bessemer converters of the Ruhr. But he knew that the Earl Marshal's family had been in re-insurance before being raised to the peerage by Lloyd George, and he did not want to appear snobbish.

'What about the element of surprise?' quavered Silver Stick, voicing the secret thoughts of all the halberdiers, pike men and rod wielders who stood impotently around.

'I think you'd find it was surprisingly stupid,' said the Earl Marshal. He had no need to articulate the odds.

Even if Silver Stick could get round the fence and skewer the lead terrorist without precipitating a torrent of Uzi or Schmidt bullets, there was the prior problem.

If Jones the Bomb was to be believed, his death would be automatically followed by a detonation that would kill them all.

'But do you think they can possibly be serious?' said Silver Stick.

'I have a terrible feeling that they are.' The flower of England's chivalry and nobility stared out at the expanse of Westminster Hall.

The heat seemed to have intensified under the TV lights and the audience flapped their programmes ever more desperately, like the spastic batting of a butterfly's wings as it dies against a window. The old English soldiers stood on the dais and looked at this innocent multitude. They looked with expressions as stony as the very sculptures that dotted the hall.

They looked with the hollow eyes of men who have failed in their first and defining constitutional duty. Black Rod clutched his eponym and was at a loss.

CHAPTER THIRTY-EIGHT
1028 HRS

Roger Barlow sat sprawled in his seat near the back, looking up at the hammerbeam ceiling, and gave way to fear, and to glassy despair. He'd bungled it. He'd bogged it up. He could have been a hero. Now he had been proved right and

Chester de Peverill had been proved wrong and the only consolation was that Chester de Peverill was as likely as any of them to get blown to smithereens.

One of the Arabs was coming down the aisle waggling his gun and urging them all to speed up. 'Give mobile,' he said, 'give mobile.'

De Peverill chucked his across on to the stone floor. 'You had better give him your phone, Rog,' he said.

'I don't have one,' said Barlow. He hoped he sounded surly, rather than frightened. He didn't like mobiles because you couldn't trust the blighters. They were technological Judases, he thought as he stared at the ceiling. There had been a godawful moment the other day when his blinking mobile had contrived quite independently to dial his wife.

He was somewhere he really shouldn't have been, not for his own good, and he was in the company of the woman in whom this ghastly reporter from the *Mirror* was now taking such an interest. The woman in question seemed deliberately to have exposed her bosom, and she was looking at him imploringly. 'Oh please,' she droned, 'you promised. Do it for Eulalie. It's a fantastic investment.'

Roger had smiled at her, because he really wanted to make her happy, or at least stop bugging him, and then he thought he must be going mad. He could hear the voice of his conscience.

It was this tiny voice squeaking at him from his breast pocket like Tinkerbell, 'Darling is that you? Hello. Hello.'

'Oh hi, darling,' he said, when he twigged. 'Hi, did you call me?'

'No I didn't call you, you must have called me.'

'No I didn't call you, you definitely called me.'

'Oh mm, oh good, how are you?'

'Oh I'm all right, how are you? You sound as though you've been running.'

It had been, all told, quite a sticky conversation. And then another time he was waiting to vote late at night and would you believe it, her mobile accidentally dialled his and left a long message. It must have jostled up against something in her handbag or been squeezed in some unexpected way and he found himself listening to his wife walking down the street when he thought she was at home. *Pok pok pok* went her heels, and then she seemed to arrive somewhere, and then he found himself listening with paranoid fascination as she engaged in some extended transaction, full of ambiguous pauses, with some chap or other; and when the message ended, Roger was so wrung out that he decided mobiles were instruments of temptation and that he would have no more to do with them.

He folded his arms, ignored Chester and gazed aloft at the woodwork.

CHAPTER THIRTY-NINE
1030 HRS

'Sweet Lord,' he thought, 'there's something moving.' He could have sworn he saw something up there where the huge transoms of oak melted into darkness. He thought of pointing it out to Chester and then decided against.

The mystery of Westminster Hall is how a space so vast can yet be so old. Even when it is bright outside, a man can stare at someone in the far corner and be unable to pick out his features. There is a total surface area of 1,547 square metres and somehow they roofed it in an age before steel girders and ferroconcrete. How? They, or rather Richard II, employed a man called Hugh Herland, who built the biggest and most technologically advanced hammerbeam roof in the world. At the end of each hammerbeam, Herland carved huge angels bearing coats of arms and staring down at the proceedings 90 feet below. The angels' faces are now a good ruddy wood colour, but for most of the six centuries of their existence, they have been black. In the winter, and indeed for much of the year, the cold seeps up through the clammy riverbank on which the flagstones are set. To take the chill off the grim mediaeval hangar, the occupants would light fires and because the braziers sent up such smoke, it was necessary to make primitive openings in the roof. These chimney holes have long since been turned into hatches for use by electricians or death-watch beetle inspectors; and the biggest chimney hole, not far from the north door, had been covered with a flèche, a folly of Victorian gothic spindles that rose from the spine of the roof.

Jason Pickel had found an inspection hatch in the bottom of the flèche; and through this he now inserted his booted feet and the knife-like creases of his fatigues. For a few seconds his legs swung in the darkness. The hatch was tight and it was hard to see below. There must be a platform beneath him, he reasoned. Why the hell else would they build a hatch here?

He lowered himself as far down as he could, straining with his biceps as though exercising on the parallel bars. He pointed his toe and probed the obscurity beneath. His toecap connected with a beam. 'Forbid it, Lord, that I should boast,' hummed Pickel, as he prepared for his plunge. 'Save in the Cross of Christ my God,' he whispered. 'All the vain things that charm me most I sacrifice them to his blood.' Yup, a sacrifice was called for and there was no higher cause. Flipping his arms above his head, like the two handles of a corkscrew when the cork is ready to be drawn, he disappeared through the hole.

In his Black Hawk Captain Ricasoli spotted the movement and jabbed with his finger. 'Whoa boy,' he said over the open mike system. 'Did you see that?'

'What's that?' said Deputy Assistant Commissioner Purnell

from the Ops Room, where sovereignty over the disaster was still alternating uneasily between the Metropolitan Police and the USSS.

'I just saw some guy go through a hole in the roof,' said Ricasoli.

'Did you authorize anyone to go through the roof?' asked Bluett.

'Nope.'

'You must have done.'

'Sorry, chummy it must be one of yours.'

'Whoo boys,' said Ricasoli, crackling in from his vantage point, 'It must be Pickel.'

Deputy Assistant Commissioner Purnell of the Metropolitan Police drew the microphone towards him, and a few inches away from his American co-gerent.

'Pickel?' he said. He knew all about Pickel.

'That's right,' said Bluett. 'He's the boy, the one we had on the roof.' A computer screen had already provided an image of Pickel's countenance looking as usual like a freshly cattle-prodded bullock. 'And he's madder than a shit house rat – at least in my experience.'

'Is he still armed?' asked Purnell.

'I'd be amazed if he wasn't.'

'But does he know the score? Does he know not to shoot?'

'How the hell would I know? All I can tell you for certain is that Lieutenant Pickel is armed with an M-24 sniper rifle capable of firing bullets at 834 metres per second and that he don't miss.'

As it happens, this was no longer true: that is, at the moment he dropped through the hatch, Pickel had his rifle strapped around his shoulders and the strap had caught on the latch of the hatch. The strap might have turned into Pickel's noose, had he not released himself before dropping ten feet on to a platform built beneath the flèche. He arrived almost silently, like Errol Flynn dropping from the mizzenmast to the deck.

He crept to the edge of the platform, and absorbed first the dreadful scene being enacted beneath him. Then he looked up and saw his gun glinting in the light from the open hatch and dangling uselessly ten feet above.

'Has everybody handed over their mobiles?' There was a silence, broken only by coughing and whimpering. The girl Bénédicte was moving up the aisle, dragging two bulging binbags of phones.

Dean looked at the audience and wished he could control his patella. It was as though it was on an invisible string, and someone was jerking it up and down. That's what people meant, he realized, when they said that their knees were shaking.

He couldn't believe the calm of Haroun and Habib, walking up and down as if they owned the place, sticking their guns in the bellies of the USSS men. He tried to control his own breathing, and to fill his lungs with the confidence of his creed. He remembered what Jones had said so many times: 'There is a special reward for those who go out and fight, and a special place for them in heaven, and a lower place for those who receive no hurt and sit at home.'

Yeah, thought Dean, and breathed out.

He hoped they were watching him in Wolverhampton; he hoped the magistrate was watching him, the one who had given him 400 hours of moss-picking; he hoped his foster-father was watching him now. Above all, in the angriest part of his teenage heart, he hoped he was being watched by that beautiful girl he had called Vanessa, Vanessa with the sweet white smile and the fat red kissy lips, whom he had trusted with his heart, and who had turned out to be a fornicating traitor.

Kill them all, thought Dean, as anger came to his aid; kill all the people who call you a coon; pluck out their eyes, cut off their heads, pull out their intestines with your bare hands.

For a moment he looked cruel and dreadful, and hung his Schmidt in the callous posture of some Sierra Leonean child guerrilla. He tried out a thin smile, and watched as Haroun, Habib and the two other Arabs started to round up the USSS men.

'Sir,' whispered an agent to the Ops Room, 'they want me to remove my two-way.'

'Me too, sir.'

'Mine too, sir. Ouch.'

'Don't worry, boys,' said Bluett. 'Just cooperate and do what they say. Hand over your stuff. We're going to git all you boys out of there in no time.' One by one the Curly-Wurlies were ripped out of the ears of the USSS men and thrown on the flags in the middle.

Then the agents were made to sit cross-legged on the floor in the central aisle.

Bluett gave a blubbering moan of grief as he saw the humiliation of his best men. 'Well, at least they haven't got Cabache yet,' he said, 'and fuck knows what we are going to do with Pickel.'

Jones the Bomb gripped the lectern and paused. The President turned and looked at the terrorist leader. He thought of making a lighthearted remark, something about carrying on with the sermon while the collection was being taken. In spite of his growing conviction that he was about to be killed, the President was conscious not of the audience in the hall – he didn't really give a stuff about them.

He was thinking about the millions of Americans who would already be watching, apathetically glomping their Cheerios and studying him on breakfast TV. They would be checking for signs of leadership, of masterfulness.

He opened his mouth.

'Shut up,' said Jones.

The President closed his mouth like a guppy.

'Here is what's going to happen now, my friends,' said Jones, 'and let me remind you that if you try to kill me then my neighbour dies too. It's like in chess: you cannot move this piece without a discovered checkmate. Yes?' The President composed his features into what he hoped was a mask of defiance.

Jones went on: 'My colleagues and I represent a group called Islamic Jihad, or the Brotherhood of the Two Mosques, and there are many injustices we would like to correct. It is now too long that the Zionist entity has been occupying illegally the homeland of my brother Arabs. We would like that to end. We would like an end to the brutal slaughter of families in Nablus, Hebron and Ramallah, the killing of people who have nothing, who have no weapons, by missiles fired from the helicopters given to the Zionist entity by the Americans. Of course we would like the final removal of the infidel bases from the lands that are holy to Islam and we would like to see an end to the corrupt and vicious regimes that are supported by the American taxpayer and by the CIA. We also demand an end to all the torture and brutality in Iraq, and all the guilty to be sent to war crimes trial in The Hague.'

This was too much for the President. He had to say something here. This was a vital part of his political identity.

'Hey,' he raised his eyebrows in that characteristic look of befuddlement. 'We sure as hell got rid of Saddam, didn't we?'

Jones kept his eyes on the crowd as he whacked the President backhanded and still holding the gun over the top of his head.

CHAPTER FORTY

1033 HRS

It was the moment for many people that the Westminster Assizes became truly frightening. It was that camera frame, the President wincing with pain, his forelock buffeted out of place, that made the front page of the evening papers around the planet.

Watching in the front row, the First Lady screamed for the first time, and began to cry. Sitting two along from her the Home Secretary realized that even if he survived this day, he would have to resign. From his vantage point in Cobra, the Prime Minister meditated not so much on the safety of the President or the crowd, but on the future of his government.

In the Shalimar all-night deli and coffee joint in Brooklyn, to take one of countless examples, the movement provoked shock. 'Shee,' said Johnson Calhoune, a security guard preparing for the morning shift, removing a doughnut from his mouth. 'That ain't right.' and the owner of the Shalimar, an Afghan, agreed that it certainly was not.

In the Ops Room, Bluett was white with hate and rage. 'Cabache,' he said to his remaining operative, 'have you still got that sucker in your sights? Why don't you just blow his head off now—?'

'NO, CABACHE,' said Deputy Assistant Commissioner Purnell, 'don't shoot. Tell him not to shoot, Colonel.'

Bluett balled his fists. He went purple. He groaned.

'OK Cabache, easy there,' he said.

'Yessir,' said Cabache.

Jones the Bomb twitched the orientation of his skull, with an almost mechanical movement, like a desert fox. He looked up and squinted into the alcove.

'You,' he said, pointing his Browning at Philippa of Hainault, 'come down.' Cabache descended, and was escorted, hands above his head, to join his colleagues in the aisle.

'I'm sorry, my friends,' said Jones, whose breathing was ragged for a second or two, 'but it is hard to think of any other way of making the point that this fellow is no longer in charge. To resume,' he said, 'there are many evils for which this man is responsible, but I'm a realist. I know how much will be quickly accomplished in your democratic system. That is why in the name of Allah, the compassionate, the merciful, we in the Brotherhood of the Two Mosques are today confining ourselves to one demand. You know the prisoners of Guantanamo Bay. You know they're being kept in brutal and degrading conditions. They're blindfolded. They're made to kneel in the sun. Some of them are just boys. Some of them are from this country. They have not even been charged. They've not been given access to lawyers and this' – he spat so plentifully that the drops hit the mike like a pebble on a drum – 'from a country that presumes to lecture the rest of the world about the application of human rights. We do not even ask for them to be released, we ask only what is natural and what is right: that they be sent back to face trial in the countries where their crimes were allegedly committed. This the President can grant. This he can do quite simply, but I believe he will need some persuasion.'

In the Ops Room in New Scotland Yard there was now barely room to stand. Psychologists, counter-terrorism gurus, hostage crisis wallahs and Special Forces representatives were trying to make themselves heard. Purnell and Bluett continued their invisible arm-wrestle, and everyone was pointedly refusing to talk to a svelte young female MP who was, so she claimed, the Under-Secretary in the new Department for Homeland Security. 'I see, yes,' she kept saying in a bewildered way, 'I see, yes.' The shambles had nothing on the

White House, where the Vice-President and the Secretary of State had both been roused from their beds and were in the cabinet rooms surrounded by the National Security adviser, the Defence Secretary and assorted other staffers, each vying to produce the most decisive response.

'I want a total news blackout.'

'Gettoudahere! This thing is running live on all channels.'

'Let's send in the Seals.'

'Yeah, right, and watch the President get turned into lasagne on breakfast TV.'

'Get me the British Prime Minister.'

'He's on line one, and he's talking to the Secretary of State.'

'But I'm the Vice-President.'

'Sweet Christ, will someone here say or do something sensible.'

Dawn was just peeping over the low hills of Missouri, when a wing of stealth bombers headed in boomerang formation for Europe, startling the ducks and convincing an itinerant drunk that he had seen the first wave of an alien invasion.

'I will not be doing the persuading,' said Jones the Bomb, 'and I hope never again to have to use my persuader here. It is up to all of us to do the persuading and up to everyone watching around the world.' He consulted his watch. 'It is now 8.34 p.m. in Australia. Some of you will be making a nice cup of Milo after your tea. I urge you, if you have views on this question, to ring up your local TV station and give a very simple answer to a very simple question: Do you believe that America should send the prisoners of Guantanamo Bay to have a fair trial in another country? Yes or No. People of the world have your say. We will stay here all day,' said Jones frothily. Dean noticed that rhetoric had given him wings. 'We will wait until Australia has gone to bed and

China has voted. We will wait until India and Russia and all the lands of Islam have given their opinion on this simple question that cries out for resolution. We will wait for Europe and for California, and if they vote to release the prisoners, and if you, sir, will come to this microphone and announce their release, then I swear that in the name of all that is holy, that you will all be released and the President of the United States will be unharmed. And if the people of this planet vote not to release the prisoners, the illegal captives of America, then of course it is very simple for us.'

In the office of the Director General of the BBC they were holding a crash meeting of a kind that was by now being held in the chancelleries, banks, newsrooms and foreign ministries of capital cities, daylit and benighted, across the planet. The honchos could see what was coming. There were rules about this, handbooks to be consulted.

They were about to be asked to collaborate on the biggest terroristic media stunt in history. 'It's very simple,' said the Editorial Director (Politics), a handsome woman in her fifties with strong traditional opinions, whose appointment was the relic of some forgotten Tory administration. 'We will have to refuse any cooperation whatsoever. Tell the switchboards immediately.'

'Hang on,' said the black polo necks.

'We can't stop people ringing up,' said a man with an earring. 'And what about everyone else?' He meant the enemy, independents and satellite television. 'They're bound to take the calls.'

'No, I'm sorry,' said the Editorial Director (Politics), 'this is really too important. We will never forgive ourselves if we respond to a terrorist outrage by going whoring after ratings.'

'Yes, well I'm sorry, too,' said one of the 40-something polo-necked men who was in fact the Political Director (Editorial), who had recently been recruited at a cost of

£113,000 to the licence payer, to neutralize the Editorial Director (Politics). 'But frankly folks, if I may interject at this point, I think we are never going to forgive ourselves if we sub-optimize the handling of a major news event.'

'But we can't be morally neutral in this.'

'It's a story, isn't it?'

'You mean you think the Corporation should do the terrorists' work for them?'

'I'm not saying that.'

'So what are you saying?'

'I'm just saying it's a matter of legitimate public interest.'

'What is?'

'Well, you know.'

'What?'

'Well, what percentage of BBC viewers think the Americans should do like he says and release all the remaining Guantanamo prisoners.'

'For God's sake, Joshua,' said the Editorial Director (Politics).

'I don't want to be provocative or anything,' said the Political Director (Editorial), 'but the last time I looked the BBC was entirely funded by the licence payers of this country and not by the CIA.'

The Editorial Director (Politics) had already gathered her papers. She walked out with as much composure as she could manage, sealed herself in the executive toilet, burst into tears, calmed down and mentally drafted a press release announcing her resignation.

Back in the office of the Director General, it fell to another black polo neck to sum up the meeting. 'I know you're all going to hate me for saying this,' he said, knowing that in fact they would be rather pleased, 'but I think we should remember that our first mission is the Reithian mission to explain and frankly,' concluded the Director of Political Editorial (£102,000 pa plus car, perks, bomb-proof state-sector pension), 'if you go for the see-no-evil option on a thing of this scale, you know what I mean, looking at the medium to long term I genuinely and sincerely believe that we could be totally and utterly stuffed in terms of what we end up with.'

'Yeah,' said several polo necks approvingly.

'I mean,' added one, 'we're the people's broadcaster aren't we? And it's up to us to let the people speak.'

CHAPTER FORTY-ONE
1036 HRS

Jones could see that his idea was taking hold in the imaginations of his audience. They were staring at him with silent respect, busily excogitating their options.

With mounting confidence he completed his conditions. 'If you vote no, people of the world . . .' he shook his head, as though to concede that this was of course an option open to the global audience, though one he doubted they would pursue . . .

'If you vote no, people of the world, if you vote in favour of the most brutal and powerful country since the Roman Empire, then it goes without saying that we will obey. We will release your Caesar to rule over you in the summary and arbitrary way with which you will all by now be familiar. In fact there is only one circumstance in which we, I, would dream of harming this man and that is if you vote yes, yes to release the Guantanamo prisoners, and they are not sent home.

'There is a flight tonight from Miami to Lahore, changing at Frankfurt. If I'm right it will become clear in the next few hours what the world thinks of American imperialism and there will be plenty of time for them to be put aboard. If the world votes yes and America says no, then I will have no choice.'

He turned and leered at the President. The President did his best to leer back. But even in long shot, the TV audience could see a hollow look, an involuntary working of the Adam's apple.

In the ministries, banks and news organizations of the earth, it was a reaction immediately detectable by those with a nose for fear, and it was viewed with every emotion from despair to satirical hilarity.

Slumped in his seat near the front, the French Ambassador saw it. He shook his Beethoven hairdo. Confounded and depressed though he was, the énarque in him admired anything cruel and brilliant, and the terrorist plan was both. 'C'est géniale, ça,' he said and decided that his chances of surviving today were about 5 per cent.

'What do you mean?' asked Cameron, gripping his arm.

'Hein?' said the French Ambassador, as though surprised to find he was in the presence of other human beings.

'You said something just now. Do you mean that you think this guy's a genius?'

'Not a genius, of course not, but the plan is certainly brilliant.'

'But do you think he is, like, cool?'

'It is certainly cool,' wheezed the French diplomat, 'to carry out an operation such as this.' Cameron tried to compute it all. She tried to make sense of the Frenchman's actions, but mainly of her own actions and the actions of the man on her right.

She turned to the love object, who was now sitting in the chair vacated by Benedicte, but facing her. She took him in slowly with the anguish of one beholding a much-loved relative on the mortuary slab. She looked first at his long tapering fingers which now held her own with the gentle and winning insistence she had felt so often. She looked at the leather patches on his tweed jacket that he wore even in the heat of London in July and which heaven knows, he wore in Baghdad during the bombing.

She looked at his strong chin with its hint of bristle and then at the humorous and intelligent crinkles around his eyes and she looked into the eyes themselves. They were still Adam Swallow's eyes: soulful, thoughtful, humane. Surely this was still a profoundly decent man.

'I know what you're thinking,' he said.

'But why did you . . . ?'

'I didn't.'

'But you made me get those passes.'

'I know, but I swear . . .'

'I signed for them,' said Cameron. As is the case, alas, with all of us, Cameron's sense of guilt was greatly exacerbated by the certain knowledge that she would be exposed. Everyone would know that she had been instrumental in importing these maniacs to the Palace of Westminster and, oh lordy, her father would know. As soon as she thought of that man whose hot-dang, straight-up and magnificently unnuanced world view had until recently served as the template for her own, she felt so bad again that she toyed with the notion of weeping. And then Cameron thought, stuff it, I'm not going to cry, I'm going to find out what's really been going on here.

'Adam.'

'Yes.'

'Do you promise that you will tell me the absolute truth?' Her voice was high, as though she had some sort of pressure on the base of her windpipe, but it was firm.

'Yes,' said Adam, and his brown eyes were unblinking, 'I swear it.'

'And that,' said Jones the Bomb, 'is more or less all I have to say. It goes without saying that there must be no attempt to tamper with the television coverage of this event. For every

238

channel that shuts off this fascinating broadcast for political reasons I will execute, shall we say, one hostage. Maybe we will start with that one over there. He seems to have survived.'

He waggled his automatic at the Dutchman, ear now swaddled like Van Gogh, and Hermanus Van Cornelijus looked back with loathing. 'Of course it is always possible that America will behave with unthinking violence, so let me say for, what, the third time, that if they kill me they will also' – he tapped his padded breast – 'kill the 43rd President. He will not be the first civilian to die from what Americans and their allies call friendly fire, but he would certainly be the first President. As to my own death and the death of my colleagues, let me quote the Holy Koran: "the nip of an ant hurts a martyr more than the thrust of a weapon, for these are more welcome to him than sweet cold water on a hot summer day".'

Recessed into the lectern was a glass carafe from which Jones the Bomb refreshed himself greedily, letting the drops trickle down his throat. He wiped his mouth and looked at the erstwhile most powerful man in the world as if to say, 'Not for you, sonny.' The President pursed his lips.

In the Ops Room at New Scotland Yard the male egos were spooling madly in all directions. They were not thinking what they were doing; they were thinking how they would be held to have done when this business was over. One mind, a young female mind, was sitting in a corner and considering logically the problem that Jones had posed. 'Hey,' she said to herself, looking up from her notes, 'hey, I know what!' she yelled. No one was listening.

The Ops Room had become an ops floor, with every computer terminal the object of discreet and overt competition between the operatives of Britain and America. Colonel Bluett of the USSS seemed slowly to be gaining the upper hand. By sheer weight of men and *matériel* at his eventual disposal, he was becoming the Eisenhower of the equation and Deputy Assistant Commissioner Purnell was being thrust into the role of Montgomery.

'Not there, you dummkopf, there!' yelled Bluett. He was now pacing around, a limp cigar hanging from his mouth in blatant imitation of Colonel Kilgore. At any moment you expected him to puff out his barrel chest and announce that Charlie don't surf or that he loved the smell of napalm in the morning.

Without looking, he took a mobile phone from an aide and yelled into it: 'Bluett! Not there, there!' He pointed at a scale model of Westminster Hall, which was hastily being bodged together with the help of a guidebook on top of one of the tables.

'Yes sir,' he said, for it was Washington on the line, in this case the Secretary of State. 'We've identified six of them, including the girl who came in with the French Ambassador. That's right, sir. The only guy we can't get a fix on is the young one. Seems to be some British kid, petty criminal, misfit, something like that. Yessir, yessir, we're working on that right now. What's that you say?'

He lunged at the model and picked up two green toy soldiers. Cradling the mobile, he grabbed a magic marker and labelled one of them POTUS, before putting them back, facing in a slightly different direction.

'Do any of them have a history of suicide bombing? Gee, sir, I don't think you can have a history of suicide bombing. I think he might have a history of attempted suicide bombing, but—'

'I've got it.' This time the female detective, whose name was Camilla, secured the attention of Deputy Assistant Commissioner Purnell, who was desperate to shut out the noise of Bluett.

'You know what, darling,' he said, smiting his forehead when it was explained to him, 'you're flaming well right.'

'Chaps,' he said, in such a way as to indicate that by 'chaps' he meant chaps as opposed to guys. 'Here is what we are going to do.' It took Bluett only seconds to realize that his British counterpart had found the solution.

CHAPTER FORTY-TWO
1037 HRS

As his eyes soaked up the room, he could see the excitement. Some of his own men were now clustering around Purnell and making animated gestures. For all his swaggering, Bluett was essentially a bureaucrat and every bureaucrat knows what to do when your rival has a brainwave.

You go along with it. You extol it; and then you secretly find a way of sabotaging it, while making sure that you have distanced yourself from it in good time.

'Fantastic,' said Bluett, when the wheeze was explained to him. 'There's only one problem I see here, and that's how do we get the guy into the hall. I don't want to rain on your parade, but if this maniac sees someone pointing a gun at him loaded with a rhino tranquillizer then he is going to pull the ripcord – no question. And anyhow, what if it doesn't knock him out?'

'It will knock him out in a trice,' said Camilla, the detective who had thought up the idea. 'Hit him in the neck and he'll be away with the fairies.'

'That's swell, that's swell,' said Bluett, pacing over to his mock-up and thinking the Brits could not be serious. What did they think this was? Daktari?

'Show me how we get him in. There are at least six entrances to Westminster Hall, but they are all obvious, and they've got men with machine guns everyplace.' With his magic marker he indicated the main access points, St

Stephen's Entrance, the entrance from New Palace Yard, the passageway entrance by which Jones & Co. had come in and then two sets of entrances on the left-hand side as the President looked at it, through doors that led to a series of debating chambers and meeting rooms.

'Of course we could take them all out just like that' – he flipped over a figurine violently, 'but then we'd run the risk of disaster. I love this idea. I love it to death. My only question is how do we get a man in there without being seen. That's why I want to hear from Pickel.'

The sharpshooter was at that moment invisible, shielded from view by the glare of the TV lights. He was filthy from soot and trying to think of a way of persuading his gun to slip off its hook and fall into his arms. He stood up to his full six foot two, and stretched his leglike arms. The gun was still several feet too high.

He gave a little jump, and landed back heavily, missing the platform and resting on a high crossbeam. The beam held up well, but Pickel wobbled as he landed. 'No,' he thought. He was a brave man, but not a funambulist. 'That's enough jumping.'

Slowly on his hands and knees, he grovelled his way to the eaves in search of a way up, and listened, as he went, to the further ravings of Jones.

'So,' said the lead terrorist, 'is there no one here in this birthplace of Parliamentary debate who has the courage to speak? Here is the building of Pitt, Fox, Disraeli, Gladstone, Churchill and the great George Galloway. Is no one prepared to say anything on the issue of the hour? Are you all cowards?' he shrieked suddenly.

'Easy, boy,' said the President. 'Last time a person tried to speak you shot him in the ear.'

'Good point, my friend,' said Jones nastily. 'This time I have a different policy. If no one speaks by the time I count

242

to ten, I will fire at a hostage. Yes, you again, why not, you miserable creature.' He once more indicated the wounded Dutchman, who opened his eyes and regarded his tormentor with herpetic inscrutability.

'Ladies and gentlemen, infidel dogs, the motion before the house is that America should release her illegal prisoners from their Cuban torture chambers. The world is watching, the world is voting. Who will have the courage to speak before the bald guy gets it?'

'ONE!'

Dean looked at the faces of the politicians nearest him. Even with his limited knowledge of current affairs, he could tell that there were some quite famous people here. Wasn't that guy the Home Secretary, inventor of FreshStart, to whose munificence with public funds he supposedly owed thanks and praise? Surely to goodness one of them would have the guts to stand up and say something snappy. Wasn't that what they were trained for?

Their faces were pale with shock, but each was inwardly engaged in that art he had made into a profession: maximizing the chance of his own survival. In the breast of each one was the traditional competition between the fear of appearing an idiot and the lust to star on television.

'TWO!'

Ziggy Roberts, best and brightest of the new intake, felt his mouth go dry. He could make his name for evermore. How many times had his speeches mentioned the concept of a 'golden opportunity' which it was necessary to 'seize with both hands' with a view to going 'forward into the future'?

'This is it, Ziggy, old man,' he told himself. 'This is the big one.'

'THREE!'

Sir Perry Grainger toyed for a heartbeat with the notion that speaking in this debate would count as dancing to the terrorist tune and be therefore unacceptable. Insofar as he had a natural human desire to be inconspicuous after the demented terrorist leader had tried to shoot him, he justified it on that ground.

'You shouldn't play their games, Perry,' one part of his brain told the other half; and the other half retorted vigorously: 'Don't be a wimp, Grainger, you fool. Did the people of South Oxfordshire send you to this place that you should keep silent on the greatest international crisis of our epoch, when hundreds of us, including the leader of Britain's oldest and most important ally, are in mortal peril? You must speak, Grainger, you great dingbat, and speak for England.'

'FOUR!'

Christ on a bike, thought Roger. I really had better get up and do the business. It was no use trying to order his thoughts, he decided. It was like one of those moments when the whips come and haul you from the tearoom, and they say you've got to speak for fifteen minutes on the Fur Trappers Compensation Bill. And you say 'awfully sorry' but (a) you're trying to finish a particularly dense and dry rock cake and (b) fascinating though the subject sounds, you don't really feel you've got quite enough to say about it in the High Court of Parliament, at which the whips look threatening, smoothly mention recent infractions and leave you with no option.

Barlow got ready to stand and knew what he wanted to say. He wanted to be as vicious and as scathing as he dared towards these terrorists without provoking them to shoot him. He was damn well going to speak up for America and for what he believed in. Apart from anything else, he had worked out one thing. Whatever happened to the President of the United States, he wasn't getting out of here alive. He had thought it through from the point of view of Jones the Bomb, and it was perfectly obvious that the loonies would have far more impact – a permanent global trauma – if they went ahead and blew the place up than if they became snared up in some double-crossing hostage deal with the Americans.

'FIVE!'

Haroun looked at his boss, histrionically waving his automatic, and felt a twinge of annoyance. He didn't hold with all this speechifying; he didn't like this silly debating-society approach that Jones had introduced. He smouldered at the crowd and spat with a *splatch* on the flagstone occupied by the front row. This was not some stupid and degenerate Western reality TV show, some kind of *Pop Idol* votathon. This wasn't *I'm the President, Get Me Out of Here*. This was a war and he, Habib and Jones and Dean and their Arab brothers and their – ahem – sister were fedayeen; they were ready to sacrifice their lives for a cause. That's what fedayeen meant. Indeed it was doctrinally vital that this action of theirs should be construed as a military action. When they all died, as they surely would, sometime in the next few hours, Haroun believed that he would die as a soldier, a man engaged in Jihad; and this was theologically essential to Haroun because it is well known that the Holy Koran forbids suicide.

'Whoever kills himself in any way will be tormented in that way in hell,' says the Koran, and it was part of the deal Haroun had made with himself that he would not be going to hell. On the contrary, he was going to a place more lovely and more perfect than you and I can possibly imagine.

Somewhere a blissful tent had been pitched for him in the clouds, piled with silken cushions, cooled by the perpetual trickle of holy water from a turquoise fountain of vaguely Mudejar design; and he would have some peace there, thought Haroun, peace after the miserable American-induced stress of this earthly existence.

He would lie back on the pillows and in one hand he would manipulate the celestial narghileh, bubbling away with hashish a thousand times more delicious than anything that could be found in the valleys of Afghanistan, and his other arm would be gently looped around the exposed stomach of the first of his statutory 72 almond-eyed virgins; and slowly he would ease off her filmy pyjama bottoms and prepare to enjoy her in a way that his imam had assured him was both decently spiritual and infinitely carnal. She would bend over him, bringing her breasts ever closer to his face, laughing low and praising him and dissolving all the onanistic wretchedness of his previous life and— Oh-oh, he thought. In the name of Allah, Haroun told himself, I had better be careful.

He found himself staring irresistibly at Cameron, just ten feet or so away in her low-cut top. He felt the surge of fundamentalist rage that inspires the pathetic Islamofascistic male. How much longer would Jones keep them among these harlots and jezebels? He stared with that perverted Wahhabi mixture of lust, terror and disgust at this portrait of sexually emancipated Western woman. He glared at her thighs and her unambiguously exuberant bosom and yearned to punish her, punish her entire society, punish America for her criminal role in pioneering feminism. He wanted to punish her for the inadequacies she made him feel, because he knew in his heart that she was more unattainable to him than the doe-eyed virgins of heaven; and there was a part of him, a secret half-acknowledged corner of his soul, that yearned for her on precisely those grounds.

It was above all that part of himself, that part that had been tempted, the part that collaborated with America and her values, that he wished to destroy. Oh, but he would purge himself, he would cleanse himself of the Western taint. With sweating fingers he touched the stitched pouch in which the one-way Nokia was stored, and waited for the moment when he could wash his soul in steep-down gulfs of liquid fire. 'Come on, Jones,' he thought.

'SIX!'

But what would he say? wondered Cameron. It was a measure of her devotion to Adam, and indeed her awful inescapable feminine deference, that as Jones began to count, she had simply assumed the love-object would take charge. He was always haranguing meetings with brilliant and mordant paradoxes. Surely he would leap to his feet, shod in lovingly polished oxblood brogues, and somehow set things straight?

But Adam Swallow just stared back. She looked into his implacable eyes, and tried to read him. Was that the glare of a proud but innocent man? Or was he a cynical abettor of terrorists? And she remembered that he knew these people anyway, or at least she assumed he knew these people, because he had suborned her into securing their access to the premises. She felt her soul-sickness deepen and she turned to the front and saw Dean with his afro hair and his proud, pale, almost Nilotic features. He looked so young and so scared.

'SEVEN! I MEAN IT!'

Dean was staring at Cameron and thinking she was one of the tastiest birds he had ever seen. Here he was, barely nineteen and about to splatter his guts over the walls. He would never know this girl, never talk to her. He might even be

247

responsible for her death. He became aware that she was returning his look. His Sierra Leonean child-guerrilla smile became a guilty smirk, and he turned his face away.

'EIGHT!!'

Verdommt Brits, thought the Dutch Ambassador and prepared to stand up himself, on the assumption that the terror chief could hardly shoot him for carrying out his orders.

Tiens, thought the French Ambassador , also girding himself for action. Perhaps he would be the first foreign diplomat in history to address a major parliamentary occasion.

They need not have worried, because at that moment, like the digits of a child's cash register, about fifteen suits sprang up across the hall and now more were rising all the time as buttock after buttock unclove itself from the little gilt chairs.

'Now that is more like it,' said Jones the Bomb, 'but I don't know whom to choose.' He turned to the President, and the President noticed how the fellow was sweating under the TV lights and how a drop had run down his brow, irrigated the cyclopean zit depression and then trickling away into the long furry undivided caterpillar of his brow.

'You choose the speaker,' said Jones the Bomb. 'Which of these people do you think will speak best for you?'

'You know what?' said the President, with a good approximation of geniality. 'It's not really my place, but I had the honour earlier today of meeting a gentleman who is in fact the Speaker of the House of Commons.' He indicated the Speaker standing glumly with Black Rod and the rest of the worthies. 'You should really ask him to take charge.'

'I think not,' said Jones, 'and I say rubbish to the snob traditions of this so-called democracy. You pick the speaker, I mean the person to speak, and you do it now.'

The President gave his squint, which was intended faintly to recall Clint Eastwood at the point of spitting out his cheroot and firing at Lee Van Cleef, but which his opponents had likened to a half-witted buzzard. 'OK, buddy,' said the President, 'let's all keep calm here.'

He shielded his eyes and looked for a conservative-seeming fellow, someone with moderate opinions who would come over well before a global audience.

Far away to the back and to the right, rocking on the balls of his heels and with his thumbs on the seam of his trousers, Roger Barlow stiffened as he saw the presidential finger pointed straight at his breastbone with the inescapable challenge of Uncle Sam.

'Oh brother,' he murmured, and had begun to say 'Ladies and g—' when 'LADEES and GENTLEMEN', screamed the man on his right.

CHAPTER FORTY-THREE
1038 HRS

It was Chester de Peverill who had risen a millisecond after him, and whose desire to star in the world's biggest televised balloon debate was now a hormonal imperative. 'Oh, I'm sorry,' said Roger, 'I thought he—'

'Don't worry, mate,' said Chester, placing his hand on Roger's shoulder and applying no uncertain pressure. 'Ladies and gentlemen, ladies and gentlemen,' he continued, puffing his chest and seeking out the cameras as though he was about to explain the secret of a really good lamb casserole. 'My name is Chester and I' – he paused – 'am a humble cook.' He waited again, as though this assertion might provoke cries of 'no, no, no' or applause.

The President stared uneasily at him. So did Jones the

Bomb. Roger sat back, folded his arms and gave way to the blackness of ungovernable shame.

'I am not a politician. I'm not a world statesman. All I really know about is eating and drinking and that gives me what you might call a gut instinct for things. What's the problem we've got here, folks? We've got a global phenomenon which is called anti-Americanism. It's people everywhere hating America, innit? That's the trouble and before we sort it out we've got to understand why people hate America and from my perspective, from where I sit, there's a lot of factors that have to be taken into account.'

'Shut up!' shrieked Jones. 'What are you trying to say? Are you an imbecile?'

Chester de Peverill looked stunned. 'I thought you wanted someone to speak, you know for or against America.'

'You must speak to the motion,' said Jones, who had studied Erskine May on parliamentary procedure, along with everything else, at Llangollen.

'The motion?'

'Yes: that this house calls for the immediate repatriation of the Guantanamo prisoners.'

'For trial,' said the President.

'Silence,' said Jones, who had the air of a rattled bus conductor about to turn vicious with a bilker. 'Do you believe the American illegally held prisoners should be sent back for trial in the place of their alleged crimes?'

Chester de Peverill went white. Like all the folksiest and most whimsical TV characters, he tended to duck hard political questions and it struck him that the stakes here were probably quite high. If only he had known. In the seventeen minutes since Jones the Bomb had first handcuffed the President, the TV audience had been growing like bacteria in a Petri dish. There were two cameras in the hall for the live coverage, going out on Sky and BBC News 24. One was trained on the President, and one on the crowd, and their terrified cameramen were feeding pictures across the world. Millions were ringing up other millions and telling them to get to a box and watch the most sensational daytime chat show ever produced anywhere. With every minute that passed the millions were turning into hundreds of millions. Within twenty minutes it is estimated that a billion people were aware by means of some electronic transmission – radio, TV or the internet – of the events in Westminster Hall. Only a small proportion had grasped Jones's idea in all its sophistication, but that small proportion was numerically huge.

They understood the concept of interactive TV, and that they were in some sense the jury. From Berlin to Baghdad, from Manchester to Manila, from Sidcup to Sydney, there were already myriads who had no principled objection to the wheeze. Of course, they were in many cases sickened and horrified by what was going on. Good people across the planet were full of loathing for Jones and his barbarous treatment of the President, and his shooting of the Dutch Ambassador; but there was also a large number of people, good people, who thought America had a case to answer, not just on the narrow question of Guantanamo Bay, but more generally.

As they prepared to ring their TV stations and record their votes, they were fascinated by this strange, long-haired, rubbery-lipped Englishman who said he was a cook. Much as their consciences warned them not to gratify the terrorists, there were millions who were also yearning to give the Americans a lesson and in the sheep-like way of all human beings, they wanted to see which way this cook would go.

Chester de Peverill goggled. Across the planet, audiences in sports bars went silent and trembling fingers turned up the volume on the zapper.

'Right,' said Chester.

'Yes or no?' said Jones.

'What? You mean, yes they should be sent back?'

'Of course that is the question: what do you think?'

'Or no they should stay in Guantanamo Bay?'

'Idiot!' barked Jones. 'Just answer the question.'

'Of course I'm going to answer the question.' The TV chef stared hopelessly around the chamber, as out of his depth as a soup-soaked crouton. Like all despairing examination candidates, he tried to get some extra purchase on the phrasing of the question.

'Should the ILLEGALLY HELD prisoners go back FOR TRIAL?' He stopped histrionically, hoping that he would give the impression that he was a man who knew exactly what he was about to say.

'Spit it out, pal,' said the President.

'Well,' said Chester, 'if you want my honest opinion . . .'

'That's right,' said Jones, flashing his teeth. 'That's the one we want. The honest one.'

'My honest opinion is, er, yes. Yes, of course the prisoners should go back and I say that without having an anti-American bone in my body. In fact some of my best friends are Americans.'

CHAPTER FORTY-FOUR
1040 HRS

It was the tipping point. Chester's moronic answer, arrived at with all the ratiocination of a donkey hesitating between two equal piles of hay, was colossally influential. Across the word this mere cook, this faux-naïve student of onions and gravy, had given cover and legitimation to the millions who wanted to vote to give America a bloody nose.

As the calls poured in, TV bosses started opportunistically whacking up the cost per minute and even though the higher prices were flashed on the screen, the viewers kept on calling.

In the upper reaches of the BBC, the hierarchs were in semi-continuous delirium of self-importance as they wondered what to do with the data. Could they responsibly publish the news? Could they not?

'Basically this is a devil and the deep blue sea job,' said the Political Director (Editorial) to the Director of Political Editorial. 'I mean, we're stuffed if we do and stuffed if we don't. If we suppress what's coming in, everyone will say we've been leant on by the government, and if we just go ahead and publish the news, everyone will start screaming about anti-American bias of the BBC.'

'Yeah,' said the Director of Political Editorial with a look of joy. He knew, they all knew, everyone who cared to look up the internet political wonk sites knew that the news was bad for America. China had recently seen a prodigious growth in the number of TVs and telephones of all kinds, not that the Chinese saw any particular need to thank America for the benefits of capitalism.

'Yes,' cried liberated young Chinese girls in pencil skirts as they dialled the TV stations. 'Yes,' said Chinese Human Rights activists into their snazzy new Sony Ericssons. Never mind all that American think tanks had done to campaign against the Laogai, the Chinese gulags.

Yes, now was the time to hold America to account. They wanted those guys sent back from Cuba. Slowly, like some storm being incubated in the armpit of Africa before it starts swirling round and round, gaining speed as it moves over the Atlantic, drenching Bermuda, then breaking out with hurricane force over the coast of North Carolina, the unthinkable was starting to become the politically correct. A global conviction was being born, that it was forgivable, this once, to comply with a terrorist stunt.

'But just because I love America,' said Chester de Peverill, 'that does not mean I support American foreign policy or American farm policy. They fill their beef with hormones and then they dump it on the markets of developing countries and destroy the livelihood of those farmers. Do you know what happened to the Vietnamese catfish industry?' he demanded.

The audience in the hall coughed and fidgeted. The audience at large watched him with fascination. Even the Vietnamese catfish fishermen watching from their pool tables wondered quite how this was relevant.

'The Americans wanted to encourage their own catfish producers, so they slapped such prohibitive duties on Vietnamese catfish that, you know, they had a very tough time of it.' Chester was conscious that this was perhaps not the most powerful point he could make, given that the anti-globalization movement, to which he was in theory affiliated, was also in favour of tariffs and protection, but he ploughed on, amid general expressions of disbelief.

'Do you know how many Americans have food poisoning every day? Two hundred thousand, and it's no wonder when you consider the kind of gloop they eat. Have you ever eaten American cheese?'

'Listen, Chester,' said Roger Barlow, 'why don't you just put a sock in it for the time being?'

Chester paused. He was being heckled and he knew from the studio audience at *Chester Minute* that a good heckle can be turned to gold.

'Well, my friends, what do we have here? It's my old friend Roger. He's a politician, you know.'

'Do shut up, Chester,' said Roger. 'These people are murderers.'

'And my old friend Roger doesn't want to hear my view of American cheese, which strikes me in a way as being not that surprising, because what you get from politicians like Roger is just like American cheese, processed and heat-treated to the point of macrobiotic extinction; and what you get from me is raw, unpasteurized – and you know, for some people like Rog here, I suppose I may be just a little bit too pungent for his taste.'

The TV chef looked down almost affectionately at the politician. Chester was quite oblivious to his surroundings, with the Asperger's syndrome, the quasi-refusal to relate to the feelings of other people, that begins to afflict those who spend their evenings in star dressing rooms and their days absent-mindedly scanning the face of everyone they pass to see if they have been 'recognized'.

'Its good to see you, Rog. You know, folks, at university he was known as Roger the Artful Todger and I wouldn't be at all surprised if he's been up to some kind of beastliness again, whanging the old donger in the kedgeree I have no doubt, no offence, Rog.'

Roger grabbed de Peverill's tie and pulled down hard.

'Stop,' cried Jones, who could hardly believe his good fortune in finding this advocate of his cause. 'You there, leave him alone and you, yes you, Mr Cook, please continue with your interesting remarks.'

'And do you know,' said Chester, scowling at Roger with magnificent disdain, 'that in spite of their pasteurized, homogenized, sterilized, emulsified, genetically modified and hormone-pumped food, the Americans eat so much of it that they are the fattest country on earth. We all know about the evils of the tobacco industry. We all know about the creeps and saddos who defend the right of every American school kid to bear arms, even if it means bearing an AK47 into the maths class and wiping out teach and sixteen pre-pubescent school children. But what, my friends, are we going to do about the real enemy of our values, I mean our European values, that have produced in France a country with 258 cheeses? The real enemy is not big oil, it's not big tobacco, it is big food.'

CHAPTER FORTY-FIVE

1043 HRS

Across the Far East the debate was going badly for America, or at least for the President. The Chinese were now voting for the return of the gagged and ski-goggled Guantanamo prisoners by 68 per cent to 32 per cent. In Malaysia the Yes vote reached a staggering 98 per cent. Even in South Korea, the country for which many young American soldiers had died, there was a 52 per cent majority of TV viewers in favour of the return of the prisoners and the story was certainly no better in Vietnam, where an apathetic public were scandalized afresh by the American insult to their catfish.

In Europe the polling was closer, and in some countries, notably Denmark, there was already strong and implacable opposition to anything that sounded like cooperation with a bunch of Islamic nutcases. Britain was proving staunch, at least so far, in that many people understood that a yes vote was a victory for the terrorists. As for America, slowly waking up, it was a different story.

Americans looked at this lank-haired chef, condescending to them about their diet, and decided they liked him about as much as they liked Osama Bin Laden. Of course, it was still early days, and even in countries like China people were delaying before casting their votes, as families feuded about the meaning of what they were doing. Phone sockets were ripped out of walls, handsets were hidden under cushions while decent people wrangled about the limits of respectable anti-Americanism. One Chinaman told his brother to go and copulate with a pangolin in a lake. He was stabbed with a letter-opener in the duodenum.

In Pakistan a man was so scandalized by his wife's refusal to vote against the awful Rumsfeld Stalag in Cuba that he shouted '*Ju te Marunga!*' which means 'I hit you with my shoe, woman', an insult she requited by braining him with an iron. All told, the internet number crunchers calculated that of the world's TV viewers who had so far expressed an opinion, a staggering 61 per cent were ready to rub America's nose in it, even if it meant going along with the boys from the Brotherhood of the Two Mosques.

And Chester de Peverill jawed on, protected by Jones. He began on the infamy of America's refusal to sign the Kyoto protocol. He went on to America's disgusting attempt to patent seeds that were the intellectual property of Third World farmers. Barlow and others had at one point tried to slow handclap him, but Jones was having none of it.

Jones wanted the debate, and yet he was growing increasingly antsy. For more than twenty minutes now he had held the Western world at his mercy, and he knew it would not be long before the imperialists struck back.

A man in a muddy tracksuit was being shown into the Ops Room in New Scotland Yard, accompanied by Sergeant Louise Botting of Horseferry Road. It was Dragan Panic, the tow-truck operative. He really didn't like being surrounded by so many policemen, but he had been told that his cooperation was essential, especially if he wanted Indefinite Leave to Remain in Britain.

He was plonked in front of a TV, which appeared to be showing some boring parliamentary debate in Westminster Hall. Nobody watched the debates in Westminster Hall, not even the MPs who took part in them.

'Is that them?' said Deputy Assistant Commissioner Purnell.

At that moment the cameras were panning across the hall, to take in Benedicte and the two other Arabs, and so Dragan began to shake his head.

'Yes!' he exclaimed, when the President and Jones the Bomb suddenly filled the frame. 'I know him anywhere, that creepy man. *Bozhe Moi*, my God,' he said, when he identified the man in the other handcuff as the President of the United States.

'What are you going to do?' he asked numbly.

'That,' said Deputy Assistant Commissioner Purnell, 'is something we are having a look at now.'

It is well known that in his younger days Henry VIII of England was very far from the bloated fat-kneed creature of caricature. He was tall and lithe, with blond locks, constantly springing into the saddle and faring forth for a spot of falconry, and then springing down again to strum his lute and knock up some imperishable masterpiece like 'Greensleeves'. He danced and sang in his lusty tenor and he also played tennis, which comes, as everyone knows, from 'tenez', the word you called out at courtly matches as you prepared to serve and as you instructed your opponent to get a grip on his racket. In 1532 he built a splendid indoor facility at Hampton Court, but at some point before that date he must have seen the possibilities of Westminster Hall, with its hard flat surface and its sheer walls offering the perfect ricochet shot. We know he must have played here because in 1923, when they were making repairs to the hammerbeams, they came across some brown and shrivelled objects in the eaves. They were of leather and stuffed with hair. They were among the first tennis balls. Their hair was shown on examination to be taken partly from a dog and partly from a human being, perhaps because the Tudors, like future generations, had a superstitious faith in composite materials.

One can imagine the scene.

It is a bright morning in the springtime of his reign, the sun strong enough outside to fill the hall with a blue smoky light. Enter Henry, determined to work up an appetite for swans stuffed with goose stuffed with vole, or whatever he is proposing to eat for lunch.

After a suitably deferential pause, he is followed by his

partner, a nervous silken-haired young courtier called Sir Charles de Spenser. The King announces that he will serve. Sir Charles says this is a first-class plan.

The King is inspired to make a joke: 'I may be born to rule,' he says, 'but I was also born to serve.' Sir Charles laughs so much he appears to be on the point of vomiting. 'Tenez!' yells the King. He then bounces the ball with his racket for an off-puttingly long time. Sir Charles sways like an osier on the chalked baseline, feebly wondering which stroke it would be most politic to play.

Twang! The monarch's first serve sails past his ear, comfortably out on all directions. 'Bien joué, sire,' cries Sir Charles, but the King is having none of it. *Phtunk!* He hits the next one with the wood and it dribbles into the net.

'Good shot, my liege,' exclaims the courtier, but no amount of flattery will coax Henry's ball into the service court. The King is beginning to go red. A certain jowly savagery is creeping over his features, later to be captured by Holbein. He serves, he misses, his racket vainly harvests the air and yet the fruit drops on his head. A sinking dread is forming in the pit of Sir Charles's belly. The King is angry.

'I' faith,' he cries, snapping his racket over his vast knee, 'I don't believe it,' and commands Sir Charles to serve. Palms wet, the courtier tosses up the little leather sphere and it plops over the net in a slow undulating dolly that even a maddened monarch cannot miss; and the King makes the most of it.

He brings his new racket forward in a gigantic forearm sweep and crashes the catgut into the leather with all the impetus of his seventeen stone. For a fraction of a second the ball is sucked back into the web of the racket, as the enormous physical force turns the strings into a kind of warped model of the space-time continuum, and then *kapoing*, it breezes off and away, far over the head of the extravagantly cowering Sir Charles, off one of the side walls, up over the hammerbeams and then *bonk bonk bonk*, it bounces into some cranny known only to the architects.

Sir Charles de Spenser sinks to his knees, deciding that he had better make the most of it. The King's shot, he declares, was glorious, it was passing glorious. 'Odd's bodkins,' he says, the world has seen nothing so awesomely ballistic since Tamburlaine the Great pelted Samarkand with his trebuchet of skulls. The King decides he likes this man's style and if Sir Charles fails to earn himself an earldom, he is at least spared execution; and if he loses graciously again, he might achieve a baronetcy.

And as for the ball, it lies alone, unseen and untouched, wedged on the upside of one of the beams, in a little dark coign, for almost half a millennium. Blacker and blacker it grows, as it is covered with the fumes of successive technologies: coal fires, gas fires, petrol engines. Empires wax and wane around it.

Britain is supplanted by America, whose very existence has only been revealed to Europeans forty years before the ball is whacked aloft.

So in principle the ball might stay there forever, lost in mid-rally, frozen in a perpetual present tense all of its own, except that it is now only inches away from Jason Pickel's scrambling foot, and about to rejoin the narrative of history.

He could make his way back up to the gun, he reckoned, if he somehow hauled himself up the joists, which were about two feet apart. It would mean crawling upwards and backwards, hanging on like Spiderman. It would need amazing prehensile strength in his hands, but Jason had confidence in his physical strength; and he needed that rifle. Mind you, if he fell, it would be almost eighty-five feet and he felt a twinge for whomsoever he might land upon.

CHAPTER FORTY-SIX

1044 HRS

'My love.' Cameron had decided to try tact, and she turned to Adam with what she hoped was a tender look.

'Yes,' said Adam, distantly.

'When we went to NATO . . .' Cameron hated to ask him this. She couldn't bear to destroy him in her own eyes as, in one way or another, she had destroyed all her previous boyfriends; but details, recollections, oddities were now crowding in upon her memory and innocent acts of the loved one now seemed pregnant with suspiciousness.

'Yes,' repeated Adam. 'When we went to NATO.'

Over their heads Chester de Peverill was ranting about GM crops and Frankenstein foods, while Haroun, Habib, Benedicte and her two accomplices played the muzzles of their Schmidts over the crowd, as if pretending to hose them with bullets.

'You know when we went inside the main building to see Brady Cunningham.'

'Of course. Brady Cunningham.' He pronounced it the American way, as though describing a particularly wily piece of pork.

'Did you know he was a friend of my father's?'

'Yes, of course I did. You told me he was.'

'I mean before we went to NATO, before all the trouble, did you know we might meet him?'

'What do you mean?'

'I don't know,' she said miserably, 'I don't know what I mean.'

What happened was this. Yesterday morning, before their drunken lunch at the Ogenblick, they had been out to NATO to protest against the President, who was making a speech to what is called the North Atlantic Council, comprising the nineteen NATO Ambassadors. As the reader will know by now, Cameron had mixed feelings about this, but went along with it because it was kind of amusing.

The dirty don and his wife were full of teenage insurrection. 'You know in 1986 I think I went to demonstrate against the Greenham Women,' he said.

'We both did,' said his wife.

'Good Lord, how plastered we must have been. Anyway look at us now,' he said, and the Mercedes shook with laughter. When they arrived at NATO HQ in Evere, on the Brussels ring road, they found themselves outside the perimeter fortifications of a building that looked like – and, indeed, had been constructed as – a suburban maternity hospital. As a quartet they did not really fit in with the rest of the crowd, who lacked their urbanity and air of mild derision. The mob was a smaller, more dedicated version of the one outside Westminster Hall today, with a higher proportion of nose rings and Socialist Worker Party badges and Yasser Arafat headscarves; and more angry brown faces.

So Cameron didn't participate in the stuck pig squealing as the cavalcade arrived, nor did they make *oink oink oink* noises in honour of the police. Nor did they try to rush the steel fence, as the hard cases did at 11 a.m., just as the President was slated to speak. But when the dirty don accidentally dropped a half-empty champagne bottle, from which they had all been swigging, a group of three riot cops converged.

Their leader was a burly Fleming with a scraggly black beard over his pockmarked cheeks. He appeared to be shaking with anger. 'I'm so sorry,' said the dirty don, hoofing the pieces together with his foot and putting them in a plastic bag. The cop, blue suited, black booted, demanded their passports. His hairy hand crawled over the shiny leather holster at his hip.

'It just sort of slipped,' said the academic.

'*Ayez la gentillesse*,' screamed the policeman, looking up from his methodical leafing, the veins standing out in his neck, '*de parler un des deux langues de mon pays.*' Speak in one of the two languages of my country. Cameron wanted to tell him that they were on his side.

She and Adam agreed: they didn't see why the whole world should speak English, just because the Americans spoke English. The don, who spoke fourteen languages fluently, and who could read the script of many more, came to her help. He tried to soothe the cop, he addressed him in good Flemish and then French and then German, since German is one of Belgium's three official languages, with substantial German minorities in the eastern towns of Eupen, Malmedy and Sankt Vith. But when faced with an outraged Flemish policeman, you have only limited options.

You can run, but he will have no hesitation in shooting you in the back. You can try to bribe him, an option which can be surprisingly successful, but which does not yet automatically occur to British people. You can weep and slobber over his boots, which is what he probably wants. What you must not do is patronize him and Stefan Van de Kerkhove, luitnant in the Belgian riot police, felt patronized by the erudition of the don.

They were all under arrest, he told them, in English. They were being taken to a nasty-looking Belgian police van, white with blue stripes, when Cameron had an idea. She took out her mobile and rang her father in North Carolina. Even at 6 a.m. eastern seaboard time, he was awake.

Her father rang Brady Cunningham, his old friend from West Point, who was now General Brady Cunningham and sitting in his office in the southern wing of NATO, not 100 feet from where they were standing. Within five minutes General Cunningham had sprung them from the clutches of the Flemish riot police and the four demonstrators were being offered coffee in the heart of the US delegation to NATO.

Cameron remembered the great tact with which Adam had handled the square-headed Costner clones of the American military. 'Oh no, sir,' he told the General, 'we weren't there as demonstrators, we were there as observers.'

In the New Scotland Yard Ops Room, they had given up trying to raise Pickel on his radio. 'OK,' said Bluett, 'here's what we do. Ricasoli says he went into the hall through a hatch in the roof, right?'

'That's correct, sir. That's what he thinks.'

'Get me a shot of the roof, an external shot.'

'You mean a picture? You want a picture of the hall.'

'We must have a camera somewhere.' In a matter of seconds the requisite camera shot was found – from the top of the Treasury – and patched through to the Ops Room screens.

'Ricasoli,' said Bluett, dialling him up, 'I want you to get someone on that roof and give some stuff to Lieutenant Pickel. I want you to land right here in the square in oh one minutes and pick it up. Have you got that?'

'Yessir,' said Ricasoli, who was just thinking that if it was all the same to Bluett he would rather not be the man to land on the roof.

'If necessary, do it yourself,' said Bluett.

'I'm only asking this because I feel obliged to ask,' said Deputy Assistant Commissioner Purnell, 'but are you sure Pickel is the right man? You know we've got a very good shot, Indira Natu, who could be deployed very quickly.'

'Pickel,' said Bluett, 'Pickel could shoot the moustache off a gnat at 1,000 paces. The guy's a phenomenon. He may be a freak, but you want a rhino dart in that man's neck, Pickel's the boy to put it there for you.'

'Fair enough.'

'Course, they do say he's a bit funny sometimes, after what happened in Baghdad.'

'I was going to mention that. In fact, the word was passed along from SO19 that he'd been acting up a bit on the roof, seemed in a bit of a state, Nam flashbacks and all that sort of thing.'

'Someone reported on Pickel?'

'Yes, that's it, the police sniper I mentioned. Of course, I should have asked you, but time was tight.'

'You should have asked me what?'

'Whether it was right to give orders to detain him.'

'And you . . . ?'

'Er, yes.'

Bluett glared, secretly delighted that his opposite number had committed such a faux pas. Was it time for Bluett to blow it? he wondered. But as the Deputy Assistant Commissioner said, time was not on their side.

'Just reassure me about one thing: this dart – you sure it's going to knock him out in time?'

'Oh yes,' said the bright young officer who had thought up the idea. 'It's thyapentine sodium. It takes three seconds to put a rhino to sleep.'

'And it won't actually kill him or set off the bomb?'

'Oh no. I mean, no, not at all.'

'History is going to judge us, Mr Commissioner,' said Bluett to Purnell, 'history is going to judge us.'

CHAPTER FORTY-SEVEN
1049 HRS

'And do you know how they make a cocktail sausage?' Chester de Peverill asked. 'They get all the fat they can't sell in other cuts of meat, and then they add something called drind, which is dried pig rind which expands when you add water, and then they add mechanically recovered meat. Mr

President, ladies and gentlemen, do you know what mechanically recovered meat is? It's what you get when you turn a fire hose on the carcass of the animal, a jet of unimaginable power, and you squirt off every scrap of fibre and gristle and tissue and you create a great slurry of unidentifiable swill, which you sieve into a pulp and then you add . . .'

Haroun walked with deliberate tread down the aisle, three paces per slab. He approached Habib, and their eyes met. Each knew what the other was thinking. Why did Jones insist on this foolery? Why were they listening to this disgusting infidel chef and his preposterous recipes for unclean food? The sooner they consummated their operation the better. Time was passing and the Americans were resourceful.

'Why don't we just kill him?' hissed Haroun to Habib as they passed.

'Soon, brother,' replied Habib, keeping his eyes travelling around the crowd. 'Soon, may it please Allah.'

Haroun listened to the change in the note of the helicopter that had been hovering above them, and then saw a shadow pass over the south window as the Black Hawk descended.

'And then do you know what Big Food puts in your cocktail sausage, Mr President? Even in the ones you serve in the White House? They put tons of sugar and salt and a load of bread crusts to make it hold water. It's disgusting, it's evil, it's' – Haroun hawked violently, as though preparing to discharge a great custard gob of phlegm. He hoped to put Chester off his stride. He did not succeed.

Haroun discovered another reason why he was starting to feel uncomfortable: his bladder was still full after a night in the ambulance, and the coffee he had drunk in the Tivoli was now bursting to be liberated from his body.

*   *   *

Cameron sieved her memory, but still couldn't think how Adam had done what she now suspected. They must have been in that office for all of fifteen minutes. They sat on oatmeal-coloured sofas, they chin-wagged absently with the General; and then they were escorted off the NATO premises with great friendliness, much to the surprise of the rest of the mob, who were still waiting for the President to reappear.

They got in a taxi; they went to the Ogenblick. How had he done it? She had to find the courage to ask him. 'Adam,' she said, still holding him by the hand, 'did you take anything from Brady Cunningham's office?'

Adam shut his eyes, feeling a weight of despair at his own folly. 'Take something?'

'That's right. This feels real dumb, but I found something.'

'You found something?' He was frowning again. 'Where did you find something?'

'Well I'm ashamed to say this, but I have to get it off my chest. I found it in your bag.'

Adam took his hand away from hers.

'My bag? You mean in the hotel? What were you doing looking in my bag?'

It must have been two in the morning. Cameron was lying awake, in a state of post-coital rapture. Outside, Brussels was subsiding into silence. The restaurants had taken in their great seafood still-lives; they had removed the huge tableaux of lobsters and langoustines and oysters and mussels, arrayed on beds of ice in whorls and fans, like mad Flemish genre paintings, trundled them inside the dining rooms and left them to drip in the dark. There was no noise save the odd police siren, the bray of some lost stag night reveller and the resistless metronomic breathing of the man she now thought she loved. As he lay there she studied the big square structure of his chest, with one muscular arm flung wide, and the hairs slowly rising and falling as he breathed. One part of her wanted him to wake up, and do that wonderful thing to her again; and as she studied him she started to feel a crushing sense of anxiety. What if he was in some way misleading her? What if he had no real feeling for her?

And in her paranoia, she remembered something earlier. Adam had been doing something with his bag when she came out of the shower.

She knew exactly what she looked like as she came back into his presence. She had dried herself and was wearing only a short silk thing with straps. She was looking – this may sound crude, but it is no less than the truth – like a lingerie model only cleverer and, if anything, with bigger breasts.

He had turned, and picked her up, and carried her on to the bed. Now, in the small hours, she remembered that just before then he had started shoving something he was reading into his bag, and zipped it up.

She brooded on this detail. There had definitely been a touch of furtiveness in his manner.

'Oh boy,' she breathed to herself in the dark, as the obvious answer struck her. He was married. He not only had a wife in Surbiton, he had a brace of kids. Make that a gaggle. And she had caught him reading their school reports. With a grim and mounting certainty, she peeled back the coverlet and placed her high-arched feet on the carpet. He was still breathing steadily.

Tiptoe, tiptoe, she went across the carpet. She bent down. Had Professor Adam Swallow woken at that moment, he would have seen a sight to make a bishop kick a hole in a stained-glass window. But he did not wake up, and as Cameron stealthily unzipped the bag, she prepared for the shock, and she constructed the necessary mental defences and excuses. She would find a moment to bring it up with him in a gentle, roundabout way, and she would try to draw him out. Maybe she would make some kind of little confession herself, as a way of getting the conversation going.

But as she reached into the bag, and prepared to extract the document, she could feel the pain preparing to course through her system. Perhaps his admiration for Islam had encouraged him to enlist a small assortment of wives. She held up a cardboard folder in the tangerine light from the street.

'SACEUR,' it said at the top, in capitals and then, 'US Military: Restricted,' and it gave that year's date. With a ludicrous sense of jubilation, she put it back and slipped into bed.

It was just some boring address book, she thought; and, believe it or not, Cameron made no connection as she eventually drifted off between its presence in Adam's bag and their earlier visit to NATO.

The anomalies had popped up only now, as a corpse will surface only some time after a drowning, and she wanted an explanation.

'OK,' said Adam. 'All right.' He spoke in dead tones, unable to meet her eyes. 'You're perfectly right. I'll explain.'

It takes huge upper body strength to climb upwards and backwards on the inside of a roof with nowhere for your hands and feet to go but the joists. And the joists offered no proper purchase, nothing about which he could curve his fingers. Insofar as he was able to grip the wood at all, it was by means of the sheer pressure he was able to exert with his fingers and thumbs.

But Pickel was remarkably strong; his hands were like those of a farmer or a manual labourer, pumped up by squeezing squash balls to double normal human size. He was also maddened with frustration, furious with himself for missing in the yard and then losing his gun, disgusted at the drivel rising like pollution from the debate below.

As soon as he had whacked the guy who was holding the President, thought Pickel, he might quietly drill a couple of holes in that hinky chef dude, the one who didn't like sausages.

He didn't know what was wrong with the world: a bunch of towelhead sickos, threatening to kill the President of the USA and some faggot Limey stands up and makes a speech attacking hamburgers.

Rage impelled him up the inside of the roof, and all he needed, he told himself, was speed and a clear run and absolute concentration. So it was unfortunate, as he looked up to check that he was aiming for the hatch, that he should receive a surprise. There was a face silhouetted in the hatch and the face was saying something to him.

'Hey Pickel,' whispered the person and removed his gun from the latch. One of Pickel's hands slipped off the joist, his foot came off the joist two below. For an instant Pickel hung above the audience, eyes bugging, joints popping, on the point of descending so violently on to the orating Chester de Peverill that he would surely have turned him into the hamburger the chef so deplored.

With a grunting convulsion, Pickel managed to regain control. He shot back down the ladder of joists as fast as he could, to take the strain off his arms, and he reached for the beam again.

He jammed his toe into the corner, just to wedge himself like a human piton. His toecap connected with the ancient tennis ball. After almost 500 years of seclusion, the ball rolled six inches off the beam and began the long drop back into play.

CHAPTER FORTY-EIGHT
1052 HRS

The President was among the first to see it: one of the advantages of having your eyes close set together, like Bjorn Borg, the tennis champion, is you can focus on balls a long way away. He thought it was a grenade, perhaps tear gas, the opening gambit of some desperate rescue plan. His first thought was that he was going to die.

Haroun didn't see it. He couldn't really concentrate on anything much at the moment except the buildup of molten lava in his lower abdomen. He was damned if he was going to urinate in front of all these shameless foreign women, like some incontinent child. It would be a haram, a disgrace; and so he was staring at the wall to avoid their eyes and hoping to distract himself from the urging of his medulla oblongata by counting every one of the big grey stones that made up the right-hand wall.

Barlow did see it, because he happened to be staring up again, praying that a thunderbolt would descend and destroy Chester de Peverill, leaving nothing but a pile of ash smoking in his Timberland loafers. He saw a small object detach itself from the area of blinding white below the TV lights. He saw the thing grow bigger in the 2.1 seconds it took to fall, and though he flinched, he knew with a sudden unarticulated joy – because he had a good eye for a ball – that there was a reasonable chance it would fall on the head of the prating prat beside him. Which it did.

Ponk went the ball on the head of the TV chef. De Peverill bellowed.

Women screamed in the rows around him. Men screamed, too, and shouted and swore. 'What was that?' shouted Jones as the Arab gunmen and woman whipped round and the ball rolled under the chairs. Everyone looked at the space in the rafters from which the ball had come. They blinked. They squinted. They listened to the noise of the helicopter, which now seemed to be directly overhead.

They couldn't be sure whether they could see something up there, or whether it was the green and purple blotches left on the retina by the scalding TV lights. Jones thought it important to assert his command of the situation.

'Die, infidel son of a whore,' he said and loosed off a round from his Browning in the general direction of Pickel. The American sniper was gone. With a single fluid lunge he had travelled up and back, wrenching his trapezius muscles but successfully gaining the hatch that led back to the flèche.

The combination of the gunshot and the little leather bomblet had frazzled the President's nerves. He had given up alcohol many years ago but seldom had he felt more in need of a stiff one, or a cigarette. 'Say buddy,' he said to Jones, 'would you have a piece of gum?'

'*Hssst*,' said Jones, as the tennis ball was recovered from under the chair of a hostage, and brought by one of the Arabs for his inspection. What in the name of the prophet? He held the sphere between finger and thumb, momentarily resting his gun on the lectern. It looked like a coprolite. He hadn't a clue what it was, but it spelled mischief.

'Come on,' he yelled at the President, putting the ball on the lectern, picking up his gun and yanking on the handcuffs. It was time to activate plan B. Jones had worked out long ago that he would need a fallback position. The British and the Americans were bound to come up with a response, and the longer he and the President stood on the dais, the more vulnerable he would be.

'Dean, follow me,' he ordered, and gave instructions to Haroun, Habib and the rest of the Arabs to keep charge of the crowd. Dragging the President in his wake and waving the automatic, he marched down the aisle. To Cameron's horror, he was staring at her as he advanced. She stared back, entranced by those wobbly brown irises in those blood-shot eyes.

'Professor Swallow,' he shouted. 'Adam,' he said, and Cameron found herself feeling no longer sick, but kind of spacey, detached in a personal bubble of horror. Oh my gosh, she thought, it's true, it's all true, and it's all a goddamn lie.

Adam said something to Jones the Bomb in Arabic.

He said: 'You'll pay for this, you moron.' But Cameron didn't know Arabic, and looked at him with wild suspicion.

'Come on, my love,' said Adam, 'we've got to go with them or they'll kill us.'

'They'll kill us anyway.'

'No they won't. Maybe. I don't know.'

The air immediately above the hall was now being churned so violently by the Black Hawk rotors that a tile was dislodged, and skittered ominously down the Himalayan shoulders of the building.

'Hurry!' shouted Jones to Adam and Cameron, and waved his Browning. Bobbing behind in the cuffs, the President hoped that the cameras could not see his expression as Jones and his party made for the exit.

On the left of Westminster Hall, as you face it from the north door, there is a curious stone balustrade with a low flight of steps leading up on either side. The banisters are decorated by carved stone heraldic beasts, chip-eared lions, a crack-horned unicorn and a stag missing part of his antler. Underneath the balustrade are steps leading to a set of swing doors which give access to a series of small meeting rooms called W1, W2, W3, W4, W5 and W6, where MPs encounter their constituents.

Here Jones hastened, having decided that room W6 was the most easily defended, being along a corridor, virtually subterranean, and only accessible by the one door from Westminster Hall. He stood on the steps and turned to ensure that his party was in order: the President, Cameron and Adam as hostages, and Dean, his skin now having an eerie Venusian tinge, bringing up the rear. 'Don't do anything stupid,' yelled Jones the Bomb at the crowd. 'If anyone tries to follow us he will die, or she.'

He was on the point of descending the steps when a voice from the crowd objected. It was Chester de Peverill, who had recovered from the shock of the ball on his head.

'Hang on,' he said. 'What about my speech: do you want me to carry on?'

CHAPTER FORTY-NINE
1053 HRS

'My dear fellow,' said Jones the Bomb, 'there is nothing that would give me greater pleasure. I will not be able to watch you in person, but I believe there may be a television down here. Carry on.' And he was gone.

'Actually,' said Chester, 'now I come to think of it, I think I've almost finished my speech. I might as well sit down.'

'So soon?' said Barlow. 'Are you sure?'

There was a silence, and a kind of power vacuum. Despite his instructions, it was not clear which of the Arabs Jones had left in charge of the debate. Habib and Haroun disapproved, and in any case Haroun was now afflicted by a Chernobyl in his underpants.

He was starting to jig up and down, as children do, waggling his hand as though playing an imaginary guitar. Nothing could mask the incontrovertible and overwhelming pressure on his urethra. Several people in the audience noticed his demeanour. I don't like the look of that one, they thought. Chap's on crack cocaine.

The two other Arabs were chauffeurs from the Kuwaiti Embassy, and they hadn't got the hang of Jones's debate at all, so it was left to Benedicte.

She marched to the vacant lectern and yelped into the

mike, 'Come on, ladies and gentlemen, *mesdames, messieurs,* who wants to be the next?'

Once again the forest of would-be speakers sprang up. Roger Barlow, Ziggy Roberts, Sir Perry Grainger, and a score of others. Benedicte's eye fell on her lover, the French Ambassador. He was standing turkey-breasted, glaring haughtily at his girlfriend.

'*Un instant, chéri,*' said Benedicte. 'Ladies first.'

Not far from the Ambassador, on the other side of the aisle, a lady had risen. Her age was unclear but she was certainly no younger than seventy. Her silvery hair was cut short, and her attire was grey and white, and of almost nunlike severity. She was a peer of the realm, a former Home Office minister, a grandmother of twenty children.

She was Elspeth, Baroness Hovell, the scourge of the gay lobby, the abominator of abortion, the defender of corporal punishment (lovingly administered), and the only politician of any party to have the guts to question whether it was the business of the Treasury to use endless fiscal incentives to drive women out to work. In short, she was one of the few people there whose views and manifesto approximated to those of an Islamic fundamentalist, which was why she was known to her enemies – the right-on columnists, the standup comedians – as Old Ironpants, or the Mullah.

'Ladies and gentlemen,' she began, 'I hope it will not be thought too much of an insult to everyone here present, if I say that I believe our conduct, our collective conduct, is pretty pathetic. Like quite a few of us in this room I am old enough to remember the war, and I must say that this is not how we won it. We are being held to ransom by a bunch of terrorist louts, just a handful of them, and we sit here, and do nothing about it. I say . . .'

'Please, madam, please,' said Benedicte, interrupting as politely as she could. 'You are not on the good path at all. You should be speaking of American abuse of human rights.'

'I beg your pardon,' said Lady Hovell, as though a ticket inspector had just sworn at her on the number 19 bus. 'Did you say American abuse of human rights?'

'That's right, you must say whether the prisoners should be released.'

'Well, I must say that strikes me as a bit hypocritical. What about your abuse of our human rights? Are you or are you not depriving us of our liberty?'

Oh Lord, thought Roger Barlow. The old bat's going to get herself killed, or at least she's going to get someone killed.

There were quite a few who seemed to agree. A neighbour tugged at her sleeve. 'Sit down, Elspeth,' hissed another.

'I will not sit down,' said the battleaxe. 'It's perfectly obvious they are relying on us to behave like sheep, and I'm afraid I don't see why I should oblige.'

On the roof Jason Pickel was being given a swift and sketchy tutorial in the use of a rhino tranquillizer gun.

'But the President's left the room, and the freaking mother's gone with him. What am I supposed to do 'n' all?'

'It's all right, Pickel: you go back down and wait for them to come out again.' Ricasoli was hanging on to a rope ladder which was hanging from the Black Hawk, bucking in the air, and the captain was green with fear. Above them the skies were gravid with monsoon, and the whole thing was like a bad scene from America's Indo-Chinese nightmare.

'What if they don't come out again?'

Ricasoli didn't know the answer to that one. 'They will, Pickel, they will.'

The burly sniper blinked his gingery lashes. 'Whyn't I abseil down into the hall, sneak into the room where he's being held, and try to save him that way? It might be our only chance.' He was thinking: it might be my only chance.

'No, Pickel,' said Ricasoli. 'You do as you're told. You're the man, Pickel,' said the quivering captain, knowing it was time to big up his subordinate. 'You're the best damn shot in the whole goddamn army.'

'Watch this,' said Pickel. And before Ricasoli could object, he picked out a leprous Victorian gryphon, ulcerated by acid rain, crouched on the roof 150 feet away. He pulled the trigger and the gryphon's head exploded. 'Clean through the eye,' said Pickel, disappearing again through the hatch. Freaking Brits could pay for it.

'And I speak up,' continued Old Ironpants, the moralizing peeress, 'because I believe we have sat through one of the most ill-judged speeches ever to have been uttered in this chamber.'

There were several strong expressions of assent. 'Hear, hear,' exploded Sir Perry Grainger, and others.

'I think it pretty disgraceful, when our country is after all playing host to the President of the United States, that anyone should stand up and say anything which could be construed as supportive of those who were preparing to murder him, and indeed us.'

'Hear, hear.' Sir Perry was on his feet clapping wildly, as were some others. Roger turned to Chester de Peverill and gave a shrug, as if to say, you can't win them all.

De Peverill also shrugged. What did he care? He needed controversy, and as his marketing people never ceased to remind him, the old bag's generation were not commercially important. They weren't the ones with the disposable income to buy his 'Ripper Tucker' © TV cassoulet, yours for £5.99 each.

'I was only trying to be diplomatic,' he grumbled. 'Read the books. You should never confront these guys.'

'All right, lady, all right, lady,' said Benedicte. She admired Lady Hovell's gumption, but it was time to show who was boss. 'Lady be quiet now or else some bad thing is going to happen, right away.'

'I will certainly not be quiet,' said Lady Hovell. At the very

277

top of the hall, behind their railing, the inspissated holders of Britain's ancient courtly offices were beginning to stir. There was something in the Agincourt spirit of Old Ironpants that sent the sap rising in their limbs, as the xylem and phloem can pump unexpectedly in a half-dead oak.

'You know what?' said Silver Stick to the Earl Marshal. 'She's bloody right. If we all just charge her now while her back's turned . . .' He glanced across at Black Rod, and he could see the light of battle in his eyes, too.

Behind them the pikes and halberds quivered, as the spirit of these objects collectively remembered their roles in battles gone by. The Earl Marshal groaned. 'But then they'll just set off their bombs,' he pointed at Habib and Haroun. 'And the other chap is bound to kill the President.'

'Oh all right,' said Silver Stick. 'Have it your way. Let's all just hang around and wait to die.' He sounded bitter, but he had to admit that the Earl Marshal had a point.

CHAPTER FIFTY
1058 HRS

As a TV spectacle, the events in Westminster Hall had lost some of their appalling fascination, after the departure of the President and Jones the Bomb. No one was really sure who the lady peeress was, though quite a few watchers agreed vehemently with what she said. The TV networks responded magnificently, however, to the shortage of more decent pictures of the President being humiliated.

At quite senior level in the BBC, it was decided they could cut away from the live coverage of Chester de Peverill and Old Ironpants. To the joy and distress of billions – still repli-cating at a Malthusian rate – they showed, again and again, the money shot of Jones clobbering the leader of the free world over the back of his head. They showed Jones firing at the Dutchman; they showed him holding up the enigmatic turd object that had dropped from the roof, while the President looked dumbly on.

The media hysteria had now reached levels not seen since the death of the Princess of Wales in 1997. And in fact the response was more hysterical because it was a running story, a breaking story, of unguessable consequences whose end could not be foretold.

Radio programmes of all kinds were being interrupted with the news that, 'the President of the United States, senior members of the Government, and hundreds of others, are being held hostage at Westminster. A group calling itself the Brotherhood of the Two Mosques is demanding the release of all the remaining prisoners held in Guantanamo Bay. At least one person is believed to have been killed by the terrorists who are threatening to detonate suicide bombs. The Prime Minister has called for calm. We go live now to Westminster.'

And the news from the voting was still bad for America, though not as bad as it had seemed at first. Some countries, such as Saudi Arabia were reporting almost 100 per cent insistence that the prisoners be sent home. But there were odd pockets of support for the President. He might have thought that Russia, after her humiliation in the Cold War, would take the chance to put her boot on the neck of the old adversary. But no, the Russians had their problems in Chechnya. They took a dim view of Islamic terror. Maybe there was some kind of fiddling of the figures by the oligarchs who ran the TV stations (and who were mainly, as some lost no time in pointing out, of Jewish origin), but it seemed that Russia, one of the most populous countries in the world, was voting heavily for America.

'We can put it out,' said the Director of Political Editorial, coming down to the BBC newsroom like Moses from Sinai.

279

'They just green-lighted it. We can report the aggregate polling figures.'

The BBC had decided that since the information was out on the net, and since all other channels were already crunching the numbers, they might as well go ahead. With elaborate editorial throat clearing and issuing of health warnings, they did the work of Jones the Bomb.

They broadcast the news that of people calling TV channels to express a preference, 58 per cent now believed that the American President should release the Guantanamo prisoners.

Jones was almost incontinent with pleasure. He cachinnated like a gibbon, as the figure was flashed on the screen. 'You see, you see,' he cried, doing a little dance, which the poor President was obliged to echo. They were standing in room W6 watching the television. It was a small, poky window-less room, with a nondescript conference table and the chairs and carpets in parliamentary green. Cameron and Adam were standing behind them, he looking calm, she preparing herself to interrogate him further.

'So go on then,' gibbered Jones, thrusting his face close to the President. 'You have seen the verdict of the world. The majority is clear. This time there are no hanging chads and stuffed ballot boxes, like you have in Florida. What do you say?'

'Well,' said the President, 'well.'

It was dawning on him that he might have to take a decision. Alone, shackled to a lunatic, with three other weirdos, besieged in some dungeon-like meeting room of the British Parliament, with no one to advise him but the blurting television, he was being called upon to make a choice of enormous moral and political implications. For the first time in his career, he was deprived of the jowly counsel of the businessmen who formed the upper reaches of his administration. 'Well, buddy,' he said, 'I think we should wait and see.

You say the verdict is clear, but I notice that the numbers have been changing a little. According to this fellow here,' he gestured at the BBC with his free hand, 'it's come down from 61 per cent to 58 per cent.'

'Coward!' yapped Jones. 'You do not even have the courage to do what the world wants you to do. We are the voice of the people of the earth. The poor people. The people that America abuses and insults and tortures. We are asking for one small thing. You do not have to give our comrades a Presidential pardon. We do not even say that they are all entirely innocent of crime. We only say they must be brought to trial in a country where they can receive a fair trial. Give the order, Mr President.'

Silence for a second. The noise of the helicopter, more muffled than in the main hall. Another crash, as though another tile had come off the roof. Then a mysterious vibration, as though the whole building were starting to shiver and purr like an ancient cat in its sleep. It was rain, falling on the roof, as a sudden drop in temperature released the thousands of gallons the heat had been holding in the sky.

'No, sir, I can't do that just yet.'

'Give the order and you will go free. But if you fail to accept the verdict of the people, then it will be my pleasure and honour to kill you, even if I lose my own life.'

The President narrowed his eyes and looked again at the screen. The fellow seemed serious. Must be to do what he'd already done. The President didn't want to die, not at all, not for the sake of the Guantanamo prisoners. His brain revolved, not normally the fastest process known to nature, but now accelerated by adrenalin.

He could pretend to capitulate and give the order, and then double-cross Jones the Bomb. But no, then people would think he was weak, and in any event, the terrorists might kill him anyway. But if he did nothing, people would also think he was passive and powerless.

'Mr Jones, sir.' It was Dean, putting his hand up to speak. Cameron watched him closely. 'Mr Jones, I think we've done enough now: can we stop?'

Again and again Dean saw the mysterious round weapon drop from the roof. In his imagination it portended the inevitable retaliation of the superpower and its lieutenants. He saw men with guns dropping from the ceiling on ropes. Violent men, who shot without questions, and then kicked their corpses.

'What do you mean, stop?' said Jones impatiently.

'Well, I think we've made our point.'

Jones glanced at the President and the others, as though to confirm that they had heard this impertinence. 'Dean,' he said in his softest and most murderous tones. 'Shut up.'

'They're going to kill us, Mr Jones, and they'll never let us out of here alive.' Dean was aware that this was a paradoxical complaint, given what he had nominally undertaken to do.

'But we've discussed this.'

'I've been thinking, and I agree with yow, Mr Jones, sir. I agree with yow about everything, but I'm not sure . . .'

'You're not sure what?'

'I'm not sure that I, like, really want to die.'

'Assuredly, Dean, if we die, angels will accompany us to our rest, and we will lay our heads on pillowy bowers, and we will live in the tabernacle of the blessed, where no rain falls, neither is there any snow, and the warm breezes play . . .'

Dean shouted: 'I don't care. Anyway, I like snow.' For the first time that day Jones the Bomb looked taken aback. It was if a snake had been hypnotizing a rabbit and the rabbit had suddenly stuck its tongue out.

He glared. Dean bit his lower lip. He had been on the wrong side of the law before. Ever since the cremation of the neighbouring cheese laboratory, he had felt a fugitive, an alien, but never had he felt so lost in a jungle of fear, and now the great white hunters were coming for him, and he was among the rabid beasts that must be put down. Cameron stood up and moved towards him.

Dean resumed. 'I'm just saying that I wanna . . .'

'You want to surrender? Will you do nothing to help our brothers who are fighting and dying in Palestine?'

'Well, I think I have helped you know, so I honestly think we've done our bit.'

'Do you want to give into this world of pornography and decadence, and the abuse of womankind . . . ?'

'And freedom and democracy and the rule of law,' said the President.

'Quiet,' said Jones the Bomb, yanking his chain. 'Dean,' said Jones, 'you took a holy oath that you would join the ranks of the Shahid, that you would be a martyr.' On the way down the corridor to room W6, Dean had looked quickly out of one of the leaded windows. He saw that the crowd was being dispersed from Parliament Square, and that the men in blue were being joined by men in green.

'Listen, mister,' said Cameron. 'I think he made it pretty clear that he doesn't want to be a suicide bomber.'

'What is it to you, woman?'

'Don't you woman me.'

'Adam,' snapped Jones at Dr Swallow, who stared levelly back. 'She is your responsibility; kindly take charge of her.'

'No one takes responsibility for me,' said Cameron.

'Yeah, Mr Jones, sir,' said the President. 'Welcome to Western civilization, buddy. Get with the programme.'

'Hold your tongues the lot of you.' He shoved his automatic into the President's temple so hard that he winced. Then Jones pulled the gun away and pointed it at Cameron and then at Dean. There was a silence.

'Well,' said Cameron to Adam. 'Aren't you going to say anything?'

'There's nothing I can say,' he told the girl he loved. 'I've been a fool, and I've been cheated. Cameron, I'm sorry.'

CHAPTER FIFTY-ONE
1103 HRS

There was something amiss with Haroun, thought Benedicte. She knew the man craved martyrdom, but he was red-faced with impatience. He walked towards her with tiny steps, as though trying to keep a walnut between his knees.

'Quickly,' he said.

'What is thees queeckly?' she whispered.

'It is time to blast these sons of goats and monkeys.'

'We must wait for Monsieur Jones to come back.'

'No! If I wait any more, something will happen.'

'What ees something?'

'Something bad. To me.'

The Palestinian girl looked closely at Haroun.

'*Mais tu veux faire pi-pi, chéri?*'

Haroun didn't like Benedicte. Her chic white T-shirt unambiguously revealed the location of her nipples. She was not attired like a black-eyed one.

He jerked his chin.

'But go on then,' she chuckled, waving the muzzle of the Uzi at the swing doors. 'We can manage.'

And if anybody laughs at me now, thought Haroun as he minced out, I will shoot them in the bladder.

'Tootle pip,' called Lady Hovell to his smouldering back, 'you clear off, and take Ulrika Meinhof here while you are at it.'

The acting terrorist leader walked towards her down the aisle, noiseless in her Nike Airs.

'I think I should warn you that you don't scare me, young lady.'

'Then you are brave but you are not smart.'

'In fact, there is only one thing that really frightens me.'

'And what is that?'

'I am frightened of the disapproval of God.'

'*Ferme ta gueule*. How do you say it in English?'

'I've no idea.'

'Shut you the fat gob.'

'My advice is to follow that young man, find the nearest policeman, and hand over that gun.'

As the two women stood next to each other, the rain outside deepened in tone. The drops swelled and thickened to the size of currants, or even gulls' eggs, and a great drumming came from the roof. A cloud of Turneresque blackness rolled across the London sky, and as the light died in the windows, strange shadows formed on the women's faces.

'Go home, dear,' said the Baroness.

Benedicte stuck her snout right next to the ancient map.

'Now is the time for the beeg silence.' She raised the Uzi to her ear. 'Or else the silence will be the long one.'

'What you need, if you ask my opinion, is a nice husband.'

'Shut your face, *vieille putain!*'

'I'm no—'

Benedicte pulled the trigger. Even as far back as Barlow and de Peverill, the shots buffeted their eustachian tubes, as though someone was ripping calico just by their ears.

Lady Hovell clapped her hand to her heart. She sat down. Her eyes fell away from Benedicte, and at once she looked like anyone's old grandma, just told a piece of bad news by the docs.

A noise went up from the audience, a small but unanimous exhalation. They knew that they had sustained a defeat.

Was Lady Hovell's chin wobbling? Was that a crinkle on the jaw that had never trembled in forty years of sneering from men who weren't fit to lick her boots? It was hard to tell. But as Silver Stick gazed at her from afar, tears formed in his ducts, of love and fright.

Frig me spastic, thought Jason Pickel, as the bullets ate into the main collar beam, just ten feet below him. That could have been a serious inguinal injury.

He squinted below, to check whether the mad A-rab bitch might fire again. Then slowly he looped the nylon rope round the crown post, tied it tight, and then began to slide it through two carabiners at his belt.

When he had finished, he crouched once again over the gathering, his big shoulders hunched, rifle ready, like an eagle as it waits for its moment.

Adam was still saying nothing, and Cameron was looking at the TV, trying not to hurt.

The BBC had a 'Russian expert', who was casting doubt on the oddly pro-American numbers from Russian TV.

She had to know about his theft. 'So how did you take it?'

'I am afraid I just put my newspapers and stuff on top of it, and then scooped it all up when we all left.'

'So what are you, a spy?'

He groaned. 'Yes, I suppose I am. But it's got nothing to do with this business.'

'And who are you supposed to be spying for?'

Dean watched their conversation. In particular, he watched Cameron, and noticed more detail: the tilt of her nose, the bangle on her wrist, the little white scar on her slender left arm. He shivered, and listened to the rattle of the rain. Not only had the temperature fallen, but the adrenalin was turning sour in his veins, leaving a hangover of fear.

Jones the Bomb spoke. 'The door is open, Dean, my young friend.'

Dean looked at the door. On the contrary, it was shut.

'But if you go through that door now, remember that you will lose all chance of bliss. You have a chance now' – he stared with his mongoose intensity – 'to obtain the stone that is more precious than the world and anything that is in it. Remember, my dear Dean, that when the first drop of blood is spilled, the shahid does not feel the pain of his wounds, and all his sins are forgiven. He sees his seat in Paradise, and he is saved from the torment of the grave—'

'Mr Jones, sir, I just don't believe in paradise.'

The President looked keenly at him. No one ever got elected President of the United States without believing in paradise.

Jones made a sad face: 'I know it is difficult, and I know it is frightening, and I know we all have moments when we feel we have lost our faith . . .'

'You bet your sweet ass,' said the President.

'But I hope you still have faith in me, Dean. Do you?'

'Do I what?'

'Have faith in the person who has liberated you from the false values of Western decadence?'

Dean rose. He moved towards the door. 'Mr Jones, I. No. Yes. I . . . No.'

That's it, thought Roger Barlow, when Benedicte fired at the roof-beams. Get me out of this thing, dear Lord, and I promise I'll be good. I'm fed up with being bad.

Here are all the good things I am going to do. I'm going to pick up my towels from the bathroom floor. I'm going to start listening properly when she talks to me. I'm going to communicate. I'm going to stay awake after lights out, because it's always worth it in the end. I'm going to understand that the important thing is not to solve problems, but to discuss them. After fifteen years, I'm going to get the point that marriage is not a final act; it's like a meeting of the European agricultural ministers, an endless negotiation of insolubles.

I won't pick the corner of my toenails with a Bic biro lid. Ditto ears, or at least not at dinner parties.

I won't open tins of tuna and then leave them under the bed. I won't go to the fridge, take out a Waitrose raspberry trifle, eat it all, and then put back the licked-out plastic container.

I won't lose my temper when we get lost, and then refuse to ask the way. I'll stop farting under the duvet . . .

His eyes met the twitchy glare of Habib, who was walking down the aisle, swinging his gun like a sadistic maths master invigilating an exam.

It occurred to Roger that if he wanted divine intervention, he had better make some real concessions.

The noise from Benedicte's gun carried out into New Palace Yard. It penetrated the ambulance, and entered the ears of William Eric Kinloch Onyeama. One lung was half-full of blood.

The pericardial puncture unit had made a neat hole in his chest. His thoracic diaphragm had been punctured, his pericardial membrane was in a bad way and his sternum was severely scraped.

But Eric Onyeama was alive, and he owed his life to the Huskie.

It was the tough little computer which had served as his breastplate, and which had borne the brunt of Haroun's attack.

He had lost about four pints of blood; but the haemorrhage had slowed, and now he was coming out of his faint. He flapped an arm, and knocked a non-glass urine bottle to the floor.

CHAPTER FIFTY-TWO

1105 HRS

'Jesus H. Christ,' said one of the Swat team that surrounded the ambulance. 'There's someone moving in there.'

'Somebody open the doors.'

'Cover me.'

With infinite care, and strictly according to the manuals, the Swat team inched towards the handle. Slowly, slowly, in the hope of not setting off some Vietcong-style booby trap, both the rear doors were swung wide. The Swat team stared within, their expressions full of the semi-sacred awe with which a man will look at the bottom of a woman's handbag.

'Strewth,' said one. 'It looks like a flaming abattoir in there.'

Eric the parkie was almost invisible in the tangle of medical equipment. His lower body was covered in a long spinal board, complete with head immobilizer and securing straps. His upper half was buried in a midden of oximeters, stethoscopes, thermometers, resuscitation masks, vomiting bags, gastric tubes, sterile surgical gloves and defibrillators. The whole assemblage was richly spattered with gore.

'I think there's someone there.'

'Sweet Mary mother of God.'

'Or part of someone, anyway. That's definitely a foot.'

'We've got to get him out.'

The Swat team leader looked at the ambulance man. 'You'd better lead the way.'

'Whoa,' said the ambulance man. 'This is an armed response situation. The rules clearly state that in armed response situations, it's down to you boys.'

'Hey, we don't want to kill him.'

'Yeah, and we don't want him to kill us.'

'Oh come off it.'

'You come off it.'

So Britain's emergency services began the now traditional act of worship before the altar of Phobia, the many-headed multiple-bosomed goddess of health and safety. With every pump of Eric Onyeama's good and loyal heart the puddle of blood beneath him grew, and with every pump the beat grew fainter.

'Help me you idiots,' he said. But only his lips moved.

Adam took Cameron's hand and led her away from the blare of the TV, to the back of room W6. As she felt those long, dark-haired pianist's fingers, she tried to remember that this was a hand she thrilled to touch.

'I'll tell you who I'm spying for,' he said, 'of course I will. I'll tell you in a minute. But I want you to believe me about something. I am not a terrorist.'

'Then why did you make me do this?'

She still loved the intensity of his intellect; she loved his broad shoulders and thick curly black hair. Despite her depression, for an instant she persuaded herself she might also love the fact that he was a spy.

'I thought – look you're not going to believe me.'

'Did you know they weren't a TV crew?'

'Yes.'

'Then you're mad. You're an active collaborator.'

'No,' said Adam with soft desperation.

'Say, who is this fellow, anyway?' The President watched as the man with the flowing grey hair was at last given the floor. 'What's that he said?'

The President reached for the zapper to turn it up.

Jones the Bomb snatched the gizmo away. 'That is His Excellency Yves Charpentier, Ambassador of the Republic of France.'

'Know him, do you?'

CHAPTER FIFTY-THREE

1108 HRS

Haroun's hasty footsteps echoed on the stone stairs. He was alone, save for the busts of dead white men and their scary dead white eyes.

He tried one door, then another. The fool English: did they expect a man to piss against the wall of their godless palaces? Well, he would have to, if this went on much longer. He turned a corner, and came face to face with a woman.

She was dressed in black from head to toe. She wore a helmet and her upper body was swaddled in Kevlar with a label saying Metropolitan Police.

She swung her gun on him. He turned his on her. By mutual consent they each slipped back around the corner and trotted in the opposite direction.

Oh, perhaps I should have asked her, thought Haroun, because things were starting to go critical in his lower abdomen. One by one the graphite rods of restraint were popping out of the radioactive pile, and meltdown was approaching.

Ah! But it was haram, a disgrace, to discuss such things with a woman.

He came to a door, of old rich oak and bossed with bronze. Praise be to the prophet, thought Haroun: it said GENTS.

Locked. Through his tears, he read a notice Sellotaped to the wood, in the name of the Clerk of Works, informing him that the convenience would be out of order, pending conversion to allow for disabled access.

'Ladies and gentlemen, *messieurs, mesdames*,' said the French Ambassador . 'Since I believe that there is a strong possibility that this will be our last day on earth, I will speak briefly, and I will speak from the heart.'

Boy, thought the President, Yves here was one hell of a snappy dresser. The Frenchman was wearing an indigo suit of the most formal possible cut, but his shirt was patterned with blue horizontal stripes of varying tones and thicknesses. The whole thing was set off by a taramasalata-coloured tie, strobing under the TV lights and – yes – giving the impression of a pulsing from-the-heart sincerity.

'I stand before you as the representative of a friendly nation, that bears nothing but amity and goodwill towards this country, which has been my home for the last three years, and also towards the United States.

'For the avoidance of doubt, I wish to join the noble lady who has just spoken, in recording my contempt for the terrorists who are holding us hostage, and who threaten murder. When these events are investigated, and the criminals punished – as they surely will be – it will be discovered that some of our captors gained access to this hall through the invitation of myself and of my former associate.'

He stuck his chin at Benedicte. 'I mean the lady with the gun. All I will say now is that I have been the slave to Aphrodite and that the goddess has ensorcelled my wits.'

Crikey, thought Barlow.

'Typical Frog,' said the President.

Jones the Bomb frowned.

'Since the hour advances, and since I repose no faith in the mental equilibrium of our captors, let me speak only to the nation which I have the honour of representing. *Français, françaises, concitoyens de la République*, there may be many millions of you who are watching and indeed preparing to vote. There may be some of you who have already made up your minds, and are doing as these people would have you do – ringing up to express your wish to release the prisoners held by the Americans. If you have already voted, that is your privilege. If you have yet to decide, I beg you to listen.

'We have a tradition, over the last fifty years or so, of

providing the intellectual opposition to what is called *le défi américain*, which I might call the challenge of American cultural and political dominance. We have our own modest culture in France, our own literary, artistic and scientific achievement, which over the centuries some foreigners have been kind enough to praise. But it would be fair to say that sometimes we become so paranoid about America, which we call the hyperpuissance, that we become exuberant in our language.

'One senior French politician recently attained notoriety by declaring that the ambition of the United States was nothing but, I quote, the organized cretinization of the French people. Our good friend the cook, who has just regaled us with his views at such generous length, alluded to the problem of the malbouffe, the hamburgerization of European cuisine. That is a discussion familiar to us in France.

'It is also true that many intelligent people, and not just in France, but also in America, are sceptical of the manner in which the US government handles the problems of the Middle East. It is my belief that an injustice has been done to the Palestinian people, that Israel could remedy that injustice, and that America could do more to assist this process. There are also many of us who believe that there were better ways of handling Monsieur Saddam – no doubt a very bad man – than the invasion and all the problems it has brought in its train.

'But, my friends, it is one thing to find fault with America. It is another thing to wish her destruction, and that, tragically, is the ambition of the deluded men, and woman, who hold us hostage today.'

Darn right, thought the President. Until that last bit, he had been meditating the modalities of a strike on Paris.

'I do not know where he has gone, the strange personage who handcuffed himself to the President. But before he went, he compared the American head of state to Caesar, and I wish to dwell for an instant on that richly suggestive analogy. Yes, it is probably true that in her pandominance, modern America surpasses the Rome of the Antonines. She has bases in countries which only fifteen years ago were part of the Soviet Union. It is a fact that Rome never conquered Scotland. It has been one of my pleasures, as Ambassador to this country, to walk along the wall the empire built to keep out the painted tribes; and yet American planes flew from Lossiemouth to Iraq.

'We all know the figures: the increment in US defence spending, the amount by which the Pentagon decided to increase defence spending last year, is greater than the combined defence budgets of Britain, France and Germany. It is surely right to call America in some sense an empire. But is she an evil empire?'

'Of course she is evil, you conceited French stupidity!' Jones the Bomb leapt up, trailing the President, and almost rubbed noses with the TV screen. 'Benedicte, you must make him shut up and sit down.'

But the French Ambassador was coming to the point.

CHAPTER FIFTY-FOUR

1112 HRS

'So you expect me to believe that?' said Cameron to Adam. 'You thought they were going to wheel in some torture victim, just to embarrass the President?'

She paused, and scanned the face of her loved one, and was amazed by how much she wanted to believe him.

'I know it sounds crazy now, but it's all I've got to say,' said Adam. 'Now let's just concentrate on getting out of here alive.'

* * *

Over the scuffed green carpet of room W6 Dean slithered in his trainers. He was now only a couple of yards from the handle. He turned and mouthed at Cameron. 'Come with me.'

Cameron looked at him, and then looked quickly back at Adam.

'Dean, my fine young friend.'

'Yes, sir,' said Dean instinctively. Jones the Bomb was still watching the TV, but he had good peripheral vision.

'I will not stand in your way. I will always remember you fondly.'

'Thank you, sir.' He edged a foot closer to the door.

'Your mother will be filled with joy over your heavenly wedding,' said Jones.

'My mother, sir?'

'The same.'

'Sir, what wedding?'

Jones smiled and slid his gunhand into the suicide jacket, and checked the Nokia.

Now Haroun was lost. He was sure he had been here before. Surely it was the same marble staircase, the one where he had met the policewoman. But if he had been here before, would he not have remembered that giant painting? It depicted the infidel Queen Elizabeth, her orange hair and pasty face, all lit up as she plotted some new act of aggression. Haroun spat and swore, and tottered on. He looked into the office of someone called the Rt Hon. John Prescott MP, and thought of urinating in the waste paper basket, but there was the risk of being interrupted by the woman. Heaven help me, he begged. Come down, O Power Divine, and give me the blessing of release. In the nuclear reactor in his loins the last carbon rod had blown out of the pile; the last drop of coolant had evaporated, and the corrupt and incompetent director had leapt into his jalopy and begun to drive for the coast.

* * *

Far above the Atlantic the boomerang of Stealth bombers was making good time, as Rome might once have sent her quinquiremes to crush a rebellion.

Jupiter Pluvius continued his percussion on the roof, and now the beat turned up again, as though the rain god were moving to some symphonic finale. Immediately beneath the tiles, Jason Pickel stared down at the sweating domes, the hats, the comb-overs and shilling-sized bald patches of the audience, ninety feet below. He looked through the sights for the umpteenth time and lined up the cross-hairs on two prominent objects, first Benedicte's left nipple, then her right nipple. 'Did e'er such love and sorrow meet?' he hummed, 'Or thorns compose so rich a crown?' He couldn't miss, he told himself. Well, he could, but he couldn't.

Away at the back, Roger Barlow was partly hoping to speak, and partly hoping that he would be spared the ordeal, not least since the Frenchman was being so colossally sound. Yves Charpentier had a slightly irritating way of pushing out his lips and making an udder-milking gesture with his hands, but what he had to say was good.

'Way to go, Froggie!' he thought.

Barlow was also wondering what the hell was going on with Cameron. To judge by the way the Arabs had treated her and that fogeyish boyfriend of hers, there seemed to be some element of complicity. Oh dear, oh dear.

And she had seemed such a nice girl. Belief, idealism, fanaticism, mania: in Barlow's mind they were all part of the same ghastly continuum. Would they blame him? Would they investigate the lackadaisical way in which he had hired her and supervised her?

Probably: once they'd finished ripping him to shreds about Eulalie. What should he do? Fire her?

Probably.

*   *   *

'All right,' said Cameron. She decided she would make up her mind about Adam later. 'So whose spy are you? The Russians? The Chinese?'

Adam gave a rueful smile. He pointed to something on his lapel.

'See that?'

'What is it? A microphone?'

'No, no. What does it look like?'

She shrugged. It looked like something from a game, a little red token of some kind. Maybe part of an army from Risk.

'It is a florette of the Grand Croix of the Légion d'Honneur.'

Cameron noticed the rather too professional way he said it, with plenty of rolling of the *r*s.

'So you are spying for the Froggies.'

'*C'est ça.*'

'*Bien je jamais.*'

'And one last thing, Dean,' said Jones as the teenager turned the handle of the door. 'I hope you will enjoy the attentions of the black-eyed ones, and remember that the black of their eyes is blacker than black, and the white of their eyes is whiter than white; and I hope that you will find them comely and submissive.' Dean shivered. He looked at Cameron and opened the door.

'Hey, Dean, wait up,' said the President.

Dean halted in amazement.

The President turned to Jones the Bomb. 'Hey, this black-eyed one stuff. Is that the black-eyed virgins, the seventy-two virgins in Paradise that you guys talk about?'

'Such is the reward of the shahid,' said Jones, stiffly.

''Cos I read something interesting 'bout that,' said the President.

'Silence,' said Jones. 'You know nothing of this.'

'Wait, wait. This might be useful for Dean to know. I read that there was a scholarly controversy about this black-eyed phrase, a real big fight.'

'Shut up,' said Jones.

'It seems, from what I read, that black-eyed ones might not mean seventy-two virgin girls. They looked at the old Arabic there, and they now think it's a mistranslation, and it really means . . .'

'What?' said Dean.

'Idiot,' said Jones the Bomb.

'. . . raisins.'

'Raisins?' said Dean.

'Isn't that something?' said the President. 'You blow your-self up thinking you're going to get seventy-two black-eyed virgins, and instead you get seventy-two raisins. Kind of makes a difference, I'd have thought.'

'Fool,' said Jones, and raised the Browning as if to whack him again.

'And another thing,' said the President bravely, 'is why is it so great if they're virgins? Most folks would say that a little experience is . . . you might want to think about that, Dean.'

'Enough,' said Jones the Bomb.

CHAPTER FIFTY-FIVE
1114 HRS

'*Non, concitoyens de France*, I do not think America is an evil empire,' said the French Ambassador. Out of that grey thatch a single drop of perspiration appeared and rolled down that high, pale forehead. He was a good-looking man, but certainly not a young man any more.

'And *franchement, mes amis*, I do not think the comparisons with Rome are apt . . .'

Cameron got up and led Adam towards the television. The President glanced at them incuriously. Jones was muttering to himself; he sounded like a bag lady.

'Look, Adam, he's got the same thing as you.' The cameras had a tight head shot, and the red thread of the Légion d'Honneur – a more discreet version of Adam's florette – was just visible on the Frenchman's lapel.

'Why don't you listen to what he has to say?' There was a strained, almost giggling note to her voice.

The Ambassador continued. He had been trained at the Ecole Nationale d'Administration in the ancient art of the suasoria, of arguing for whatever side of the case he happened to be on. Should Hannibal have crossed the Alps by the Iser Valley? Or should he have stuck to the Riviera? There was a time when Yves Charpentier would have been equally learned and fluent in support of either case. Today, as happens with all of us from time to time, he found his voice taking on the choky timbre of absolute sincerity.

'Our friend the cook has told us that America would dominate the world with her nasty fast food. He deplores the hamburger, and so do I. And yet I must ask you all: Are you forced to eat this thing? Are you obliged to buy the dreaded Newman's Own Balsamic Vinegar, instead of making your own vinaigrette? Are you obliged to support the ruthless profiteering of Ben and Jerry's ice cream? But no!

'Yes, the men from McDonald's have built their triumphant yellow arches across Europe, and it may interest you to know that in our country, people of France, the hamburger chain is growing faster than anywhere else on earth. But do they compel us to erect these monstrosities, as the victorious Roman generals erected their triumphal arches over the defeated Gauls? *Non, mes amis.* We build the arches ourselves, to gratify our own appetites.

'Our friend the cook – whose recipes for dock leaf soup and placenta pie I have not yet had the good fortune to sample

– told us of the many American soldiers who are deployed overseas. Well, I should not have to remind you, but there are many thousands of American soldiers still in France . . .'

'Say what?' said the President, scandalized for a second that his extensive briefing on Yurp did not contain this fact.

'Chap doesn't know what he's on about,' said Silver Stick, who had once been something in NATO.

'Yes of course,' said the Frenchman to those around him. 'Do not look so surprised. Go to Normandy; go to Omaha, and Gold and Juno and Sword; and then go to see the receding vistas of white crosses on the huge green lawns which contain the remains of thousands upon thousands of the Americans who gave their lives for the freedom of my country, of our country, who sacrificed themselves for the freedom of Europe. Go to Flanders, and the Ardennes; go there, you fools who despise and deprecate America, go there and tell me that we the people of France do not owe the Americans an eternal debt, a debt which it is our privilege, in some small way, to pay back today.'

'Well I'll be danged,' said the President, breathing out. He snapped a salute. '*Allons, enfants de la patrie, le jour de gloire est arrivé.*'

The Frenchman was about to make some other points; for instance that the ideological links between the American and French republics were in some ways stronger than the link between the United Kingdom and her former colony. He was going to point out that the Statue of Liberty had been presented to the people of America by the people of France, in 1885, in recognition of the centenary of America's war of liberation from government by the very place in which they stood.

But by now his job was done. It is a feature of human nature to believe in that which is evidently strongly believed in; and there were millions in France who were deeply impressed by the passion of their distinguished representative. Many had picked up their mobiles to express one point of view, and were suddenly overcome with a sense of the frivolity of anti-Americanism, and voted the other way.

In the diners and lounges of America there was shock at this sign of gratitude from an unexpected quarter. There was amazement. There were fits of piteous blubbing.

'Yay!' whooped Cameron. She was blushing, and there were tears in her eyes of innocent joy. 'See,' she said, turning to Adam, 'see what Yves really thinks.'

'Of course he thinks that, and that's exactly what I think, too.'

Jones stared at the Frenchman on the screen. His nostrils were as white and rigid as porcelain.

'Shut up the pair of you,' he said out of the corner of his mouth. 'We will see what happens when the votes come in.'

The BBC announced that there had been some very heavy polling in India, where intercommunal riots had broken out in Mumbai and Delhi, so ferocious was the disagreement between Muslims and Hindus. The percentage in favour of release of the Guantanamo prisoners was back up to 55.

Jones's eyes went to the door, whence he could hear Dean's retreating footsteps.

Oh sweet Prophet, praise and honour to your name and may a thousand blessings be upon you, thought Haroun as he struggled with his fly. As he did so he noticed the horrible graffiti: 'Vote Labour!' 'Death to the middle class.' 'Applications to be next Tory leader,' someone had written on the bog roll dispenser. 'Please take one.' Was there no end to the degeneracy of these people and their politics?

His gun had been left in the sink, and the door, marked Gentlemen Members Only, was unlocked. But what did he care? In an instant he would attain relief.

Now the fly was open, and – what in the name of Allah? He had forgotten about the prophylactic towel. He swore, and with a lung-bursting, drowning desperation he tore at his trousers and sought out the safety pin he had used to fasten the towel to his loins.

His imam had given him a tip, you see: that he would need his genitals intact, in order to enjoy the seventy-two heavenly benefits of martyrdom. Now he couldn't undo the beastly towel. He jabbed his finger on the pin. He bled on the sacred nappy.

He yanked and pulled on the towel, formerly the property – for some reason – of the Creech Castle Hotel, Taunton, and now the O-ring seal of his urethra began to expand. He couldn't stop it. Shame was coming down the tracks like a derailed Cannonball Express.

America has an astonishing 99.3 televisions per 100 households, a density exceeded only by Taiwan. Almost the entire population of the East Coast was now watching the debate in Westminster Hall, and they were voting with a patriotism that stunned the data collators of the BBC.

'It can't be true,' said one polo neck to the Director of Political Editorial. 'There's something on the wires saying that 127 million Americans have voted to keep the prisoners in Cuba. How many people live in America anyway?'

'Sounds dead dodgy to me,' said the BBC hierarch.

'We can't suppress it, can we?'

'Nah, put it out,' said the executive with a vanishingly tiny smile. 'But if you can think of a health warning, so much the better.'

CHAPTER FIFTY-SIX

1118 HRS

'It is lies, all lies!' railed Jones. 'It is the Fox TV. It is propaganda and bullshit.' But Jones could not stop the earth turning, and as dawn continued to break over America, and as the alarm clocks went off and the TVs went on, Americans voted in huge numbers to vindicate their right to bang up the towelhead nutters. In Iowa, Wanda Pickel and Jason Jr voted solidly for the President, and so did Mom's new friend Howie, a realtor whom she had met on the set of a daytime TV show.

Now Jones could feel his majority slipping away; he was like one of those candidates who thinks he has won, on the night of the election, because they count the votes from the liberal urban areas first. Only as the votes start to come in from the shires, from the boneheaded conservative villages where they know right from wrong, does it dawn on the candidate that the race may be closer than he thought.

Dean, he noted, was now out of the door; and Jones began to count his protégé's footfalls down the corridor. Another couple of seconds, he thought, and stroked the Nokia.

'So I say in conclusion,' perorated the Frenchman, 'that to hate America is in a way to hate ourselves. It is a fact of human psychology that all our most vehement opinions, all our most passionate prejudices, are but the result of some internal argument, some unresolved tension in our own souls. If I may borrow the words of a great Anglo-Saxon writer, the rage of those who despise America is the rage of Caliban, staring at his face in the glass. It may seem odd to some of my countrymen that I should end my speech with the same slogan that you might hear from the lips of the President, if he were still with us. But I say these words with the utmost sincerity and respect. God Bless America, ladies and gentlemen, *messieurs*, *mesdames*, and I say it again—'

As Haroun finally disentangled himself from the towel, he was filled with that infantile ballistic joy that comes in the last second before the weapon is discharged. I am a missile, a sidewinder, a tank, he thought. I will shoot them all, he thought as he aimed at the sign saying 'Shanks'. I will tear their bodies into little pieces and cause them more pain than they will ever know.

'God . . .'

High over the Atlantic warm Gulf winds were pushing the Stealth bombers faster than they had ever flown before.

Parliament Square was now a parade ground of crack troops: the Paras, the SAS. Men with blackened faces were running on rubber soles to take up positions all over Pugin and Barry's palace. They scoped the gryphons in their sights. They primed the stun grenades. They checked the rope ladders.

In the Ops Room of Scotland Yard the Deputy Assistant Commissioner of the Metropolis was twitching like a palsied ant. These lunatics could blow themselves up any moment, and yet Bluett the Yank seemed paralysed.

'I really think we should give the command, Colonel,' he said. 'Of course the odds are not particularly bright, but we've got to give it a go.'

Colonel Bluett was staring at the cornflake-packet and Lego model of Westminster Hall. He could see the conflagration in his mind's eye, the flesh charred and shrivelled like something left on a barbecue.

'Waco,' he said. 'Waco had nothing on this.'

'. . . bless . . .'

And I tell you what, thought Roger Barlow, as he cast around for other undertakings he could offer the Almighty, I really promise that I'll put a lot more into my marriage, 'cos I know that you only get out what you put in. Tell you what, God old bean, I'll clean up the puddles on the bathroom floor, and I'll even remember to put the sodding electric toothbrush on the charger . . . And oh all right (he winced), I'll make stuff to eat, fish pie and whatnot, and perhaps I'll roll up my sleeves and wear some gay pinafore like little Chester here . . .

'. . . America!'

'Goodbye, Dean, my child,' said Jones. He pressed the button marked Yes on the Nokia. The number came up in the blue square on the screen. DIALLING, said the machine, and began to count the seconds.

'No, I certainly wasn't in on it,' said Adam to Cameron, and for the first time in their relationship, it seemed, she noticed the odd little lentil-shaped convexity, the relic of a trapped follicle, perhaps, on his cheek. Was her love dying? She couldn't believe it could; and perhaps, indeed, it was not. 'Don't be angry. The only thing I can assume is that Benedicte took us all for a ride.'

CONNECTING, said the machine. Somewhere in the ether one gang of chirruping electrons was introduced to another gang. They snuffled round each other; they started to speak each other's language. They seriously clicked and began electronic intercourse. The corresponding mobile phone vibrated once.

The explosion could be heard all over the Palace, and in the square outside. It wasn't a car backfiring, or a firework, or someone inadvertently putting a match to the intestinal vapours of a cow. It was an aggressive, percussive noise, the rattling of demons on the gates of Hell.

'You morons!' screamed Raimondo Charles, who was being made to kneel on the ground in Whitehall, not far from the Cenotaph, with his hands cuffed behind his back. 'You hear that? Now they're sending in the freaking Swat guys like this is *Raid on Entebbe.* Frigging idiotic cowboy shit-for-brains!'

'Hey, knock it off, man,' said a British captive.

'Yeah,' said another captive, a gloomy-looking pony-tailed fellow with a Motorhead T-shirt. 'Whose side are you on, anyway?'

Adam threw his arm around Cameron, but she hunched her shoulders and pulled away from him. 'No,' she said in a small voice. 'Don't.'

The President hurled himself to the floor; not out of any particular cowardice, but simply in deference to the many lessons he had been given in protecting POTUS in the event of a bomb. It is a measure of the violence with which he hurled himself that Jones the Bomb, still handcuffed to his captive, came too.

Benedicte spun round to see where the explosion had come from. So did Habib, and 1,600 eyes bugged from their sockets as the audience prepared to surrender to a full-blown Gadarene hysteria, kicking over the little gilt chairs and thinking, at last, of making a break for it.

Silver Stick dropped his silver stick, and then caught it again, like a conjurer, before raising it in the en garde position.

Dean jumped out of his skin, but only metaphorically. His

skin remained attached to his body. He turned round, and rushed back down the corridor to room W6.

Pickel barely moved. Frig me dead, he thought.

And it was Haroun, of course, who Jackson Pollocked the walls and ceiling of the Gentlemen Members' conveniences with his blood and brains. Perhaps it was because his circumstances were so confined, but the 5-kilo bomb did remarkably little damage to anything else. A light bulb was lost to his levitating brain-pan, and his teeth chipped the tiles. Various parts of him were trapped in the U-bend of the lavatory, but they presented no real problems to the forensic plumbers.

Did he attain Paradise, beyond that final orgasmic delivery of urine? Was he transported on wings of angels to the soft bowers that await the martyrs in the islands of the blessed?

Does Haroun now live in a dome decorated with pearls, aquamarine and rubies, a sunny pleasure-dome as wide as the distance between al-Jabiyyah, a suburb of Damascus, and the Yemeni capital of Sana'a? Is he attended by 80,000 servants?

Does he eat of honeydew and drink the milk of Paradise? And finally, is this menu brought to him by seventy-two black-eyed virgins, so decorous and submissive as to assuage all the sexual indignities of this earth?

Or has he by now eaten his pitiful ration of raisins?

My friends, I have not the faintest idea. There, as they say in German, I am over-questioned. No narrator, whatever omniscience he may claim, can give you the answer to that one.

But I have my suspicions.

CHAPTER FIFTY-SEVEN

1119 HRS

Barry White had seen enough war zones to know when it was time to be gone. 'Let's make like hockey players,' he said to Chester de Peverill, 'and get the puck out of here.' They rose to their feet. Across the hall, people were doing the same.

Their faces were pale and their ears were singing; but tongues that had cloven to the roofs of mouths were suddenly able to speak. It briefly occurred to those members of the British cabinet, who had sat for more than an hour in tapioca-like terror, that this was it: this was the moment for self-preservation.

Behind the black-painted rail at the top of the hall, Silver Stick and Black Rod and the Earl Marshal exchanged meaningful glances, like an escape committee at Colditz. They knew that the authority of the terrorists had been momentarily dissipated; and that if the whole crowd went amok together, they might yet prevail.

As soon as Habib heard the bomb, he whirled and stared at the door that led into the hall. He knew what had happened, and in spite of his religious training, which had taught him to feel nothing but gladness for the death of his brother, the tears ran down his cheeks.

He stood still, and closed his eyes. 'Call out in joy, O my mother; distribute sweets, O my father and brother. A wedding with the black-eyed virgins awaits your sons in Paradise. Go with God, Haroun,' he said, and for a second he listened with brimming eyelashes to the pagan mutterings of the crowd, growing in strength like pigs who have found their way out of the sty.

He heard them milling from their seats, knocking over the chairs, and he felt a sudden contempt. They were a different species. They were unclean. They were dogs and the sons of dogs. They had no right to be reckoned in the same category as Haroun, the pure, the martyr, the shahid.

He opened his eyes. He looked at the sweaty old peeresses, the New Labour MPs with their cruel and unfeeling promotion of liberal values, and the perpetually compromised Tories.

How could they rival the moral depth of a man who gave his life for a cause? He felt overcome by the hot hate of righteousness, and waved his Schmidt.

'Sit down,' he shouted, 'or I shoot you.'

'Sit down, everybody, or it will be the shooting time!' yelled Benedicte, and she invisibly painted the crowd with her bullets.

The moment of opportunity passed. There is something very particular about the sensation of watching the black O of a loaded gun barrel moving across your abdomen, and several members of the crowd felt it now. In many cases, it loosens the alimentary system, and causes the pulse to rise and a green moment to happen to the cheeks. People sat down again. Resignation descended.

'For crying out loud,' said the Deputy Assistant Commissioner, 'I am going to call Downing Street. Look,' he said, and he found himself bubbling over with a point he had been wanting to make all morning. 'It's our bloody country, it's our bloody city, it's our bloody Parliament, and I am in charge here.'

'Stephen,' said Bluett, champing his cigar and bugging out one bright blue eye, so as to look like Colonel Kilgore at his most demented, 'I want you to know how much I respect your right to say those things. But it's my fucking President whose life is at risk there, Stephen, and we have a plan.'

'But your plan isn't working.'

'Well, I wanna remind you here, Stephen, that this was a plan originally proposed by one of your officers.'

'But it still isn't working.'

'It's been cleared with the Vice-President, Stephen. It's been approved at the highest possible level in the White House.'

'But this is just bonkers. It's only because the SAS are British. And where is this bloody man Pickel, anyway?'

'Listen, buddy, we've got 800 hostages in there, including the President of the United States. You talk about your SAS, and I want you to know I have the highest respect for the SAS, but I am a keen student of military history, and whenever those guys come through the windows a whole lot of people get killed.'

He grabbed the model, and pointed at room W6, which had been constructed out of an empty PG Tips box. 'The President is here. Anyway, he's outta sight. I say we wait for Pickel to get a shot at this leader guy.'

Purnell looked at his counterpart, and behind the braggart mask he saw the worry and the fear in those flickering blue eyes. There were several obvious points he could have made.

'Yeah, Pickel,' repeated Bluett, his voice fading to bleakness. 'He's our only hope.'

'My dear Dean,' said Jones, without skipping a beat. 'My dear, dear Dean. I am glad you decided to come back. Perhaps you will come with us now and finish the job.'

The young Wulfrunian stepped through the doorway and back into room W6.

'What happened, man?' asked the President. 'What was the bang?'

'Someone died, I expect,' said Dean.

He stared at Jones the Bomb. Somehow he seemed bigger, older, at least to Cameron's eyes.

'Well,' she said brightly. 'Now what happens?'

'Ask the boss,' said Dean evenly, staring at Jones.

* * *

A kidney bowl fell with a clang to the floor of the ambulance. Then a head brace, and a defibrillator. There was definitely something moving in there.

The police and paramedics had found a periscope for use in armed sieges, and they were peering into the dimness, one of the paramedics lying flat on the cobbles beneath the running board.

'He's alive,' said the scout.

'Can you see a gun?' said another.

'I can't see a gun, though it's hard to tell with all this mess. There's blood everywhere.'

'Of course there's blood everywhere,' said one of the nurses. 'The guy's been bleeding to death. I think we should just take a chance and go in.'

'The rules are the rules. We've got armed and dangerous here.'

'I think we're all being pathetic,' said the nurse.

'You go if you want to,' said the paramedic, 'but we won't be insured and it's ten to one he's a fruitcake who wants to take one of us with him on the way to the seventy-two virgins of Paradise.'

'I'm going in,' said the nurse.

'Well, at least wait until they bring the protective gloves.'

Jones was about to tell room W6 what to do, when the television said something that made Dean jump out of his skin. 'I want to appeal now to my son, Dean,' said a voice he had never heard before. He looked at the screen, and saw a curious middle-aged man, with a proud nose and curly hair, sitting in a lilac tracksuit on a beige sofa.

'Who is that?' asked Cameron, coming up and standing next to him.

'Bogged if I know,' said Dean. It was Sammy Katz.

As the feature writers would discover, to their immense pleasure, the former wiper manufacturer had known about

Dean all his life. Five months after the night of his conception, Katz had come across the same girl, again, in the same godforsaken spot on the Bilston Road, plying the same miserable trade.

But now she was pregnant, and she had recognized Sammy Katz as a man who might well be the father of her child. We do not need to know the details of the subsequent desultory relationship (the embarrassed letters to Dennis Faulkner, Faulkner's attempts to shrug him off, the pathetic presents, every five years, of low-denomination bills). All we need accept is that at this critical point in his life, Dean's biological father had sprung from nowhere, and was sitting slumped before the cameras on the oatmeal settee of his lounge, and moaning about his feelings. 'I feel I let yow down, Dean,' he said. He looked fittingly weepy, since he was in TV's traditional defeated sofa-ridden posture in which parents announce some terrible fact about their children. 'I appeal to yow, Dean,' he said, again. He didn't care much what he said, since his overriding feeling was pleasure, after all these years, at appearing on TV.

'You hear that, Dean, old pal,' said the President. 'He's appealing to you.'

'He doesn't look much like you,' said Cameron.

But Sammy Katz could not expect to last long at the epicentre of the biggest ever global media event; and after thirty-five seconds the moaning man on the Wolverhampton settee was banished by the schedulers in favour of news – amazing news – from the TV stations across the planet. Perhaps it was the explosion, muffled but audible on screen; perhaps it was more than an hour of being exposed to Jones & Co., but the peoples of the earth were beginning to change their collective mind. It might be that the global consciousness of our species – as Blake or Rousseau understood it – was being affected by considerations of right and wrong. It might have been a statistical error. But at the bottom of the screen was a big bi-coloured bar, rather like that used in televised rugby internationals to show which side has had the higher percentage of ball possession. For the first time the right-hand, blue side of the bar was bigger than the left-hand, red side of the bar. By 51 to 49 per cent, people appeared to be voting for America – even if it meant the retention of the prisoners in Cuba.

'It is bullshit,' said Jones. 'It is the Jewish cabal who run the American media complex.'

'Too bad, buddy. You lose,' said the President. 'If I were you I'd stick to your promise and let us all out of here.'

'Shut up!' said Jones the Bomb. He stuffed his Browning into his trousers and started waving his Nokia under the President's nose.

'See this?' he said, wielding it like a TV zapper. 'If I want, I kill you with this. If I want I kill us all.'

'I don't want,' said the President. 'Fact is, you sure as hell misunderestimated the great world public.'

'You come with me, stinky pig,' said Jones the Bomb, and yanked the presidential handcuffs in the direction of the door. 'Follow me!' he yelled at the others. Adam wearily obeyed, and Cameron and Dean brought up the rear.

''Ere,' said Dean, as they moved down the subterranean green-carpeted corridor, with its old yellowy electric light, in the direction of Westminster Hall. 'Is your name Cameron?'

'And you're Dean, right?'

'Is he your boyfriend?' said Dean, pointing at Adam, who was striding after Jones the Bomb.

Cameron chose not to answer this question, and asked: 'That man on the TV, was he really your father?'

'The hell should I know? What was his name again?'

'I think it was Katz.'

'Is that like the animals?'

'It was with a K, I think.'

Dean pondered the ethnic implications of this. They passed the small window that gave on to Parliament Square, whose mullions were now treacly with water; and once again Dean snatched a glimpse of the hundreds – thousands? – of running, booted men, the APCs, the helicopters. It was almost twilit in the square, and there was something orange and thundery in the light.

CHAPTER FIFTY-EIGHT
1123 HRS

In the hall, Benedicte had once more subdued the crowd, and now she handed over to Jones. 'We're back, my friends.' As announcements go, this one was less popular than Gary Glitter announcing his comeback to a thousand skinheads at the Slough Apollo. But this audience had neither the energy nor the courage to boo. There had been death in this building, and they knew there would be more before the day was done.

'I know some of you have just heard a noise, a bang, and you may be worried. Let me reassure you that it was the American imperialists, who tried to recapture this ancient British Parliament, and who have been violently repelled, with great loss of American life.'

The President was about to speak, and then said nothing. Jones could tell that many of them didn't believe him; but some of them did.

'So let us show we are not afraid, by continuing our debate. I know it is the custom to speak for many hours here. Who would like the floor?'

* * *

314

Up in the rafters, beneath the flèche, Pickel now prepared his shot. He lined up the lead terrorist in his sights, and began to sing his executioner's song, the moaning hymn to his own calvary.

> 'Were the whole realm of nature mine,
> That were an offering far too small.
> Love so amazing, so divine,
> Demands my soul, my life, my all.'

He'd missed in the yard, but there were extenuating circumstances there, with that pisser Barry White. This time he would do the business.

The neck was presenting itself to the cross-hairs, a stretch of stringy brown neck, with the muscles and veins standing out, there where the drug had to go in. It was a tough shot, but it was doable, and it had to be done now.

Well stuff this for a game of soldiers, thought Roger Barlow. He'd been waiting to speak for ages, and it was just like the Commons: you stood up and walked to the end of the diving board; you girded your Speedos and stared at the terrors below; and then someone else was called, and you sat back down again, and the adrenalin turned all manky and stale in your system. There was only one thing to be said for his terror of making his speech – every phrase of which was now supermasticated in his mind – and that was that it obscured his terror of being shot.

And if he spoke well, they might just knock that story on the head.

Listen, the editors would say to the sadistic girl who was persecuting him, we can't do down Roger Barlow any more. Did you hear his speech on America? Did you hear him speak up for the President, and the transatlantic alliance?

Bad luck, they'd say to the vicious wheedling little Debbie

Gujaratne. We don't want any anti-Barlow stuff. Barlow is in, they'd say; Barlow is cool. And Debbie would gnash and spike her rotten little story.

Oh God, oh Gawd, thought Roger Barlow: why had he done it? Why had he put himself in this ludicrous position? And he thought back to the moment of failure, the woman with her shirt seemingly open to the waist, with her lip gloss, her black hair, her busy little fingers on his arm.

'Oh Roger,' she'd droned, 'oh please. You promised,' and he'd touched her cheek – Oh strewth, had they been snapped? – and reached for his wallet.

Oh Eulalie, Eulalie, he moaned. Unless he spoke up forcefully now, Eulalie was going to be his ruin.

He rose to his feet and tried to catch the eye of Jones the Bomb; and as he did so he tried to envisage the reaction of the Oedipal four-year-old, when the news of his folly broke over London like a thunderclap, and he was the butt of a thousand jokes.

'Who is that man, Mummy?'

'You are not necessary. Goodbye.'

'Mr Chairman terrorist,' he said firmly, causing a bit of a gasp in the back rows. 'Ahoy there.'

Gently, gently, said Pickel the ace marksman to himself, drawing a bead on that hectic pockmarked neck.

Jones bowed his head, shaded his eyes, and squinted in the TV lights. Who was that at the back? He jerked his head forward again for a better view . . .

Keep still, you pisser, muttered Pickel. The neck was big in his scope; he could see the grime around the white neck of the T-shirt; he could see the pulse.

But it was no goddamn use if the sucker kept jigging,

because the neck would just pass out of view, and he would be focusing on stone again.

'My dear sir,' said Jones the Bomb to Roger, thinking that whatever happened, this was the last speech. 'The world awaits!' And he stepped back to the lectern, and almost eighty-five feet above him Pickel cursed and felt the ache begin in his fingers.

Standing in a clot of embarrassment next to Jones and the President were Cameron, Adam and Dean. Cameron had started to cry, big tears chasing each other down her cheeks: not because she was terrified – though she was – but because the whole thing seemed so mad, and so interminable.

Dean felt at once overcome with sadness to see her tears, and appalled at the thought that he might be responsible. He was about to touch her arm, and comfort her, when Habib approached him.

'It should have been you to die, not Haroun,' said the Arab quietly, and Dean dropped his hand and stared out in misery once more at the audience, who stared in misery back.

And then he saw her. Yes it was. There could be no question. Five rows back. He looked straight into her beseeching eyes.

'Mr Chairman terrorist, my lords, honourable members, ladies and gentlemen,' said Barlow, 'I really don't have much to add to what speakers today have already said . . .'

'Then shut up,' said Jones the Bomb, bending to reach for the Nokia in his jacket pouch.

'Damn,' said Pickel.

* * *

'. . . but on behalf of all the electorate of Cirencester, whom it is my privilege to represent, I believe I would be remiss if I . . .'

'Get on with it!' said Jones the Bomb, and looked down again at the green liquid crystal display of the Nokia, as he prepared to bring the operation to its predestined end.

'Pisser,' hissed Pickel, squinting again through the sight.

'. . . did not say a few words on a subject which . . .'

In the ambulance in New Palace Yard, William Eric Kinloch Onyeama had fully regained consciousness, with no assistance from the emergency services, and was struggling to get up. His chest hurt like hell, as though he had been involved in a car crash.

His long brown fingers reached for something to help him upright, and wrapped themselves round some wires which were protruding from a box.

'. . . is evidently controversial, and which arouses strong opinions across the globe . . .'

'Say something interesting, you silly man!' yelled Jones the Bomb, who was fed up to the back teeth with British parliamentary procedure. He stood still and pressed the button to activate the automatic dialling system.

Pickel had the vein in his sights. He began the squeeze on the trigger, so delicately that he could not possibly disturb the barrel.

'All right, you tosser,' said Roger Barlow. 'I say to hell with you and the rest of you chippy, pathetic, pretentious, evil, envious, Islamic nutcases. I say vote for America!'

'Sit down!' screamed Jones the Bomb. 'Sit down and shut up.'

And just as Pickel pulled the trigger, Jones jerked the President forward a foot and a half, and placed the crown of the presidential head in the path of the thyapentine sodium dart as it was dispatched with a muzzle velocity of 3,100 feet per second.

'Ow,' said the President. 'What the fuuurggghh . . .'

CHAPTER FIFTY-NINE
1125 HRS

'You fools,' said Jones. The Yanks were attacking. He pushed again at the mobile, and the number flashed on the screen.

DIALLING, said the mobile.

It took only a second for the stuff to begin to work on the President, who weighed less than a sixth of the average white rhino. He toppled forward. The dart was sticking out of the top of his head. It looked terrible on TV.

DIALLING, said the mobile.

And as the President went down he dragged Jones down with him. The mobile spilled out of his hand.

DIALLING, said the screen as the mobile spun across the flags.

Pickel knew what he had to do. With what the citations would call a characteristic disregard for his own safety, he flung his seventeen stone off the little wooden platform beneath the flèche, and abseiled from the ceiling. He aimed at the form of Jones, and in order to hit him he threw himself forward. He went too far and too fast.

ENGAGED, said the mobile.

Pickel landed awkwardly, at 34 miles an hour, on the fifth step, twelve away from Jones the Bomb. Oxlike though it was in dimension and construction, his left tibia was cleanly snapped by the violence of his arrival.

Jones was now crawling towards the mobile, and thinking what an idiot he had been. He had dialled himself! He panted as he tried to lug the inert mass of the President across the old striated shale. All he had to do was dial Dean or Habib, he thought; and it may or may not be an indication of some ultimate failure of his character that he did not think to activate by hand the detonator on his own jacket.

ENGAGED, said the mobile. RETRY?

As Jones crawled towards the mobile the broken-limbed Pickel crawled up the steps towards Jones. His gun was gone, but he had his knife, and he had the courage of a wounded lion as it charges down the rifle of some mock-brave white hunter.

Hardly bothering to look, Jones turned his Browning round and shot Pickel in the chest. The 9 mm bullet ripped through the trapezius of his right breast, scraped a rib and a scapula, and lodged in his vast sternocleidomastoid withers. The damage was very severe. And still that great heart beat on. Army knife to the fore, he slithered on up the stairs to save his Head of State and Commander in Chief.

In his shame and rage, Adam made forward, to help the injured man. But Cameron held him back.

* * *

Five steps to go, reckoned Pickel, now in tremendous pain from both his chest and his leg. Four more agonizing tiger-crawling steps, and he would give Wanda and Jason Jr something they could be eternally proud of.

Three more steps and he would expunge any guilty memory of the incinerated car in Baghdad.

Two more steps and he would wash away the stain that had been left on his name by that pisser Barry White.

If he had managed one more step, he would have been upon Jones the Bomb and the President, as they advanced in a crumpled pushme-pullyou across the floor.

ENGAGED, said the mobile. RETRY?

But Jones did not wait for Pickel's arms to come within swinging distance. He aimed the Browning at Pickel's head and shot at him again.

And that might have been the end of Jason Pickel. By the laws of ballistics the bullet should have entered his brain and killed him instantly. He would have died far from home, fighting on a foreign flagstone, in the protection not just of the President, but of British citizens, as many brave Americans have died before.

And later the news would have been brought to his wife, at that moment running the early morning bath for another man.

Except that Jones's trigger finger was just closing when his gun arm was kicked sharply at the elbow by Roger Barlow, who felt that his speech had not been exactly coherent, and that now was the time for action, not words.

'You idiot MP!' said Jones, and would have blown Roger away with the bullet meant for Pickel; only his gun now jammed.

'Yo! Roger!' sang out his beautiful research assistant, and Adam saw her exultant eyes, and wished they had been turned on him.

But Jones the Bomb was not finished yet. By dragging and shoving the recumbent President, whose anaesthetic dart waggled absurdly from the top of his skull, he had at last extended his fingers to within six inches of the master Nokia.

At which point Dean stepped forward, and kicked it aside. 'No!' shrieked Jones the Bomb, and Habib ran after it, directing a hideous Arab imprecation at the Wulfrunian recruit.

Across Westminster Hall, the audience was now screaming and shouting instructions, and rising from their places in fear.

Adam was saying how much he wished he had a gun, but Cameron was not listening to Adam. She was looking at the back of the head of Jones the Bomb, as he crouched over the President, spitting and waving his Browning.

There was a little bald spot in the greying crown. She knew what she wanted to do. Her eyes went to the group of heraldic figures behind the black railing. Before she could ask to borrow it, the necessary object was thrust without a word into her hand.

'Come on, you idle bastard,' shrieked Jones at the comatose form of the President, as he scrabbled feebly after Habib and the Nokia, trying with one hand to slide the bolt and unjam the Browning. Now he would shoot him. No, he had better shoot himself. Or should he shoot Dean?

He realized that he must have only one or two bullets left in the magazine. He was sitting there, crouched over and grizzling with irritation when Cameron came up behind him . . .

And before she could act she found that Roger had materialized beside her, and taken the ancient artefact with a wink; and because he was her boss, she naturally deferred to him.

Then Roger drew back his arm with a wristy motion he had first learned as a child when thwacking the tops of the thistles in the meadow, and hit him very hard, on the base of the skull.

Jones the Bomb said not a word, and subsided prone over the President's motionless shins. Black Rod smiled to see his eponym put to such good use. It was there to protect the House of Commons, and it had done its job.

But now Habib had found the phone, and handed it to Benedicte. 'Wait,' she said, 'or I will detonate the dirty bomb. There is another bomb in the ambulance, my friends, and this time it is the beeg one!' She called up the menu screen, found what she wanted, and pressed.

DIALLING, said the screen of the master mobile.

'It is all your fault!' screamed Benedicte. 'We played fair, and you did not, and now we must all die!'

In the ambulance in New Palace Yard, Eric Onyeama the parking warden was feeling woozy again, and his bloodied hand pulled harder on the wires that were linked to the funny little box on the floor of the ambulance.

CONNECTING, said the mobile.

'*Ooof*,' said Eric, and sat up on the gurney, and out of the box popped first a red wire, and then a green one.

CONNECTING, said the mobile.

'Death to America!' cried Benedicte. 'Death to imperialism! I die for Palestine and to avenge injustice.'

CONNECTION FAILURE, said the mobile.

* * *

And then the klieg lights went *phut*, and the hall was plunged into comparative darkness, and the upper air of the chamber was full of a blizzard of glass. Through every window in the building crashed the special forces of Britain and America, and they executed their task of saving life with pent-up rage and professionalism. Of the Brotherhood of the Two Mosques, all the four who were still conscious and willing – Benedicte, Habib and the two Arabs – were arrested unharmed. The only casualties were Barry White and Chester de Peverill, who were running to escape at the North End, when they contrived to cushion the fall of the left arm and right breast of Philippa of Hainault, which had been dislodged by Agent Cabache, and now fell victim to a stun grenade. These objects, as a result, were undamaged, and able to be replaced with no obvious ill effects. Which was more than could be said for Chester and Barry, who sustained a range of contusions, none of them very severe.

In less than thirty seconds, about 200 officers had surrounded Dean, Cameron and the odd tableau of Jones and the President. But as the squads of black catsuits with guns moved among the crowd, Dean spotted her again; and this time, shyly, she waved.

It was Lucy Goodbody, aka Vanessa, she who had infil-trated RitePrice in Wolverhampton, and who had been sent by the *Guardian* to cover what they had imagined would be a torpid speech about the Special Relationship.

As Dean looked, he realized she wasn't the Lucy Goodbody of his tortured imagination, the Lucy Goodbody whose flagrant X-rated enjoyment of sex with his best friend had so fried his ego and moved him half to madness. She was just a tired and frightened reporter with a spot on her forehead, visible even at this distance; and it wasn't her fault, thought Dean, that she had fancied his friend more than him.

'Yow roight, Vanessa?' he waved, and began to grow up.

* * *

The cordite settled around them, and the fluffy wadding stuff from the inside of the warning shots, and the broken glass crunched underfoot as people made for the exits. No one took much notice of Dean and Cameron as they now huddled together on the stairs. He had his arm round her, and noticed that she smelled lovely. She was crying and crying and crying from shock and exhaustion.

'Oi,' said Dean, 'don't cry. Yer man – wotsisname?'

'Adam.'

'He really didn't know anything about it. We told him a load of crap. I promise you.'

'Really?' She stopped and snivelled.

'Yeah. Yow'll be foine, love.' She turned to him and because her lips were so trembling and vulnerable he kissed them. To his astonishment, they opened a little, and for a second she returned his kiss, and he could taste the inside of her mouth, and remembered why people talked about kisses being sweet. He knew she didn't mean anything by it. He knew she was just kissing for the joy of being alive, and she knew she would never do it again. But for Dean it was a possession forever, and the joyous phenylethylamines coursed in his veins.

Well, thought Roger Barlow as he sat back down again, stone me. He was a bit stunned by his own recklessness; but one thing was for sure – they'd never bother with the Eulalie business now.

Eulalie! What a prat he'd been. Twenty thousand of his own hard-earned pre-tax pounds, sunk without trace in a lingerie shop called Eulalie, which, at least according to the *Daily Mirror*'s pestilential Debbie Gujaratne, was a front for a brothel. MP RUNS KNOCKING-SHOP was the headline he was dreading, but if tomorrow's front pages were about his drivelling escapades with Eulalie, he would eat his hat. It was, no doubt about it, a good day to bury bad news.

* * *

Deep in their respective unconsciousnesses, Jones and the President lay on the stone dais, curled like twins awaiting their rebirth into a weird and unfair world.

Outside the rain had stopped. In that sudden summery way, the heat was on the street again, and the smell of dust and warmed-up dogshit up rose from the paving stones. The flags of Britain and America fluttered in the sun.

Up above London the clouds were no longer threatening, but high and white, fleecy and friendly. As he was passed carefully out of the ambulance, Eric Onyeama admired them, and knew he had a word for that fat, beautiful look. It would come back to him.

'Wait,' he said to his stretcher-bearers as he was carried round the front of the ambulance. He printed off a ticket from the Sanderson machine, and stuck it under the wiper.

'*Tee hee hee*,' said Eric Onyeama, and fainted again from loss of blood.

And later that day Roger cycled home, having dealt with Mrs Betts, the respite centre, and many other matters. He received something approaching a hero's welcome. 'You were on TV,' said the four-year-old, and climbed his knee, with the others, the envied kiss to share; and they all daubed him with tomato ketchup, so he could be like the other people they'd seen on TV.

Lend Me Your Ears

Boris Johnson

An anthology of pieces selected to illustrate the history of our times, from the fall of Thatcher to the presidency of Blair, with new commentary on some of the major developments as seen from today's perspective.

Boris Johnson was there at Maastricht and in Kosovo; he was at Bush's ranch during his early career and in the Clinton White House during the days of trouble. His material also covers the consequences of the end of the Cold War.

But much of his writing concerns the domestic issues of our times: the time of Diana, the age of self-expression, the end of culture, the moment of the Yuppies, liberty versus freedom. Boris Johnson has also interviewed many of the key figures in the political and cultural worlds and addresses what these personalities tell of our age.

'Johnson has cracked the art of making politics invigorating.'
Daily Telegraph

ISBN 0-00-717334-2

Friends, Voters, Countrymen

Boris Johnson

Have you ever wondered about becoming a Member of Parliament? Or why other people do? Or thought about the process of getting from being a regular person, through the selection procedure, to becoming that candidate for whom we may (or may not) vote? Or considered what the prospective parliamentary candidates do as they stump around the constituency – making speeches, kissing babies, knocking on front doors, providing newspaper copy? Or what difference it makes to us?

As a journalist, Boris Johnson is used to writing about politicians. But he decided that he should become one. Now he is himself being interviewed. So what does it feel like, with the tables turned? What made him decide to become an MP?

In his own inimitable style, Boris Johnson writes about his views on the role of MPs and their historical place: what they can achieve today. He comments on life on the stump, and the pleasure (mostly) of meeting voters, on political parties, current issues, and how to persuade people to vote – all interwoven with stories of what happened to him on his way to a meeting...

'It is very funny...and has, in short, all the idiosyncrasies of its author.'   JEREMY PAXMAN, *The Spectator*

ISBN 0-00-711914-3